OXFORD WORLD'S CLASSICS

THE NETHER WORLD

GEORGE GISSING was born in Wakefield in 1857. His promising academic career was cut short when, in 1876, he was dismissed from Owens College, Manchester, after stealing money in order to help the prostitute, Nell Harrison, start a new life. After a month's hard labour and a year in the United States, he returned to England, married Nell, and began a life of constant literary activity. The early years were spent in poverty and domestic discord; his wife died in 1888. A series of novels, beginning with *Workers in the Dawn* (1880) and culminating in *The Nether World* (1889), attracted some notice, but financial security continued to elude him. It was not until 1891, with the publication of *New Grub Street*, that Gissing was acknowledged as a major writer. In the same year he married for a second time, no less disastrously than before. Many novels followed, notably *Born in Exile* (1892), *The Odd Women* (1893), *In the Year of Jubilee* (1894), and *The Crown of Life* (1899): the dominant note was one of dour pessimism. Gissing moved to France in 1899 to live with Gabrielle Fleury. Widespread acclaim greeted *The Private Papers of Henry Ryecroft* in 1903, but at the end of that year Gissing died.

STEPHEN GILL is a Professor of English in the University of Oxford and a Fellow of Lincoln College, Oxford. His first publication was on Dickens, and he has since edited novels by Trollope, Gaskell, Gissing, and George Eliot. He has written *William Wordsworth: A Life* (1989) and *Wordsworth and the Victorians* (1998).

OXFORD WORLD'S CLASSICS

*For almost 100 years Oxford World's Classics have brought
readers closer to the world's great literature. Now with over 700
titles—from the 4,000-year-old myths of Mesopotamia to the
twentieth century's greatest novels—the series makes available
lesser-known as well as celebrated writing.*

*The pocket-sized hardbacks of the early years contained
introductions by Virginia Woolf, T. S. Eliot, Graham Greene,
and other literary figures which enriched the experience of reading.
Today the series is recognized for its fine scholarship and
reliability in texts that span world literature, drama and poetry,
religion, philosophy and politics. Each edition includes perceptive
commentary and essential background information to meet the
changing needs of readers.*

OXFORD WORLD'S CLASSICS

══

GEORGE GISSING

The Nether World

══

Edited with an Introduction and Notes by
STEPHEN GILL

OXFORD
UNIVERSITY PRESS

Oxford University Press, Great Clarendon Street, Oxford OX2 6DP

Oxford New York

Athens Auckland Bangkok Bogotá Buenos Aires Calcutta
Cape Town Chennai Dar es Salaam Delhi Florence Hong Kong Istanbul
Karachi Kuala Lumpur Madrid Melbourne Mexico City Mumbai
Nairobi Paris São Paulo Singapore Taipei Tokyo Toronto Warsaw

and associated companies in Berlin Ibadan

Oxford is a registered trade mark of Oxford University Press

Published in the United States
by Oxford University Press Inc., New York

First published as a World's Classics paperback 1992
Reissued as an Oxford World's Classics paperback 1999

British Library Cataloguing in Publication Data
Data available

Library of Congress Cataloging in Publication Data
Gissing, George, 1857–1903.
The nether world/ George Gissing; edited with an introduction by
Stephen Gill.
p. cm.—(Oxford world's classics)
Includes bibliographical references.
I. Gill, Stephen Charles. II. Title. III. Series.
PR4716.N42 1992 823'.8—dc20 91–34844

ISBN 0-19-283767-2

1 3 5 7 9 10 8 6 4 2

Printed in Great Britain by
Cox & Wyman Ltd.
Reading, Berkshire

CONTENTS

INTRODUCTION

Note: Readers who do not wish to know the plot in advance may prefer to read the Introduction after the novel itself.

The Nether World is the last of Gissing's novels specifically about the working class and the urban poor, and it is generally judged the best. *Workers in the Dawn* (1880), *The Unclassed* (1884), *Demos* (1886), and *Thyrza* (1887) are intriguing works, which deserve to be better known than they are, but the fact that they are generally treated as if their main interest lies in what they reveal about Gissing at the start of his career indicates that, as novels, they are somewhat raw. *The Nether World*, by contrast, is a complete artistic success. The vision it projects is a very bleak one (in fairness to a reader new to Gissing, that warning needs to be given at the outset), but it is compellingly realized. It is an angry book, whose intensity of focus and dramatic economy marks it out as the beginning of Gissing's major phase and one of his finest achievements.

It is, however, a very discomfiting book, and I want in this introduction to suggest briefly why a reader familiar with other Victorian novels is likely to find it so.

The Nether World subverts the established procedures of the genre to which it seems to belong. Consider, as a way into the novel, a chapter which ought to be ending happily, as a newly married couple sink into sleep on their first night together. Chapter xii, in fact, closes as Bob Hewett, stupefied with drink and exhausted from blows taken in a street-fight, falls dead away, 'breathing stertorously'. His wife, Penelope ('Pennyloaf') Candy, her face bloody too, lies awake. Down in the slum court of Shooter's Gardens she can hear her father punching her mother, who has once again celebrated a Bank Holiday by breaking her vow of total abstinence. As she stares into the darkness Pennyloaf is 'thinking all the time that on the morrow it would be necessary to pawn her wedding-ring'.

This appalling reversal of the traditional fade-out as a couple climb into the nuptial bed concludes a sequence which is an epitome of *The Nether World*. It begins with a foolish marriage. Bob is 19 and Pennyloaf only 17. For neither has family life provided a positive model to encourage them to marriage. Bob's father and stepmother are slipping fast in the nether world, as child after child enfeebles the mother and makes financial demands the father cannot meet. (Later in the novel Bob is to greet the death of one of his own infants with the unfeeling, but rational, 'Thank goodness for that'). For a moment Pennyloaf is happy, twirling her wedding-ring and enjoying new clothes, quietly exultant too that she has won her man from the sexually much-more-alluring Clem Peckover. A Bank Holiday excursion to the Crystal Palace brings her back to reality and opens up the vista of her future. Her husband finds her tiresome and gets drunk, largely to demonstrate manly independence. (He later neglects her altogether and knocks her about, only demonstrating manliness by continuing to make her pregnant.) Bob also cannot resist sparkling before Clem (a premonition of the chilling sequence later in the novel when Clem puts Bob to the test, by setting the price of her sexual favours at the murder of her husband, and ideally of his wife too.) On the way home 'to the black hole which was [their] wedding-chamber', tribal status is settled in a violent brawl, man on man and woman on woman. And Pennyloaf goes to bed knowing that since all their money has been spent on this 'honeymoon' day, she will have to pawn her wedding-ring in the morning.

Such a chapter, which discloses both the attitudes,

expectations, and customs of these inhabitants of the nether world, and their social and economic determinants, would seem to place the book firmly in the tradition of the social-problem novel, a placing which is supported, it would seem, by Gissing himself. In 1880 he dedicated his art

to bring home to people the ghastly condition (material, mental, and moral) of our poor classes, to show the hideous injustice of our whole system of society, to give light upon the plan of altering it, and above all, to preach an enthusiasm for high *ideals* in this age of unmitigated egotism and 'shop'. I shall never write a book which does not keep these ends in view. (Letter, 3 November 1880)

In the next few years this fervent tone was little heard, but it returned with power shortly before Gissing began *The Nether World*. Early in 1888 Gissing was summoned to the house where his estranged wife lay dead. The sight of the emaciated woman, who had died of alcoholism exacerbated by hunger and cold, lying in a bare room with only a few scraps of food and pawn-tickets as signs of her struggle to survive, so moved Gissing that he declared afresh: 'Henceforth I never cease to bear testimony against the accursed social order that brings about things of this kind' (Diary, 1 March 1888). Both statements echo Elizabeth Gaskell's declaration in the Preface to *Mary Barton* (1848), that she was compelled 'to give some utterance to the agony which, from time to time, convulses this dumb people', or Dickens's promise after he had seen conditions in the industrial north: 'I mean to strike the heaviest blow in my power.' It might be added, also, that *The Nether World* was received as belonging to the 'Condition-of-England' tradition. The Archdeacon of Westminster, F. W. Farrar, pronounced it 'well fitted to bring the careless, the indolent, the selfish, the luxurious face to face with problems which it will be impossible for Government or Society much longer to ignore'. *Fraser's Magazine* had made the same claims, in the same language, about *Mary Barton* forty years earlier.

Clearly there is a considerable similarity between Gissing and the social-problem novelists—Disraeli, Gaskell, Kingsley, Dickens, and Reade. Each of these supplemented first-hand experience by research into government blue books, statistical enquiries, and similar investigative writing, and so did Gissing. Though he knew poverty in a way which Gaskell or Kingsley never did, he too did research to ensure that his facts—about wages, conditions and hours of work, rents, and so on—were *accurate*. Like the other novelists, Gissing was conscientious about providing information. He was no more a naïve realist than Dickens: 'every novelist beholds a world of his own, and the supreme endeavour of his art must be to body forth that world as it exists for him. The novelist works, and must work, subjectively' ('The Place of Realism in Fiction', 1895). But there was no necessary conflict between working subjectively and recording ineluctable fact. As his diary and scrap-book reveal, Gissing gathered information about the lives of the poor and introduced it directly into *The Nether World*.

The range of topics touched on is remarkable. At one point, for example, he notes that Mrs Candy is paying four shillings and sixpence a week for a room in Shooter's Gardens. The detail is not inert. In a paragraph Gissing lays bare an intractable social evil. Mrs Candy and the twenty-six other people living in the seven-roomed house are victims of the 'house-knacker', men who bought up properties whose leases were nearing an end and for a year or two sublet at outrageous rents to the sort of undesirable tenants who had to take what they could get. (Clerkenwell was notorious: see Gareth Stedman Jones, *Outcast London: A Study in the Relationship Between Classes in Victorian Society* (1971; rev. edn. 1984), 210–12). What four-and-six means is made clear: Stephen Candy, the potman, earns ten shillings a week for a sixteen-hour day. Elsewhere in the novel Gissing touches on the 'Five-percent philanthropy' of the Model Lodgings associations, and why their barracks-like

blocks were so unappealing to the very poor; on the
rootlessness of people who, never owning a house, could
rent rooms by the week, or even by the day; on fertility and
infant mortality; on the home-workers and sweaters; on
diet; on the ravages of drink; on the significance of ageing to
a labouring man; on shoddy building and lack of sanitation.
The list could be lengthened. Much of what horrified the
archdeacon is conveyed, of course, not through conscien-
tiously recorded facts, but through imaginative realization
of their implications—that overcrowding drives people into
the streets when they want privacy, for example, or that
decency, such as separate bedrooms for male and female
children, costs money.

The specificity and directness of this social exposé
connects *The Nether World* not only to the earlier 'Condition-
of-England' novels, but to contemporary social-protest
discourse. Despite what the tone of Farrar's expostulation
might suggest, *The Nether World* did not burst on an
unprepared public. Artists such as Gustave Doré and Luke
Fildes depicted the plight of the urban masses. Journalists
such as James Greenwood in *Low Life Deeps* (1876) and *The
Wilds of London* (1879), and George R. Sims in *How the Poor
live* (1883) investigated it. The Revd Andrew Mearns
uttered *The Bitter Cry of Outcast London* (1883); Arnold White
identified *The Problems of a Great City* (1886). And in the
same year as *The Nether World* was published, Charles Booth
issued the first volume of *Labour and Life of the People*, in
which the occupations, income, dwellings, and family
circumstances of the London working class were tabulated
on a scale and with a thoroughness not previously
attempted. The line continued (well documented in P. J.
Keating's *The Working-Classes in English Fiction* and *Into
Unknown England 1866–1913*) in such works as 'General'
William Booth's *In Darkest England and the Way Out* (1890)
and the Revd A. Osborne Jay's *Life in Darkest London* (1891).

Although *The Nether World* is situated in a vigorous

contemporary discourse, which itself had a solid mid-century ancestry, it is, however, fundamentally different from, even at odds with, the representative titles just listed.

All Victorian 'Condition-of-England' writing (save for the flimsier newspaper reportage), discloses the intolerable and suggests ways towards amelioration. Non-fiction works very directly: facts are countered by proposals. In *The Problems of a Great City*, for example, Arnold White heads one of his chapters, 'Sterilisation of the Unfit', an indication of the no-nonsense firmness with which he puts forward various measures for dealing with what he identifies as the main threats to civilization. Even Charles Booth, who insists in *Labour and Life of the People* that he supports free enterprise and the individualist ethic, calls for 'limited Socialism' to help his 'Class B' poor, the 'unfortunate people [who] form a sort of quagmire underlying the social structure'. For each of society's cancers—bad housing, casual labour, sweating, drunkenness, and malnutrition—specific remedies were proposed.

Novels, of course, work differently. In *Mary Barton*, for example, Gaskell identifies the great gulf fixed between Dives and Lazarus as essentially one of ignorance. Dramatic episodes and set-piece descriptions depict its effects in contemporary life, but the unfolding of the plot serves to project a moral vision. As the mill-owner, Mr Carson, cradles the dying murderer, John Barton, in his arms, the documentary gives way to parable. Kingsley grounds *Alton Locke* in a Mayhew-like exposure of horrors and in the recent history of Chartism, but as the novel unfolds the wrongs the poor endure and the political movement which failed are set over against Christian millenarianism and the presentation of the only power which Kingsley believes can prevail.

Different though they are (so different that some will think it ridiculous to yoke Arnold White with Elizabeth

Gaskell), fictions and non-fictions are alike in one vital respect. They project a vision of possibilities. Whether it be through the presentation of practical measures or through the appeal to aroused imagination and sympathy as the motors for a restructuring of social relationships, a fable such as Dickens's *A Christmas Carol* on the one hand, and a non-fictional polemic such as General Booth's *In Darkest London and the Way Out* on the other, are written in the conviction that exposure of intolerable wrong will ignite the energy for change.

The Nether World extirpates such optimism. Gissing's 'testimony against the accursed social order' is eloquent, unflinching, and without hope.

The novel projects a closed world from which there is no escape. Other writers who exploit the motif of 'the nether world' or 'the abyss' lead the reader on an exploration *from* the upper world *to* the lower. When George R. Sims, for example, described the East End as 'a dark continent that is within easy walking distance of the General Post Office', his map reference pin-points the symbol of advanced civilization of which the Victorians were most proud. *The Nether World* employs no such framing device. It opens with an old man crossing Clerkenwell Green, and most of the rest of the novel is set within a mile or so of this spot. Characters are continuously on the move, walking, searching out one another, but the fact that their movements are plotted precisely by naming the streets they traverse claustrophobically emphasizes the fact that they are bounded by bricks and cobble-stones. Apparent escapes only serve to reinforce the truth that there is no escape. Clara Hewett disappears into the touring theatre, only to crawl back into hiding in the nether world, defeated. Far from offering Wordsworthian nourishment on which they can always feed, their holiday in Essex is only an interlude for Jane and Sidney before return to the inexorable condition of their lives.

In other novels alternative worlds exist as real possibilities. When Oliver Twist encounters Mr Brownlow and the Maylies, he enters a world which not only exists as certainly as Fagin's but which, in this fable, proves more powerful. Gissing, by contrast, refuses any possible lead into another world. At one point he declares: 'Really, we shall soon be coming to the conclusion that the differences between the nether and the upper world are purely superficial.' Dickens builds the whole of *Bleak House* on this observation; in *The Nether World* it is a sarcastic aside. The 'upper world' remains an abstraction. It exists, of course. Sidney Kirkwood toils at making jewellery to adorn its bosom. But it exists in the novel only as the other, of which the characters have no knowledge and to which they have no access. Sidney declares: 'We have to fight against the rich world that's always crushing us down, down, whether it means to or not', but he doesn't and can't. His words are meaningless. All he can do is struggle to make life less intolerable for those who are his responsibility in the nether world.

If Gissing refuses to explore the economic and social interdependence of the upper world and the lower, he presents the economic realities of the latter relentlessly. Other novels, *Little Dorrit* or *The Way We Live Now*, for example, deploy the *idea* of money more variously and imaginatively, but none conveys the *reality* more starkly than *The Nether World*. Only money commands food, drink, and a roof over one's head. Money has to be earned laboriously, at a jewellery workshop, an artificial-flower maker's, a die-sinker's, or a cabinet-maker's. Money pits the poor against the poor. John Hewett takes to dyeing his hair in a vain attempt to get a job against younger, stronger men. Mrs Candy sinks into alcoholism, but every penny she spends helps Mrs Green who runs the beer-shop. Where would pawnbrokers be without the poor? Money is a site of potent fantasy. Bob Hewett hits on the idea of using his skills to make it, not metaphorically but literally, by forging. Joseph Snowdon dreams of inheriting it, so that money's power will transform his life without any effort. Mrs Peckover and Clem scheme to wrest old Snowdon's money away from him and Jane, even though strictly they are not in need of it and the price is Clem's marrying a man she despises. No one is free from its power. The Byass family lives in a better-class street, comfortable enough on a clerk's income, but when the wage-earner begins to neglect his family it is clear how fragile their security is. Bessie Byass's heart is full when she learns that Jane is, after all, not an heiress, but even as she consoles she is calculating what it means to her that Jane will no longer be able to afford the rent she has been paying. Money even determines Sidney Kirkwood's life. At the beginning of the novel he is the one independent character—unmarried, in regular work, temperate and thrifty enough to save a little from his wages. By its end, burdened with an embittered wife, a decayed father-in-law, and feckless children from John Hewett's second marriage, Kirkwood's waking thoughts are dominated by money. As are everyone else's. The narrator comments that, for this family, 'life had no illusions. Of every mouthful they ate, the price was known to them.'

What is so striking about *The Nether World* is how little is presented as a counter-force to this economic pressure. Christianity, for example, is notably absent. During the latter third of the century a number of heroic clergymen attempted to revivify the Church as a force within working-class communities in London, and alongside them, inspired by Christian ideals, worked the volunteers for the university settlements. This limited but positive action is not even glanced at in *The Nether World*. Philanthropy is represented by Miss Lant, a joyless woman who is said to belong to a whole class of such, 'who substitute for the old religious acerbity a narrow and oppresive zeal for good works', and by Michael Snowdon, whose dedication to his philanthropic project increasingly dehumanizes him. As for religion, there is none, only the crazed witness of 'Mad Jack', gabbling psalms and screaming: 'This life you are now leading is that of the damned; this place to which you are confined is Hell! This is Hell—Hell—Hell!'

It is ironic that it should be 'Mad Jack' who places the experience of life in Clerkenwell in a wider, metaphysical perspective, for no one else does, not excepting the narrator. In *Jude the Obscure*, when the corpses of the children are discovered, a local doctor, 'an advanced man', tries to console the distraught parents by telling them that their children's death partakes of 'the coming universal wish not to live'. Outside in the street two clergymen 'of different views [are] arguing about the eastward position'. Both metaphysical discourses, the new and the old, in their irrelevance only intensify the agony of Sue and Jude, but they also serve to place the tragedy in a wider frame. Perhaps life is meaningless, but Schopenhauerians and Christians alike continue the attempt to render it intelligible. Throughout *The Nether World* Gissing eschews all opportunity to place events in a larger setting. At one point, for example, he states that the inhabitants of Shooter's Gardens preferred it to more salubrious model lodgings, for in the Gardens they could be 'as vile as they pleased'. He adds: 'How they came to love vileness, well, that is quite another matter, and shall not for the present concern us.' The refusal to speculate reinforces the impression that this novel deals with an enclosed world, whose reality is the prime fact, not its position in any interpretative frame of social or historical or metaphysical discourse.

Another significant absence is any reference to trades-unionism or other forms of concerted action. All positive evidence—and there was plenty from the 1870s onwards—that working people were making efforts to improve their lot by organizing from within their own world go unnoticed. Shouting himself hoarse on Clerkenwell Green, wild-eyed and foaming at the mouth, John Hewett embodies the impotence of radical activity in a world whose law is enunciated by his daughter: 'We have to fight, fight for everything, and the weak get beaten.' Sidney Kirkwood has passed through his radical phase. It is presented as a sign of his strength that he no longer agitates himself with dreams.

The most striking absence of all is romantic love. That Gissing ignored church missions and trades-unionism is not surprising. For various reasons he had no faith in either, and there is no reason to enter here into biographical explanations for why this should have been so. That he refuses to privilege romantic love, however, is extraordinary, the clearest indication of the extremity of vision realized in this novel, for it has always been the transhistorical power to which artists appeal as the one element in life which surmounts social and economic determinism. When Mary Barton finally marries Jem Wilson, when Margaret Hale unites with the mill-owner Thornton, when Little Dorrit and Arthur Clennam walk down the steps of the church 'inseparable and blessed', romantic love, consecrated in marriage, has triumphed over all obstacles. The couple is not a nostrum for society's ills, but a locus for values, and hopes, and potentialities which even the worst of environmental circumstances cannot suppress. Gissing confounds this literary tradition as totally as Hardy did later in *Jude the Obscure*. Sidney Kirkwood and Jane Snowdon—the two main figures in the novel—ought to marry. Marriage for all of the other characters in *The Nether World* is at best—the Byasses—tolerable, and at worst—the Candys—bestial. Sidney and Jane, though, are not married but falling in love, and any reader familiar with Victorian fiction can see the way the story ought to unfold. However, having awakened Jane's love, Sidney draws back for reasons which every other inhabitant of the nether world would deem absurd, and then, self-deluded and in no little spirit of self-sacrifice, he marries the now-disfigured Clara Hewett. He ends up still unable to look his wife in the face without

flinching, desperately beseeching Clara to realize that if
they cannot act kindly to one another they will join the
other 'poor creatures who let their misery degrade them'.

At the novel's close Jane and Sidney meet by the grave-
side of Michael Snowdon, whose money and crazy scheme
drove them apart. A few words and they separate, Jane to
spend her life helping such unfortunates as Pennyloaf
Candy, with the love that alone inspires genuine philanthropy, and Sidney to spend his keeping his wife from
suicidal despair and his adopted children away from the
edge of the abyss. The narrator comments:

Unmarked, unencouraged save by their love of uprightness and
mercy, they stood by the side of those more hapless, brought some
comfort to hearts less courageous than their own. Where they
abode it was not all dark. Sorrow certainly awaited them,
perchance defeat in even the humble aims they had set themselves;
but at least their lives would remain a protest against those brute
forces of society which fill with wreck the abysses of the nether
world.

Comparison with the similar last sentence of *Middlemarch*
will indicate what a sad and muted statement this is.
Something is wrested from defeat, but how little and at
what cost.

The second reason why *The Nether World* is so discomfiting
is, to put it simply, that it is not Dickens. Low-life London
was Dickens's territory. There were, in fact, many Victorian
novels set in London's unfashionable quarters, but it was
Dickens's vision which prevailed over all others. The City
and the Inns of court, Saffron Hill and Limehouse—by the
time Gissing wrote *The Nether World* these places were
known all over the English-speaking world as if Dickens
had created them. They were known, that is to readers who
would never visit London, only as Dickens had created
them. In setting *The Nether World* in a named part of

London, Gissing was entering the domain which Dickens had commanded.

The Nether World, however, is not a work of discipleship. It continually invokes Dickens only to subvert the Dickensian. It is disconcerting inasmuch as the reader senses how completely Gissing refuses alternative modes of imaginative treatment.

Much in the novel brings Dickens to mind. The scene in the work-room of the artificial-flower factory, for example, where a sunbeam 'touched the skirt, the arms, the head of one of the girls, who, as if gladdened by the kindly warmth, looked round and smiled', recalls the similar moment in *Hard Times* when a sunbeam falling across the schoolroom gives Sissy Jupe 'a deeper and more lustrous colour', but draws out of Bitzer 'what little colour he ever possessed'. Again, Bob Hewett blindly seeking refuge in a place where he is certain to be hunted down recalls Bill Sikes in *Oliver Twist*, while Shooter's Gardens in its last days is strikingly reminiscent of Staggs's Gardens in *Dombey and Son*.

Examples could be multiplied, and to explore them all would lengthen this introduction into a monograph. One might dwell, for example, on Gissing's refusal to 'harlequinize' (John Sloan's term in *George Gissing: The Cultural Challenge*, 11). Consider what the creator of Mrs Pardiggle would have made of the opportunity presented by Miss Lant. Dickens's power of creating characters who live in their own fantasy world would certainly have been lavished on Mr Eagles, who, obsessed by financial reform, lives contentedly on two pounds a week while 'for ever engaged in the theoretic manipulation of millions'. Gissing notes the pathos of their lives but, unlike Dickens, he never allows Miss Lant or Mr Eagles to be centre-stage in their own pathetic scene, however brief, nor to exhibit comic vitality. To do either would jeopardize the singleness of focus and effect aimed for. To endow such characters with comic vitality, or the capacity for awakening sentimental emotion, would be, moreover, to empower them, to release them from their status as victims alongside other victims in the total structure of the nether world.

Two elements in Gissing's relationship to Dickens, however, are especially important and deserve more than summary treatment. The first can be reached through the scene in Chapter I in which Clem Peckover tortures Jane. Jane, saved from the workhouse only by the 'kindness' of Mrs Peckover, as she is constantly reminded, is used to the older Clem's habitual bullying. On this night, however, Clem, sated with food and drink, is at leisure to inflict pain with finesse, and terrifies Jane with the order she knows the younger girl most dreads—to go, in the dark, into the room where a coffin awaits burial. Clem's sadism recalls Noah Claypole's cruelty to Oliver Twist. He too is replete and at leisure to torment a child who is orphaned and dependent. Noah and Clem, who both degenerate as the novel proceeds, are 'rank, evilly-fostered growth' of the nether world.

It is, though, the difference between the two scenes that matters. Dickens plays up Noah's brutality in order to maximize the effect when puny Oliver Twist turns on his tormentor and thrashes him. And this reversal leads into one of the funniest moments in the novel, as the now-furious and emboldened Oliver, locked in the cupboard, defies Mr Bumble. In Gissing's world victims don't suddenly become strong, nor is their plight susceptible to comic treatment. Jane succumbs, as she must, to Clem's power, and for the rest of her life, as the novel makes explicit, the memory of her terror remains with her. In a Dickens novel there is always the moment of retribution—as Mr Micawber unmasks Uriah Heep, for example—when the reader's carefully nourished desire for emotional release is satisfied. In *The Nether World* there never is.

The second element concerns the nature of plot. Adrian Poole claims that the 'creative core of the novel lies in its images rather than the components of "character" and "plot" ' (*Gissing in Context*, 86). Poole's emphasis is right, and his own account of the cumulative power of the novel's images is persuasive, but he underestimates, I think, the importance of the plot of *The Nether World* as the agent which deploys them to such effect. For *The Nether World* certainly has a plot—it is not a series of impressions or loosely connected scenes—and the plot is Dickensian. More exactly, it is like *Great Expectations*.

An old man returns from Australia, apparently wealthy. He has a scheme for using his money for the betterment of the lower orders, through the agency of a young woman. Once it is clear that he does have money, despite his humble way of living, schemers get to work to acquire it for themselves. Ultimately the fortune is wasted. In detail *The Nether World* diverges from *Great Expectations*: whereas Magwitch wants to 'make' Pip a gentleman, for example, to enjoy revenge on a society which discarded him as a criminal, Michael Snowdon is determined that Jane shall not become a lady. But viewed overall it is clear that most of the ingredients of the Dickens plot figure in *The Nether World*—mystery, a missing will, machination, an heiress, disappointed claimants and dubious lawyers—and that it operates dynamically, bringing characters into significant relationships, establishing moral dilemmas, and involving the reader in predicting the outcome.

The plot of *The Nether World*, however, systematically and discomfitingly denies its parentage. Michael Snowdon is not Mr Brownlow nor Mr Boffin. He is not even Magwitch, for Magwitch's money does ultimately do some good, though not in the way he had intended. Snowdon's money oppresses Jane, who is too passive to resist the old man's demands that she should dedicate her life to his philanthropic scheme. Instead of enabling the union of the two figures who are clearly meant for each other—Jane and Sidney—it separates them. And at the denouement, through the merest accident of timing, the fortune passes to the one person who should not inherit it, the idle schemer Joseph Snowdon.

In a Dickens plot, gaining or losing money can both establish correct order and promote virtue. Oliver Twist comes into his inheritance and Fagin and Monks are rightly destroyed. Pip loses his, again rightly. John Harmon becomes rich, while Silas Wegg ends up being pitched into a scavenger's cart. In every case the plot identifies a hierarchy of deserving and undeserving, humbles the proud, unmasks the hypocrite, and in at least one site of domestic virtue—the new Bleak House—establishes happiness. The plot of *The Nether World* refuses all of this. The deserving are damaged, irreparably; the undeserving Joseph is rewarded. Gissing even gives one further twist, to complete the thoroughness of the reversal. Joseph Snowdon dies in America and so, after all, old Snowdon's money should pass to Jane, as Joseph's daughter. But there isn't any. Joseph lost it in commercial speculation. Jane ends the novel working once again to pay the rent on her single room.

NOTE ON THE TEXT

ALTHOUGH *The Nether World* is clearly related to Gissing's previous novels and draws on his own recent experiences, actual composition seems to have been spurred by his response to the appalling circumstances of the death of his estranged wife, Helen. At the end of February 1888 Gissing was summoned to a house in Lambeth, where his wife lay dead in a miserable room. He began to write *The Nether World* a little less than three weeks later, on 19 March 1888.

The diary records fitful progress, but Volume One was finished on 2 May. Gissing was extremely wretched and complained about slow progress; none the less, Volume Two was finished on 18 June. Volume Three, however, did not go smoothly. On 8 July Gissing recorded that 'of a sudden, like the snapping of a cord, I became aware that the plot of my story, as arranged for the next few days, would not do'. The following day: 'Woke to the most miserable distress; striving vainly to see my way in the story. Seldom have I suffered keener mental pain.' After some rewriting of earlier sections, Gissing drove on to the end, the only hiccup being that writing the capture of Bob Hewett so excited him that he had to walk the streets instead of finishing his daily quota (13 July). Volume Three was completed on 22 July. The following morning he deposited the novel with Smith, Elder, and Co.

The manuscript is now in the Huntington Library, Pasadena. It is foliated in three separate volumes, each fos. 1–90. Chapter-breaks (referring to the chapter numbers in this edition), are 1–13; 14–27; 28–40. There is evidence of substantial revision in Volume Three of the manuscript, but of a kind which for the most part makes the original irrecoverable. Gissing has cut up sheets and made up fresh folios by joining old to new with gummed paper. Some renumbering of folios was required, and the renumbering of the chapter 'Mad Jack's Dream' suggests that 'The Heir' was a late insertion. The manuscript bears compositors' marks throughout.

Gissing received £150 for *The Nether World*. It was published by Smith, Elder, in three volumes, on 3 April 1889, in an edition of 500 copies. A one-volume edition followed in 1890 (issued December 1889) and it provides the text for this edition. For bibliographical details see Michael Collie, *George Gissing: A Bibliography* (1975), 46–8.

I am grateful to the Trustees of the Huntington Library for allowing me to examine the manuscript and to the administrators of the Astor Travel Fund and the research funds of the English Faculty Board, Oxford University, for financial assistance.

SELECT BIBLIOGRAPHY

THIS is a list of books which will be found helpful in further study of *The Nether World* and other early Gissing novels. There is a bibliography of Gissing's writings by Michael Collie, *George Gissing: A Bibliographical Study* (Winchester: St Paul's Bibliographies, 1985), but it is judged wholly inadequate by all Gissing scholars.

The following are indispensable resources: *The Collected Letters of George Gissing*, ed. Paul F. Mattheisen, Arthur C. Young, and Pierre Coustillas, 9 vols. (Athens, Oh.: Ohio University Press, 1990–7). *London and the Life of Literature in Late Victorian England: The Diary of George Gissing, Novelist*, ed. Pierre Coustillas (Hassocks: Harvester Press, 1978); *George Gissing's Commonplace Book*, ed. Jacob Korg (New York: New York Public Library, 1962); *George Gissing on Ficton*, ed. Jacob and Cynthia Korg (London: Enitharmon Press, 1978); *George Gissing: Essays and Fiction*, ed. Pierre Coustillas (Baltimore: Johns Hopkins University Press, 1970); Pierre Coustillas and Patrick Bridgwater, *George Gissing at Work: A Study of his Notebook 'Extracts from My Reading'* (Greenboro, NC: ELT Press, 1988); *Gissing: The Critical Heritage*, ed. Pierre Coustillas and Colin Partridge (London: Routledge and Kegan Paul, 1972).

A fresh biography of Gissing, which takes into account the collected letters and recent work on Gissing's early life, is much needed. At the time of writing (1998) the best biography remains Jacob Korg, *George Gissing: A Critical Biography* (London: Methuen, 1965). Gillian Tindall, *The Born Exile: George Gissing* (London: Temple Smith, 1974) and John Halperin, *Gissing: A Life in Books* (Oxford: Oxford University Press, 1982) are also of interest.

The following critical and scholarly books are recommended: David Howard, John Lucas, and John Goode,

Tradition and Tolerance in Nineteenth-Century Fiction (London: Routledge and Kegan Paul, 1966); P. J. Keating, *The Working-Classes in Victorian Fiction* (London: Routledge and Kegan Paul, 1971); Adrian Poole, *Gissing in Context* (London: Macmillan, 1975); John Goode, *George Gissing: Ideology and Fiction* (London: Vision Press, 1978); Frederic Jameson, *The Political Unconscious: Narrative as a Socially Symbolic Act* (Ithaca, NY: Cornell University Press, 1981); David Grylls, *The Paradox of Gissing* (London: Allen and Unwin, 1986); P. J. Keating, *The Haunted Study: A Social History of the English Novel 1875–1914* (London: Secker and Warburg, 1989); John Sloan, *George Gissing: The Cultural Challenge* (London: Macmillan, 1989); William H. Greenslade, *Degeneration, Culture and the Novel 1880–1940* (Cambridge: Cambridge University Press, 1994); and Peter D. McDonald, *British Literary Culture and Publishing Practice, 1880–1914* (Cambridge: Cambridge University Press, 1997).

The *Gissing Newsletter*, now called the *Gissing Journal*, is valuable for its articles on every aspect of Gissing's life and work and especially for its reviews of scholarship and criticism. Joseph J. Wolff surveyed the field in *George Gissing: An Annotated Bibliography of Writings about Him* (De Kalb, Ill.: Northern Illinois University Press, 1974). Writings on Gissing are listed in the annual bibliography issue of *Victorian Studies*, in the annual bibliography published by the Modern Language Association (available in good libraries on CD ROM), and in the annual *Bibliography of Victorian Studies* (Edmonton, Alberta: LITR Database, 1984–   ).

The following works of social history are of especial interest for readers of Gissing: H. Pfautz, *Charles Booth on the City: Physical Pattern and Social Structure* (Chicago: University of Chicago Press, 1967); Brian Harrison, *Drink and the Victorians: The Temperance Question in England 1815–1872* (London: Faber and Faber, 1971); Gareth Stedman Jones, *Outcast London: A Study in the Relationship Between Classes in Victorian Society* (Oxford: Oxford University Press, 1971; revised edn.

Harmondsworth: Penguin Books, 1984); H. J. Dyos and Michael Wolff (eds.), *The Victorian City: Images and Realities*, 2 vols. (London: Routledge and Kegan Paul, 1973); John Nelson Tarn, *Five Per Cent Philanthropy: An Account of Housing in Urban Areas between 1840 and 1914* (Cambridge: Cambridge University Press, 1973); Enid Gauldie, *Cruel Habitations: A History of Working-Class Housing 1780–1918* (London: Allen and Unwin, 1974); Donald J. Olsen, *The Growth of Victorian London* (London: Batsford, 1976); Anthony S. Wohl, *The Eternal Slum: Housing and Social Policy in Victorian London* (London: E. Arnold, 1977); F. B. Smith, *The People's Health 1830–1910* (London: Croom Helm, 1979); Gareth Stedman Jones, *Languages of Class: Studies in English Working Class History 1832–1982* (Cambridge: Cambridge University Press, 1983); William J. Fishman, *East End 1881: A Year in a London Borough among the Labouring Poor* (London: Duckworth, 1988); Jack Simmons, *The Victorian Railway* (London: Thames and Hudson, 1991); Jose Harris, *Private Lives Public Spirit: A Social History of Britain 1870–1914* (Oxford: Oxford University Press, 1993).

A CHRONOLOGY OF
GEORGE GISSING

1857   Born in Wakefield, Yorkshire (22 November); his father, Thomas Gissing, is a pharmacist, who dies when George is 13.

1872   Wins scholarship to Owens College, Manchester; a multiple prize-winner, clearly destined for a successful academic career.

1876   Meets prostitute Marianne Helen ('Nell') Harrison; (31 May) caught stealing money in college to further plan to save Nell from prostitution; expelled and stripped of honours, he serves one month's imprisonment; sails for America (September), where he supports himself by teaching and, latterly, short-story writing.

1877   Returns to England (October) and begins life in London; lives with Nell Harrison; publishes short stories written in America and begins first novel, unpublished.

1879   Having come of age he receives £300 from his aunt's estate; marries Nell (27 October); finishes *Workers in the Dawn*.

1880   *Workers in the Dawn* published; gets to know leading positivist Frederic Harrison and for four years tutors his sons.

1882   Separates from wife, now alcoholic; rejects positivism and writes essay, 'The Hope of Pessimism', much influenced by Schopenhauer.

1884   Publication of *The Unclassed* (June) marks real beginning of his career as a novelist.

1886   *Demos* published to generally favourable reviews, but he is living in constant poverty; manages first visit to France; *Isabel Clarendon* published.

1887   *Thyrza* published.

1888 Death of Nell (February); *A Life's Morning* published; visits Italy for first time and is overwhelmed.

1889 *The Nether World* published; visits Greece.

1890 Meets Edith Underwood (September); *The Emancipated* published.

1891 Marries Edith (25 February); moves to Exeter; *New Grub Street* published (April), to acclaim; son Walter born (10 December).

1892 *Denzil Quarrier* and *Born in Exile* published.

1893 Returns to London (June); *The Odd Women* published.

1894 Moves to Epsom (September); *In the Year of Jubilee* published; during this period his reputation grows, and there is a modest improvement in finances.

1895 *Eve's Ransom* and *Sleeping Fires* published; also many short stories, which now become a staple of income.

1896 Son Alfred born (20 January); meets H. G. Wells (20 November); *The Paying Guest* published.

1897 Leaves wife and home (February); slight emphysema diagnosed; moves to Devon, but returns after four months; *The Whirlpool* published to better sales than any previous novel; finally parts from Edith (September), and makes another visit to Italy; away seven months.

1898 *Charles Dickens: A Critical Study* published; settles in Dorking; receives letter from 29-year-old Gabrielle Fleury (June), enquiring after French translation rights of *New Grub Street*; meets her (6 July) and soon decides to live with her.

1899 Leaves England for France; eventually settles in Paris with Gabrielle and her mother; *The Crown of Life* published; health begins to deteriorate.

1901 *Our Friend the Charlatan* published; returns to England and stays with H. G. Wells; *By the Ionian Sea* published; returns to France (August), eventually settling in St Jean de Luz, south-west France.

The Nether World

*'La peinture d'un fumier peut être justifiée
pourvu qu'il y pousse une belle fleur; sans
cela, le fumier n'est que repoussant.'*

(M. Renan, at the Académie Française, Feb 21, 1889)*

CONTENTS

———◆———

THE NETHER WORLD

—◆◆—

CHAPTER I

A THRALL OF THRALLS

In the troubled twilight of a March evening ten years ago, an old man, whose equipment and bearing suggested that he was fresh from travel, walked slowly across Clerkenwell Green,* and by the graveyard of St. James's Church stood for a moment looking about him. His age could not be far from seventy, but, despite the stoop of his shoulders, he gave little sign of failing under the burden of years; his sober step indicated gravity of character rather than bodily feebleness, and his grasp of a stout stick was not such as bespeaks need of support. His attire was neither that of a man of leisure, nor of the kind usually worn by English mechanics.* Instead of coat and waistcoat, he wore a garment something like a fisherman's guernsey, and over this a coarse short cloak, picturesque in appearance as it was buffeted by the wind. His trousers were of moleskin; his boots reached almost to his knees; for head-covering he had the cheapest kind of undyed felt, its form exactly that of the old petasus.* To say that his aspect was venerable would serve to present him in a measure, yet would not be wholly accurate, for there was too much of past struggle and present anxiety in his countenance to permit full expression of the natural dignity of the features. It was a fine face and might have been distinctly noble, but circumstances had marred the purpose of Nature; you perceived that his cares had too often been of the kind which are created by ignoble necessities, such as leave to most men of his standing a bare humanity of visage. He had long thin white hair; his beard was short and merely grizzled. In his left hand he carried a bundle, which probably contained clothing.

The burial-ground by which he had paused was as little restful to the eye as are most of those discoverable in the by-ways of London. The small trees that grew about it shivered in their leaflessness; the rank grass was wan under the failing day; most of the stones leaned this way or that, emblems of neglect (they were very white at the top, and darkened downwards till the damp soil made them black), and certain cats and dogs were prowling or sporting among the graves. At this corner the east wind blew with malice such as it never puts forth save where there are poorly clad people to be pierced; it swept before it thin clouds of unsavoury dust, mingled with the light refuse of the streets. Above the shape-less houses night was signalling a murky approach; the sky —if sky it could be called—gave threatening of sleet, per-chance of snow. And on every side was the rumble of traffic, the voiceful evidence of toil and of poverty; hawkers were cry-ing their goods; the inevitable organ was clanging before a public-house hard by; the crumpet-man was hastening along, with monotonous ringing of his bell and hoarse rhythmic wail.

The old man had fixed his eyes half absently on the in-scription of a gravestone near him; a lean cat springing out between the iron railings seemed to recall his attention, and with a slight sigh he went forward along the narrow street which is called St. James's Walk. In a few minutes he had reached the end of it, and found himself facing a high grey-brick wall, wherein, at this point, was an arched gateway closed with black doors. He looked at the gateway, then fixed his gaze on something that stood just above—something which the dusk half concealed, and by so doing made more impressive. It was the sculptured counterfeit of a human face, that of a man distraught with agony. The eyes stared wildly from their sockets, the hair struggled in maniac disorder, the forehead was wrung with torture, the cheeks sunken, the throat fearsomely wasted, and from the wide lips there seemed to be issuing a horrible cry. Above this hideous effigy was carved the legend: 'MIDDLESEX HOUSE OF DETENTION.'

Something more than pain came to the old man's face as he looked and pondered; his lips trembled like those of one in anger, and his eyes had a stern resentful gleaming. He walked on a few paces, then suddenly stopped where a woman was standing at an open door.

'I ask your pardon,' he said, addressing her with the courtesy which owes nothing to refined intercourse, 'but do you by chance know anyone of the name of Snowdon hereabouts?'

The woman replied with a brief negative; she smiled at the appearance of the questioner, and, with the vulgar instinct, looked about for someone to share her amusement.

'Better inquire at the 'ouse at the corner,' she added, as the man was moving away. 'They've been here a long time, I b'lieve.'

He accepted her advice. But the people at the public-house could not aid his search. He thanked them, paused for a moment with his eyes down, then again sighed slightly and went forth into the gathering gloom.

Less than five minutes later there ran into the same house of refreshment a little slight girl, perhaps thirteen years old; she carried a jug, and at the bar asked for 'a pint of old six.' The barman, whilst drawing the ale, called out to a man who had entered immediately after the child:

'Don't know nobody called Snowdon about 'ere, do you, Mr. Squibbs?'

The individual addressed was very dirty, very sleepy, and seemingly at odds with mankind. He replied contemptuously with a word which, in phonetic rendering may perhaps be spelt 'Nay-oo.'

But the little girl was looking eagerly from one man to the other; what had been said appeared to excite keen interest in her. She forgot all about the beer-jug that was waiting, and, after a brief but obvious struggle with timidity, said in an uncertain voice:

'Has somebody been asking for that name, sir?'

'Yes, they have,' the barman answered, in surprise. 'Why?'

'My name's Snowdon, sir—Jane Snowdon.'

She reddened over all her face as soon as she had given utterance to the impulsive words. The barman was regarding her with a sort of semi-interest, and Mr. Squibbs also had fixed his bleary (or beery) eyes upon her. Neither would have admitted an active interest in so pale and thin and wretchedly-clad a little mortal. Her hair hung loose, and had no covering; it was hair of no particular colour, and seemed to have been for a long time utterly untended; the wind, on her run hither, had tossed it into much disorder. Signs there

were of some kind of clothing beneath the short, dirty, worn
dress, but it was evidently of the scantiest description. The
freely exposed neck was very thin, but, like the outline of her
face, spoke less of a feeble habit of body than of the present
pinch of sheer hunger. She did not, indeed, look like one of
those children who are born in disease and starvation, and
put to nurse upon the pavement; her limbs were shapely
enough, her back was straight, she had features that were not
merely human, but girl-like, and her look had in it the light
of an intelligence generally sought for in vain among the
children of the street. The blush and the way in which she
hung her head were likewise tokens of a nature endowed with
ample sensitiveness.

'Oh, your name's Jane Snowdon, is it?' said the barman.
'Well, you're just three minutes an' three-quarters too late.
P'r'aps it's a fortune a-runnin' after you. He was a rum old
party as inquired. Never mind; it's all in a life. There's
fortunes lost every week by a good deal less than three
minutes when it's 'orses—eh, Mr. Squibbs?'

Mr. Squibbs swore with emphasis.

The little girl took her jug of beer and was turning away.

'Hollo!' cried the barman. 'Where's the money, Jane?
—if you don't mind.'

She turned again in increased confusion, and laid coppers*
on the counter. Thereupon the man asked her where she
lived; she named a house in Clerkenwell Close, near at hand.

'Father live there?'

She shook her head.

'Mother?'

'I haven't got one, sir.'

'Who is it as you live with, then?'

'Mrs. Peckover, sir.'

'Well, as I was sayin', he was a queer old joker as arsted
for the name of Snowdon. Shouldn't wonder if you see him
goin' round.'

And he added a pretty full description of this old man, to
which the girl listened closely. Then she went thoughtfully—
a little sadly—on her way.

In the street, all but dark by this time, she cast anxious
glances onwards and behind, but no old man in an odd hat
and cloak and with white hair was discoverable. Linger she
might not. She reached a house of which the front-door
stood open; it looked black and cavernous within; but she

advanced with the step of familiarity, and went downstairs to a front-kitchen. Through the half-open door came a strong odour and a hissing sound, plainly due to the frying of sausages. Before Jane could enter she was greeted sharply in a voice which was young and that of a female, but had no other quality of graciousness.

'You've taken your time, my lady! All right! just wait till I've 'ad my tea, that's all! Me an' you'll settle accounts to-night, see if we don't. Mother told me as she owed you a lickin', and I'll pay it off, with a little on my own account too. Only wait till I've 'ad my tea, that's all. What are you standin' there for, like a fool? Bring that beer 'ere, an' let's see 'ow much you've drank.'

'I haven't put my lips near it, miss; indeed I haven't,' pleaded the child, whose face of dread proved both natural timidity and the constant apprehension of ill-usage.

'Little liar! that's what you always was, an' always will be.—Take that!'

The speaker was a girl of sixteen, tall, rather bony, rudely handsome; the hand with which she struck was large and coarse-fibred, the muscles that impelled it vigorous. Her dress was that of a work-girl, unsubstantial, ill-fitting, but of ambitious cut; her hair was very abundant, and rose upon the back of her head in thick coils, an elegant fringe depending in front. The fire had made her face scarlet, and in the lamplight her large eyes glistened with many joys.

First and foremost, Miss Clementina Peckover rejoiced because she had left work much earlier than usual, and was about to enjoy what she would have described as a 'blow out.' Secondly, she rejoiced because her mother, the landlady of the house, was absent for the night, and consequently she would exercise sole authority over the domestic slave, Jane Snowdon—that is to say, would indulge to the uttermost her instincts of cruelty in tormenting a defenceless creature. Finally—a cause of happiness antecedent to the others, but less vivid in her mind at this moment—in the next room lay awaiting burial the corpse of Mrs. Peckover's mother-in-law, whose death six days ago had plunged mother and daughter into profound delight, partly because they were relieved at length from making a pretence of humanity to a bed-ridden old woman, partly owing to the fact that the deceased had left behind her a sum of seventy-five pounds, exclusive of moneys due from a burial-club.

'Ah!' exclaimed Miss Peckover (who was affectionately known to her intimates as 'Clem'), as she watched Jane stagger back from the blow, and hide her face in silent endurance of pain. 'That's just a morsel to stay your appetite, my lady! You didn't expect me back 'ome at this time, did you? You thought as you was goin' to have the kitchen to yourself when mother went. Ha ha! ho ho!—These sausages is done; now you clean that fryin'-pan; and if I can find a speck of dirt in it as big as 'arlf a farden,* I'll take you by the 'air of the 'ed an' clean it with your face, *that's* what I'll do! Understand? Oh, I mean what I say, my lady! Me an' you's a-goin' to spend a evenin' together, there's no two ways about that. Ho ho! he he!'

The frankness of Clem's brutality went far towards redeeming her character. The exquisite satisfaction with which she viewed Jane's present misery, the broad joviality with which she gloated over the prospect of cruelties shortly to be inflicted, put her at once on a par with the noble savage running wild in woods. Civilisation could bring no charge against this young woman; it and she had no common criterion. Who knows but this lust of hers for sanguinary domination was the natural enough issue of the brutalising serfdom of her predecessors in the family line of the Peckovers? A thrall suddenly endowed with authority will assuredly make bitter work for the luckless creature in the next degree of thraldom.

A cloth was already spread across one end of the deal table, with such other preparations for a meal as Clem deemed adequate. The sausages—five in number—she had emptied from the frying-pan directly on to her plate, and with them all the black rich juice that had exuded in the process of cooking—particularly rich, owing to its having several times caught fire and blazed triumphantly. On sitting down and squaring her comely frame to work, the first thing Clem did was to take a long draught out of the beer-jug; refreshed thus, she poured the remaining liquor into a glass. Ready at hand was mustard, made in a tea-cup; having taken a certain quantity of this condiment on to her knife, she proceeded to spread each sausage with it from end to end, patting them in a friendly way as she finished the operation. Next she sprinkled them with pepper, and after that she constructed a little pile of salt on the side of the plate, using her fingers to convey it from the salt-cellar. It remained to cut a thick slice of bread —she held the loaf pressed to her bosom whilst doing this—

and to crush it down well into the black grease beside the sausages ; then Clem was ready to begin.

For five minutes she fed heartily, showing really remarkable skill in conveying pieces of sausage to her mouth by means of the knife alone. Finding it necessary to breathe at last, she looked round at Jane. The hand-maiden was on her knees near the fire, scrubbing very hard at the pan with successive pieces of newspaper. It was a sight to increase the gusto of Clem's meal, but of a sudden there came into the girl's mind a yet more delightful thought. I have mentioned that in the back-kitchen lay the body of a dead woman ; it was already encoffined, and waited for interment on the morrow, when Mrs. Peckover would arrive with a certain female relative from St. Albans. Now the proximity of this corpse was a ceaseless occasion of dread and misery to Jane Snowdon ; the poor child had each night to make up a bed for herself in this front-room, dragging together a little heap of rags when mother and daughter were gone up to their chamber, and since the old woman's death it was much if Jane had enjoyed one hour of unbroken sleep. She endeavoured to hide these feelings, but Clem, with her Red Indian scent, divined them accurately enough. She hit upon a good idea.

'Go into the next room,' she commanded suddenly, 'and fetch the matches off of the mantel-piece. I shall want to go upstairs presently, to see if you've scrubbed the bed-room well.'

Jane was blanched ; but she rose from her knees at once, and reached a candlestick from above the fireplace.

'What's that for?' shouted Clem, with her mouth full. 'You've no need of a light to find the mantel-piece. If you're not off——'

Jane hastened from the kitchen. Clem yelled to her to close the door, and she had no choice but to obey. In the dark passage outside there was darkness that might be felt. The child all but fainted with the sickness of horror as she turned the handle of the other door and began to grope her way. She knew exactly where the coffin was ; she knew that to avoid touching it in the diminutive room was all but impossible. And touch it she did. Her anguish uttered itself, not in a mere sound of terror, but in a broken word or two of a prayer she knew by heart, including a name which sounded like a charm against evil. She had reached the mantel-piece ; oh, she could not, could not find the matches ! Yes, at last her hand closed on them. A blind rush, and she was out

again in the passage. She re-entered the front-kitchen with
limbs that quivered, with the sound of dreadful voices ringing
about her, and blankness before her eyes.

Clem laughed heartily, then finished her beer in a long,
enjoyable pull. Her appetite was satisfied; the last trace of
oleaginous matter had disappeared from her plate, and now
she toyed with little pieces of bread lightly dipped into the
mustard-pot. These *bonnes bouches** put her into excellent
humour; presently she crossed her arms and leaned back.
There was no denying that Clem was handsome; at sixteen
she had all her charms in apparent maturity, and they were
of the coarsely magnificent order. Her forehead was low and
of great width; her nose was well shapen, and had large
sensual apertures; her cruel lips may be seen on certain fine
antique busts; the neck that supported her heavy head was
splendidly rounded. In laughing, she became a model for an
artist, an embodiment of fierce life independent of morality.
Her health was probably less sound than it seemed to be; one
would have compared her, not to some piece of exuberant
normal vegetation, but rather to a rank, evilly-fostered growth.
The putrid soil of that nether world yields other forms besides
the obviously blighted and sapless.

'Have you done any work for Mrs. Hewett to-day?' she
asked of her victim, after sufficiently savouring the spectacle
of terror.

'Yes, miss; I did the front-room fireplace, an' fetched
fourteen of coals, an' washed out a few things.'

'What did she give you?'

'A penny, miss. I gave it to Mrs. Peckover before she
went.'

'Oh, you did? Well, look 'ere; you'll just remember in
future that all you get from the lodgers belongs to me, an' not
to mother. It's a new arrangement, understand. An' if you
dare to give up a 'apenny to mother, I'll lick you till you're
nothin' but a bag o' bones. Understand?'

Having on the spur of the moment devised this ingenious
difficulty for the child, who was sure to suffer in many ways
from such a conflict of authorities, Clem began to consider
how she should spend her evening. After all, Jane was too
poor-spirited a victim to afford long entertainment. Clem
would have liked dealing with some one who showed fight—
some one with whom she could try savage issue in real tooth-
and-claw conflict. She had in mind a really exquisite piece

of cruelty, but it was a joy necessarily postponed to a late hour of the night. In the meantime, it would perhaps be as well to take a stroll, with a view of meeting a few friends as they came away from the work-rooms. She was pondering the invention of some long and hard task to be executed by Jane in her absence, when a knocking at the house-door made itself heard. Clem at once went up to see who the visitor was.

A woman in a long cloak and a showy bonnet stood on the step, protecting herself with an umbrella from the bitter sleet which the wind was now driving through the darkness. She said that she wished to see Mrs. Hewett.

'Second-floor front,' replied Clem in the offhand, impertinent tone wherewith she always signified to strangers her position in the house.

The visitor regarded her with a look of lofty contempt, and, having deliberately closed her umbrella, advanced towards the stairs. Clem drew into the back regions for a few moments, but as soon as she heard the closing of a door in the upper part of the house, she too ascended, going on tip-toe, with a noiselessness which indicated another side of her character. Having reached the room which the visitor had entered, she brought her ear close to the keyhole, and remained in that attitude for a long time—nearly twenty minutes, in fact. Her sudden and swift return to the foot of the stairs was followed by the descent of the woman in the showy bonnet.

'Miss Peckover!' cried the latter when she had reached the foot of the stairs.

'Well, what is it?' asked Clem, seeming to come up from the kitchen.

'Will you 'ave the goodness to go an' speak to Mrs. Hewett for a hinstant?' said the woman, with much affectation of refined speech.

'All right! I will just now, if I've time.'

The visitor tossed her head and departed, whereupon Clem at once ran upstairs. In five minutes she was back in the kitchen.

'See 'ere,' she addressed Jane. 'You know where Mr. Kirkwood works in St. John's Square? You've been before now. Well, you're to go an' wait at the door till he comes out, and then you're to tell him to come to Mrs. Hewett at wunst. Understand?—Why ain't these tea-things all cleared away? All right! Wait till you come back, that's all. Now be off, before I skin you alive!'

On the floor in a corner of the kitchen lay something that had once been a girl's hat. This Jane at once snatched up and put on her head. Without other covering, she ran forth upon her errand.

CHAPTER II

A FRIEND IN REQUEST

It was the hour of the unyoking of men. In the highways and byways of Clerkenwell there was a thronging of released toilers, of young and old, of male and female. Forth they streamed from factories and workrooms, anxious to make the most of the few hours during which they might live for themselves. Great numbers were still bent over their labour, and would be for hours to come, but the majority had leave to wend stablewards. Along the main thoroughfares the wheeltrack was clangorous; every omnibus that clattered by was heavily laden with passengers; tarpaulins gleamed over the knees of those who sat outside. This way and that the lights were blurred into a misty radiance; overhead was mere blackness, whence descended the lashing rain. There was a ceaseless scattering of mud; there were blocks in the traffic, attended with rough jest or angry curse; there was jostling on the crowded pavement. Public-houses began to brighten up, to bestir themselves for the evening's business. Streets that had been hives of activity since early morning were being abandoned to silence and darkness and the sweeping wind.

At noon to-day there was sunlight on the Surrey hills; the fields and lanes were fragrant with the first breath of spring, and from the shelter of budding copses many a primrose looked tremblingly up to the vision of blue sky. But of these things Clerkenwell takes no count; here it had been a day like any other, consisting of so many hours, each representing a fraction of the weekly wage. Go where you may in Clerkenwell, on every hand are multiform evidences of toil, intolerable as a nightmare. It is not as in those parts of London where the main thoroughfares consist of shops and warehouses and workrooms, whilst the streets that are hidden away on either hand are devoted in the main to dwellings. Here every alley is thronged with small industries; all but every door and window exhibits the advertisement of a craft that is carried on within. Here you may see how men have multiplied toil for toil's sake, have wrought to devise work superfluous, have worn their lives away in imagining new forms of weariness. The energy, the ingenuity daily put forth in these grimy burrows task the brain's power of wondering. But that those who sit here through the livelong day, through every season, through all the years of the life that is granted them, who strain their eyesight, who overtax their muscles, who nurse disease in their frames, who put resolutely from them the thought of what existence *might* be—that these do it all without prospect or hope of reward save the permission to eat and sleep and bring into the world other creatures to strive with them for bread, surely that thought is yet more marvellous.

Workers in metal, workers in glass and in enamel, workers in wood, workers in every substance on earth, or from the waters under the earth, that can be made commercially valuable. In Clerkenwell the demand is not so much for rude strength as for the cunning fingers and the contriving brain. The inscriptions on the house-fronts would make you believe that you were in a region of gold and silver and precious stones. In the recesses of dim byways, where sunshine and free air are forgotten things, where families herd together in dear-rented garrets and cellars, craftsmen are for ever handling jewellery, shaping bright ornaments for the necks and arms of such as are born to the joy of life. Wealth inestimable is ever flowing through these workshops, and the hands that have been stained with gold-dust may, as likely as not, some day extend themselves in petition for a crust. In this house, as the announcement tells you, business is carried on by a trader in diamonds, and next door is a den full of children who wait for their day's one meal until their mother has come home with her chance earnings. A strange enough region wherein to wander and muse. Inextinguishable laughter were perchance the fittest result of such musing; yet somehow the heart grows heavy, somehow the blood is troubled in its course, and the pulses begin to throb hotly.

Amid the crowds of workpeople, Jane Snowdon made what speed she might. It was her custom, whenever dispatched on an errand, to run till she could run no longer, then to hasten along panting until breath and strength were recovered. When it was either of the Peckovers who sent her, she knew that reprimand was inevitable on her return, be she ever so speedy;

but her nature was incapable alike of rebellion and of that
sullen callousness which would have come to the aid of most
girls in her position. She did not serve her tyrants with
willingness, for their brutality filled her with a sense of injustice; yet the fact that she was utterly dependent upon them
for her livelihood, that but for their grace—as they were perpetually reminding her—she would have been a workhouse
child, had a mitigating effect upon the bitterness she could
not wholly subdue.

There was, however, another reason why she sped eagerly
on her present mission. The man to whom she was conveying
Mrs. Hewett's message was one of the very few persons who
had ever treated her with human kindness. She had known
him by name and by sight for some years, and since her
mother's death (she was eleven when that happened) he had
by degrees grown to represent all that she understood by the
word 'friend.' It was seldom that words were exchanged
between them; the opportunity came scarcely oftener than
once a month; but whenever it did come, it made a bright
moment in her existence. Once before she had fetched him
of an evening to see Mrs. Hewett, and as they walked together
he had spoken with what seemed to her wonderful gentleness,
with consideration inconceivable from a tall, bearded man,
well-dressed, and well to do in the world. Perhaps he would
speak in the same way to-night; the thought of it made her
regardless of the cold rain that was drenching her miserable
garment, of the wind that now and then, as she turned a corner,
took away her breath, and made her cease from running.

She reached St. John's Square, and paused at length by
a door on which was the inscription: 'H. Lewis, Working
Jeweller.' It was just possible that the men had already left;
she waited for several minutes with anxious mind. No; the
door opened, and two workmen came forth. Jane's eagerness
impelled her to address one of them.

'Please, sir, Mr. Kirkwood hasn't gone yet, has he?'

'No, he ain't,' the man answered pleasantly; and turning
back, he called to some one within the doorway; 'Hollo, Sidney! here's your sweetheart waiting for you.'

Jane shrank aside; but in a moment she saw a familiar
figure; she advanced again, and eagerly delivered her message.

'All right, Jane! I'll walk on with you,' was the reply.
And whilst the other two men were laughing good-naturedly,

Kirkwood strode away by the girl's side. He seemed to be absent-minded, and for some hundred yards' distance was silent; then he stopped of a sudden and looked down at his companion.

'Why, Jane,' he said, 'you'll get your death, running about in weather like this.' He touched her dress. 'I thought so; you're wet through.'

There followed an inarticulate growl, and immediately he stripped off his short overcoat.

'Here, put this on, right over your head. Do as I tell you, child!'

He seemed impatient to-night. Wasn't he going to talk with her as before? Jane felt her heart sinking. With her hunger for kind and gentle words, she thought nothing of the character of the night, and that Sidney Kirkwood might reasonably be anxious to get over the ground as quickly as possible.

'How is Mrs. Hewett?' Sidney asked, when they were walking on again. 'Still poorly, eh? And the baby?'

Then he was again mute. Jane had something she wished to say to him—wished very much indeed, yet she felt it would have been difficult even if he had encouraged her. As he kept silence and walked so quickly, speech on her part was utterly forbidden. Kirkwood, however, suddenly remembered that his strides were disproportionate to the child's steps. She was an odd figure thus disguised in his over-jacket; he caught a glimpse of her face by a street lamp, and smiled, but with a mixture of pain.

'Feel a bit warmer so?' he asked.

'Oh yes, sir.'

'Haven't you got a jacket, Jane?'

'It's all to pieces, sir. They're goin' to have it mended, I think.'

'They' was the word by which alone Jane ventured to indicate her aunt.

'Going to, eh? I think they'd better be quick about it.'

Ha! that was the old tone of kindness! How it entered into her blood and warmed it! She allowed herself one quick glance at him.

'Do I walk too quick for you?'

'Oh no, sir. Mr. Kirkwood, please, there's something I——'

The sentence had, as it were, begun itself, but timidity cut
it short.   Sidney stopped and looked at her.

'What?   Something you wanted to tell me, Jane?'

He encouraged her, and at length she made her disclosure.
It was of what had happened in the public-house.   The young
man listened with much attention, walking very slowly.   He
got her to repeat her second-hand description of the old man
who had been inquiring for people named Snowdon.

'To think that you should have been just too late!' he
exclaimed with annoyance.   'Have you any idea who he
was?'

'I can't think, sir,' Jane replied sadly.

Sidney took a hopeful tone—thought it very likely that the
inquirer would pursue his search with success, being so near
the house where Jane's parents had lived,

'I'll keep my eyes open,' he said.   'Perhaps I might see
him.   He'd be easy to recognise, I should think.'

'And would you tell him, sir?' Jane asked eagerly.

'Why, of course I would.   You'd like me to, wouldn't you?'

Jane's reply left small doubt on that score.   Her companion looked down at her again, and said with compassionate
gentleness:

'Keep a good heart, Jane.   Things'll be better some day,
no doubt.'

'Do you think so, sir?'

The significance of the simple words was beyond all that
eloquence could have conveyed.   Sidney muttered to himself,
as he had done before, like one who is angry.   He laid his
hand on the child's shoulder for a moment.

A few minutes more, and they were passing along by the
prison wall, under the ghastly head, now happily concealed
by darkness.   Jane stopped a little short of the house and
removed the coat that had so effectually sheltered her.

'Thank you, sir,' she said, returning it to Sidney.

He took it without speaking, and threw it over his arm.
At the door, now closed, Jane gave a single knock; they were
admitted by Clem, who, in regarding Kirkwood, wore her
haughtiest demeanour.   This young man had never paid
homage of any kind to Miss Peckover, and such neglect was
by no means what she was used to.   Other men who came to
the house took every opportunity of paying her broad compliments, and some went so far as to offer practical testimony of
their admiration.   Sidney merely had a 'How do you do,

miss?' at her service. Coquetry had failed to soften him; Clem accordingly behaved as if he had given her mortal offence on some recent occasion. She took care, moreover, to fling a few fierce words at Jane before the latter disappeared into the house. Thereupon Sidney looked at her sternly; he said nothing, knowing that interference would only result in harsher treatment for the poor little slave.

'You know your way upstairs, I b'lieve,' said Clem, as if he were all but a stranger.

'Thank you, I do,' was Sidney's reply.

Indeed he had climbed these stairs innumerable times during the last three years; the musty smells were associated with ever so many bygone thoughts and states of feeling; the stains on the wall (had it been daylight), the irregularities of the bare wooden steps, were remembrancers of projects and hopes and disappointments. For many months now every visit had been with heavier heart; his tap at the Hewetts' door had a melancholy sound to him.

A woman's voice bade him enter. He stepped into a room which was not disorderly or unclean, but presented the chill discomfort of poverty. The principal, almost the only, articles of furniture were a large bed, a washhand stand,* a kitchen table, and two or three chairs, of which the cane seats were bulged and torn. A few meaningless pictures hung here and there, and on the mantel-piece, which sloped forward somewhat, stood some paltry ornaments, secured in their places by a piece of string stretched in front of them. The living occupants were four children and their mother. Two little girls, six and seven years old respectively, were on the floor near the fire; a boy of four was playing with pieces of firewood at the table. The remaining child was an infant, born but a fortnight ago, lying at its mother's breast. Mrs. Hewett sat on the bed, and bent forward in an attitude of physical weakness. Her age was twenty-seven, but she looked several years older. At nineteen she had married; her husband, John Hewett, having two children by a previous union. Her face could never have been very attractive, but it was good-natured, and wore its pleasantest aspect as she smiled on Sidney's entrance. You would have classed her at once with those feeble-willed, weak-minded, yet kindly-disposed women, who are only too ready to meet affliction half-way, and who, if circumstances be calamitous, are more harmful than an enemy to those they hold dear. She was rather wrapped up than dressed, and her hair, thin and pale-coloured, was tied in a ragged knot. She wore slippers, the upper parts of which still adhered to the soles only by miracle. It looked very much as if the same relation subsisted between her frame and the life that informed it, for there was no blood in her cheeks, no lustre in her eye. The baby at her bosom moaned in the act of sucking; one knew not how the poor woman could supply sustenance to another being.

The children were not dirty nor uncared for, but their clothing hung very loosely upon them; their flesh was unhealthy, their voices had an unnatural sound.

Sidney stepped up to the bed and gave his hand.

'I'm so glad you've come before Clara,' said Mrs. Hewett. 'I hoped you would. But she can't be long, an' I want to speak to you first. It's a bad night, isn't it? Yes, I feel it in my throat, and it goes right through my chest—just 'ere, look! And I haven't slep' not a hour a night this last week; it makes me feel that low. I want to get to the Orspital, if I can, in a day or two.'

'But doesn't the doctor come still?' asked Sidney, drawing a chair near to her.

'Well, I didn't think it was right to go on payin' him, an' that's the truth. I'll go to the Orspital, an' they'll give me somethin'. I look bad, don't I, Sidney?'

'You look as if you'd no business to be out of bed,' returned the young man in a grumbling voice.

'Oh, I *can't* lie still, so it's no use talkin'! But see, I want to speak about Clara. That woman Mrs. Tubbs has been here to see me, talkin' an' talkin'. She says she'll give Clara five shillin' a week, as well as board an' lodge her. I don't know what to do about it, that I don't. Clara, she'ꞌ that set on goin', an' her father's that set against it. It seems as if it 'ud be a good thing, don't it, Sidney? I know *you* don't want her to go, but what's to be done? What *is* to be done?'

Her wailing voice caused the baby to wail likewise. Kirkwood looked about the room with face set in anxious discontent.

'Is it no use, Mrs. Hewett?' he exclaimed suddenly, turning to her. 'Does she mean it? Won't she ever listen to me?'

The woman shook her head miserably; her eyes filled with tears.

'I've done all I could,' she replied, half sobbing. 'I

have; you know I have, Sidney! She's that 'eadstrong, it seems as if she wouldn't listen to nobody—at least nobody as we knows anything about.'

'What do you mean by that?' he inquired abruptly. 'Do you think there's any one else?'

'How can I tell? I've got no reason for thinkin' it, but how can I tell? No, I believe it's nothin' but her self-will an' the fancies she's got into her 'ead. Both her an' Bob, there's no doin' nothin' with them. Bob, he's that wasteful with his money; an' now he talks about goin' an' gettin' a room in another 'ouse, when he might just as well make all the savin' he can. But no, that ain't his idea, nor yet his sister's. I suppose it's their mother as they take after, though their father he won't own to it, an' I don't blame him for not speakin' ill of her as is gone. I should be that wretched if I thought my own was goin' to turn out the same. But there's John, he ain't a wasteful man; no one can't say it of him. He's got his fancies, but they've never made him selfish to others, as well you know, Sidney. He's been the best 'usband to me as ever a poor woman had, an' I'll say it with my last breath.'

She cried pitifully for a few moments. Sidney, mastering his own wretchedness, which he could not altogether conceal, made attempts to strengthen her.

'When things are at the worst they begin to mend,' he said. 'It can't be much longer before he gets work. And look here, Mrs. Hewett, I won't hear a word against it; you must and shall let me lend you something to go on with!'

'I dursn't, I dursn't, Sidney! John won't have it. He's always a-saying: "Once begin that, an' it's all up; you never earn no more of your own." It's one of his fancies, an' you know it is. You'll only make trouble, Sidney.'

'Well, all I can say is, he's an unreasonable and selfish man!'

'No, no; John ain't selfish! Never say that! It's only his fancies, Sidney.'

'Well, there's one trouble you'd better get rid of, at all events. Let Clara go to Mrs. Tubbs. You'll never have any peace till she does, I can see that. Why shouldn't she go, after all? She's seventeen; if she can't respect herself now, she never will, and there's no help for it. Tell John to let her go.'

There was bitterness in the tone with which he gave

this advice; he threw out his hands impatiently, and then flung himself back, so that the cranky chair creaked and tottered.

'An' if 'arm comes to her, what then?' returned Mrs. Hewett plaintively. 'We know well enough why Mrs. Tubbs wants her; it's only because she's good-lookin', an' she'll bring more people to the bar. John knows that, an' it makes him wild. Mind what I'm tellin' you, Sidney; if any 'arm comes to that girl, her father'll go out of his 'ead. I know he will! I know he will! He worships the ground as she walks on, an' if it hadn't been for that, she'd never have given him the trouble as she is doin'. It 'ud a been better for her if she'd had a father like mine, as was a hard, careless man. I don't wish to say no 'arm of him as is dead an' buried, an' my own father too, but he was a hard father to us, an' as long as he lived we dursn't say not a word as he didn't like. He'd a killed me if I'd gone on like Clara. It was a good thing as he was gone, before——'

'Don't, don't speak of that,' interposed Kirkwood, with kindly firmness. 'That's long since over and done with and forgotten.'

'No, no; not forgotten. Clara knows, an' that's partly why she makes so little of me; I know it is.'

'I don't believe it! She's a good-hearted girl——'

A heavy footstep on the stairs checked him. The door was thrown open, and there entered a youth of nineteen, clad as an artisan. He was a shapely fellow, though not quite so stout as perfect health would have made him, and had a face of singular attractiveness, clear-complexioned, delicate featured, a-gleam with intelligence. The intelligence was perhaps even too pronounced; seen in profile, the countenance had an excessive eagerness; there was selfish force about the lips, moreover, which would have been better away. His noisy entrance indicated an impulsive character, and the nod with which he greeted Kirkwood was self-sufficient.

'Where's that medal I cast last night, mother?' he asked, searching in various corners of the room and throwing things about.

'Now, do mind what you're up to, Bob!' remonstrated Mrs. Hewett. 'You'll find it on the mantel in the other room. Don't make such a noise.'

The young man rushed forth, and in a moment returned. In his hand, which was very black, and shone as if from the manipulation of metals, he held a small bright medal. He showed it to Sidney, saying, ' What d'you think o' that ? '

The work was delicate and of clever design ; it represented a racehorse at full speed, a jockey rising in the stirrups and beating it with orthodox brutality.

' That's " Tally-ho " at the Epsom Spring Meetin',' he said. ' I've got money on him ! '

And, with another indifferent nod, he flung out of the room.

Before Mrs. Hewett and Kirkwood could renew their conversation, there was another step at the door, and the father of the family presented himself.

CHAPTER III

A SUPERFLUOUS FAMILY

KIRKWOOD'S face, as he turned to greet the new-comer, changed suddenly to an expression of surprise.

' Why, what have you been doing to your hair ? ' he asked abruptly.

A stranger would have seen nothing remarkable in John Hewett's hair, unless he had reflected that, being so sparse, it had preserved its dark hue and its gloss somewhat unusually. The short beard and whiskers were also of richer colour than comported with the rest of the man's appearance. Judging from his features alone, one would have taken John for sixty at least ; his years were in truth not quite two-and-fifty. He had the look of one worn out with anxiety and hardship ; the lines engraven upon his face were of extraordinary depth and frequency ; there seemed to be little flesh between the dry skin and the bones which sharply outlined his visage. The lips were, like those of his son, prominent and nervous, but none of Bob's shrewdness was here discoverable ; feeling rather than intellect appeared to be the father's characteristic. His eyes expressed self-will, perhaps obstinacy, and he had a peculiarly dogged manner of holding his head. At the present moment he was suffering from extreme fatigue ; he let himself sink upon a chair, threw his hat on to the floor, and rested a hand on each knee. His boots were thickly covered with mud ; his corduroy trousers were splashed with the same. Rain had drenched him ; it trickled to the floor from all his garments.

For answer to Sidney's question, he nodded towards his wife, and said in a thick voice, ' Ask her.'

' He's dyed it,' Mrs. Hewett explained, with no smile. ' He thought one of the reasons why he couldn't get work was his lookin' too old.'

' An' so it was,' exclaimed Hewett, with an angry vehemence which at once declared his position and revealed much of his history. ' So it was! My hair was a bit turned, an' nowadays there's no chance for old men. Ask any one you like. Why, there's Sam Lang couldn't even get a job at gardenin' 'cause his hair was a bit turned. It was him as told me what to do. " Dye your hair, Jack," he says ; " it's what I've had to myself," he says. " They won't have old men nowadays, at no price." Why, there's Jarvey the painter ; you know him, Sidney. His guvnor sent him on a job to Jones's place, an' they sent him back. " Why, he's an old man," they says. " What good's a man of that age for liftin' ladders about ? " An' Jarvey's no older than me.'

Sidney knitted his brows. He had heard the complaint from too many men to be able to dispute its justice.

' When there's twice too many of us for the work that's to be done,' pursued John, ' what else can you expect ? The old uns have to give way, of course. Let 'em beg; let 'em starve ! What use are they ? '

Mrs. Hewett had put a kettle on the fire, and began to arrange the table for a meal.

' Go an' get your wet things off, John,' she said. ' You'll be havin' your rheumatics again.'

' Never mind me, Maggie. What business have you to be up an' about ? You need a good deal more takin' care of than I do. Here, let Amy get the tea.'

The three children, Amy, Annie, and Tom, had come forward, as only children do who are wont to be treated affectionately on their father's return. John had a kiss and a caress for each of them ; then he stepped to the bed and looked at his latest born. The baby was moaning feebly ; he spoke no word to it, and on turning away glanced about the room absently. In the meantime his wife had taken some clothing from a chest of drawers, and at length he was persuaded to go into the other room and change. When he returned, the meal was ready. It consisted of a scrap of cold steak, left over from yesterday, and still upon the original dish amid congealed fat ; a spongy half-quartern loaf, that

species of baker's bread of which a great quantity can be consumed with small effect on the appetite ; a shapeless piece of
something purchased under the name of butter, dabbed into a
shallow basin ; some pickled cabbage in a tea-cup; and, lastly,
a pot of tea, made by adding a teaspoonful or two to the
saturated leaves which had already served at breakfast and
mid-day. This repast was laid on a very dirty cloth. The
cups were unmatched and chipped, the knives were in all
stages of decrepitude ; the teapot was of dirty tin, with a
damaged spout.

Sidney began to affect cheerfulness. He took little Annie
on one of his knees, and Tom on the other. The mature Amy
presided. Hewett ate the morsel of meat, evidently without
thinking about it ; he crumbled a piece of bread, and munched
mouthfuls in silence. Of the vapid liquor called tea he drank
cup after cup.

'What's the time?' he asked at length. 'Where's
Clara?'

'I daresay she's doin' overtime,' replied his wife. 'She
won't be much longer.'

The man was incapable of remaining in one spot for more
than a few minutes. Now he went to look at the baby ; now
he stirred the fire ; now he walked across the room aimlessly.
He was the embodiment of worry. As soon as the meal was
over, Amy, Annie, and Tom were sent off to bed. They occupied the second room, together with Clara ; Bob shared the
bed of a fellow-workman upstairs. This was great extrava-
gance, obviously; other people would have made two rooms
sufficient for all, and many such families would have put up
with one. But Hewett had his ideas of decency, and stuck to
them with characteristic wilfulness.

'Where do you think I've been this afternoon?' John
began, when the three little ones were gone, and Mrs. Hewett
had been persuaded to lie down upon the bed. 'Walked to
Enfield an' back. I was told of a job out there; but it's no
good; they're full up. They say exercise is good for the
'ealth. I shall be a 'ealthy man before long, it seems to me.
What do *you* think?'

'Have you been to see Corder again?' asked Sidney, after
reflecting anxiously.

'No, I haven't!' was the angry reply; 'an' what's more,
I ain't goin' to! He's one o' them men I can't get on with.
As long as you make yourself small before him, an' say " sir "

to him with every other word, an' keep tellin' him as he's
your Providence on earth, an' as you don't know how ever
you'd get on without him—well, it's all square, an' he'll keep
you on the job. That's just what I *can't* do—never could, an'
never shall. I should have to hear them children cryin' for
food before I could do it. So don't speak to me about Corder
again. It makes me wild ! '

Sidney tapped the floor with his foot. Himself a single
man, without responsibilities, always in fairly good work, he
could not invariably sympathise with Hewett's sore and impracticable pride. His own temper did not err in the direction
of meekness, but as he looked round the room he felt that a
home such as this would drive him to any degree of humiliation. John knew what the young man's thoughts were ; he
resumed in a voice of exasperated bitterness.

' No, I haven't been to Corder—I beg his pardon ; *Mister*
Corder—James Corder, Esquire. But where do you think I
went this mornin' ? Mrs. Peckover brought up a paper an'
showed me an advertisement. Gorbutt in Goswell Road
wanted a man to clean windows an' sweep up, an' so on ;—
offered fifteen bob a week. Well, I went. Didn't I, mother?
Didn't I go after that job ? I got there at half-past eight ;
an' what do you think I found ? If there was one man
standin' at Gorbutt's door, *there was five hundred* ! Don't
you believe me ? You go an' ask them as lives about there.
If there was one, there was five hundred ! Why, the p'lice
had to come an' keep the road clear. Fifteen bob ! What
was the use o' me standin' there, outside the crowd ? What
was the use, I say ? Such a lot o' poor starvin' devils you
never saw brought together in all your life. There they was,
lookin' ready to fight with one another for the fifteen bob a
week. Didn't I come back and tell you about it, mother ? An'
if they'd all felt like me, they'd a turned against the shop an'
smashed it up—ay, an' every other shop in the street ! What
use ? Why, no use ; but I tell you that's how I felt. If any
man had said as much as a rough word to me, I'd a gone at
him like a bulldog. I felt like a beast. I wanted to fight, I
tell you—to fight till the life was kicked an' throttled out of
me ! '

' John, don't, don't go on in that way,' cried his wife,
sobbing miserably. ' Don't let him go on like that, Sidney.'

Hewett jumped up and walked about.

' What's the time ? ' he asked the next moment. And

when Sidney told him that it was half-past nine, he exclaimed, 'Then why hasn't Clara come 'ome? What's gone with her?'

'Perhaps she's at Mrs. Tubbs's,' replied his wife, in a low voice, looking at Kirkwood.

'An' what call has she to be there? Who gave her leave to go there?'

There was another exchange of looks between Sidney and Mrs. Hewett; then the latter with hesitation and timidity told of Mrs. Tubbs's visit to her that evening, and of the proposals the woman had made.

'I won't hear of it!' cried John. 'I won't have my girl go for a barmaid, so there's an end of it. I tell you she shan't go!'

'I can understand you, Mr. Hewett,' said Sidney, in a tone of argument softened by deference; 'but don't you think you'd better make a few inquiries, at all events? You see, it isn't exactly a barmaid's place. I mean to say, Mrs. Tubbs doesn't keep a public-house where people stand about drinking all day. It is only a luncheon-bar, and respectable enough.'

John turned and regarded him with astonishment.

'Why, I thought you was as much set against it as me? What's made you come round like this? I s'pose you've got tired of her, an' that's made you so you don't care.'

The young man's eyes flashed angrily, but before he could make a rejoinder Mrs. Hewett interposed.

'For shame o' yourself, John! If you can't talk better sense than that, don't talk at all. He don't mean it, Sidney. He's half drove off his head with trouble.'

'If he does think it,' said Kirkwood, speaking sternly but with self-command, 'let him say what he likes. He can't say worse than I should deserve.'

There was an instant of silence. Hewett's head hung with more than the usual doggedness. Then he addressed Sidney, sullenly, but in a tone which admitted his error.

'What have you got to say? Never mind me. I'm only the girl's father, an' there's not much heed paid to fathers nowadays. What have you got to say about Clara? If you've changed your mind about her goin' there, just tell me why.'

Sidney could not bring himself to speak at once, but an appealing look from Mrs. Hewett decided him.

'Look here, Mr. Hewett,' he began, with blunt earnestness.
'If any harm came to Clara I should feel it every bit as much
as you, and that you ought to know by this time. All the
same, what I've got to say is this : Let her go to Mrs. Tubbs
for a month's trial. If you persist in refusing her, mark my
words, you'll be sorry. I've thought it all over, and I know
what I'm talking about. The girl can't put up with the work-
room any longer. It's ruining her health, for one thing, anybody can see that, and it's making her so discontented, she'll
soon get reckless. I understand your feeling well enough,
but I understand her as well ; at all events, I believe I do.
She wants a change ; she's getting tired of her very life.'

'Very well,' cried the father in shrill irritation, 'why
doesn't she take the change that's offered to her ? She's no
need to go neither to workroom nor to bar. There's a good
home waiting for her, isn't there ? What's come to the girl ?
She used to go on as if she liked you well enough.'

'A girl alters a deal between fifteen and seventeen,'
Sidney replied, forcing himself to speak with an air of calmness, of impartiality. 'She wasn't old enough to know her
own mind. I'm tired of plaguing her. I feel ashamed to
say another word to her, and that's the truth. She only gets
more and more set against me. If it's ever to come right,
it'll have to be by waiting ; we won't talk about that any
more. Think of her quite apart from me, and what I've been
hoping. She's seventeen years old. You can't deal with a
girl of that age like you can with Amy and Annie. You'll
have to trust her, Mr. Hewett. You'll have to, because
there's no help for it. We're working people, we are ; we're
the lower orders ; our girls have to go out and get their
livings. We teach them the best we can, and the devil knows
they've got examples enough of misery and ruin before their
eyes to help them to keep straight. Rich people can take
care of their daughters as much as they like ; they can treat
them like children till they're married ; people of our kind
can't do that, and it has to be faced.'

John sat with dark brow, his eyes staring on vacancy.

'It's right what Sidney says, father,' put in Mrs. Hewett ;
'we can't help it.'

'You may perhaps have done harm when you meant only
to do good,' pursued Sidney. 'Always being so anxious, and
showing what account you make of her, perhaps you've led
her to think a little too much of herself. She knows other

fathers don't go on in that way. And now she wants more freedom, she feels it worse than other girls do when you begin to deny her. Talk to her in a different way ; talk as if you trusted her. Depend upon it, it's the only hold you have upon her. Don't be so much afraid. Clara has her faults— I see them as well as any one—but I'll never believe she'd darken your life of her own free will.'

There was an unevenness, a jerky vehemence, in his voice, which told how difficult it was for him to take this side in argument. He often hesitated, obviously seeking phrases which should do least injury to the father's feelings. The expression of pain on his forehead and about his lips testified to the sincerity with which he urged his views, at the same time to a lurking fear lest impulse should be misleading him. Hewett kept silence, in aspect as far as ever from yielding. Of a sudden he raised his hand, and said, ' Husht ! ' There was a familiar step on the stairs. Then the door opened and admitted Clara.

The girl could not but be aware that the conversation she interrupted had reference to herself. Her father gazed fixedly at her ; Sidney glanced towards her with self-consciousness, and at once averted his eyes ; Mrs. Hewett examined her with apprehension. Having carelessly closed the door with a push, she placed her umbrella in the corner and began to unbutton her gloves. Her attitude was one of affected unconcern ; she held her head stiffly, and let her eyes wander to the farther end of the room. The expression of her face was cold, preoccupied ; she bit her lower lip so that the under part of it protruded.

' Where have you been, Clara ? ' her father asked.

She did not answer immediately, but finished drawing off her gloves and rolled them up by turning one over the other. Then she said indifferently :

' I've been to see Mrs. Tubbs.'

' And who gave you leave ? ' asked Hewett with irritation.

' I don't see that I needed any leave. I knew she was coming here to speak to you or mother, so I went, after work, to ask what you'd said.'

She was not above the middle stature of women, but her slimness and erectness, and the kind of costume she wore, made her seem tall as she stood in this low-ceiled room. Her features were of very uncommon type, at once sensually attractive and bearing the stamp of intellectual vigour. The profile was cold, subtle, original; in full face, her high cheek-bones and the heavy, almost horizontal line of her eyebrows were the points that first drew attention, conveying an idea of force of character. The eyes themselves were hazel-coloured, and, whatever her mood, preserved a singular pathos of expression, a look as of self-pity, of unconscious appeal against some injustice. In contrast with this her lips were defiant, insolent, unscrupulous; a shadow of the naïveté of childhood still lingered upon them, but, though you divined the earlier pout of the spoilt girl, you felt that it must have foretold this danger-signal in the mature woman. Such cast of countenance could belong only to one who intensified in her personality an inheritance of revolt; who, combining the temper of an ambitious woman with the forces of a man's brain, had early learnt that the world was not her friend nor the world's law.

Her clothing made but poor protection against the rigours of a London winter. Its peculiarity (bearing in mind her position) was the lack of any pretended elegance. A close-fitting, short jacket of plain cloth made evident the grace of her bust; beneath was a brown dress with one row of kilting. She wore a hat of brown felt, the crown rising from back to front, the narrow brim closely turned up all round. The high collar of the jacket alone sheltered her neck. Her gloves, though worn, were obviously of good kid; her boots—strangest thing of all in a work-girl's daily attire—were both strong and shapely. This simplicity seemed a declaration that she could not afford genuine luxuries and scorned to deck herself with shams.

The manner of her reply inflamed Hewett with impotent wrath. He smote the table violently, then sprang up and flung his chair aside.

'Is that the way you've learnt to speak to your father?' he shouted. 'Haven't I told you you're not to go nowhere without my leave or your mother's? Do you pay no heed to what I bid you? If so, say it! Say it at once, and have done with it.'

Clara was quietly removing her hat. In doing so, she disclosed the one thing which gave proof of regard for personal appearance. Her hair was elaborately dressed. Drawn up from the neck, it was disposed in thick plaits upon the top of her head; in front were a few rows of crisping. She affected to be quite unaware that words had been spoken to her, and stood smoothing each side of her forehead.

John strode forward and laid his hands roughly upon her shoulders.

' Look at me, will you ? Speak, will you ? '

Clara jerked herself from his grasp and regarded him with insolent surprise. Of fear there was no trace upon her countenance ; she seemed to experience only astonishment at such unwonted behaviour from her father, and resentment on her own behalf. Sidney Kirkwood had risen, and advanced a step or two, as if in apprehension of harm to the girl, but his interference was unneeded. Hewett recovered his self-control as soon as Clara repelled him. It was the first time he had ever laid a hand upon one of his children other than gently ; his exasperation came of over-tried nerves, of the experiences he had gone through in search of work that day, and the keen suffering occasioned by his argument with Sidney. The practical confirmation of Sidney's warning that he must no longer hope to control Clara like a child stung him too poignantly ; he obeyed an unreasoning impulse to recover his authority by force.

The girl's look entered his heart like a stab ; she had never faced him like this before, saying more plainly than with words that she defied him to control her. His child's face, the face he loved best of all ! yet at this moment he was searching it vainly for the lineaments that were familiar to him. Something had changed her, had hardened her against him, in a moment. It seemed impossible that there should come such severance between them. John revolted against it, as against all the other natural laws that visited him harshly.

' What's come to you, my girl ? ' he said in a thick voice. ' What's wrong between us, Clara ? Haven't I always done my best for you ? If I was the worst enemy you had, you couldn't look at me crueller.'

' I think it's [me that should ask what's come to *you*, father,' she returned with her former self-possession. ' You treat me as if I was a baby. I want to know what you're going to say about Mrs. Tubbs. I suppose mother's told you what she offers me ? '

Sidney had not resumed his chair. Before Hewett could reply he said :

' I think I'll leave you to talk over this alone.'

' No ; stay where you are,' said John gruffly. ' Look here,

Clara. Sidney's been talkin' to me; he's been sayin' that I ought to let you have your own way in this. Yes, you may well look as if it surprised you.' Clara had just glanced at the young man, slightly raising her eyebrows, but at once looked away again with a careless movement of the head. 'He says what it's hard an' cruel for me to believe, though I half begin to see that he's right; he says you won't pay no more heed to what *I* wish, an' it's me now must give way to you. I didn't use to think me an' Clara would come to that; but it looks like it—it looks like it.'

The girl stood with downcast eyes. Once more her face had suffered a change; the lips were no longer malignant, her forehead had relaxed from its haughty frown. The past fortnight had been a period of contest between her father's stubborn fears and her own determination to change the mode of her life. Her self-will was only intensified by opposition. John had often enough experienced this, but hitherto the points at issue had been trifles, matters in which the father could yield for the sake of pleasing his child. Serious resistance brought out for the first time all the selfish forces of her nature. She was prepared to go all lengths rather than submit, now the question of her liberty had once been broached. Already there was a plan in her mind for quitting home, regardless of all the misery she would cause, reckless of what future might be in store for herself. But the first sign of yielding on her father's part touched the gentler elements of her nature. Thus was she constituted; merciless in egotism when put to the use of all her weapons, moved to warmest gratitude as soon as concession was made to her. To be on ill terms with her father had caused her pain, the only effect of which, however, was to heighten the sullen impracticability of her temper. At the first glimpse of relief from overstrained emotions, she desired that all angry feeling should be at an end. Having gained her point, she could once more be the affectionately wilful girl whose love was the first necessity of John Hewett's existence.

'Well,' John pursued, reading her features eagerly, 'I'll say no more about that, and I won't stand in the way of what you've set your mind on. But understand, Clara, my girl! It's because Sidney persuaded me. Sidney answers for it, mind you that!'

His voice trembled, and he looked at the young man with something like anger in his eyes.

'I'm willing to do that, Mr. Hewett,' said Kirkwood in a low but firm voice, his eyes turned away from Clara. 'No human being can answer for another in the real meaning of the word; but I take upon myself to say that Clara will bring you no sorrow. She hears me say it. They're not the kind of words that a man speaks without thought of what they mean.'

Clara had seated herself by the table, and was moving a finger along the pattern of the dirty white cloth. She bit her under-lip in the manner already described, seemingly her habit when she wished to avoid any marked expression of countenance.

'I can't see what Mr. Kirkwood's got to do with it at all,' she said, with indifference, which now, however, was rather good-humoured than the reverse. 'I'm sure I don't want anybody to answer for *me*.' A slight toss of the head. 'You'd have let me go in any case, father; so I don't see you need bring Mr. Kirkwood's name in.'

Hewett turned away to the fireplace and hung his head. Sidney, gazing darkly at the girl, saw her look towards him, and she smiled. The strange effect of that smile upon her features! It gave gentleness to the mouth, and, by making more manifest the intelligent light of her eyes, emphasised the singular pathos inseparable from their regard. It was a smile to which a man would concede anything, which would vanquish every prepossession, which would inspire pity and tenderness and devotion in the heart of sternest resentment.

Sidney knew its power only too well; he averted his face. Then Clara rose again and said:

'I shall just walk round and tell Mrs. Tubbs. It isn't late, and she'd like to know as soon as possible.'

'Oh, surely it'll do in the mornin'!' exclaimed Mrs. Hewett, who had followed the conversation in silent anxiety.

Clara paid no attention, but at once put on her hat again. Then she said, 'I won't be long, father,' and moved towards the door.

Hewett did not look round.

'Will you let me walk part of the way with you?' Sidney asked abruptly.

'Certainly, if you like.'

He bade the two who remained 'Good-night,' and followed Clara downstairs.

CHAPTER IV

CLARA AND JANE

RAIN no longer fell, but the gusty and bitter wind still swept about the black streets. Walking side by side without speech, Clara and her companion left the neighbourhood of the prison, and kept a northward direction till they reached the junction of highways where stands the 'Angel.' Here was the wonted crowd of loiterers and the press of people waiting for tramcar or omnibus—east, west, south, or north; newsboys, eager to get rid of their last batch, were crying as usual, 'Ech-ow! Exteree speciul! Ech-ow! Steendard!' and a brass band was blaring out its saddest strain of merry dance-music. The lights gleamed dismally in rain-puddles and on the wet pavement. With the wind came whiffs of tobacco and odours of the drinking-bar.

They crossed, and walked the length of Islington High Street, then a short way along its continuation, Upper Street. Once or twice Clara had barely glanced at Kirkwood, but his eyes made no reply, and his lips were resolutely closed. She did not seem offended by this silence; on the contrary, her face was cheerful, and she smiled to herself now and then. One would have imagined that she found pleasure in the sombreness of which she was the cause.

She stopped at length, and said :

'I suppose you don't want to go in with me?'

'No.'

'Then I'll say good-night. Thank you for coming so far out of your way.'

'I'll wait. I may as well walk back with you, if you don't mind.'

'Oh, very well. I shan't be many minutes.'

She passed on and entered the place of refreshment that was kept by Mrs. Tubbs. Till recently it had been an ordinary eating-house or coffee-shop; but having succeeded in obtain a license to sell strong liquors, Mrs. Tubbs had converted the establishment into one of a more pretentious kind. She called it 'Imperial Restaurant and Luncheon Bar.' The front shone with vermilion paint; the interior was aflare with many gas-jets; in the window was disposed a tempting exhibition of 'snacks' of fish, cold roast fowls, ham-sandwiches, and the like; whilst farther back stood a cooking-stove, whereon frizzled and vapoured a savoury mess of sausages and onions.

Sidney turned away a few paces. The inclemency of the night made Upper Street—the promenade of a great district on account of its spacious pavement—less frequented than usual; but there were still numbers of people about, some hastening homewards, some sauntering hither and thither in the familiar way, some gathered into gossiping groups. Kirkwood was irritated by the conversation and laughter that fell on his ears, irritated by the distant strains of the band, irritated above all by the fume of frying that pervaded the air for many yards about Mrs. Tubbs's precincts. He observed that the customers tending that way were numerous. They consisted mainly of lads and young men who had come forth from neighbouring places of entertainment. The locality and its characteristics had been familiar to him from youth upwards; but his nature was not subdued to what it worked in, and the present fit of disgust was only an accentuation of a mood by which he was often possessed. To the Hewetts he had spoken impartially of Mrs. Tubbs and her bar; probably that was the right view; but now there came back upon him the repugnance with which he had regarded Clara's proposal when it was first made.

It seemed to him that he had waited nearly half an hour when Clara came forth again. In silence she walked on beside him. Again they crossed by the 'Angel' and entered St. John Street Road.

'You've made your arrangements?' Sidney said, now that there were few people passing.

'Yes; I shall go on Monday.'

'You're going to live there altogether?'

'Yes; it'll be more convenient, and then it'll give them more room at home. Bob can sleep with the children, and save money.'

'To be sure!' observed the young man with bitter irony.

Clara flashed a glance at him. It was a new thing for Sidney to take this tone with her; not seldom he had expressed unfavourable judgments by silence, but he had never spoken to her otherwise than with deference and gentleness.

'You don't seem in a very good temper to-night, Mr Kirkwood,' she remarked in a suave tone.

He disregarded her words, but in a few moments turned
upon her and said scornfully :

'I hope you'll enjoy the pleasant, ladylike work you've
found ! I should think it'll improve your self-respect to wait
on the gentlemen of Upper Street !'

Irony is not a weapon much in use among working people ;
their wits in general are too slow. With Sidney, however, it
had always been a habit of speech in indignant criticism, and
sympathy made him aware that nothing would sting Clara
more acutely. He saw that he was successful when she
turned her head away and moved it nervously.

'And do you suppose I go there because the place pleases
me ?' she asked in a cold, hostile voice. 'You make a great
mistake, as you always do when you pretend to know anything
about *me*. Wait till I've learned a little about the business ;
you won't find me in Upper Street then.'

'I understand.'

Again they walked on in silence. They were nearing
Clerkenwell Close, and had to pass a corner of the prison in a
dark lane, where the wind moaned drearily. The line of the
high blank wall was relieved in colourless gloom against a sky
of sheer night. Opposite, the shapes of poverty-eaten houses
and grimy workshops stood huddling in the obscurity. From
near at hand came shrill voices of children chasing each other
about—children playing at midnight between slum and gaol !

'We're not likely to see much of each other after to-night,'
said Sidney, stopping.

'The less the better, I should say, if this is how you're
going to talk to me.'

'The less the better, perhaps—at all events for a time.
But there's one or two things on my mind, and I'll say them
now. I don't know whether you think anything about it, but
you must have seen that things are getting worse and worse
at home. Your mother——'

'She's no mother of mine !' broke in Clara angrily.

'She's been a mother to you in kindness, that's certain,
and you've repaid her almost as ill as you could have done.
Another girl would have made her hard life a bit easier. No ;
you've only thought of yourself. Your father walks about
day after day trying to get work, and how do you meet him
when he comes home ? You fret him and anger him ; you
throw him back ill-tempered words when he happens to think
different from you ; you almost break his heart, because you

won't give way in things that he only means for your good—
he that would give his life for you! It's as well you should
hear the truth for once, and hear it from me, too. Anyone
else might speak from all sorts of motives; as for me, it
makes me suffer more to say such things than it ever could
you to hear them. Laugh if you like! I don't ask you to
pay any heed to what *I*'ve wished and hoped; but just give a
thought to your father, and the rest of them at home. I told
him to-night he'd only to trust you, that you never could do
anything to make him ashamed of you. I said so, and I
believe it. Look, Clara! with all my heart I believe it. But
now you've got your way, think of them a little.'

'It isn't your fault if I don't know how bad I am,' said
the girl with a half-smile. That she did not resent his lecture
more decidedly was no doubt due to its having afforded new
proof of the power she had over him. Sidney was shaken
with emotion; his voice all but failed him at the last.

'Good-bye,' he said, turning away.

Clara hesitated, looked at him, but finally also said ' Good-
bye,' and went on alone.

She walked with bent head, and almost passed the house-
door in absence of thought. On the threshold was standing
Miss Peckover; she drew aside to let Clara pass. Between
these two was a singular rivalry. Though by date a year
younger than Clara, Clem gave no evidence of being physically
less mature. In the matter of personal charms she regarded
herself as by far Miss Hewett's superior, and resented vigo-
rously the tone of the latter's behaviour to her. Clara, on
the other hand, looked down upon Miss Peckover as a mere
vulgar girl; she despised her brother Bob because he had
allowed himself to be inveigled by Clem; in intellect, in social
standing, she considered herself out of all comparison with
the landlady's daughter. Clem had the obvious advantage
of being able to ridicule the Hewetts' poverty, and did so
without sparing. Now, for instance, when Clara was about
to pass with a distant ' Good-night,' Clem remarked:

'It's cold, ain't it? I wonder you don't put on a ulster, a
night like this.'

' Thank you,' was the reply. 'I shan't consult you about
how I'm to dress.'

Clem laughed, knowing she had the best of the joke.

The other went upstairs, and entered the back-room,
where it was quite dark.

'That you, Clara?' asked Amy's voice. 'The candle's on the mantel-shelf.'

'Why aren't you asleep?' Clara returned sharply. But the irritation induced by Clem's triumph quickly passed in reflection on Sidney's mode of leave-taking. That had not at all annoyed her, but it had made her thoughtful. She lit the candle. Its light disclosed a room much barer than the other one. There was one bed, in which Amy and Annie lay (Clara had to share it with them), and a mattress placed on the floor, where reposed little Tom; a low chest of drawers with a very small looking-glass upon it, a washstand, a few boxes. Handsome girls, unfortunate enough to have brains to boot, do not cultivate the patient virtues in chambers of this description.

There was a knock at the door. Clara found her father standing there.

'Have you anything to tell me, my girl?' he asked in a subdued voice, furtively regarding her.

'I shall go on Monday.'

He drew back a step, and seemed about to return to the other room.

'Father, I shall have to give Mrs. Tubbs the five shillings for a few weeks. She's going to let me have a new dress.'

'Your earnin's is your own, Clara.'

'Yes; but I hope very soon to be able to give you something. It's hard for you, having no work.'

John brightened wonderfully.

'Don't you trouble, my dear. That's all right. Things'll come round somehow. You're a good girl. Good-night, my darlin'!'

He kissed her, and went consoled to his rest.

Miss Peckover kept going up and down between the kitchen and the front-door. Down below, Jane was cleaning a copper kettle. Clem, who had her sweetest morsel of cruelty yet in store, had devised this pleasant little job as a way of keeping the child employed till all was quiet.

She had just come down to watch the progress of the work, and to give a smart rap or two on the toiling fingers, when a heavy footstep in the passage caused her to dart upstairs again. It was Bob Hewett, returned from his evening recreations.

'Oh, that's you, is it?' cried Clem. 'Come down; I want to speak to you.'

'Wait till to-morrow,' answered Bob, advancing towards the stairs.

'Wait! we'll see about that!'

She sprang forward, and with a prompt exertion of muscle, admirable in its way, whirled Bob round and dragged him to the head of the kitchen flight. The young fellow took it in good part, and went down with her.

'You go up into the passage,' said Clem to her servant, and was immediately obeyed.

'Now,' resumed Miss Peckover, when she had closed the door, ' who have you been goin' about with to-night?'

'What are you talking about?' returned Bob, who had seated himself on the table, and was regarding Clem jocosely. 'I've been with some pals, that's all.'

'Pals! what sort o' pals? Do you call Pennyloaf Candy one o' your pals?'

She stood before him in a superb attitude, her head poised fiercely, her arms quivering at her sides, all the stature and vigour of her young body emphasised by muscular strain.

'Pennyloaf Candy!' Bob repeated, as if in scorn of the person so named. 'Get on with you! I'm sick of hearing you talk about her. Why I haven't seen her not these three weeks.'

'It's a —— lie!' Clem's epithet was too vigorous for reproduction. ' Sukey Jollop saw you with her down by the meat-market, an' Jeck Bartley saw you too.'

'Jeck did?' He laughed with obstreperous scorn. ' Why, Jeck's gone to Homerton to his mother till Saturday night. Don't be such a bloomin' fool! Just because Suke Jollop's dead nuts on me, an' I won't have nothin' to say to her, she goes tellin' these bloomin' lies. When I see her next, I'll make her go down on her marrow-bones an' beg my pardon. See if I don't just!'

There was an engaging frankness in Bob's way of defending himself which evidently impressed Miss Peckover, though it did not immediately soothe her irritation. She put her arms a-kimbo, and examined him with a steady suspicion which would have disconcerted most young men. Bob, however, only laughed more heartily. The scene was prolonged. Bob had no recourse to tenderness to dismiss the girl's jealousy. His self-conceit was supreme, and had always stood him in such stead with the young ladies who, to use his own expression, were 'dead nuts on him,' that his love-

D 2

making, under whatever circumstances, always took the form of genial banter *de haut en bas*. 'Don't be a bloomin' fool!' was the phrase he deemed of most efficacy in softening the female heart; and the result seemed to justify him, for after some half-hour's wrangling, Clem abandoned her hostile attitude, and eyed him with a savage kind of admiration.

'When are you goin' to buy me that locket, Bob, to put a bit of your 'air in?' she inquired pertinently.

'You just wait, can't you? There's a event coming off next week. I won't say nothing, but you just wait.'

'I'm tired o' waitin'. See here; you ain't goin' to best me out of it?'

'Me best you? Don't be a bloomin' fool, Clem!'

He laughed heartily, and in a few minutes allowed himself to be embraced and sent off to his chamber at the top of the house.

Clem summoned her servant from the passage. At the same moment there entered another lodger, the only one whose arrival Clem still awaited. His mode of ascending the stairs was singular; one would have imagined that he bore some heavy weight, for he proceeded very slowly, with a great clumping noise, surmounting one step at a time in the manner of a child. It was Mr. Marple, the cab-driver, and his way of going up to bed was very simply explained by the fact that a daily sixteen hours of sitting on the box left his legs in a numb and practically useless condition.

The house was now quiet. Clem locked the front-door and returned to the kitchen, eager with anticipation of the jest she was going to carry out. First of all she had to pick a quarrel with Jane; this was very easily managed. She pretended to look about the room for a minute, then asked fiercely:

'What's gone with that sixpence I left on the dresser?'

Jane looked up in terror. She was worn almost to the last point of endurance by her day and night of labour and agitation. Her face was bloodless, her eyelids were swollen with the need of sleep.

'Sixpence!' she faltered, 'I'm sure I haven't seen no sixpence, miss.'

'You haven't? Now, I've caught you at last. There's been nobody 'ere but you. Little thief! We'll see about this in the mornin', an' to-night *you shall sleep in the back-kitchen!*'

The child gasped for breath. The terror of sudden death could not have exceeded that which rushed upon her heart when she was told that she must pass her night in the room where lay the coffin.

'An' you shan't have no candle, neither,' proceeded Clem, delighted with the effect she was producing. 'Come along! I'm off to bed, an' I'll see you safe locked in first, so as no one can come an' hurt you.'

'Miss! please!—I can't, I durstn't!'

Jane pleaded in inarticulate anguish. But Clem had caught her by the arm, was dragging her on, on, till she was at the very door of that ghastly death-cellar. Though thirteen years old, her slight frame was as incapable of resisting Clem Peckover's muscles as an infant's would have been. The door was open, but at that moment Jane uttered a shriek which rang and echoed through the whole house. Startled, Clem relaxed her grasp. Jane tore herself away, fled up the kitchen stairs, fled upwards still, flung herself at the feet of someone who had come out on to the landing and held a light.

'Oh, help me! Don't let her! Help me!'

'What's up with you, Jane?' asked Clara, for it was she who, not being yet in bed, had come forth at once on hearing the scream.

Jane could only cling to her garment, pant hysterically, repeat the same words of entreaty again and again. Another door opened, and John Hewett appeared half-dressed.

'What's wrong?' he cried. 'The 'ouse o' fire? Who yelled out like that?'

Clem was coming up; she spoke from the landing below.

'It's that Jane, just because I gave her a rap as she deserved. Send her down again.'

'Oh, no!' cried the poor girl. 'Miss Hewett! be a friend to me! She's goin' to shut me up all night with the coffin. Don't let her, miss! I durstn't! Oh, be a friend to me!'

'Little liar!' shouted Clem. 'Oh, that bloomin' little liar! when I never said a word o' such a thing!'

'I'll believe her a good deal sooner than you,' returned Clara sharply. 'Why, anybody can see she's tellin' the truth—can't they, father? She's half-scared out of her life. Come in here, Jane; you shall stay here till morning.'

By this time all the grown-up people in the house were on the staircase; the clang of tongues was terrific. Clem held her ground stoutly, and in virulence was more than a match for all her opponents. Even Bob did not venture to take her part; he grinned down over the banisters, and enjoyed the entertainment immensely. Dick Snape, whose room Bob shared, took the opportunity of paying off certain old scores he had standing against Clem. Mr. Marple, the cab-driver, was very loud and very hoarse in condemnation of such barbarity. Mrs. Hewett, looking as if she had herself risen from a coffin, cried shame on the general heartlessness with which Jane was used.

Clara held to her resolve. She led Jane into the bedroom, then, with a parting shot at Miss Peckover, herself entered and locked the door.

'Drink some water, Jane,' she said, doing her best to reassure the child. 'You're safe for to-night, and we'll see what Mrs. Peckover says about this when she comes back to-morrow.'

Jane looked at her rescuer with eyes in which eternal gratitude mingled with fear for the future. She could cry now, poor thing, and so little by little recover herself. Words to utter her thanks she had none; she could only look something of what she felt. Clara made her undress and lie down with little Tom on the mattress. In a quarter of an hour the candle was extinguished, and but for the wind, which rattled sashes and doors, and made ghostly sounds in the chimneys, there was silence throughout the house.

Something awoke Clara before dawn. She sat up, and became aware that Jane was talking and crying wildly, evidently re-acting in her sleep the scene of a few hours ago. With difficulty Clara broke her slumber.

'Don't you feel well, Jane?' she asked, noticing a strangeness in the child's way of replying to her.

'Not very, miss. My head's bad, an' I'm so thirsty. May I drink out of the jug, miss?'

'Stay where you are. I'll bring it to you.'

Jane drank a great deal. Presently she fell again into slumber, which was again broken in the same way. Clara did not go to sleep, and as soon as it was daylight she summoned her father to come and look at the child. Jane was ill, and, as everyone could see, rapidly grew worse.

CHAPTER V

JANE IS VISITED

At ten o'clock next morning Mrs. Peckover reached home. She was a tall, big-boned woman of fifty, with an arm like a coalheaver's. She had dark hair, which shone and was odorous with unguents; a sallow, uncomely face, and a handsome moustache. Her countenance was more difficult to read than Clem's; a coarse, and most likely brutal, nature was plain enough in its lines, but there was also a suggestion of self-restraint, of sagacity, at all events of cunning—qualities which were decidedly not inherited by her daughter. With her came the relative whose presence had been desired at the funeral to-day. This was Mrs. Gully, a stout person with a very red nose and bleared eyes. The credit of the family demanded that as many relatives as possible should follow the hearse, and Mrs. Peckover's reason for conducting Mrs. Gully hither was a justifiable fear lest, if she came alone, the latter would arrive in too manifest a state of insobriety. A certain amount of stimulant had been permitted on the way, just enough to assist a genteel loquacity, for which Mrs. Gully had a reputation. She had given her word to abstain from further imbibing until after the funeral.

The news which greeted her arrival was anything but welcome to Mrs. Peckover. In the first place, there would be far more work than usual to be performed in the house to-day, and Jane could be ill spared. Worse than that, however, Clara Hewett, who was losing half a day's work on Jane's account, made a very emphatic statement as to the origin of the illness, and said that if anything happened to Jane, there would be disagreeable facts forthcoming at a coroner's inquest. Having looked at the sick child, Mrs. Peckover went downstairs and shut herself up with Clem. There was a stormy interview.

'So you thought you'd have yer fling, did you, just because I wasn't 'ere? You must go makin' trouble, just to suit yer own fancies! I'll pay you, my lady! Gr-r-r!'

Whereupon followed the smack of a large hand on a fleshy cheek, so vigorous and unexpected a blow that even the sturdy Clem staggered back.

'You leave me alone, will you?' she roared out, her

smitten cheek in a flame. 'Do that again, an' I'll give you somethin' for yerself! See if I don't! You just try it on!'

The room rang with uproarious abuse, with disgusting language, with the terrific threats which are such common flowers of rhetoric in that world, and generally mean nothing whatever. The end of it all was that Clem went to fetch a doctor,* one in whom Mrs. Peckover could repose confidence. The man was, in fact, a druggist, with a shop in an obscure street over towards St. Luke's ; in his window was exhibited a card which stated that a certain medical man could be consulted here daily. The said medical man had, in fact, so much more business than he could attend to—his name appearing in many shops—that the druggist was deputed to act as his assistant, and was considerately supplied with death-certificates, already signed, and only needing to be filled in with details. Summoned by Mrs. Peckover, whose old acquaintance he was, the druggist left the shop in care of his son, aged fifteen, and sped to Clerkenwell Close. He made light of Jane's ailment. 'A little fever, that was all—soon pull her round. Any wounds, by-the-by ? No ? Oh, soon pull her round. Send for medicines.'

'We'll have her down in the back-kitchen as soon as the corffin's away,' said Mrs. Peckover to Mrs. Hewett. 'Don't you upset yerself about it, my dear ; you've got quite enough to think about. Yer 'usband got anythink yet ? Dear, dear! Don't you put yerself out. I'm sure it was a great kindness of you to let the troublesome thing lay 'ere all night.'

Funeral guests were beginning to assemble. On arriving, they were conducted first of all into the front-room on the ground-floor, the Peckovers' parlour. It was richly furnished. In the centre stood a round table, which left small space for moving about, and was at present covered with refreshments. A polished sideboard supported a row of dessert-plates propped on their edges, and a number of glass vessels, probably meant for ornament alone, as they could not possibly have been put to any use. A low cupboard in a recess was surmounted by a frosted cardboard model of St. Paul's under a glass case, behind which was reared an oval tray painted with flowers. Over the mantel-piece was the regulation mirror, its gilt frame enveloped in coarse yellow gauze ; the mantel-piece itself bore a 'wealth' of embellishments in glass and crockery. On each side of it hung a framed silhouette, portraits of ancestors. Other pictures there were many, the most impressive being

an ancient oil-painting, of which the canvas bulged forth
from the frame; the subject appeared to be a ship, but
was just as likely a view of the Alps. Several German
prints* conveyed instruction as well as delight; one represented the trial of Strafford in Westminster Hall; another,
the trial of William Lord Russell, at the Old Bailey. There
was also a group of engraved portraits, the Royal Family of
England early in the reign of Queen Victoria; and finally,
'The Destruction of Nineveh,' by John Martin. Along the
window-sill were disposed flower-pots containing artificial
plants; one or other was always being knocked down by the
curtains or blinds.

Each guest having taken a quaff of ale or spirits or what
was called wine, with perhaps a mouthful of more solid sustenance, was then led down into the back-kitchen to view the
coffin and the corpse. I mention the coffin first, because in
everyone's view this was the main point of interest. Could
Mrs. Peckover have buried the old woman in an orange-crate,
she would gladly have done so for the saving of expense; but
with relatives and neighbours to consider, she drew a great
deal of virtue out of necessity, and dealt so very handsomely
with the undertaker, that this burial would be the talk of the
Close for some weeks. The coffin was inspected inside and
out, was admired and appraised, Mrs. Peckover being at hand
to check the estimates. At the same time every most revolting
detail of the dead woman's last illness was related and discussed and mused over and exclaimed upon. 'A lovely corpse,
considerin' her years,' was the general opinion. Then all
went upstairs again, and once more refreshed themselves.
The house smelt like a bar-room.

'Everythink most respectable, I'm sure!' remarked the
female mourners to each other, as they crowded together in
the parlour.

'An' so it had ought to be!' exclaimed one, in an indignant
tone, such as is reserved for the expression of offence among
educated people, but among the poor—the London poor, least
original and least articulate beings within the confines of
civilisation—has also to do duty for friendly emphasis. 'If
Mrs. Peckover can't afford to do things respectable, who
can?'

And the speaker looked defiantly about her, as if daring
contradiction. But only approving murmurs replied. Mrs.
Peckover had, in fact, the reputation of being wealthy; she

was always inheriting, always accumulating what her friends called 'interess,' never expending as other people needs must. The lodgings she let enabled her to live rent-free and rate-free. Clem's earnings at an artificial-flower factory more than paid for that young lady's board and clothing, and all other outlay was not worth mentioning as a deduction from the income created by her sundry investments. Her husband—ten years deceased—had been a 'moulder';* he earned on an average between three and four pounds a week, and was so prudently disposed that, for the last decade of his life, he made it a rule never to spend a farthing of his wages. Mrs. Peckover at that time kept a small beer-shop in Rosoman Street—small and unpretending in appearance, but through it there ran a beery Pactolus.* By selling the business shortly after her husband's death, Mrs. Peckover realised a handsome capital. She retired into private life, having a strong sense of personal dignity, and feeling it necessary to devote herself to the moral training of her only child.

At half-past eleven Mrs. Peckover was arrayed in her mourning robes—new, dark-glistening. During her absence Clem had kept guard over Mrs. Gully, whom it was very difficult indeed to restrain from the bottles and decanters; the elder lady coming to relieve, Clem could rush away and don her own solemn garments. The undertaker with his men arrived; the hearse and coaches drove up; the Close was in a state of excitement. 'Now that's what I call a respectable turn-out!' was the phrase passed from mouth to mouth in the crowd gathering near the door. Children in great numbers had absented themselves from school for the purpose of beholding this procession. 'I do like to see spirited 'orses at a funeral!' remarked one of the mourners, who had squeezed his way to the parlour window. 'It puts the finishin' touch, as you may say, don't it?' When the coffin was borne forth, there was such a press in the street that the men with difficulty reached the hearse. As the female mourners stepped across the pavement with handkerchiefs held to their mouths, a sigh of satisfaction was audible throughout the crowd; the males were less sympathetically received, and some jocose comments from a costermonger,* whose business was temporarily interrupted, excited indulgent smiles.

The procession moved slowly away, and the crowd, unwilling to disperse immediately, looked about for some new source of entertainment. They were fortunate, for at this mo-

ment came round the corner an individual notorious throughout Clerkenwell as 'Mad Jack.'* Mad he presumably was—
at all events, an idiot. A lanky, raw-boned, red-headed man,
perhaps forty years old; not clad, but hung over with the
filthiest rags; hatless, shoeless. He supported himself by
singing in the streets, generally psalms, and with eccentric
modulations of the voice which always occasioned mirth in
hearers. Sometimes he stood at a corner and began the delivery of a passage of Scripture in French; how, where, or
when he could have acquired this knowledge was a mystery,
and Jack would throw no light on his own past. At present,
having watched the funeral coaches pass away, he lifted up
his voice in a terrific blare, singing, 'All ye works of the Lord,
bless ye the Lord, praise Him and magnify Him for ever.'
Instantly he was assailed by the juvenile portion of the throng,
was pelted with anything that came to hand, mocked merci-
lessly, buffeted from behind. For a while he persisted in his
psalmody, but at length, without warning, he rushed upon his
tormentors, and with angry shrieks endeavoured to take revenge. The uproar continued till a policeman came and
cleared the way. Then Jack went off again, singing, 'All
ye works of the Lord.' With his voice blended that of the
costermonger, 'Penny a bundill!'

Up in the Hewetts' back-room lay Jane Snowdon, now
seemingly asleep, now delirious. When she talked, a name
was constantly upon her lips; she kept calling for 'Mr.
Kirkwood.' Amy was at school; Annie and Tom frequently
went into the room and gazed curiously at the sick girl. Mrs.
Hewett felt so ill to-day that she could only lie on the bed
and try to silence her baby's crying.

The house-door was left wide open between the departure
and return of the mourners; a superstition of the people
demands this. The Peckovers brought back with them some
half a dozen relatives and friends, invited to a late dinner.
The meal had been in preparation at an eating-house close by,
and was now speedily made ready in the parlour. A liberal
supply of various ales was furnished by the agency of a pot-
boy (Jane's absence being much felt), and in the course of
half an hour or so the company were sufficiently restored to
address themselves anew to the bottles and decanters. Mrs.
Gully was now permitted to obey her instincts; the natural
result could be attributed to overstrung feelings.

Just when the mourners had grown noisily hilarious,

testifying thereby to the respectability with which things were
being conducted to the very end, Mrs. Peckover became aware
of a knocking at the front-door. She bade her daughter go
and see who it was. Clem, speedily returning, beckoned her
mother from among the guests.

'It's somebody wants to know if there ain't somebody
called Snowdon livin' 'ere,' she whispered in a tone of alarm.
'An old man.'

Mrs. Peckover never drank more than was consistent with
the perfect clearness of her brain. At present she had very
red cheeks, and her cat-like eyes gleamed noticeably, but any
kind of business would have found her as shrewdly competent
as ever.

'What did you say?' she whispered savagely

'Said I'd come an' ask.'

'You stay 'ere. Don't say nothink.'

Mrs. Peckover left the room, closed the door behind her,
and went along the passage. On the doorstep stood a man
with white hair, wearing an unusual kind of cloak and a
strange hat. He looked at the landlady without speaking.

'What was you wantin', mister?'

'I have been told,' replied the man in a clear, grave voice,
'that a child of the name of Snowdon lives in your house,
ma'am.'

'Eh? Who told you that?'

'The people next door but one. I've been asking at many
houses in the neighbourhood. There used to be relations
of mine lived somewhere here; I don't know the house,
nor the street exactly. The name isn't so very common.
If you don't mind, I should like to ask you who the child's
parents was.'

Mrs. Peckover's eyes were searching the speaker with the
utmost closeness.

'I don't mind tellin' you,' she said, 'that there *is* a child
of that name in the 'ouse, a young girl, at least. Though I
don't rightly know her age, I take her for fourteen or fifteen.'

The old man seemed to consult his recollections.

'If it's anyone I'm thinking of,' he said slowly, 'she can't
be quite as old as that.'

The woman's face changed; she looked away for a moment.

'Well, as I was sayin', I don't rightly know her age. Any
way, I'm responsible for her. I've been a mother to her, an'

a good mother—though I say it myself—these six years or more. I look on her now as a child o' my own. I don't know who you may be, mister. P'r'aps you've come from abroad?'

'Yes, I have. There's no reason why I shouldn't tell you that I'm trying to find any of my kin that are still alive. There was a married son of mine that once lived somewhere about here. His name was Joseph James Snowdon. When I last heard of him, he was working at a 'lectroplater's in Clerkenwell. That was thirteen years ago. I deal openly with you; I shall thank you if you'll do the like with me.'

'See, will you just come in? I've got a few friends in the front-room; there's been a death in the 'ouse, an' there's sickness, an' we're out of order a bit. I'll ask you to come downstairs.'

It was late in the afternoon, and though lights were not yet required in the upper rooms, the kitchen would have been all but dark save for the fire. Mrs. Peckover lit a lamp and bade her visitor be seated. Then she re-examined his face, his attire, his hands. Everything about him told of a life spent in mechanical labour. His speech was that of an untaught man, yet differed greatly from the tongue prevailing in Clerkenwell; he was probably not a Londoner by birth, and—a point of more moment—he expressed himself in the tone of one who is habitually thoughtful, who, if the aid of books has been denied to him, still has won from life the kind of knowledge which develops character. Mrs. Peckover had small experience of faces which bear the stamp of simple sincerity. This man's countenance put her out. As a matter of course, he wished to overreach her in some way, but he was obviously very deep indeed. And then she found it so difficult to guess his purposes. How would he proceed if she gave him details of Jane's history, admitting that she was the child of Joseph James Snowdon? What, again, had he been told by the people of whom he had made inquiries? She needed time to review her position.

'As I was sayin',' she resumed, poking the fire, 'I've been a mother to her these six years or more, an' I feel I done the right thing by her. She was left on my 'ands by them as promised to pay for her keep; an' a few months, I may say a few weeks, was all as ever I got. Another woman would a sent the child to the 'Ouse;' but that's always the way with me; I'm always actin' against my own interesses.'

'You say that her parents went away and left her?' asked the old man, knitting his brows.

'Her father did. Her mother, she died in this very 'ouse, an' she was buried from it. He gave her a respectable burial, I'll say that much for him. An' I shouldn't have allowed anything but one as was respectable to leave this 'ouse; I'd sooner a paid money out o' my own pocket. That's always the way with me. Mr. Willis, he's my undertaker; you'll find him at Number 17 Green Passage. He buried my 'usband; though that wasn't from the Close; but I never knew a job turned out more respectable. He was 'ere to-day; we've only just buried my 'usband's mother. That's why I ain't quite myself—see?'

Mrs. Peckover was not wont to be gossippy. She became so at present, partly in consequence of the stimulants she had taken to support her through a trying ceremony, partly as a means of obtaining time to reflect. Jane's unlucky illness made an especial difficulty in her calculations. She felt that the longer she delayed mention of the fact, the more likely was she to excite suspicion; on the other hand, she could not devise the suitable terms in which to reveal it. The steady gaze of the old man was disconcerting. Not that he searched her face with a cunning scrutiny, such as her own eyes expressed; she would have found that less troublesome, as being familiar. The anxiety, the troubled anticipation, which her words had aroused in him, were wholly free from shadow of ignoble motive; he was pained, and the frequent turning away of his look betrayed that part of the feeling was caused by observation of the woman herself, but every movement visible on his features was subdued by patience and mildness. Suffering was a life's habit with him, and its fruit in this instance that which (spite of moral commonplace) it least often bears —self-conquest.

'You haven't told me yet,' he said, with quiet disregard of her irrelevancies, 'whether or not her father's name was Joseph Snowdon.'

'There's no call to hide it. That was his name. I've got letters of his writin'. "J. J. Snowdon" stands at the end, plain enough. And he was your son, was he?'

'He was. But have you any reason to think he's dead?'

'Dead! I never heard as he was. But then I never heard as he was livin', neither. When his wife went, poor thing—an' it was a chill on the liver, they said; it took her very sudden—he says to me, "Mrs. Peckover," he says, "I

know you for a motherly woman "—just like that—see ?—" I
know you for a motherly woman," he says, " an' the idea I
have in my 'ed is as I should like to leave Janey in your care,
'cause," he says, " I've got work in Birmingham, an' I don't
see how I'm to take her with me. Understand me ? " he says.
" Oh ! " I says—not feelin' quite sure what I'd ought to do—
see ?   " Oh ! " I says.   " Yes," he says ; " an' between you
an' me," he says, " there won't be no misunderstanding.   If
you'll keep Janey with you "—an' she was goin' to school at
the time, 'cause she went to the same as my own Clem—
that's Clemintiner—understand ?—" if you'll keep Janey with
you," he says, " for a year, or maybe two years, or maybe
three years—'cause that depends on cirkinstances "—understand ?—" I'm ready," he says, " to pay you what it's right
that pay I should, an' I'm sure," he says, " as we shouldn't
misunderstand one another."   Well, of course I had my own
girl to bring up, an' my own son to look after too.   A nice
sort o' son ; just when he was beginnin' to do well, an' ought
to a paid me back for all the expense I was at in puttin'
him to a business, what must he do but take his 'ook to
Australia.'

Her scrutiny discerned something in the listener's face
which led her to ask :

' Perhaps you've been in Australia yourself, mister ? '

' I have.'

The woman paused, speculation at work in her eyes.

' Do you know in what part of the country your son is ?
inquired the old man absently.

' He's wrote me two letters, an' the last, as come more
than a year ago, was from a place called Maryborough.'

The other still preserved an absent expression ; his eyes
travelled about the room.

' I always said,' pursued Mrs. Peckover, ' as it was Snowdon as put Australia into the boy's 'ed.   He used to tell us
he'd got a brother there, doin' well.   P'r'aps it wasn't true.'

' Yes, it was true,' replied the old man coldly.   ' But you
haven't told me what came to pass about the child.'

An exact report of all that Mrs. Peckover had to say on
this subject would occupy more space than it merits.   The
gist of it was that for less than a year she had received certain
stipulated sums irregularly ; that at length no money at all was
forthcoming ; that in the tenderness of her heart she had still
entertained the child, sent her to school, privately instructed

her in the domestic virtues, trusting that such humanity would not lack even its material reward, and that either Joseph Snowdon or someone akin to him would ultimately make good to her the expenses she had not grudged.

'She's a child as pays you back for all the trouble you take, so much I *will* say for her,' observed the matron in conclusion. 'Not as it hasn't been a little 'ard to teach her tidiness, but she's only a young thing still. I shouldn't wonder but she's felt her position a little now an' then; it's only natural in a growin' girl, do what you can to prevent it. Still, she's willin'; that nobody can deny, an' I'm sure *I* should never wish to. Her cirkinstances has been peculiar; that you'll understand, I'm sure. But I done my best to take the place of the mother as is gone to a better world. An' now that she's layin' ill, I'm sure no mother could feel it more——'

'Ill? Why didn't you mention that before?'

'Didn't I say as she was ill? Why, I thought it was the first word I spoke as soon as you got into the 'ouse. You can't a noticed it, or else it was me as is so put about. What with havin' a burial——'

'Where is she?' asked the old man anxiously.

'Where? Why, you don't think as I'd a sent her to be looked after by strangers? She's layin' in Mrs. Hewett's room—that's one o' the lodgers—all for the sake o' comfort. A better an' kinder woman than Mrs. Hewett you wouldn't find, not if you was to——'

With difficulty the stranger obtained a few details of the origin and course of the illness—details wholly misleading, but devised to reassure. When he desired to see Jane, Mrs. Peckover assumed an air of perfect willingness, but reminded him that she had nothing save his word to prove that he had indeed a legitimate interest in the girl.

'I can do no more than tell you that Joseph James Snowdon was my younger son,' replied the old man simply. 'I've come back to spend my last years in England, and I hoped—I hope still—to find my son. I wish to take his child into my own care; as he left her to strangers—perhaps he didn't do it willingly; he may be dead—he could have nothing to say against me giving her the care of a parent. You've been at expense——'

Mrs. Peckover waited with eagerness, but the sentence remained incomplete. Again the old man's eyes strayed about the room. The current of his thoughts seemed to change, and he said :

'You could show me those letters you spoke of—of my son's writing ?'

'Of course I could,' was the reply, in the tone of coarse resentment whereby the scheming vulgar are wont to testify to their dishonesty.

'Afterwards—afterwards. I should like to see Jane, if you'll be so good.'

The mild voice, though often diffident, now and then fell upon a note of quiet authority which suited well with the speaker's grave, pure countenance. As he spoke thus, Mrs. Peckover rose, and said she would first go upstairs just to see how things were. She was absent ten minutes, then a little girl—Amy Hewett—came into the kitchen and asked the stranger to follow her.

Jane had been rapidly transferred from the mattress to the bedstead, and the room had been put into such order as was possible. A whisper from Mrs. Peckover to Mrs. Hewett, promising remission of half a week's rent, had sufficed to obtain for the former complete freedom in her movements. The child, excited by this disturbance, had begun to moan and talk inarticulately. Mrs. Peckover listened for a moment, but heard nothing dangerous. She bade the old man enter noiselessly, and herself went about on tip-toe, speaking only in a hoarse whisper.

The visitor had just reached the bedside, and was gazing with deep, compassionate interest at the unconscious face, when Jane, as if startled, half rose and cried painfully, 'Mr. Kirkwood ! oh, Mr. Kirkwood !' and she stretched her hand out, appearing to believe that the friend she called upon was near her.

'Who is that ?' inquired the old man, turning to his companion.

'Only a friend of ours,' answered Mrs. Peckover, herself puzzled and uneasy.

Again the sick girl called 'Mr. Kirkwood !' but without other words. Mrs. Peckover urged the danger of this excitement, and speedily led the way downstairs.

CHAPTER VI

GLIMPSES OF THE PAST

SIDNEY KIRKWOOD had a lodging in Tysoe Street, Clerkenwell. It is a short street, which, like so many in London, begins reputably and degenerates in its latter half. The cleaner end leads into Wilmington Square, which consists of decently depressing houses, occupied in the main, as the lower windows and front-doors indicate, by watchmakers, working jewellers, and craftsmen of allied pursuits. The open space, grateful in this neighbourhood, is laid out as a garden, with trees, beds, and walks. Near the iron gate, which, for certain hours in the day, gives admission, is a painted notice informing the public that, by the grace of the Marquis of Northampton,* they may here take their ease on condition of good behaviour; to children is addressed a distinct warning that ' This is not a playing ground.' From his window Sidney had a good view of the Square. The house in which he lived was of two storeys; a brass plate on the door showed the inscription, ' Hodgson, Dial Painter.' The window on the ground-floor was arched, as in the other dwellings at this end of the street, and within stood an artistic arrangement of wax fruit under a glass shade, supported by a heavy volume of Biblical appearance. The upper storey was graced with a small iron balcony, on which straggled a few flower-pots. However, the exterior of this abode was, by comparison, promising; the curtains and blinds were clean, the step was washed and whitened, the brass plate shone, the panes of glass had at all events acquaintance with a duster. A few yards in the direction away from the Square, and Tysoe Street falls under the dominion of dry-rot.

It was not until he set forth to go to work next morning that Sidney called to mind his conversation with Jane. That the child should have missed by five minutes a meeting with someone who perchance had the will and the power to befriend her, seemed to him, in his present mood, merely an illustration of a vice inherent in the nature of things. He determined to look in at the public-house of which she had spoken, and hear for himself what manner of man had made inquiries for people named Snowdon. The name was not a common one; it was worth while to spend a hope or two on the chance of doing Jane a kindness. Her look and voice when he bade her be of good courage had touched him. In his rejected state, he felt that it was pleasant to earn gratitude even from so humble a being as the Peckovers' drudge.

His workshop, it has been mentioned, was in St. John's Square. Of all areas in London thus defined, this Square of St. John is probably the most irregular in outline. It is cut in two by Clerkenwell Road, and the buildings which compose it form such a number of recesses, of abortive streets, of shadowed alleys, that from no point of the Square can anything like a general view of its totality be obtained. The exit from it on the south side is by St. John's Lane, at the entrance to which stands a survival from a buried world—the embattled and windowed archway which is all that remains above ground of the great Priory of St. John of Jerusalem. Here dwelt the Knights Hospitallers, in days when Clerkenwell was a rural parish, distant by a long stretch of green country from the walls of London. But other and nearer memories are revived by St. John's Arch. In the rooms above the gateway dwelt, a hundred and fifty years ago, one Edward Cave, publisher of the *Gentleman's Magazine*, and there many a time has sat a journeyman author of his, by name Samuel Johnson, too often *impransus*.* There it was that the said Samuel once had his dinner handed to him behind a screen, because of his unpresentable costume, when Cave was entertaining an aristocratic guest. In the course of the meal, the guest happened to speak with interest of something he had recently read by an obscure Mr. Johnson; whereat there was joy behind the screen, and probably increased appreciation of the unwonted dinner. After a walk amid the squalid and toil-infested ways of Clerkenwell, it impresses one strangely to come upon this monument of old time. The archway has a sad, worn, grimy aspect. So closely is it packed in among buildings which suggest nothing but the sordid struggle for existence, that it looks depressed, ashamed, tainted by the ignobleness of its surroundings. The wonder is that it has not been swept away, in obedience to the great law of traffic and the spirit of the time.

St. John's Arch had a place in Sidney Kirkwood's earliest memories. From the window of his present workshop he could see its grey battlements, and they reminded him of the days when, as a lad just beginning to put questions about the surprising world in which he found himself, he used to listen to such stories as his father could tell him of the history of

Clerkenwell. Mr. Kirkwood occupied part of a house in St. John's Lane, not thirty yards from the Arch; he was a printers' roller maker, and did but an indifferent business. A year after the birth of Sidney, his only child, he became a widower. An intelligent, warm-hearted man, the one purpose of his latter years was to realise such moderate competency as should place his son above the anxieties which degrade. The boy had a noticeable turn for drawing and colouring; at ten years old, when (as often happened) his father took him for a Sunday in the country, he carried a sketch-book and found his delight in using it. Sidney was to be a draughtsman of some kind; perhaps an artist, if all went well. Unhappily things went the reverse of well. In his anxiety to improve his business, Mr. Kirkwood invented a new kind of 'composition' for printers' use; he patented it, risked capital upon it, made in a short time some serious losses. To add to his troubles, young Sidney was giving signs of an unstable character; at fifteen he had grown tired of his drawing, wanted to be this, that, and the other thing, was self-willed, and showed no consideration for his father's difficulties. It was necessary to take a decided step, and, though against his will, Sidney was apprenticed to an uncle, a Mr. Roach, who also lived in Clerkenwell, and was a working jeweller. Two years later the father died, all but bankrupt. The few pounds realised from his effects passed into the hands of Mr. Roach, and were soon expended in payment for Sidney's board and lodging.

His bereavement possibly saved Sidney from a young-manhood of foolishness and worse. In the upper world a youth may 'sow his wild oats' and have done with it; in the nether, 'to have your fling' is almost necessarily to fall among criminals. The death was sudden; it affected the lad profoundly, and filled him with a remorse which was to influence the whole of his life. Mr. Roach, a thick-skinned and rather thick-headed person, did not spare to remind his apprentice of the most painful things wherewith the latter had to reproach himself. Sidney bore it, from this day beginning a course of self-discipline of which not many are capable at any age, and very few indeed at seventeen. Still, there had never been any sympathy between him and his uncle, and before very long the young man saw his way to live under another roof and find work with a new employer.

It was just after leaving his uncle's house that Sidney

came to know John Hewett; the circumstances which fostered their friendship were such as threw strong light on the characters of both. Sidney had taken a room in Islington, and two rooms on the floor beneath him were tenanted by a man who was a widower and had two children. In those days, our young friend found much satisfaction in spending his Sunday evenings on Clerkenwell Green, where fervent, if ungrammatical, oratory was to be heard, and participation in debate was open to all whom the spirit moved. One whom the spirit did very frequently move was Sidney's fellow-lodger; he had no gift of expression whatever, but his brief, stammering protests against this or that social wrong had such an honest, indeed such a pathetic sound, that Sidney took an opportunity of walking home with him and converting neighbourship into friendly acquaintance. John Hewett gave the young man an account of his life. He had begun as a lath-render; later he had got into cabinet-making, started a business on his own account, and failed. A brother of his, who was a builder's foreman, then found employment for him in general carpentry on some new houses; but John quarrelled with his brother, and after many difficulties fell to the making of packing-cases; that was his work at present, and with much discontent he pursued it. John was curiously frank in owning all the faults in himself which had helped to make his career so unsatisfactory. He confessed that he had an uncertain temper, that he soon became impatient with work 'which led to nothing,' that he was tempted out of his prudence by anything which seemed to offer 'a better start.' With all these admissions, he maintained that he did well to be angry. It was wrong that life should be so hard; so much should not be required of a man. In body he was not strong; the weariness of interminable days over-tried him and excited his mind to vain discontent. His wife was the only one who could ever keep him cheerful under his lot, and his wedded life had lasted but six years; now there was his lad Bob and his little girl Clara to think of, and it only made him more miserable to look forward and see them going through hardships like his own. Things were wrong somehow, and it seemed to him that 'if only we could have universal suffrage——'

Sidney was only eighteen, and strong in juvenile Radicalism, but he had a fund of common sense, and such a conclusion as this of poor John's half-astonished, half-amused him. However, the man's personality attracted him; it was

honest, warm-hearted, interesting ; the logic of his plead-
ings might be at fault, but Sidney sympathised with him, for
all that. He too felt that 'things were wrong somehow,'
and had a pleasure in joining the side of revolt for revolt's
sake.

Now in the same house with them dwelt a young woman
of about nineteen years old ; she occupied a garret, was seldom seen about, and had every appearance of being a simple,
laborious girl, of the kind familiar enough as the silent victims
of industrialism. One day the house was thrown into consternation by the news that Miss Barnes—so she was named—
had been arrested on a charge of stealing her employer's goods.
It was true, and perhaps the best way of explaining it will be
to reproduce a newspaper report which Sidney Kirkwood thereafter preserved.

' On Friday, Margaret Barnes, nineteen, a single woman,
was indicted for stealing six jackets, value 5*l.*, the property of
Mary Oaks, her mistress. The prisoner, who cried bitterly
during the proceedings, pleaded guilty. The prosecutrix is a
single woman, and gets her living by mantle-making.* She
engaged the prisoner to do what is termed " finishing off,"
that is, making the button-holes and sewing on the buttons.
The prisoner was also employed to fetch the work from the
warehouse, and deliver it when finished. On September 7th
her mistress sent her with the six jackets, and she never returned. Sergeant Smith, a detective, who apprehended the
prisoner, said he had made inquiries in the case, and found
that up to this time the prisoner had borne a good character as an honest, hard-working girl. She had quitted her
former lodgings, which had no furniture but a small table
and a few rags in a corner, and he discovered her in a room
which was perfectly bare. Miss Oaks was examined, and
said the prisoner was employed from nine in the morning to
eight at night. The Judge : How much did you pay her per
week ? Miss Oaks : Four shillings. The Judge : Did you
give her her food ? Miss Oaks : No ; I only get one shilling
each for the jackets myself when completed. I have to use
two sewing-machines, find my own cotton and needles, and I
can, by working hard, make two in a day. The Judge said it
was a sad state of things. The prisoner, when called upon,
said she had had nothing to eat for three days, and so gave
way to temptation, hoping to get better employment. The
Judge, while commiserating with the prisoner, said it could

not be allowed that distress should justify dishonesty, and sentenced the prisoner to six weeks' imprisonment.'

The six weeks passed, and about a fortnight after that, John Hewett came into Sidney's room one evening with a strange look on his face. His eyes were very bright, the hand which he held out trembled.

'I've something to tell you,' he said. 'I'm going to get married again.'

'Really? Why, I'm glad to hear it!'

'And who do you think? Miss Barnes.'

Sidney was startled for a moment. John had had no acquaintance with the girl prior to her imprisonment. He had said that he should meet her when she came out and give her some money, and Sidney had added a contribution. For a man in Hewett's circumstances this latest step was somewhat astonishing, but his character explained it.

'I'm goin' to marry her,' he exclaimed excitedly, 'and I'm doing the right thing! I respect her more than all the women as never went wrong because they never had occasion to. I'm goin' to put her as a mother over my children, and I'm goin' to make a happier life for her. She's a good girl, I tell you. I've seen her nearly every day this fortnight; I know all about her. She wouldn't have me when I first asked her—that was a week ago. She said no; she'd disgrace me. If you can't respect her as you would any other woman, never come into my lodging!'

Sidney was warm with generous glow. He wrung Hewett's hand and stammered incoherent words.

John took new lodgings in an obscure part of Clerkenwell, and seemed to have become a young man once more. His complaints ceased; the energy with which he went about his work was remarkable. He said his wife was the salvation of him. And then befell one of those happy chances which supply mankind with instances for its pathetic faith that a good deed will not fail of reward. John's brother died, and bequeathed to him some four hundred pounds. Hereupon, what must the poor fellow do but open workshops on his own account, engage men, go about crying that his opportunity had come at last. Here was the bit of rock by means of which he could save himself from the sea of competition that had so nearly whelmed him! Little Clara, now eleven years old, could go on steadily at school; no need to think of how the poor child should earn a wretched living. Bob, now

thirteen, should shortly be apprenticed to some better kind of
trade. New rooms were taken and well furnished. Maggie,
the wife, could have good food, such as she needed in her constant ailing, alas! The baby just born was no longer a cause
of anxious thought, but a joy in the home. And Sidney Kirkwood came to supper as soon as the new rooms were in order,
and his bright, manly face did everyone good to look at. He
still took little Clara upon his knee. Ha! there would come
a day before long when he would not venture to do that, and
then perhaps—perhaps! What a supper that was, and how
smoothly went the great wheels of the world that evening!

One baby, two babies, three babies; before the birth of
the third, John's brow was again clouded, again he had begun
to rail and fume at the unfitness of things. His business was
a failure, partly because he dealt with a too rigid honesty,
partly because of his unstable nature, which left him at the
mercy of whims and obstinacies and airy projects. He did
not risk the ordinary kind of bankruptcy, but came down and
down, until at length he was the only workman in his own
shop; then the shop itself had to be abandoned; then he was
searching for someone who would employ him.

Bob had been put to the die-sinker's craft;* Clara was still
going to school, and had no thought of earning a livelihood—
ominous state of things. When it shortly became clear even
to John Hewett that he would wrong the girl if he did not
provide her with some means of supporting herself, she was
sent to learn 'stamping' with the same employer for whom
her brother worked. The work was light; it would soon
bring in a little money. John declared with fierceness that his
daughter should never be set to the usual needle-slavery, and
indeed it seemed very unlikely that Clara would ever be fit for
that employment, as she could not do the simplest kind of
sewing. In the meantime the family kept changing their
abode, till at length they settled in Mrs. Peckover's house. All
the best of their furniture was by this time sold; but for the
two eldest children, there would probably have been no home
at all. Bob, aged nineteen, earned at this present time a pound
weekly; his sister, an average of thirteen shillings. Mrs.
Hewett's constant ill-health (the result, doubtless, of semi-
starvation through the years of her girlhood), would have excused defects of housekeeping; but indeed the poor woman
was under any circumstances incapable of domestic manage-
ment, and therein represented her class. The money she

received was wasted in comparison with what might have been done with it. I suppose she must not be blamed for bringing children into the world when those already born to her were but half-clothed, half-fed ; she increased the sum total of the world's misery in obedience to the laws of the Book of Genesis. And one virtue she had which compensated for all that was lacking—a virtue merely negative among the refined, but in that other world the rarest and most precious of moral distinctions—she resisted the temptations of the public-house.

This was the story present in Sidney Kirkwood's mind as often as he climbed the staircase in Clerkenwell Close. By contrast, his own life seemed one of unbroken ease. Outwardly it was smooth enough. He had no liking for his craft, and being always employed upon the meaningless work which is demanded by the rich vulgar, he felt such work to be paltry and ignoble ; but there seemed no hope of obtaining better. and he made no audible complaint. His wages were considerably more than he needed, and systematically he put money aside each week.

But this orderly existence concealed conflicts of heart and mind which Sidney himself could not have explained, could not lucidly have described. The moral shock which he experienced at his father's death put an end to the wanton play of his energies, but it could not ripen him before due time ; his nature was not of the sterile order common in his world, and through passion, through conflict, through endurance, it had to develop such maturity as fate should permit. Saved from self-indulgence, he naturally turned into the way of political enthusiasm ; thither did his temper point him. With some help—mostly negative—from Clerkenwell Green, he reached the stage of confident and aspiring Radicalism, believing in the perfectibility of man, in human brotherhood, in—anything you like that is the outcome of a noble heart sheltered by ignorance. It had its turn, and passed.

To give place to nothing very satisfactory. It was not a mere coincidence that Sidney was going through a period of mental and moral confusion just in those years which brought Clara Hewett from childhood to the state of woman. Among the acquaintances of Sidney's boyhood there was not one but had a chosen female companion from the age of fifteen or earlier ; he himself had been no exception to the rule in his class, but at the time of meeting with Hewett he was companionless, and remained so. The Hewetts became his closest friends; in their brief prosperity he rejoiced with them, in their hardships he gave them all the assistance to which John's pride would consent; his name was never spoken among them but with warmth and gratitude. And of course the day came to which Hewett had looked forward—the day when Sidney could no longer take Clara upon his knee and stroke her brown hair and joke with her about her fits of good and ill humour. Sidney knew well enough what was in his friend's mind, and, though with no sense of constraint, he felt that this handsome, keen-eyed, capricious girl was destined to be his wife. He liked Clara; she always attracted him and interested him; but her faults were too obvious to escape any eye, and the older she grew, the more was he impressed and troubled by them. The thought of Clara became a preoccupation, and with the love which at length he recognised there blended a sense of fate fulfilling itself. His enthusiasms, his purposes, never defined as education would have defined them, were dissipated into utter vagueness. He lost his guiding interests, and found himself returning to those of boyhood. The country once more attracted him; he took out his old sketch-books, bought a new one, revived the regret that he could not be a painter of landscape. A visit to one or two picture-galleries, and then again profound discouragement, recognition of the fact that he was a mechanic and never could be anything else.

It was the end of his illusions. For him not even passionate love was to preserve the power of idealising its object. He loved Clara with all the desire of his being, but could no longer deceive himself in judging her character. The same sad clearness of vision affected his judgment of the world about him, of the activities in which he had once been zealous, of the conditions which enveloped his life and the lives of those dear to him. The spirit of revolt often enough stirred within him, but no longer found utterance in the speech which brings relief; he did his best to dispel the mood, mocking at it as folly. Consciously he set himself the task of becoming a practical man, of learning to make the best of life as he found it, of shunning as the fatal error that habit of mind which kept John Hewett on the rack. Who was he that he should look for pleasant things in his course through the world? 'We are the lower orders; we are the working classes,' he said bitterly to his friend, and that seemed the final answer to all his aspirations.

This was a dark day with him. The gold he handled stung him to hatred and envy, and every feeling which he had resolved to combat as worse than profitless. He could not speak to his fellow-workmen. From morning to night it had rained. St. John's Arch looked more broken-spirited than ever, drenched in sooty moisture.

During the dinner-hour he walked over to the public-house of which Jane had spoken, and obtained from the barman as full a description as possible of the person he hoped to encounter. Both then and on his return home in the evening he shunned the house where his friends dwelt.

It came round to Monday. For the first time for many months he had allowed Sunday to pass without visiting the Hewetts. He felt that to go there at present would only be to increase the parents' depression by his own low spirits. Clara had left them now, however, and if he still stayed away, his behaviour might be misinterpreted. On returning from work, he washed, took a hurried meal, and was on the point of going out when someone knocked at his door. He opened, and saw an old man who was a stranger to him.

CHAPTER VII

MRS. BYASS'S LODGINGS

'You are Mr. Kirkwood?' said his visitor civilly. 'My name is Snowdon. I should be glad to speak a few words with you, if you could spare the time.'

Sidney's thoughts were instantly led into the right channel; he identified the old man by his white hair and the cloak. The hat, however, which had been described to him, was now exchanged for a soft felt of a kind common enough; the guernsey, too, had been laid aside. With ready goodwill he invited Mr. Snowdon to enter.

There was not much in the room to distinguish it from the dwelling of any orderly mechanic. A small bed occupied one side; a small table stood before the window; the toilet apparatus was, of course, unconcealed; a half-open cupboard allowed a glimpse of crockery, sundries, and a few books. The walls, it is true, were otherwise ornamented than is usual; engravings, chromo-lithographs, and some sketches of landscape in pencil.

were suspended wherever light fell, and the choice manifested in this collection was nowise akin to that which ruled in Mrs. Peckover's parlour, and probably in all the parlours of Tysoe Street. To select for one's chamber a woodcut after Constable or Gainsborough is at all events to give proof of a capacity for civilisation.

The visitor made a quick survey of these appearances; then he seated himself on the chair Sidney offered. He was not entirely at his ease, and looked up at the young man twice or thrice before he began to speak again.

'Mr. Kirkwood, were you ever acquainted with my son, by name Joseph Snowdon?'

'No; I never knew him,' was the reply. 'I have heard his name, and I know where he once lived—not far from here.'

'You're wondering what has brought me to you. I have heard of you from people a grandchild of mine is living with. I dare say it is the house you mean—in Clerkenwell Close.'

'So you have found it!' exclaimed Sidney with pleasure. 'I've been looking about for you as I walked along the streets these last two or three days.'

'Looking for me?' said the other, astonished.

Sidney supplied the explanation, but without remarking on the circumstances which made Jane so anxious to discover a possible friend. Snowdon listened attentively, and at length, with a slight smile; he seemed to find pleasure in the young man's way of expressing himself. When silence ensued, he looked about absently for a moment; then, meeting Sidney's eyes, said in a grave voice:

'That poor child is very ill.'

'Ill? I'm sorry to hear it.'

'The reason I've come to you, Mr. Kirkwood, is because she's called out your name so often. They don't seem able to tell me how she came into this state, but she's had a fright of some kind, or she's been living very unhappily. She calls on your name, as if she wanted you to protect her from harm. I didn't know what to think about it at first. I'm a stranger to everybody—I may tell you I've been abroad for several years—and they don't seem very ready to put trust in me; but I decided at last that I'd come and speak to you. It's my grandchild, and perhaps the only one of my family left; nobody can give me news of her father since he went away four or five years ago. She came to herself this morning for a little, but I'm afraid she couldn't understand what I tried to tell her; then I mentioned your name, and I could see it did her good at once. What I wish to ask of you is, would you come to her bedside for a few minutes? She might know you, and I feel sure it would be a kindness to her.'

Sidney appeared to hesitate. It was not, of course, that he dreamt of refusing, but he was busy revolving all he knew of Jane's life with the Peckovers, and asking himself what it behoved him to tell, what to withhold. Daily experience guarded him against the habit of gossip, which is one of the innumerable curses of the uneducated (whether poor or wealthy), and, notwithstanding the sympathy with which his visitor inspired him, he quickly decided to maintain reserve until he understood more of the situation.

'Yes, yes; I'll go with you at once,' he made haste to reply, when he perceived that his hesitancy was occasioning doubt and trouble. 'In fact, I was just starting to go and see the Hewetts when you knocked at the door. They're friends of mine—living in Mrs. Peckover's house. That's how I came to know Jane. I haven't been there for several days, and when I last saw her, as I was saying, she seemed as well as usual.'

'I'm afraid that wasn't much to boast of,' said Snowdon. 'She's a poor, thin-looking child.'

Sidney was conscious that the old man did not give expression to all he thought. This mutual exercise of tact seemed, however, to encourage a good understanding between them rather than the reverse.

'You remain in the house?' Kirkwood asked as they went downstairs.

'I stay with her through the night. I didn't feel much confidence in the doctor that was seeing her, so I made inquiries and found a better man.'

When they reached the Close, the door was opened to them by Clem Peckover. She glared haughtily at Sidney, but uttered no word. To Kirkwood's surprise, they went up to the Hewetts' back-room. The mattress that formerly lay upon the floor had been removed; the bed was occupied by the sick girl, with whom at present Mrs. Peckover was sitting. That benevolent person rose on seeing Sidney, and inclined her head with stateliness.

'She's just fell asleep,' was her whispered remark. 'I shouldn't say myself as it was good to wake her up, but of course you know best.'

This was in keeping with the attitude Mrs. Peckover had adopted as soon as she understood Snowdon's resolve to neglect no precaution on the child's behalf. Her sour dignity was meant to express that she felt hurt at the intervention of others where her affections were so nearly concerned. Sidney could not help a certain fear when he saw this woman installed as sick-nurse. It was of purpose that he caught her eye and regarded her with a gravity she could scarcely fail to comprehend.

Jane awoke from her fitful slumber. She looked with but half-conscious fearfulness at the figures darkening her view. Sidney moved so that his face was in the light, and, bending near to her, asked if she recognised him. A smile—slow-forming, but unmistakable at last—amply justified what her grandfather had said. She made an effort to move her hand towards him. Sidney responded to her wish, and again she smiled, self-forgetfully, contentedly.

Snowdon turned to Mrs. Peckover, and, after a few words with regard to the treatment that was being pursued, said that he would now relieve her; she lingered, but shortly left the room. Sidney, sitting by the bed, in a few minutes saw that Jane once more slept, or appeared to do so. He whispered to Snowdon that he was going to see his friends in the next room, and would look in again before leaving.

His tap at the door was answered by Amy, who at once looked back and said:

'Can Mr. Kirkwood come in, mother?'

'Yes; I want to see him,' was the answer.

Mrs. Hewett was lying in bed; she looked, if possible, more wretchedly ill than four days ago. On the floor were two mattresses, covered to make beds for the children. The baby, held in its mother's arms, was crying feebly.

'Why, I hoped you were getting much better by now,' said Sidney.

Mrs. Hewett told him that she had been to the hospital on Saturday, and seemed to have caught cold. A common enough occurrence; hours of waiting in an out-patients' room frequently do more harm than the doctor's advice can remedy. She explained that Mrs. Peckover had requested the use of the other room.

'There's too many of us to be livin' an' sleepin' in this little place,' she said; 'but, after all, it's a savin' of rent. It's

a good thing Clara isn't here. An' you've heard as John's got
work ? '

He had found a job at length with a cabinet-maker; to-
night he would probably be working till ten or eleven o'clock.
Good news so far. Then Mrs. Hewett began to speak with
curiosity of the old man who claimed Jane as his grandchild.
Sidney told her what had just happened.

' An' what did you say about the girl ? ' she asked anxiously.

' I said as little as I could; I thought it wisest. Do you
know what made her ill ? '

' It was that Clem as did it,' Mrs. Hewett replied, subduing
her voice. And she related what had befallen after Sidney's
last visit. ' Mrs. Peckover, she's that afraid the truth should
get out. Of course I don't want to make no bother, but I do
feel that glad the poor thing's got somebody to look after her
at last. I never told you half the things as used to go on.
That Clem's no better than a wild-beast tiger; but then what
can you do? There's never any good comes out of makin' a
bother with other people's business, is there? Fancy him
comin' to see you ! Mrs. Peckover's afraid of him, I can see
that, though she pretends she isn't goin' to stand him inter-
ferin'. What do you think about him, Sidney ? He's sent
for a doctor out of Islington; wouldn't have nothin' to say to
the other. He must have plenty of money, don't you think ?
Mrs. Peckover says he's goin' to pay the money owin' to her
for Jane's keep. As if the poor thing hadn't more than paid
for her bits of meals an' her bed in the kitchen ! Do you
think that woman 'ud ever have kept her if it wasn't she could
make her a servant with no wages ? If Jane 'ud been a boy,
she'd a gone to the workhouse long ago. She's been that
handy, poor little mite ! I've always done what I could for her ;
you know that, Sidney. I do hope she'll get over it. If anything happens, mind my word, there'll be a nice to-do ! Clara
says she'll go to a magistrate an' let it all out, if nobody else
will. She hates the Peckovers, Clara does.'

' It won't come to that,' said Sidney. ' I can see the old
man'll take her away as soon as possible. He may have a
little money; he's just come back from Australia. I like the
look of him myself.'

He began to talk of other subjects; waxed wrath at the
misery of this housing to which the family had shrunk; urged
a removal from the vile den as soon as ever it could be

managed. Sidney always lost control of himself when he
talked with the Hewetts of their difficulties; the people were,
from his point of view, so lacking in resource, so stubbornly
rooted in profitless habit. Over and over again he had implored them to take a rational view of the case, to borrow a
few pounds of him, to make a new beginning on clean soil.
It was like contending with some hostile force of nature; he
spent himself in vain.

As Hewett did not return, he at length took his leave, and
went into the back-room for a moment.

'She's asleep,' said Snowdon, rising from the chair where
he had been sitting deep in thought. 'It's a good sign.'

Sidney just looked towards the bed, and nodded with
satisfaction. The old man gave him a warm pressure of the
hand, and he departed. All the way home, he thought with
singular interest of the bare sick-room, of the white-headed
man watching through the night; the picture impressed him
in a way that could not be explained by its natural pathos
merely; it kept suggesting all sorts of fanciful ideas, due in
a measure, possibly, to Mrs. Hewett's speculations. For an
hour he was so lost in musing on the subject that he even
rested from the misery of his ceaseless thought of Clara.

He allowed three days to pass, then went to inquire about
Jane's progress. It had been satisfactory. Subsequent visits
brought him to terms of a certain intimacy with Snowdon.
The latter mentioned at length that he was looking for two
rooms, suitable for himself and Jane. He wished them to be
in a decent house, somewhere in Clerkenwell, and the rent
was not to be more than a working man could afford.

'You don't know of anything in your street?' he asked
diffidently.

Something in the tone struck Sidney. It half expressed
a wish to live in his neighbourhood if possible. He looked at
his companion (they were walking together), and was met in
return with a glance of calm friendliness; it gratified him,
strengthened the feeling of respect and attachment which had
already grown out of this intercourse. In Tysoe Street, however, no accommodation could be found. Sidney had another
project in his thoughts; pursuing it, he paid a visit the next
evening to certain acquaintances of his named Byass, who
had a house in Hanover Street, Islington, and let lodgings.
Hanover Street lies to the north of City Road; it is a quiet
byway, of curving form, and consists of dwellings only.

Squalor is here kept at arm's length; compared with regions close at hand, this and the contiguous streets have something of a suburban aspect.

Three or four steps led up to the house-door. Sidney's knock summoned a young, healthy-faced, comely woman, who evinced hearty pleasure on seeing who her visitor was. She brought him at once into a parlour on the ground-floor.

'Well, an' I was only this mornin' tellin' Sam to go an' look after you, or write a note, or somethin'! Why can't you come round oftener? I've no patience with you! You just sit at 'ome an' get humped, an' what's the good o' that, I should like to know? I thought you'd took offence with me, an' so I told Sam. Do you want to know how baby is? Why don't you ask, then, as you ought to do the first thing? He's a good deal better than he deserves to be, young rascal—all the trouble he gives me! He's fast asleep, I'm glad to say, so you can't see him. Sam 'll be back in a few minutes; at least I expect him, but there's no knowin' nowadays when he can leave the warehouse. What's brought you to-night, I wonder? You needn't tell me anything about the Upper Street business; _I_ know all about _that_!'

'Oh, do you? From Clara herself?'

'Yes. Don't talk to me about her! There! I'm sick an' tired of her—an' so are you, I should think, if you've any sense left. Her an' me can't get along, an' that's the truth. Why, when I met her on Sunday afternoon, she was that patronisin' you'd have thought she'd got a place in Windsor Castle. Would she come an' have a cup of tea? Oh dear, no! Hadn't time! The Princess of Wales, I suppose, was waitin' round the corner!'

Having so relieved her mind, Mrs. Byass laughed with a genuine gaiety which proved how little malice there was in her satire. Sidney could not refuse a smile, but it was a gloomy one.

'I'm not sure you've done all you might have to keep her friends with you,' he said seriously, but with a good-natured look.

'There you go!' exclaimed Mrs. Byass, throwing back her head. 'Of course everybody must be in fault sooner than _her_! She's an angel is Miss Hewett! Poor dear! to think how shameful she's been used! Now I do wonder how you've the face to say such things, Mr. Kirkwood! Why, there's nobody else livin' would have been as patient with her as I always was. I'm not bad-tempered, I will say that for myself, an' I've put up with all sorts of things (me, a married woman), when anyone else would have boxed her ears an' told her she was a conceited minx. I used to be fond of Clara; you know I did. But she's got beyond all bearin'; and if you wasn't just as foolish as men always are, you'd see her in her true colours. Do shake yourself a bit, do! Oh, you silly, silly man!'

Again she burst into ringing laughter, throwing herself backwards and forwards, and at last covering her face with her hands. Sidney looked annoyed, but the contagion of such spontaneous merriment in the end brought another smile to his face. He moved his head in sign of giving up the argument, and, as soon as there was silence, turned to the object of his visit.

'I see you've still got the card in the window. I shouldn't wonder if I could find you a lodger for those top-rooms.'

'And who's that? No children, mind.'

Sidney told her what he could of the old man. Of Jane he only said that she had hitherto lived with the Hewetts' landlady, and was now going to be removed by her grand-father, having just got through an illness. Dire visions of infection at once assailed Mrs. Byass; impossible to admit under the same roof with her baby a person who had just been ill. This scruple was, however, overcome; the two rooms at the top of the house—unfurnished—had been long vacant, owing to fastidiousness in Mr. and Mrs. Byass, since their last lodger, after a fortnight of continuous drunkenness, broke the windows, ripped the paper off the walls, and ended by trying to set fire to the house. Sidney was intrusted with an outline treaty, to be communicated to Mr. Snowdon.

This discussion was just concluded when Mr. Samuel Byass presented himself—a slender, large-headed young man, with very light hair cropped close upon the scalp, and a foolish face screwed into an expression of facetiousness. He was employed in some clerkly capacity at a wholesale stationer's in City Road. Having stepped into the room, he removed a very brown silk hat and laid it on a chair, winking the while at Sidney with his right eye; then he removed his overcoat, winking with the left eye. Thus disembarrassed, he strode gravely to the fireplace, took up the poker, held it in the manner of a weapon upright against his shoulder, and ex-claimed in a severe voice, 'Eyes right!' Then, converting the poker into a sword, he drew near to Sidney and affected to practise upon him the military cuts, his features distorted into grotesque ferocity. Finally, assuming the attitude of a juggler, he made an attempt to balance the poker perpendicularly upon his nose, until it fell with a crash, just missing the ornaments on the mantel-piece. All this time Mrs. Byass shrieked with laughter, with difficulty keeping her chair.

'Oh, Sam,' she panted forth, her handkerchief at her eyes, 'what a fool you are! Do stop, or you'll kill me!'

Vastly gratified, Samuel advanced with ludicrous gestures towards the visitor, held out his hand, and said with affected nasality, 'How do you do, sir? It's some time since I had the pleasure of seeing you, sir. I hope you have been pretty tolerable.'

'*Isn't* he a fool, Mr. Kirkwood?' cried the delighted wife. 'Do just give him a smack on the side of the head, to please me! Sam, go an' wash, an' we'll have supper. What do you mean by being so late to-night?'

'Where's the infant?' asked Mr. Byass, thrusting his hands into his waistcoat pockets and peering about the room. 'Bring forth the infant! Let a fond parent look upon his child.'

'Go an' wash, or I'll throw something at you. Baby's in bed, and mind, you wake him if you dare!'

Sidney would have taken his leave, but found it impossible. Mrs. Byass declared that if he would not stay to supper he should never enter the house again.

'Let's make a night of it!' cried Sam, standing in the doorway. 'Let's have three pots of six ale and a bottle of old Tom! Let us be reckless!'

His wife caught up the pillow from the sofa and hurled it at him. Samuel escaped just in time. The next moment his head was again thrust forward.

'Let's send to the High Street for three cold roast fowls and a beef-steak pie! Let's get custards and cheese-cakes and French pastry! Let's have a pine-apple and preserved ginger! Who says, Go it for once?'

Mrs. Byass caught up the poker and sprang after him. From the passage came sounds of scuffling and screaming, and in the end of something produced by the lips. Mrs. Byass then showed a very red face at the door, and said:

'*Isn't* he a fool? Just wait a minute while I get the table laid.'

Supper was soon ready in the comfortable kitchen. A cold shoulder of mutton, a piece of cheese, pickled beetroot, a seed-cake, and raspberry jam; such was the fare to which Bessie Byass invited her husband and her guest. On a side-table were some open cardboard boxes containing artificial flowers and leaves; for Bessie had now and then a little 'mounting' to do for a shop in Upper Street, and in that way aided the income of the family. She was in even better spirits than usual at the prospect of letting her top-rooms. On hearing that piece of news, Samuel, who had just come from the nearest public-house with a foaming jug, executed a wild dance round the room and inadvertently knocked two plates from the dresser. This accident made his wife wrathful, but only for a moment; presently she was laughing as unre-strainedly as ever, and bestowing upon the repentant young man her familiar flattery.

At eleven o'clock Sidney left them, and mused with smiles on his way home. This was not exactly his ideal of domestic happiness, yet it was better than the life led by the Hewetts—better than that of other households with which he was acquainted—better far, it seemed to him, than the aspirations which were threatening to lead poor Clara—who knew whither? A temptation beset him to walk round into Upper Street and pass Mrs. Tubbs's bar. He resisted it, knowing that the result would only be a night of sleepless anger and misery.

The next day he again saw Snowdon, and spoke to him of Mrs. Byass's rooms. The old man seemed at first indisposed to go so far; but when he had seen the interior of the house and talked with the landlady, his objections disappeared. Before another week had passed the two rooms were furnished in the simplest possible way, and Snowdon brought Jane from Clerkenwell Close.

Kirkwood came by invitation as soon as the two were fairly established in their home. He found Jane sitting by the fire in her grandfather's room; a very little exertion still out-wearied her, and the strange things that had come to pass had made her habitually silent. She looked about her wonder-ingly, seemed unable to realise her position, was painfully con-scious of her new clothes, ever and again started as if in fear.

'Well, what did I say that night?' was Sidney's greeting. 'Didn't I tell you it would be all right soon?'

Jane made no answer in words, but looked at him timidly;

and then a smile came upon her face, an expression of joy that could not trust itself, that seemed to her too boldly at variance with all she had yet known of life.

CHAPTER VIII

PENNYLOAF CANDY

IN the social classification of the nether world—a subject which so eminently adapts itself to the sportive and gracefully picturesque mode of treatment—it will be convenient to distinguish broadly, and with reference to males alone, the two great sections of those who do, and those who do not, wear collars. Each of these orders would, it is obvious, offer much scope to an analyst delighting in subtle gradation. Taking the collarless, how shrewdly might one discriminate between the many kinds of neckcloth which our climate renders necessary as a substitute for the nobler article of attire! The navvy, the scaffolder, the costermonger, the cab-tout—innumerable would be the varieties of texture, of fold, of knot, observed in the ranks of unskilled labour. And among those whose higher station is indicated by the linen or paper symbol, what a gap between the mechanic with collar attached to a flannel shirt, and just visible along the top of a black tie, and the shopman whose pride it is to adorn himself with the very ugliest neck-encloser put in vogue by aristocratic sanction! For such attractive disquisition I have, unfortunately, no space; it must suffice that I indicate the two genera. And I was led to do so in thinking of Bob Hewett.

Bob wore a collar. In the die-sinking establishment which employed him there were, it is true, two men who belonged to the collarless; but their business was down in the basement of the building, where they kept up a furnace, worked huge stamping-machines, and so on. Bob's workshop was upstairs, and the companions with whom he sat, without exception, had something white and stiff round their necks; in fact, they were every bit as respectable as Sidney Kirkwood, and such as he, who bent over a jeweller's table. To John Hewett it was no slight gratification that he had been able to apprentice his son to a craft which permitted him always to wear a collar. I would not imply that John thought of the matter in these terms, but his reflections bore this significance. Bob was raised for ever above the rank of those who depend merely upon their muscles, even as Clara was saved from the dismal destiny of the women who can do nothing but sew.

There was, on the whole, some reason why John Hewett should feel pride in his eldest son. Like Sidney Kirkwood, Bob had early shown a faculty for draughtsmanship; when at school, he made decidedly clever caricatures of such persons as displeased him, and he drew such wonderful horses (on the race-course or pulling cabs), such laughable donkeys in costers' carts, such perfect dogs, that on several occasions some friend had purchased with a veritable shilling a specimen of his work. 'Put him to the die-sinking,' said an acquaintance of the family, himself so employed; 'he'll find a use for this kind of thing some day.' Die-sinking is not the craft it once was; cheap methods, vulgarising here as everywhere, have diminished the opportunities of capable men; but a fair living was promised the lad if he stuck to his work, and at the age of nineteen he was already earning his pound a week. Then he was clever in a good many other ways. He had an ear for music, played (nothing else was within his reach) the concertina, sang a lively song with uncommon melodiousness—a gift much appreciated at the meetings of a certain Mutual Benefit Club, to which his father had paid a weekly subscription, without fail, through all adversities. In the regular departments of learning Bob had never shown any particular aptitude; he wrote and read decently, but his speech, as you have had occasion for observing, was not marked by refinement, and for books he had no liking. His father, unfortunately, had spoilt him, just as he had spoilt Clara. Being of the nobly independent sex, between fifteen and sixteen he practically freed himself from parental control. The use he made of his liberty was not altogether pleasing to John, but the time for restraint and training had hopelessly gone by. The lad was selfish, that there was no denying; he grudged the money demanded of him for his support; but in other matters he always showed himself so easy-tempered, so disposed to a genial understanding, that the great fault had to be blinked. Many failings might have been forgiven him in consideration of the fact that he had never yet drunk too much, and indeed cared little for liquor.

Men of talent, as you are aware, not seldom exhibit low tastes in their choice of companionship. Bob was a case in point; he did not sufficiently appreciate social distinctions.

He, who wore a collar, seemed to prefer associating with the collarless. There was Jack—more properly 'Jeck'—Bartley, for instance, his bosom friend until they began to cool in consequence of a common interest in Miss Peckover. Jack never wore a collar in his life, not even on Sundays, and was closely allied with all sorts of blackguards, who somehow made a living on the outskirts of turf-land. And there was Eli Snape, compared with whom Jack was a person of refinement and culture. Eli dealt surreptitiously in dogs and rats, and the mere odour of him was intolerable to ordinary nostrils; yet he was a species of hero in Bob's regard, such invaluable information could he supply with regard to 'events' in which young Hewett took a profound interest. Perhaps a more serious aspect of Bob's disregard for social standing was revealed in his relations with the other sex. Susceptible from his tender youth, he showed no ambition in the bestowal of his amorous homage. At the age of sixteen did he not declare his resolve to wed the daughter of old Sally Budge, who went about selling watercress? and was there not a desperate conflict at home before this project could be driven from his head? It was but the first of many such instances. Had he been left to his own devices, he would already, like numbers of his coevals, have been supporting (or declining to support) a wife and two or three children. At present he was 'engaged' to Clem Peckover; that was an understood thing. His father did not approve it, but this connection was undeniably better than those he had previously declared or concealed. Bob, it seemed evident, was fated to make a *mésalliance*—a pity, seeing his parts and prospects. He might have aspired to a wife who had scarcely any difficulty with her *h*'s; whose bringing-up enabled her to look with compassion on girls who could not play the piano; who counted among her relatives not one collarless individual.

Clem, as we have seen, had already found, or imagined, cause for dissatisfaction with her betrothed. She was well enough acquainted with Bob's repute, and her temper made it improbable, to say the least, that the course of wooing would in this case run very smoothly. At present, various little signs were beginning to convince her that she had a rival, and the hints of her rejected admirer, Jack Bartley, fixed her suspicions upon an acquaintance whom she had hitherto regarded merely with contempt. This was Pennyloaf Candy, formerly, with her parents, a lodger in Mrs. Peckover's house.

The family had been ousted some eighteen months ago on
account of failure to pay their rent and of the frequent intoxi-
cation of Mrs. Candy.   Pennyloaf's legal name was Penelope,
which, being pronounced as a trisyllable, transformed itself by
further corruption into a sound at all events conveying some
meaning. Applied in the first instance jocosely, the title grew
inseparable from her, and was the one she herself always
used.   Her employment was the making of shirts for export;
she earned on an average tenpence a day, and frequently
worked fifteen hours between leaving and returning to her
home.   That Bob Hewett could interest himself, with whatever motive, in a person of this description, Miss Peckover at
first declined to believe.   A hint, however, was quite enough
to excite her jealous temperament; as proof accumulated,
cunning and ferocity wrought in her for the devising of such
a declaration of war as should speedily scare Pennyloaf from
the field.   Jane Snowdon's removal had caused her no little
irritation; the hours of evening were heavy on her hands,
and this new emotion was not unwelcome as a temporary
resource.

As he came home from work one Monday towards the end
of April, Bob encountered Pennyloaf; she had a bundle in her
hands and was walking hurriedly.

'Hallo! that you?' he exclaimed, catching her by the
arm.   'Where are you going?'

'I can't stop now.   I've got some things to put away, an'
it's nearly eight.'

'Come round to the Passage to-night.   Be there at ten.'

'I can't give no promise.   There's been such rows at 'ome.
You know mother summonsed father this mornin'?'

'Yes, I've heard.   All right! come if you can; I'll be
there.'

Pennyloaf hastened on.   She was a meagre, hollow-eyed,
bloodless girl of seventeen, yet her features had a certain
charm—that dolorous kind of prettiness which is often enough
seen in the London needle-slave.   Her habitual look was one
of meaningless surprise; whatever she gazed upon seemed a
source of astonishment to her, and when she laughed, which
was not very often, her eyes grew wider than ever.   Her attire
was miserable, but there were signs that she tried to keep it
in order; the boots upon her feet were sewn and patched into
shapelessness; her limp straw hat had just received a new
binding.

By saying that she had things ' to put away,' she meant
that her business was with the pawnbroker, who could not
receive pledges after eight o'clock. It wanted some ten
minutes of the hour when she entered a side-doorway, and,
by an inner door, passed into one of a series of compartments
constructed before the pawnbroker's counter. She deposited
her bundle, and looked about for someone to attend to her.
Two young men were in sight, both transacting business ; one
was conversing facetiously with a customer on the subject of
a pledge. Two or three gas-jets lighted the interior of the
shop, but the boxes were in shadow. There was a strong
musty odour ; the gloom, the narrow compartments, the low
tones of conversation, suggested stealth and shame.

Pennyloaf waited with many signs of impatience, until one
of the assistants approached, a smartly attired youth, with
black hair greased into the discipline he deemed becoming,
with an aquiline nose, a coarse mouth, a large horseshoe pin
adorning his necktie, and rings on his fingers. He caught
hold of the packet and threw it open ; it consisted of a petti-
coat and the skirt of an old dress.

' Well, what is it ? ' he asked, rubbing his tongue along his
upper lip before and after speaking.

' Three an' six, please, sir.'

He rolled the things up again with a practised turn of the
hand, and said indifferently, glancing towards another box,
' Eighteenpence.'

' Oh, sir, we had two shillin's on the skirt not so long ago,'
pleaded Pennyloaf, with a subservient voice. ' Make it two
shillin's—please do, sir ! '

The young man paid no attention ; he was curling his
moustache and exchanging a smile of intelligence with
his counter-companion with respect to a piece of business
the latter had in hand. Of a sudden he turned and said
sharply :

' Well, are you goin' to take it or not ? '

Pennyloaf sighed and nodded.

' Got a 'apenny ? ' he asked.

' No.'

He fetched a cloth, rolled the articles in it very tightly,
and pinned them up ; then he made out ticket and duplicate,
handling his pen with facile flourish, and having blotted the
little piece of card on a box of sand (a custom which survives
in this conservative profession), he threw it to the customer.

Lastly, he counted out one shilling and fivepence halfpenny. The coins were sandy, greasy, and of scratched surface.

Pennyloaf sped homewards. She lived in Shooter's Gardens, a picturesque locality which demolition and rebuilding have of late transformed. It was a winding alley, with paving raised a foot above the level of the street whence was its main approach. To enter from the obscurer end, you descended a flight of steps, under a low archway, in a court itself not easily discovered. From without, only a glimpse of the Gardens was obtainable; the houses curved out of sight after the first few yards, and left surmise to busy itself with the characteristics of the hidden portion. A stranger bold enough to explore would have discovered that the Gardens had a blind offshoot, known simply as ' The Court.' Needless to burden description with further detail; the slum was like any other slum; filth, rottenness, evil odours, possessed these dens of superfluous mankind and made them gruesome to the peering imagination. The inhabitants of course felt nothing of the sort; a room in Shooter's Gardens was the only kind of home that most of them knew or desired. The majority preferred it, on all grounds, to that offered them in a block of model lodgings* not very far away; here was independence, that is to say, the liberty to be as vile as they pleased. How they came to love vileness, well, that is quite another matter, and shall not for the present concern us.

Pennyloaf ran into the jaws of this black horror with the indifference of habit; it had never occurred to her that the Gardens were fearful in the night's gloom, nor even that better lighting would have been a convenience. Did it happen that she awoke from her first sleep with the ring of ghastly shrieking in her ears, that was an incident of too common occurrence to cause her more than a brief curiosity; she could wait till the morning to hear who had half-killed whom. Four days ago it was her own mother's turn to be pounded into insensibility; her father (a journeyman baker, often working nineteen hours out of the twenty-four, which probably did not improve his temper), maddened by his wife's persistent drunkenness, was stopped just on the safe side of murder. To the amazement and indignation of the Gardens, Mrs. Candy prosecuted her sovereign lord; the case had been heard to-day, and Candy had been cast in a fine. The money was paid, and the baker went his way, remarking that his family were to 'expect him back when they saw him.' Mrs. Candy, on her return, was hooted through all the length of the Gardens, a demonstration of public feeling probably rather of base than of worthy significance.

As Pennyloaf drew near to the house, a wild, discordant voice suddenly broke forth somewhere in the darkness, singing n a high key, 'All ye works of the Lord, bless ye the Lord, praise Him and magnify Him for ever!' It was Mad Jack, who had his dwelling in the Court, and at all hours was wont to practise the psalmody which made him notorious throughout Clerkenwell. A burst of laughter followed from a group of men and boys gathered near the archway. Unheeding, the girl passed in at an open door and felt her way up a staircase; the air was noisome, notwithstanding a fierce draught which swept down the stairs. She entered a room lighted by a small metal lamp hanging on the wall—a precaution of Pennyloaf's own contrivance. There was no bed, but one mattress lay with a few rags of bed-clothing spread upon it, and two others were rolled up in a corner. This chamber accommodated, under ordinary circumstances, four persons : Mr. and Mrs. Candy, Pennyloaf, and a son named Stephen, whose years were eighteen. (Stephen pursued the occupation of a potman ;* his hours were from eight in the morning till midnight on week-days, and on Sunday the time during which a public-house is permitted to be open; once a month he was allowed freedom after six o'clock.) Against the window was hung an old shawl pierced with many rents. By the fire sat Mrs. Candy ; she leaned forward, her head, which was bound in linen swathes, resting upon her hands.

' What have you got?' she asked, in the thick voice of a drunkard, without moving.

' Eighteenpence ; it's all they'd give me.'

The woman cursed in her throat, but exhibited no anger with Pennyloaf.

' Go an' get some tea an' milk,' she said, after a pause. ' There is sugar. An' bring seven o' coals; there's only a dust.'

She pointed to a deal box which stood by the hearth. Pennyloaf went out again.

Over the fireplace, the stained wall bore certain singular ornaments. These were five coloured cards, such as are signed by one who takes a pledge of total abstinence ;* each presented the signature, ' Maria Candy,' and it was noticeable that at each progressive date the handwriting had become more unsteady. Yes, five times had Maria Candy promised, with the help of God, to abstain,' &c. &c.; each time she was in earnest. But it appeared that the help of God availed little against the views of one Mrs. Green, who kept the beer-shop in Rosoman Street, once Mrs. Peckover's, and who could on no account afford to lose so good a customer. For many years that house, licensed for the sale of non-spirituous liquors, had been working Mrs. Candy's ruin; not a particle of her frame but was vitiated by the drugs retailed there under the approving smile of civilisation. Spirits would have been harmless in comparison. The advantage of Mrs. Green's ale was that the very first half-pint gave conscience its bemuddling sop; for a penny you forgot all the cares of existence; for threepence you became a yelling maniac.

Poor, poor creature! She was sober to-night, sitting over the fire with her face battered into shapelessness; and now that her fury had had its way, she bitterly repented invoking the help of the law against her husband. What use? what use? Perhaps he had now abandoned her for good, and it was certain that the fear of him was the only thing that ever checked her on the ruinous road she would so willingly have quitted. But for the harm to himself, the only pity was he had not taken her life outright. She knew all the hatefulness of her existence; she knew also that only the grave would rescue her from it. The struggle was too unequal between Mrs. Candy with her appeal to Providence, and Mrs. Green with the forces of civilisation at her back.

Pennyloaf speedily returned with a ha'p'orth of milk, a pennyworth of tea, and seven pounds (also price one penny) of coals in an apron. It was very seldom indeed that the Candys had more of anything in their room than would last them for the current day. There being no kettle, water was put on to boil in a tin saucepan; the tea was made in a jug. Pennyloaf had always been a good girl to her mother; she tended her as well as she could to-night; but there was no word of affection from either. Kindly speech was stifled by the atmosphere of Shooter's Gardens.

Having drunk her tea, Mrs. Candy lay down, as she was, on the already extended mattress, and drew the ragged coverings about her. In half an hour she slept.

Pennyloaf then put on her hat and jacket again and left the house. She walked away from the denser regions of

Clerkenwell, came to Sadler's Wells Theatre*(gloomy in its profitless recollection of the last worthy manager that London knew), and there turned into Myddelton Passage. It is a narrow paved walk between brick walls seven feet high; on the one hand lies the New River Head, on the other are small gardens behind Myddelton Square. The branches of a few trees hang over; there are doors, seemingly never opened, belonging one to each garden; a couple of gas-lamps shed feeble light. Pennyloaf paced the length of the Passage several times, meeting no one. Then a policeman came along with echoing tread, and eyed her suspiciously. She had to wait more than a quarter of an hour before Bob Hewett made his appearance. Greeting her with a nod and a laugh, he took up a leaning position against the wall, and began to put questions concerning the state of things at her home.

'And what'll your mother do if the old man don't give her nothing to live on?' he inquired, when he had listened good-naturedly to the recital of domestic difficulties.

'Don't know,' replied the girl, shaking her head, the habitual surprise of her countenance becoming a blank interrogation of destiny.

Bob kept kicking the wall, first with one heel, then with the other. He whistled a few bars of the last song he had learnt at the music-hall.

'Say, Penny,' he remarked at length, with something of shamefacedness, 'there's a namesake of mine here as I shan't miss, if you can do any good with it.'

He held a shilling towards her under his hand. Pennyloaf turned away, casting down her eyes and looking troubled.

'We can get on for a bit,' she said indistinctly.

Bob returned the coin to his pocket. He whistled again for a moment, then asked abruptly:

'Say! have you seen Clem again?'

'No,' replied the girl, examining him with sudden acuteness. 'What about her?'

'Nothing much. She's got her back up a bit, that's all.'

'About me?' Pennyloaf asked anxiously.

Bob nodded. As he was making some further remarks on the subject, a man's figure appeared at a little distance, and almost immediately withdrew again round a winding of the Passage. A moment after there sounded from that direction a shrill whistle. Bob and the girl regarded each other.

'Who was that?' said the former suspiciously. 'I half

believe it was Jeck Bartley.   If Jeck is up to any of his larks,
I'll make him remember it.   You wait here a minute !'

He walked at a sharp pace towards the suspected quarter.
Scarcely had he gone half a dozen yards, when there came
running from the other end of the Passage a girl whom
Pennyloaf at once recognised.   It was Clem Peckover; with
some friend's assistance she had evidently tracked the couple
and was now springing out of ambush.   She rushed upon
Pennyloaf, who for very alarm could not flee, and attacked
her with clenched fists.   A scream of terror and pain caused
Bob to turn and run back.   Pennyloaf could not even ward
off the blows that descended upon her head ; she was pinned
against the wall, her hat was torn away, her hair began to
fly in disorder.   But Bob effected a speedy rescue.   He
gripped Clem's muscular arms, and forced them behind her
back as if he meant to dismember her.   Even then it was
with no slight effort that he restrained the girl's fury.

' You run off 'ome !' he shouted to Pennyloaf.   ' If she
tries this on again, I'll murder her !'

Pennyloaf's hysterical cries and the frantic invectives of
her assailant made the Passage ring.   Again Bob roared to
the former to be off, and was at length obeyed.   When Pennyloaf was out of sight he released Clem.   Her twisted arms
caused her such pain that she threw herself against the wall,
mingling maledictions with groans.   Bob burst into scornful
laughter.

Clem went home vowing vengeance.   In the nether world
this trifling dissension might have been expected to bear its
crop of violent language and straightway pass into oblivion ;
but Miss Peckover's malevolence was of no common stamp,
and the scene of to-night originated a feud which in the end
concerned many more people than those immediately interested.

CHAPTER IX

PATHOLOGICAL

THROUGH the day and through the evening Clara Hewett had
her place behind Mrs. Tubbs's bar.   For daylight wear, the
dress which had formerly been her best was deemed sufficient;
it was simple, but not badly made, and became her figure.
Her evening attire was provided by Mrs. Tubbs, who recouped

herself by withholding the promised wages for a certain number of weeks. When Clara had surveyed this garment in the bar mirror, she turned away contemptuously; the material was cheap, the mode vulgar. It must be borne with for the present, like other indignities which she found to be inseparable from her position. As soon as her employer's claim was satisfied, and the weekly five shillings began to be paid, Clara remembered the promise she had volunteered to her father. But John was once more at work; for the present there really seemed no need to give him any of her money, and she herself, on the other hand, lacked so many things. This dress plainly would not be suitable for the better kind of engagement she had in view; it behoved her first of all to have one made in accordance with her own taste. A mantle, too, a silk umbrella, gloves—— It would be unjust to herself to share her scanty earnings with those at home.

Yes; but you must try to understand this girl of the people, with her unfortunate endowment of brains and defect of tenderness. That smile of hers, which touched and fascinated and made thoughtful, had of course a significance discoverable by study of her life and character. It was no mere affectation; she was not conscious, in smiling, of the expression upon her face. Moreover, there was justice in the sense of wrong discernible upon her features when the very self looked forth from them. All through his life John Hewett had suffered from the same impulse of revolt; less sensitively constructed than his daughter, uncalculating, inarticulate, he fumed and fretted away his energies in a conflict with forces ludicrously personified. In the matter of his second marriage he was seen at his best, generously defiant of social cruelties; but self-knowledge was denied him, and circumstances condemned his life to futility. Clara inherited his temperament; transferred to her more complex nature, it gained in subtlety and in power of self-direction, but lost in its nobler elements. Her mother was a capable and ambitious woman, one in whom active characteristics were more prominent than the emotional. With such parents, every probability told against her patient acceptance of a lot which allowed her faculties no scope. And the circumstances of her childhood were such as added a peculiar bitterness to the trials waiting upon her maturity.

Clara, you remember, had reached her eleventh year when her father's brother died and left the legacy of which came

so little profit. That was in 1873. State education had recently made a show of establishing itself, and in the Hewetts'
world much argument was going on with reference to the new
Board schools, and their advantages or disadvantages when
compared with those in which working-folk's children had
hitherto been taught. Clara went to a Church school, and
the expense was greater than the new system rendered necessary. Her father's principles naturally favoured education on
an independent basis, but a prejudice then (and still) common
among workpeople of decent habits made him hesitate about
sending his girl to sit side by side with the children of the
street ; and he was confirmed by Clara's own view of the
matter. She spoke with much contempt of Board schools,
and gave it to be understood that her religious convictions
would not suffer her to be taught by those who made light of
orthodoxy.* This attitude was intelligible enough in a child
of sharp wit and abundant self-esteem. Notwithstanding her
father's indifferentism, little Clara perceived that a regard for
religion gave her a certain distinction at home, and elsewhere
placed her apart from 'common girls.' She was subject also
to special influences : on the one hand, from her favourite
teacher, Miss Harrop ; on the other, from a school-friend,
Grace Rudd.

Miss Harrop was a good, warm-hearted woman of about
thirty, one of those unhappy persons who are made for
domestic life, but condemned by fate to school-celibacy.
Lonely and impulsive, she drew to herself the most interesting
girl in her classes, and, with complete indiscretion, made a
familiar, a pet, a prodigy of one whose especial need was
discipline. By her confidences and her flatteries she set Clara
aflame with spiritual pride. Ceaselessly she excited her to
ambition, remarked on her gifts, made dazzling forecast of
her future. Clara was to be a teacher first of all, but only
that she might be introduced to the notice of people who
would aid her to better things. And the child came to regard
this as the course inevitably before her. Had she not already
received school-prizes, among them a much-gilded little
volume 'for religious knowledge'? Did she not win universal
applause when she recited a piece of verse on prize-day—Miss
Harrop (disastrous kindness!) even saying that the delivery
reminded her of Mrs. ——, the celebrated actress!

Grace Rudd was busy in the same fatal work. Four years
older than Clara, weakly pretty, sentimental, conceited, she

had a fancy for patronising the clever child, to the end that
she might receive homage in return. Poor Grace! She left
school, spent a year or two at home with parents as foolish
as herself, and—disappeared. Prior to that, Miss Harrop had
also passed out of Clara's ken, driven by restlessness to try
another school, away from London.

These losses appeared to affect Clara unfavourably. She
began to neglect her books, to be insubordinate, to exhibit
arrogance, which brought down upon her plenty of wholesome
reproof. Her father was not without a share in the responsibility for it all. Entering upon his four hundred pounds, one
of the first things John did was to hire a piano, that his child
might be taught to play. Pity that Sidney Kirkwood could
not then cry with effective emphasis, ' We are the working
classes! we are the lower orders!' It was exactly what
Hewett would not bring himself to understand. What! His
Clara must be robbed of chances just because her birth was
not that of a young lady? Nay, by all the unintelligible Powers,
she should enjoy every help that he could possibly afford her.
Bless her bright face and her clever tongue! Yes, it was
now a settled thing that she should be trained for a school-
teacher. An atmosphere of refinement must be made for her;
she must be better dressed, more delicately fed.

The bitter injustice of it! In the outcome you are already
instructed. Long before Clara was anything like ready to
enter upon a teacher's career, her father's ill-luck once more
darkened over the home. Clara had made no progress since
Miss Harrop's day. The authorities directing her school
might have come forward with aid of some kind, had it appeared to them that the girl would repay such trouble; but
they had their forebodings about her. Whenever she chose,
she could learn in five minutes what another girl could
scarcely commit to memory in twenty; but it was obviously
for the sake of display. The teachers disliked her ; among
the pupils she had no friends. So at length there came the
farewell to school and the beginning of practical life, which
took the shape of learning to stamp crests and addresses on
note-paper. There was hope that before long Clara might
earn thirteen shillings a week.

The bitter injustice of it! Clara was seventeen now, and
understood the folly of which she had been guilty a few years
ago, but at the same time she felt in her inmost heart the
tyranny of a world which takes revenge for errors that are

inevitable, which misleads a helpless child and then condemns
it for being found astray. She could judge herself, yes, better
than Sidney Kirkwood could judge her. She knew her defects,
knew her vices, and a feud with fate caused her to accept them
defiantly. Many a time had she sobbed out to herself, ' I wish
I could neither read nor write ! I wish I had never been told
that there is anything better than to work with one's hands
and earn daily bread!' But she could not renounce the claims
that Nature had planted in her, that her guardians had fostered.
The better she understood how difficult was every way of advancement, the more fiercely resolute was she to conquer satisfactions which seemed beyond the sphere of her destiny.

Of late she had thought much of her childish successes in
reciting poetry. It was not often that she visited a theatre
(her father had always refused to let her go with any one save
himself or Sidney), but on the rare occasions when her wish
was gratified, she had watched each actress with devouring
interest, with burning envy, and had said to herself, 'Couldn't
I soon learn to do as well as that ? Can't I see where it
might be made more lifelike ? Why should it be impossible
for me to go on the stage ?' In passing a shop-window where
photographs were exposed, she looked for those of actresses,
and gazed at them with terrible intensity. ' I am as good-
looking as she is. Why shouldn't *my* portrait be seen some
day in the windows ? ' And then her heart throbbed, smitten
with passionate desire. As she walked on there was a turbid
gloom about her, and in her ears the echoing of a dread
temptation. Of all this she spoke to nobody.

For she had no friends. A couple of years ago something
like an intimacy had sprung up between her and Bessie Jones
(since married and become Bessie Byass), seemingly on the
principle of contrast in association. Bessie, like most London
workgirls, was fond of the theatre, and her talk helped to
nourish the ambition which was secretly developing in Clara.
But the two could not long harmonise. Bessie, just after her
marriage, ventured to speak with friendly reproof of Clara's
behaviour to Sidney Kirkwood. Clara was not disposed to
admit freedoms of that kind ; she half gave it to be understood
that, though others might be easily satisfied, she had views of
her own on such subjects. Thereafter Mrs. Byass grew decidedly cool. The other girls with whom Clara had formal
intercourse showed no desire to win her confidence; they were
kept aloof by her reticent civility.

As for Sidney himself, it was not without reason that he had seen encouragement in the girl's first reply to his advances. At sixteen, Clara found it agreeable to have her good graces sought by the one man in whom she recognised superiority of mind and purpose. Of all the unbetrothed girls she knew not one but would have felt flattered had Kirkwood thus distinguished her. Nothing common adhered to his demeanour, to his character; he had the look of one who will hold his own in life; his word had the ring of truth. Of his generosity she had innumerable proofs, and it contrasted nobly with the selfishness of young men as she knew them; she appreciated it all the more because her own frequent desire to be unselfish was so fruitless. Of awakening tenderness towards him she knew nothing, but she gave him smiles and words which might mean little or much, just for the pleasure of completing a conquest. Nor did she, in truth, then regard it as impossible that, sooner or later, she might become his wife. If she *must* marry a workman, assuredly it should be Sidney. He thought so highly of her, he understood things in her to which the ordinary artisan would have been dead; he had little delicacies of homage which gave her keen pleasure. And yet—well, time enough!

Time went very quickly, and changed both herself and Sidney in ways she could not foresee. It was true, all he said to her in anger that night by the prison wall—true and deserved every word of it. Even in acknowledging that, she hardened herself against him implacably. Since he chose to take this tone with her, to throw aside all his graceful blindness to her faults, he had only himself to blame if she considered everything at an end between them. She tried to believe herself glad this had happened; it relieved her from an embarrassment, and made her absolutely free to pursue the ambitions which now gave her no rest. For all that, she could not dismiss Sidney from her mind; indeed, throughout the week that followed their parting, she thought of him more persistently than for many months. That he would before long seek pardon for his rudeness she felt certain, she felt also that such submission would gratify her in a high degree. But the weeks were passing and no letter came; in vain she glanced from the window of the bar at the faces which moved by. Even on Sunday, when she went home for an hour or two, she neither saw nor heard of Kirkwood. She could not bring herself to ask a question.

Under any circumstances Clara would ill have borne a suspense that irritated her pride, and at present she lived amid conditions so repugnant, that her nerves were ceaselessly strung almost beyond endurance. Before entering upon this engagement she had formed but an imperfect notion of what would be demanded of her. To begin with, Mrs. Tubbs belonged to the order of women who are by nature slave-drivers ; though it was her interest to secure Clara for a permanency, she began by exacting from the girl as much labour as could possibly be included in their agreement. The hours were insufferably long ; by nine o'clock each evening Clara was so outworn that with difficulty she remained standing, yet not until midnight was she released. The unchanging odours of the place sickened her, made her head ache, and robbed her of all appetite. Many of the duties were menial, and to perform them fevered her with indignation. Then the mere waiting upon such men as formed the majority of the customers, vulgarly familiar, when not insolent, in their speech to her, was hateful beyond anything she had conceived. Had there been no one to face but her father, she would have returned home and resumed her old occupation at the end of the first fortnight, so extreme was her suffering in mind and body ; but rather than give Sidney Kirkwood such a triumph, she would work on, and breathe no word of what she underwent. Even in her anger against him, the knowledge of his forgiving disposition, of the sincerity of his love, was an unavowed support. She knew he could not utterly desert her ; when some day he sought a reconciliation, the renewal of conflict between his pride and her own would, she felt, supply her with new courage.

Early one Saturday afternoon she was standing by the windows, partly from heavy idleness of thought, partly on the chance that Kirkwood might go by, when a young, well-dressed man, who happened to be passing at a slow walk, turned his head and looked at her. He went on, but in a few moments Clara, who had moved back into the shop, saw him enter and come forwards. He took a seat at the counter and ordered a luncheon. Clara waited upon him with her customary cold reserve, and he made no remark until she returned him change out of the coin he offered.

Then he said with an apologetic smile :

' We are old acquaintances, Miss Hewett, but I'm afraid you've forgotten me.'

Clara regarded him in astonishment. His age seemed to

be something short of thirty; he had a long, grave, intelligent face, smiled enigmatically, spoke in a rather slow voice. His silk hat, sober necktie drawn through a gold ring, and dark morning-coat, made it probable that he was 'in the City.'

'We used to know each other very well about five years ago,' he pursued, pocketing his change carelessly. 'Don't you remember a Mr. Scawthorne, who used to be a lodger with some friends of yours called Rudd?'

On the instant memory revived in Clara. In her school-days she often spent a Sunday afternoon with Grace Rudd, and this Mr. Scawthorne was generally at the tea-table. Mr. and Mrs. Rudd made much of him, said that he held a most important post in a lawyer's office, doubtless had private designs concerning him and their daughter. Thus aided, she even recognised his features.

'And you knew me again after all this time?'

'Yours isn't an easy face to forget,' replied Mr. Scaw-thorne, with the subdued polite smile which naturally accom-panied his tone of unemotional intimacy. 'To tell you the whole truth, however, I happened to hear news of you a few days ago. I met Grace Rudd; she told me you were here. Some old friend had told *her*.'

Grace's name awoke keen interest in Clara. She was startled to hear it, and did not venture to make the inquiry her mind at once suggested. Mr. Scawthorne observed her for an instant, then proceeded to satisfy her curiosity. Grace Rudd was on the stage; she had been acting in provincial theatres under the name of Miss Danvers, and was now waiting for a promised engagement at a minor London theatre.

'Do you often go to the theatre?' he added carelessly. 'I have a great many acquaintances connected with the stage in one way or another. If you would like, I should be very glad to send you tickets now and then. I always have more given me than I can well use.'

Clara thanked him rather coldly, and said that she was very seldom free in the evening. Thereupon Mr. Scawthorne again smiled, raised his hat, and departed.

Possibly he had some consciousness of the effect of his words, but it needed a subtler insight, a finer imagination than his, to interpret the pale, beautiful, harassed face which stu-diously avoided looking towards him as he paused before step-ping out on to the pavement. The rest of the evening, the hours of night that followed, passed for Clara in hot tumult

of heart and brain. The news of Grace Rudd had flashed
upon her as revelation of a clear possibility where hitherto she
had seen only mocking phantoms of futile desire. Grace was
an actress; no matter by what course, to this she had attained.
This man, Scawthorne, spoke of the theatrical life as one to
whom all its details were familiar; acquaintance with him of a
sudden bridged over the chasm which had seemed impassable.
Would he come again to see her? Had her involuntary
reserve put an end to any interest he might have felt in her?
Of him personally she thought not at all; she could not have
recalled his features; he was a mere abstraction, the representative of a wild hope which his conversation had inspired.

From that day the character of her suffering was altered;
it became less womanly, it defied weakness and grew to a fever
of fierce, unscrupulous rebellion. Whenever she thought of
Sidney Kirkwood, the injury he was inflicting upon her pride
rankled into bitter resentment, unsoftened by the despairing
thought of self-subdual which had at times visited her sick
weariness. She bore her degradations with the sullen indifference of one who is supported by the hope of a future
revenge. The disease inherent in her being, that deadly outcome of social tyranny which perverts the generous elements
of youth into mere seeds of destruction, developed day by day,
blighting her heart, corrupting her moral sense, even setting
marks of evil upon the beauty of her countenance. A passionate desire of self-assertion familiarised her with projects,
with ideas, which formerly she had glanced at only to dismiss
as ignoble. In proportion as her bodily health failed, the
worst possibilities of her character came into prominence.
Like a creature that is beset by unrelenting forces, she summoned and surveyed all the crafty faculties lurking in the dark
places of her nature; theoretically she had now accepted every
debasing compact by which a woman can spite herself on the
world's injustice. Self-assertion; to be no longer an unregarded atom in the mass of those who are born only to labour
for others; to find play for the strength and the passion
which, by no choice of her own, distinguished her from the
tame slave. Sometimes in the silence of night she suffered
from a dreadful need of crying aloud, of uttering her anguish
in a scream like that of insanity. She stifled it only by
crushing her face into the pillow until the hysterical fit had
passed, and she lay like one dead.

A fortnight after his first visit Mr. Scawthorne again presented himself, polite, smiling, perhaps rather more familiar. He stayed talking for nearly an hour, chiefly of the theatre. Casually he mentioned that Grace Rudd had got her engagement—only a little part in a farce. Suppose Clara came to see her play some evening? Might he take her? He could at any time have places in the dress-circle.

Clara accepted the invitation. She did so without consulting Mrs. Tubbs, and when it became necessary to ask for the evening's freedom, difficulties were made. 'Very well,' said Clara, in a tone she had never yet used to her employer, 'then I shall leave you.' She spoke without a moment's reflection; something independent of her will seemed to direct her in speech and act. Mrs. Tubbs yielded.

Clara had not yet been able to obtain the dress she wished for. Her savings, however, were sufficient for the purchase of a few accessories, which made her, she considered, not unpresentable. Scawthorne was to have a cab waiting for her at a little distance from the luncheon-bar. It was now June, and at the hour of their meeting still broad daylight, but Clara cared nothing for the chance that acquaintances might see her; nay, she had a reckless desire that Sidney Kirkwood might pass just at this moment. She noticed no one whom she knew, however; but just as the cab was turning into Pentonville Road, Scawthorne drew her attention to a person on the pavement.

'You see that old fellow,' he said. 'Would you believe that he is very wealthy?'

Clara had just time to perceive an old man with white hair, dressed as a mechanic.

'But I know him,' she replied. 'His name's Snowdon.'

'So it is. How do you come to know him?' Scawthorne inquired with interest.

She explained.

'Better not say anything about it,' remarked her companion. 'He's an eccentric chap. I happen to know his affairs in the way of business. I oughtn't to have told secrets, but I can trust you.'

A gentle emphasis on the last word, and a smile of more than usual intimacy. But his manner was, and remained through the evening, respectful almost to exaggeration. Clara seemed scarcely conscious of his presence, save in the act of listening to what he said. She never met his look, never smiled. From entering the theatre to leaving it, she

had a high flush on her face. Impossible to recognise her
friend in the actress whom Scawthorne indicated; features
and voice were wholly strange to her. In the intervals, Scawthorne spoke of the difficulties that beset an actress's career
at its beginning.

'I suppose you never thought of trying it?' he asked.
'Yet I fancy you might do well, if only you could have a few
months' training, just to start you. Of course it all depends
on knowing how to go about it. A little money would be
necessary—not much.'

Clara made no reply. On the way home she was mute.
Scawthorne took leave of her in Upper Street, and promised
to look in again before long. . . .

Under the heat of these summer days, in the reeking atmosphere of the bar, Clara panted fever-stricken. The weeks
went on; what strength supported her from the Monday
morning to the Saturday midnight she could not tell. Acting
and refraining, speaking and holding silence, these things were
no longer the consequences of her own volition. She wished
to break free from her slavery, but had not the force to do so;
something held her voice as often as she was about to tell
Mrs. Tubbs that this week would be the last. Her body
wasted so that all the garments she wore were loose upon
her. The only mental process of which she was capable was
reviewing the misery of days just past and anticipating that
of the days to come. Her only feelings were infinite self-pity
and a dull smouldering hatred of all others in the world.
A doctor would have bidden her take to bed, as one in danger
of grave illness. She bore through it without change in her
habits, and in time the strange lethargy passed.

Scawthorne came to the bar frequently. He remarked
often on her look of suffering, and urged a holiday. At length,
near the end of July, he invited her to go up the river with
him on the coming Bank-holiday. Clara consented, though
aware that her presence would be more than ever necessary at
the bar on the day of much drinking. Later in the evening
she addressed her demand to Mrs. Tubbs. It was refused.

Without a word of anger, Clara went upstairs, prepared
herself for walking, and set forth among the by-ways of
Islington. In half an hour she had found a cheap bedroom,
for which she paid a week's rent in advance. She purchased
a few articles of food and carried them to her lodging, then
lay down in the darkness.

CHAPTER X

THE LAST COMBAT

DURING these summer months Sidney Kirkwood's visits to
the house in Clerkenwell Close were comparatively rare. It
was not his own wish to relax in any degree the close friendship so long subsisting between the Hewetts and himself, but
from the day of Clara's engagement with Mrs. Tubbs John
Hewett began to alter in his treatment of him. At first there
was nothing more than found its natural explanation in regret
of what had happened, a tendency to muteness, to troubled
brooding; but before long John made it unmistakable that
the young man's presence was irksome to him. If, on coming
home, he found Sidney with Mrs. Hewett and the children, a
cold nod was the only greeting he offered; then followed signs
of ill-humour, such as Sidney could not in the end fail to
interpret as unfavourable to himself. He never heard Clara's
name on her father's lips, and himself never uttered it when
John was in hearing.

'She told him what passed between us that night,' Sidney
argued inwardly. But it was not so. Hewett had merely
abandoned himself to an unreasonable resentment. Notwithstanding his concessions, he blamed Sidney for the girl's
leaving home, and, as his mood grew more irritable, the
more hopeless it seemed that Clara would return, he nursed
the suspicion of treacherous behaviour on Sidney's part. He
would not take into account any such thing as pride which
could forbid the young man to urge a rejected suit. Sidney
had grown tired of Clara, that was the truth, and gladly
caught at any means of excusing himself. He had made
new friends. Mrs. Peckover reported that he was a constant
visitor at the old man Snowdon's lodgings; she expressed her
belief that Snowdon had come back from Australia with a
little store of money, and if Kirkwood had knowledge of that,
would it not explain his interest in Jane Snowdon?

'For shame to listen to such things!' cried Mrs. Hewett
angrily, when her husband once repeated the landlady's words.
'I'd be ashamed of myself, John! If you don't know him no
better than that, you ought to by this time.'

And John did, in fact, take to himself no little shame, but
his unsatisfied affection turned all the old feelings to bitter-

ness. In spite of himself, he blundered along the path of perversity. Sidney, too, had his promptings of obstinate humour. When he distinctly recognised Hewett's feeling it galled him; he was being treated with gross injustice, and temper suggested reprisals which could answer no purpose but to torment him with self-condemnation. However, he must needs consult his own dignity; he could not keep defending himself against ignoble charges. For the present, there was no choice but to accept John's hints, and hold apart as much as was possible without absolute breach of friendly relations. Nor could he bring himself to approach Clara. It was often in his mind to write to her; had he obeyed the voice of his desire he would have penned such letters as only the self-abasement of a passionate lover can dictate. But herein, too, the strain of sternness that marked his character made its influence felt. He said to himself that the only hope of Clara's respecting him lay in his preservation of the attitude he had adopted, and as the months went on he found a bitter satisfaction in adhering so firmly to his purpose. The self-flattery with which no man can dispense whispered assurance that Clara only thought the more of him the longer he held aloof. When the end of July came, he definitely prescribed to his patience a trial of yet one more month. Then he would write Clara a long letter, telling her what it had cost him to keep silence, and declaring the constancy he devoted to her.

This resolve he registered whilst at work one morning. The triumphant sunshine, refusing to be excluded even from London workshops, gleamed upon his tools and on the scraps of jewellery before him; he looked up to the blue sky, and thought with heavy heart of many a lane in Surrey and in Essex where he might be wandering but for this ceaseless necessity of earning the week's wage. A fly buzzed loudly against the grimy window, and by one of those associations which time and change cannot affect, he mused himself back into boyhood. The glimpse before him of St. John's Arch aided the revival of old impressions; his hand ceased from its mechanical activity, and he was absorbed in a waking dream, when a voice called to him and said that he was wanted. He went down to the entrance, and there found Mrs. Hewett. Her coming at all was enough to signal some disaster, and the trouble on her face caused Sidney to regard her with silent interrogation.

'I couldn't help comin' to you,' she began, gazing at him fixedly. 'I know you can't do anything, but I had to speak to somebody, an' I know nobody better than you. It's about Clara.'

'What about her?'

'She's left Mrs. Tubbs. They had words about Bank-holiday last night, an' Clara went off at once. Mrs. Tubbs thought she'd come 'ome, but this mornin' her box was sent for, an' it was to be took to a house in Islington. An' then Mrs. Tubbs came an' told me. An' there's worse than that, Sidney. She's been goin' about to the theatre an' such places with a man as she got to know at the bar, an' Mrs. Tubbs says she believes it's him has tempted her away.'

She spoke the last sentences in a low voice, painfully watching their effect.

'And why hasn't Mrs. Tubbs spoken about this before?' Sidney asked, also in a subdued voice, but without other show of agitation.

'That's just what I said to her myself. The girl was in her charge, an' it was her duty to let us know if things went wrong. But how am I to tell her father? I dursn't do it, Sidney; for my life, I dursn't! I'd go an' see her where she's lodging—see, I've got the address wrote down here—but I should do more harm than good; she'd never pay any heed to me at the best of times, an' it isn't likely she would now.'

'Look here! If she's made no attempt to hide away, you may be quite sure there's no truth in what Mrs. Tubbs says. They've quarrelled, and of course the woman makes Clara as black as she can. Tell her father everything as soon as he comes home; you've no choice.'

Mrs. Hewett averted her face in profound dejection. Sidney learnt at length what her desire had been in coming to him; she hoped he would see Clara and persuade her to return home.

'I dursn't tell her father,' she kept repeating. 'But perhaps it isn't true what Mrs. Tubbs says. Do go an' speak to her before it's too late. Say we won't ask her to come 'ome, if only she'll let us know what she's goin' to do.'

In the end he promised to perform this service, and to communicate the result that evening. It was Saturday; at half-past one he left the workroom, hastened home to prepare himself for the visit, and, without thinking of dinner, set out to find the address Mrs. Hewett had given him. His steps

were directed to a dull street on the north of Pentonville Road;
the house at which he made inquiry was occupied by a drum-
manufacturer. Miss Hewett, he learnt, was not at home;
she had gone forth two hours ago, and nothing was known of
her movements. Sidney turned away and began to walk up
and down the shadowed side of the street; there was no
breath of air stirring, and from the open windows radiated
stuffy odours. A quarter of an hour sufficed to exasperate
him with anxiety and physical malaise. He suffered from his
inability to do anything at once, from conflict with himself as
to whether or not it behoved him to speak with John Hewett;
of Clara he thought with anger rather than fear, for her
behaviour seemed to prove that nothing had happened save
the inevitable breach with Mrs. Tubbs. Just as he had said
to himself that it was no use waiting about all the afternoon,
he saw Clara approaching. At sight of him she manifested
neither surprise nor annoyance, but came forward with eyes
carelessly averted. Not having seen her for so long, Sidney
was startled by the change in her features; her cheeks had
sunk, her eyes were unnaturally dark, there was something
worse than the familiar self-will about her lips.

'I've been waiting to see you,' he said. 'Will you walk
along here for a minute or two?'

'What do you want to say? I'm tired.'

'Mrs. Tubbs has told your mother what has happened,
and she came to me. Your father doesn't know yet.'

'It's nothing to me whether he knows or not. I've left
the place, that's all, and I'm going to live here till I've got
another.'

'Why not go home?'

'Because I don't choose to. I don't see that it concerns
you, Mr. Kirkwood.'

Their eyes met, and Sidney felt how little fitted he was to
reason with the girl, even would she consent to hear him.
His mood was the wrong one; the torrid sunshine seemed to
kindle an evil fire in him, and with difficulty he kept back
words of angry unreason; he even—strangest of inconsistencies—experienced a kind of brutal pleasure in her obvious
misery. Already she was reaping the fruit of obstinate folly.
Clara read what his eyes expressed; she trembled with respon-
sive hostility.

'No, it doesn't concern me,' Sidney replied, half turning
away. 'But it's perhaps as well you should know that Mrs.

Tubbs is doing her best to take away your good name. However little we are to each other, it's my duty to tell you that, and put you on your guard. I hope your father mayn't hear these stories before you have spoken to him yourself.'

Clara listened with a contemptuous smile.

'What has she been saying?'

'I shan't repeat it.'

As he gazed at her, the haggardness of her countenance smote like a sword-edge through all the black humours about his heart, piercing the very core of love and pity. He spoke in a voice of passionate appeal.

'Clara, come home before it is too late! Come with me—now—come at once? Thank heaven you have got out of that place! Come home, and stay there quietly till we can find you something better.'

'I'll die rather than go home!' was her answer, flung at him as if in hatred. 'Tell my father that, and tell him anything else you like. I want no one to take any thought for me; and I wouldn't do as *you* wish, not to save my soul!'

How often, in passing along the streets, one catches a few phrases of discord such as this! The poor can seldom command privacy; their scenes alike of tenderness and of anger must for the most part be enacted on the peopled ways. It is one of their misfortunes, one of the many necessities which blunt feeling, which balk reconciliation, which enhance the risks of dialogue at best semi-articulate.

Clara, having uttered the rancour which had so long poisoned her mind, straightway crossed the street and entered the house where she was lodging. She had just returned from making several applications for employment—futile, as so many were likely to be, if she persevered in her search for a better place than the last. The wages due to her for the present week she had of course sacrificed; her purchases of clothing—essential and superfluous—had left only a small sum out of her earnings. Food, fortunately, would cost her little; the difficulty, indeed, was to eat anything at all.

She was exhausted after her long walk, and the scene with Sidney had made her tremulous. In thrusting open the windows, as soon as she entered, she broke a pane which was already cracked; the glass cut into her palm, and blood streamed forth. For a moment she watched the red drops falling to the floor, then began to sob miserably, almost as a child might have done. The exertion necessary for binding the wound seemed beyond her strength ; sobbing and moaning, she stood in the same attitude until the blood began to congeal. The tears, too, she let dry unheeded upon her eyelashes and her cheeks ; the mist with which for a time they obscured her vision was nothing amid that cloud of misery which blackened about her spirit as she brooded. The access of self-pity was followed, as always, by a persistent sense of intolerable wrong, and that again by a fierce desire to plunge herself into ruin, as though by such act she could satiate her instincts of defiance. It is a phase of exasperated egotism common enough in original natures frustrated by circumstance—never so pronounced as in those who suffer from the social disease. Such mood perverts everything to cause of bitterness. The very force of sincerity, which Clara could not but recognise in Kirkwood's appeal, inflamed the resentment she nourished against him ; she felt that to yield would be salvation and happiness, yet yield she might not, and upon him she visited the anger due to the evil impulses in her own heart. He spoke of her father, and in so doing struck the only nerve in her which conveyed an emotion of tenderness ; instantly the feeling begot self-reproach, and of self-reproach was born as quickly the harsh self-justification with which her pride ever answered blame. She had made her father's life even more unhappy than it need have been, and to be reminded of that only drove her more resolutely upon the recklessness which would complete her ingratitude.

The afternoon wore away, the evening, a great part of the night. She ate a few mouthfuls of bread, but could not exert herself to make tea. It would be necessary to light a fire, and already the air of the room was stifling.

After a night of sleeplessness, she could only lie on her bed through the Sunday morning, wretched in a sense of abandonment. And then began to assail her that last and subtlest of temptations, the thought that already she had taken an irrevocable step, that an endeavour to return would only be trouble spent in vain, that the easy course was, in truth, the only one now open to her. Mrs. Tubbs was busy circulating calumnies; that they were nothing more than calumnies could never be proved ; all who heard them would readily enough believe. Why should she struggle uselessly to justify herself in the eyes of people predisposed to condemn her ? Fate was busy in all that had happened during the last two days. Why had she quitted her situation at a moment's notice ? Why on this occasion rather than fifty times previously? It was not her own doing; something impelled her, and the same force—call it chance or destiny—would direct the issue once more. All she could foresee was the keeping of her appointment with Scawthorne to-morrow morning; what use to try and look further, when assuredly a succession of circumstances impossible to calculate would in the end constrain her? The best would be if she could sleep out the interval.

At mid-day she rose, ate and drank mechanically, then contemplated the hours that must somehow be killed. There was sunlight in the sky, but to what purpose should she go out? She went to the window, and surveyed the portion of street that was visible. On the opposite pavement, at a little distance, a man was standing; it was Sidney Kirkwood. The sight of him roused her from apathy; her blood tingled, rushed into her cheeks and throbbed at her temples. So, for all she had said, he was daring to act the spy! He suspected her; he was lurking to surprise visitors, to watch her outgoing and coming in. Very well; at least he had provided her with occupation.

Five minutes later she saw that he had gone away. Thereupon—having in the meantime clad herself—she left the house and walked at a quick step towards a region of North London with which she had no acquaintance. In an hour's time she had found another lodging, which she took by the day only. Then back again to Islington. She told her landlady that a sudden necessity compelled her to leave; she would have a cab and remove her box at once. There was the hazard that Sidney might return just as she was leaving; she braved it, and in another ten minutes was out of reach. . . .

Let his be the blame. She had warned him, and he chose to disregard her wish. Now she had cut the last bond that fretted her, and the hours rushed on like a storm-wind driving her whither they would.

Her mind was relieved from the stress of conflict; despair had given place to something that made her laugh at all the old scruples. So far from dreading the judgments that would follow her disappearance, she felt a pride in evil repute. Let them talk of her! If she dared everything, it would be well understood that she had not done so without a prospect worthy of herself. If she broke away from the obligations of a life that could never be other than poor and commonplace, those who knew her would estimate the compensation she had found.

Sidney Kirkwood was aware of her ambitions; for his own
sake he had hoped to keep her on the low level to which she
was born ; now let him recognise his folly ! Some day she
would present herself before him :—' Very sorry that I could
not oblige you, my dear sir, but you see that my lot was to
be rather different from that you kindly planned for me.'
Let them gossip and envy !

It was a strange night that followed. Between one and
two o'clock the heavens began to be overflashed with summer
lightning ; there was no thunder, no rain. The blue gleams
kept illuminating the room for more than an hour. Clara
could not lie in bed. The activity of her brain became all
but delirium ; along her nerves, through all the courses of her
blood, seemed to run fires which excited her with an indescribable mingling of delight and torment. She walked to
and fro, often speaking aloud, throwing up her arms. She
leaned from the open window and let the lightning play freely
upon her face : she fancied it had the effect of restoring her
wasted health. Whatever the cause, she felt stronger and
more free from pain than for many months.

At dawn she slept. The striking of a church-clock woke
her at nine, giving her just time to dress with care and set
forth to keep her appointment.

CHAPTER XI

A DISAPPOINTMENT

On ordinary Sundays the Byasses breakfasted at ten o'clock;
this morning the meal was ready at eight, and Bessie's
boisterous spirits declared the exception to be of joyous
significance. Finding that Samuel's repeated promises to
rise were the merest evasion, she rushed into the room where
he lay fly-fretted, dragged the pillows from under his tousled
head, and so belaboured him in schoolboy fashion that he had
no choice but to leap towards his garments. In five minutes
he roared down the kitchen-stairs for shaving-water, and in
five minutes more was seated in his shirt-sleeves, consuming
fried bacon with prodigious appetite. Bessie had the twofold
occupation of waiting upon him and finishing the toilet of the
baby; she talked incessantly and laughed with an echoing

shrillness which would have given a headache for the rest of
the day to any one of average nervous sensibility.

They were going to visit Samuel's parents, who lived at
Greenwich. Bessie had not yet enjoyed an opportunity of ex-
hibiting her first-born to the worthy couple ; she had, however,
written many and long letters on the engrossing subject, and
was just a little fluttered with natural anxiety lest the infant's
appearance or demeanour should disappoint the expectations
she had excited. Samuel found his delight in foretelling the
direst calamities.

'Don't say I didn't advise you to draw it mild,' he remarked
whilst breakfasting, when Bessie had for the tenth time obliged
him to look round and give his opinion on points of costume.
'Remember it was only last week you told them that the imp
had never cried since the day of his birth, and I'll bet you
three half-crowns to a bad halfpenny he roars all through to-
night.'

'Hold your tongue, Sam, or I'll throw something at
you!'

Samuel had just appeased his morning hunger, and was
declaring that the day promised to be the hottest of the year,
such a day as would bring out every vice inherent in babies,
when a very light tap at the door caused Bessie to abandon
her intention of pulling his ears.

'That's Jane,' she said. 'Come in!'

The Jane who presented herself was so strangely unlike
her namesake who lay ill at Mrs. Peckover's four months ago,
that one who had not seen her in the interval would with difficulty have recognised her. To begin with, she had grown a
little; only a little, but enough to give her the appearance of
her full thirteen years. Then her hair no longer straggled in
neglect, but was brushed very smoothly back from her forehead, and behind was plaited in a coil of perfect neatness ; one
could see now that it was soft, fine, mouse-coloured hair, such
as would tempt the fingers to the lightest caress. No longer
were her limbs huddled over with a few shapeless rags ; she
wore a full-length dress of quiet grey, which suited well with
her hair and the pale tones of her complexion. As for her
face—oh yes, it was still the good, simple, unremarkable countenance, with the delicate arched eyebrows, with the diffident
lips, with the cheeks of exquisite smoothness, but so sadly
thin. Here too, however, a noteworthy change was beginning
to declare itself. You were no longer distressed by the shrink-

ing fear which used to be her constant expression; her eyes
no longer reminded you of a poor animal that has been beaten
from every place where it sought rest and no longer expects
anything but a kick and a curse. Timid they were, drooping
after each brief glance, the eyes of one who has suffered and
cannot but often brood over wretched memories, who does not
venture to look far forward lest some danger may loom inevitable—meet them for an instant, however, and you saw that
lustre was reviving in their still depths, that a woman's soul
had begun to manifest itself under the shadow of those gently
falling lids. A kind word, and with what purity of silent gratitude the grey pupils responded! A merry word, and mark
if the light does not glisten on them, if the diffident lips do not
form a smile which you would not have more decided lest
something of its sweetness should be sacrificed.

'Now come and tell me what you think about baby,' cried
Bessie. 'Will he do? Don't pay any attention to my husband; he's a vulgar man!'

Jane stepped forward.

'I'm sure he looks very nice, Mrs. Byass.'

'Of course he does, bless him! Sam, get your coat on,
and brush your hat, and let Miss Snowdon teach you how to
behave yourself. Well, we're going to leave the house in your
care, Jane. We shall be back *some time* to-morrow night, but
goodness knows when. Don't you sit up for us.'

'You know where to wire to if there's a fire breaks out in
the back kitchen,' observed Samuel facetiously. 'If you hear
footsteps in the passage at half-past two to-morrow morning
don't trouble to come down; wait till daylight to see whether
they've carried off the dresser.'

Bessie screamed with laughter.

'What a fool you are, Sam! If you don't mind, you'll be
making Jane laugh. You're sure you'll be home before dark
to-morrow, Jane?'

'Oh, quite sure. Mr. Kirkwood says there's a train gets
to Liverpool Street about seven, and grandfather thought that
would suit us.'

'You'll be here before eight then. Do see that your fire's
out before you leave. And you'll be sure to pull the door to?
And see that the area-gate's fastened.'

'Can't you find a few more orders?' observed Samuel.

'Hold your tongue! Jane doesn't mind; do you, Jane?
Now, Sam, are you ready? Bless the man, if he hasn't got a

great piece of bread sticking in his whiskers! How *did* it get there? Off you go!'

Jane followed them, and stood at the front door for a moment, watching them as they departed.

Then she went upstairs. On the first floor the doors of the two rooms stood open, and the rooms were bare. The lodgers who had occupied this part of the house had recently left; a card was again hanging in the window of Bessie's parlour. Jane passed up the succeeding flight and entered the chamber which looked out upon Hanover Street. The truckle-bed*on which her grandfather slept had been arranged for the day some two hours ago; Snowdon rose at six, and everything was orderly in the room when Jane came to prepare breakfast an hour later. At present the old man was sitting by the open window, smoking a pipe. He spoke a few words with reference to the Byasses, then seemed to resume a train of thought, and for a long time there was unbroken silence. Jane seated herself at a table, on which were a few books and writing materials. She began to copy something, using the pen with difficulty, and taking extreme pains. Occasionally her eyes wandered, and once they rested upon her grandfather's face for several minutes. But for the cry of a milkman or a paperboy in the street, no sound broke the quietness of the summer morning. The blessed sunshine, so rarely shed from a London sky—sunshine, the source of all solace to mind and body—reigned gloriously in heaven and on earth.

When more than an hour had passed, Snowdon came and sat down beside the girl. Without speaking she showed him what she had written. He nodded approvingly.

'Shall I say it to you, grandfather?'

'Yes.'

Jane collected her thoughts, then began to repeat the parable of the Samaritan.* From the first words it was evident that she frequently thus delivered passages committed to memory; evident, too, that instruction and a natural good sense guarded her against the gabbling method of recitation. When she had finished Snowdon spoke with her for awhile on the subject of the story. In all he said there was the earnestness of deep personal feeling. His theme was the virtue of Compassion; he appeared to rate it above all other forms of moral goodness, to regard it as the saving principle of human life.

'If only we had pity on one another, all the worst things

we suffer from in this world would be at an end. It's because men's hearts are hard that life is so full of misery. If we could only learn to be kind and gentle and forgiving—never mind anything else. We act as if we were all each other's enemies; we can't be merciful, because we expect no mercy; we struggle to get as much as we can for ourselves and care nothing for others. Think about it; never let it go out of your mind. Perhaps some day it'll help you in your own life.'

Then there was silence again. Snowdon went back to his seat by the window and relit his pipe; to muse in the sunshine seemed sufficient occupation for him. Jane opened another book and read to herself.

In the afternoon they went out together. The old man had grown more talkative. He passed cheerfully from subject to subject, now telling a story of his experiences abroad, now reviving recollections of London as he had known it sixty years ago. Jane listened with quiet interest. She did not say much herself, and when she did speak it was with a noticeable effort to overcome her habit of diffidence. She was happy, but her nature had yet to develop itself under these strangely novel conditions.

A little before sunset there came a knocking at the house-door. Jane went down to open, and found that the visitor was Sidney Kirkwood. The joyful look with which she recognised him changed almost in the same moment; his face wore an expression that alarmed her; it was stern, hard-set in trouble, and his smile could not disguise the truth. Without speaking, he walked upstairs and entered Snowdon's room. To Sidney there was always something peculiarly impressive in the first view of this quiet chamber; simple as were its appointments, it produced a sense of remoteness from the common conditions of life. Invariably he subdued his voice when conversing here. A few flowers such as can be bought in the street generally diffused a slight scent through the air, making another peculiarity which had its effect on Sidney's imagination. When Jane moved about, it was with a sound-less step; if she placed a chair or arranged things on the table, it was as if with careful avoidance of the least noise. When his thoughts turned hitherwards, Sidney always pictured the old man sitting in his familiar mood of reverie, and Jane, in like silence, bending over a book at the table. Peace, the thing most difficult to find in the world that Sidney knew, had here made itself a dwelling.

He shook hands with Snowdon and seated himself. A few friendly words were spoken, and the old man referred to an excursion they had agreed to make together on the morrow, the general holiday.

'I'm very sorry,' replied Kirkwood, 'but it'll be impossible for me to go.'

Jane was standing near him; her countenance fell, expressing uttermost disappointment.

'Something has happened,' pursued Sidney, 'that won't let me go away, even for a few hours. I don't mean to say that it would really prevent me, but I should be so uneasy in my mind all the time that I couldn't enjoy myself, and I should only spoil your pleasure. Of course you'll go just the same?'

Snowdon reassured him on this point. Jane had just been about to lay supper; she continued her task, and Sidney made a show of sharing the meal. Soon after, as if conscious that Sidney would speak with more freedom of his trouble but for her presence, Jane bade them good-night and went to her own room. There ensued a break in the conversation; then Kirkwood said, with the abruptness of one who is broaching a difficult subject:

'I should like to tell you what it is that's going wrong with me. I don't think anyone's advice would be the least good, but it's a miserable affair, and I shall feel better for speaking about it.'

Snowdon regarded him with eyes of calm sympathy. There is a look of helpful attention peculiar to the faces of some who have known much suffering; in this instance, the grave force of character which at all times made the countenance impressive heightened the effect of its gentleness. In external matters, the two men knew little more of each other now than after their first meeting, but the spiritual alliance between them had strengthened with every conversation. Each understood the other's outlook upon problems of life, which are not commonly discussed in the top rooms of lodging-houses; they felt and thought differently at times, but in essentials they were at one, and it was the first time that either had found such fruitful companionship.

'Did you hear anything from the Peckovers of Clara Hewett?' Sidney began by asking.

'Not from them. Jane has often spoken of her.'

Sidney again hesitated, then, from a fragmentary begin-

ning, passed into a detailed account of his relations with
Clara. The girl herself, had she overheard him, could not
have found fault with the way in which the story was narrated.
He represented his love as from the first without response
which could give him serious hope ; her faults he dealt with
not as characteristics to be condemned, but as evidences of
suffering, the outcome of cruel conditions. Her engagement
at the luncheon-bar he spoke of as a detestable slavery, which
had wasted her health and driven her in the end to an act of
desperation. What now could be done to aid her ? John
Hewett was still in ignorance of the step she had taken, and
Sidney described himself as distracted by conflict between
what he felt to be his duty, and fear of what might happen if
he invoked Hewett's authority. At intervals through the day
he had been going backwards and forwards in the street where
Clara had her lodging. He did not think she would seek to
escape from her friends altogether, but her character and circumstances made it perilous for her to live thus alone.

'What does she really wish for ? ' inquired Snowdon, when
there had been a short silence.

'She doesn't know, poor girl ! Everything in the life she
has been living is hateful to her—everything since she left
school. She can't rest in the position to which she was born;
she aims at an impossible change of circumstances. It comes
from her father ; she can't help rebelling against what seem
to her unjust restraints. But what's to come of it ? She
may perhaps get a place in a large restaurant—and what does
that mean ? '

He broke off, but in a moment resumed even more passionately :

'What a vile, cursed world this is, where you may see
men and women perish before your eyes, and no more chance
of saving them than if they were going down in mid-ocean !
She's only a child—only just seventeen—and already she's
gone through a lifetime of miseries. And I, like a fool, I've
often been angry with her ; I was angry yesterday. How can
she help her nature ? How can we any of us help what
we're driven to in a world like this ? Clara isn't made to be
one of those who slave to keep themselves alive. Just a
chance of birth ! Suppose she'd been the daughter of a rich
man ; then everything we now call a fault in her would either
have been of no account or actually a virtue. Just because
we haven't money we may go to perdition, and comfortable

people tell us we've only ourselves to blame. Put *them* in our place!'

Snowdon's face had gone through various changes as Sidney flung out his vehement words. When he spoke, it was in a tone of some severity.

'Has she no natural affection for her father? Does she care nothing for what trouble she brings him?'

Sidney did not reply at once; as he was about to speak, Snowdon bent forward suddenly and touched his arm.

'Let me see her. Let me send Jane to her to-morrow morning, and ask her to come here. I might—I can't say—but I might do some good.'

To this Sidney gave willing assent, but without sanguine expectation. In further talk it was agreed between them that, if this step had no result, John Hewett ought to be immediately informed of the state of things.

This was at ten o'clock on Sunday evening. So do we play our tragi-comedies in the eye of fate.

The mention of Jane led to a brief conversation regarding her before Sidney took his leave. Since her recovery she had been going regularly to school, to make up for the time of which she had been defrauded by Mrs. Peckover. Her grandfather's proposal was, that she should continue thus for another six months, after which, he said, it would be time for her to learn a business. Mrs. Byass had suggested the choice of artificial-flower making, to which she herself had been brought up; possibly that would do as well as anything else.

'I suppose so,' was Sidney's reluctant acquiescence. 'Or as ill as anything else, would be a better way to put it.'

Snowdon regarded him with unusual fixedness, and seemed on the point of making some significant remark; but immediately his face expressed change of purpose, and he said, without emphasis:

'Jane must be able to earn her own living.'

Sidney, before going home, walked round to the street in which he had already lingered several times to-day, and where yesterday he had spoken with Clara. The windows of the house he gazed at were dark.

CHAPTER XII

' IO SATURNALIA ! '

So at length came Monday, the first Monday in August, a day gravely set apart for the repose and recreation of multitudes who neither know how to rest nor how to refresh themselves with pastime. To-day will the slaves of industrialism don the *pileus*.* It is high summertide. With joy does the awaking publican look forth upon the blue-misty heavens, and address his adorations to the Sun-god, inspirer of thirst. Throw wide the doors of the temple of Alcohol ! Behold, we come in our thousands, jingling the coins that shall purchase us this one day of tragical mirth. Before us is the dark and dreary autumn ; it is a far cry to the foggy joys of Christmas. Io Saturnalia !

For certain friends of ours this morning brought an event of importance. At a church in Clerkenwell were joined together in holy matrimony Robert Hewett and Penelope (otherwise Pennyloaf) Candy, the former aged nineteen, the latter less than that by nearly three years. John Hewett would have nothing to do with an alliance so disreputable ; Mrs. Hewett had in vain besought her stepson not to marry so unworthily. Even as a young man of good birth has been known to enjoy a subtle self-flattery in the thought that he graciously bestows his name upon a maiden who, to all intents and purposes, may be said never to have been born at all, so did Bob Hewett feel when he put a ring upon the scrubby finger of Pennyloaf. Proudly conscious was Bob that he had ' married beneath him '—conscious also that Clem Peckover was gnawing her lips in rage.

Mrs. Candy was still sober at the hour of the ceremony. Her husband, not a bad fellow in his way, had long since returned to her, and as yet had not done more than threaten a repetition of his assault. Both were present at church. A week ago Bob had established himself in a room in Shooter's Gardens, henceforth to be shared with him by his bride. Probably he might have discovered a more inviting abode for the early days of married life, but Bob had something of the artist's temperament and could not trouble about practical details; for the present this room would do as well as another. It was cheap, and he had need of all the money he could save from everyday expenses. Pennyloaf would go on with her shirt-making, of course, and all they wanted was a roof over their heads at night.

And in truth he was fond of Pennyloaf. The poor little slave worshipped him so sincerely; she repaid his affectionate words with such fervent gratitude; and there was no denying that she had rather a pretty face, which had attracted him from the first. But above all, this preference accorded to so humble a rival had set Clem Peckover beside herself. It was all very well for Clem to make pretence of having transferred her affections to Jack Bartley. Why, Suke Jollop (ostensibly Clem's bosom friend, but treacherous at times because she had herself given an eye to Jack)—Suke Jollop reported that Clem would have killed Pennyloaf had she dared. Pennyloaf had been going about in fear for her life since that attack upon her in Myddelton Passage. 'I dursn't marry you, Bob! I dursn't!' she kept saying, when the proposal was first made. But Bob laughed with contemptuous defiance. He carried his point, and now he was going to spend his wedding-day at the Crystal Palace—choosing that resort because he knew Clem would be there, and Jack Bartley, and Suke Jollop, and many another acquaintance, before whom he was resolved to make display of magnanimity.

Pennyloaf shone in most unwonted apparel. Everything was new except her boots—it had been decided that these only needed soleing. Her broad-brimmed hat of yellow straw was graced with the reddest feather purchasable in the City Road; she had a dolman* of most fashionable cut, blue, lustrous; blue likewise was her dress, hung about with bows and streamers. And the gleaming ring on the scrubby small finger! On that hand most assuredly Pennyloaf would wear no glove. How proud she was of her ring! How she turned it round and round when nobody was looking! Gold, Pennyloaf, real gold! The pawnbroker would lend her seven-and-sixpence on it, any time.

At Holborn Viaduct there was a perpetual rush of people for the trains to the 'Paliss.' As soon as a train was full, off it went, and another long string of empty carriages drew up in its place. No distinction between 'classes' to-day; get in where you like, where you can. Positively, Pennyloaf found herself seated in a first-class carriage; she would have been awe-struck, but that Bob flung himself back on the cushions

with such an easy air, and nodded laughingly at her. Among
their companions was a youth with a concertina; as soon as
the train moved he burst into melody. It was the natural
invitation to song, and all joined in the latest ditties learnt at
the music-hall. Away they sped, over the roofs of ¦South
London, about them the universal glare of sunlight, the
carriage dense with tobacco-smoke. Ho for the bottle of
muddy ale, passed round in genial fellowship from mouth to
mouth! Pennyloaf would not drink of it; she had a dread
of all such bottles. In her heart she rejoiced that Bob knew
no craving for strong liquor. Towards the end of the journey the young man with the concertina passed round his
hat.

Clem Peckover had come by the same train; she was one
of a large party which had followed close behind Bob and
Pennyloaf to the railway station. Now they followed along
the long corridors into the 'Paliss,' with many a loud expression of mockery, with hee-hawing laughter, with coarse
jokes. Depend upon it, Clem was gorgeously arrayed; amid
her satellites she swept on 'like a stately ship of Tarsus,
bound for the isles of Javan or Gadire;' her face was aflame,
her eyes flashed in enjoyment of the uproar. Jack Bartley
wore a high hat—Bob never had owned one in his life—and
about his neck was a tie of crimson; yellow was his waistcoat, even such a waistcoat as you may see in Pall Mall, and
his walking-stick had a nigger's head for handle. He was
the oracle of the maidens around him; every moment the
appeal was to 'Jeck! Jeck!' Suke Jollop, who would in
reality have preferred to accompany Bob and his allies, whispered it about that Jack had two-pound-ten in his pocket, and
was going to spend every penny of it before he left the 'Paliss'
—yes, 'every bloomin' penny!'

Thus early in the day, the grounds were of course preferred to the interior of the glass house. Bob and Pennyloaf
bent their steps to the fair. Here already was gathered much
goodly company; above their heads hung a thick white
wavering cloud of dust. Swing-boats and merry-go-rounds
are from of old the chief features of these rural festivities;
they soared and dipped and circled to the joyous music of
organs which played the same tune automatically for any
number of hours, whilst raucous voices invited all and sundry
to take their turn. Should this delight pall, behold on every
hand such sports as are dearest to the Briton, those which

call for strength of sinew and exactitude of aim. The philosophic mind would have noted with interest how ingeniously these games were made to appeal to the patriotism of the throng. Did you choose to 'shy' sticks in the contest for cocoa-nuts, behold your object was a wooden model of the treacherous Afghan or the base African. If you took up the mallet to smite upon a spring and make proof of how far you could send a ball flying upwards, your blow descended upon the head of some other recent foeman. Try your fist at the indicator of muscularity, and with zeal you smote full in the stomach of a guy made to represent a Russian. If you essayed the pop-gun, the mark set you was on the flank of a wooden donkey, so contrived that it would kick when hit in the true spot. What a joy to observe the tendency of all these diversions! How characteristic of a high-spirited people that nowhere could be found any amusement appealing to the mere mind, or calculated to effeminate by encouraging a love of beauty.

Bob had a sovereign*to get rid of. He shied for cocoa-nuts, he swung in the boat with Pennyloaf, he rode with her on the whirligigs. When they were choked, and whitened from head to foot, with dust, it was natural to seek the nearest refreshment-booth. Bob had some half-dozen male and female acquaintances clustered about him by now; of course he must celebrate the occasion by entertaining all of them. Consumed with thirst, he began to drink without counting the glasses. Pennyloaf plucked at his eldow, but Bob was beginning to feel that he must display spirit. Because he was married, that was no reason for his relinquishing the claims to leadership in gallantry which had always been recognised. Hollo! Here was Suke Jollop! She had just quarrelled with Clem, and had been searching for the hostile camp. 'Have a drink, Suke!' cried Bob, when he heard her acrimonious charges against Clem and Jack. A pretty girl, Suke, and with a hat which made itself proudly manifest a quarter of a mile away. Drink! of course she would drink; that thirsty she could almost drop! Bob enjoyed this secession from the enemy. He knew Suke's old fondness for him, and began to play upon it. Elated with beer and vanity, he no longer paid the least attention to Pennyloaf's remonstrances; nay, he at length bade her 'hold her bloomin' row!' Pennyloaf had a tear in her eye; she looked fiercely at Miss Jollop.

The day wore on. For utter weariness Pennyloaf was
constrained to beg that they might go into the 'Paliss' and
find a shadowed seat. Her tone revived tenderness in Bob;
again he became gracious, devoted; he promised that not
another glass of beer should pass his lips, and Suke Jollop,
with all her like, might go to perdition. But heavens! how
sweltering it was under this glass canopy! How the dust
rose from the trampled boards ! Come, let's have tea. The
programme says there'll be a military band playing presently,
and we shall return refreshed to hear it.

So they made their way to the 'Shilling Tea-room.'
Having paid at the entrance, they were admitted to feed
freely on all that lay before them. With difficulty could a
seat be found in the huge room; the uproar of voices was
deafening. On the tables lay bread, butter, cake in hunches,
tea-pots, milk-jugs, sugar-basins—all things to whomso could
secure them in the conflict. Along the gangways coursed
perspiring waiters, heaping up giant structures of used plates
and cups, distributing clean utensils, and miraculously sharp
in securing the gratuity expected from each guest as he rose
satiate. Muscular men in aprons wheeled hither the supplies
of steaming fluid in immense cans on heavy trucks. Here
practical joking found the most graceful of opportunities,
whether it were the deft direction of a piece of cake at the
nose of a person sitting opposite, or the emptying of a saucer
down your neighbour's back, or the ingenious jogging of an
arm which was in the act of raising a full tea-cup. Now and
then an ill-conditioned fellow, whose beer disagreed with him,
would resent some piece of elegant trifling, and the waiters
would find it needful to request gentlemen not to fight until
they had left the room. These cases, however, were exceptional. On the whole there reigned a spirit of imbecile
joviality. Shrieks of female laughter testified to the success
of the entertainment.

As Bob and his companion quitted this sphere of delight,
ill-luck brought it to pass that Mr. Jack Bartley and his train
were on the point of entering. Jack uttered a phrase of
stinging sarcasm with reference to Pennyloaf's red feather;
whereupon Bob smote him exactly between the eyes. Yells
arose; there was a scuffle, a rush, a tumult. The two were
separated before further harm came of the little misunderstanding, but Jack went to the tea-tables vowing vengeance.

Poor Pennyloaf shed tears as Bob led her to the place

where the band had begun playing. Only her husband's anger prevented her from yielding to utter misery. But now they had come to the centre of the building, and by dint of much struggle in the crowd they obtained a standing whence they could see the vast amphitheatre, filled with thousands of faces. Here at length was quietness, intermission of folly and brutality. Bob became another man as he stood and listened. He looked with kindness into Pennyloaf's pale, weary face, and his arm stole about her waist to support her. Ha! Pennyloaf was happy! The last trace of tears vanished. She too was sensible of the influences of music; her heart throbbed as she let herself lean against her husband.

Well, as every one must needs have his panacea for the ills of society, let me inform you of mine. To humanise the multitude two things are necessary—two things of the simplest kind conceivable. In the first place, you must effect an entire change of economic conditions: a preliminary step of which every tyro will recognise the easiness; then you must bring to bear on the new order of things the constant influence of music. Does not the prescription recommend itself? It is jesting in earnest. For, work as you will, there is no chance of a new and better world until the old be utterly destroyed. Destroy, sweep away, prepare the ground; then shall music the holy, music the civiliser, breathe over the renewed earth, and with Orphean magic raise in perfected beauty the towers of the City of Man.

Hours yet before the fireworks begin. Never mind; here by good luck we find seats where we can watch the throng passing and repassing. It is a great review of the People. On the whole how respectable they are, how sober, how deadly dull! See how worn-out the poor girls are becoming, how they gape, what listless eyes most of them have! The stoop in the shoulders so universal among them merely means over-toil in the workroom. Not one in a thousand shows the elements of taste in dress; vulgarity and worse glares in all but every costume. Observe the middle-aged women; it would be small surprise that their good looks had vanished, but whence comes it they are animal, repulsive, absolutely vicious in ugliness? Mark the men in their turn: four in every six have visages so deformed by ill-health that they excite disgust; their hair is cut down to within half an inch of the scalp; their legs are twisted out of shape by evil conditions of life from birth upwards. Whenever a youth and a girl come along arm-in-arm, how flagrantly shows the man's coarseness ! They are pretty, so many of these girls, delicate of feature, graceful did but their slavery allow them natural development; and the heart sinks as one sees them side by side with the men who are to be their husbands.

One of the livelier groups is surging hitherwards; here we have frolic, here we have humour. The young man who leads them has been going about all day with the lining of his hat turned down over his forehead; for the thousandth time those girls are screaming with laughter at the sight of him. Ha, ha! He has slipped and fallen upon the floor, and makes an obstruction; his companions treat him like a horse that is ' down ' in the street. ' Look out for his 'eels ! ' cries one; and another, ' Sit on his 'ed ! ' If this doesn't come to an end we shall die of laughter. Lo ! one of the funniest of the party is wearing a gigantic cardboard nose and flame-coloured whiskers. There, the stumbler is on his feet again. ' 'Ere he comes up smilin'!' cries his friend of the cardboard nose, and we shake our diaphragms with mirth. One of the party is an unusually tall man. ' When are you comin' down to have a look at us?' cries a pert lass as she skips by him.

A great review of the People. Since man came into being did the world ever exhibit a sadder spectacle ?

Evening advances; the great ugly building will presently be lighted with innumerable lamps. Away to the west yonder the heavens are afire with sunset, but at that we do not care to look; never in our lives did we regard it. We know not what is meant by beauty or grandeur. Here under the glass roof stand white forms of undraped men and women—casts of antique statues—but we care as little for the glory of art as for that of nature; we have a vague feeling that, for some reason or other, antiquity excuses the indecent, but further than that we do not get.

As the dusk descends there is a general setting of the throng towards the open air ; all the pathways swarm with groups which have a tendency to disintegrate into couples ; universal is the protecting arm. Relief from the sweltering atmosphere of the hours of sunshine causes a revival of hilarity ; those who have hitherto only bemused themselves with liquor now pass into the stage of jovial recklessness, and others, determined to prolong a flagging merriment, begin to depend upon their companions for guidance. On the terraces dancing has commenced; the players of violins, concertinas, and penny-whistles do a brisk trade among the groups eager for a rough-and-tumble valse; so do the pickpockets. Vigorous and varied is the jollity that occupies the external galleries, filling now in expectation of the fireworks; indescribable the mingled tumult that roars heavenwards. Girls linked by the half-dozen arm-in-arm leap along with shrieks like grotesque mænads; a rougher horseplay finds favour among the youths, occasionally leading to fisticuffs. Thick voices bellow in fragmentary chorus; from every side comes the yell, the cat-call, the ear-rending whistle; and as the bass, the never-ceasing accompaniment, sounds myriad-footed tramp, tramp along the wooden flooring. A fight, a scene of bestial drunkenness, a tender whispering between two lovers, proceed concurrently in a space of five square yards.—Above them glimmers the dawn of starlight.

For perhaps the first time in his life Bob Hewett has drunk more than he can well carry. To Pennyloaf's remonstrances he answers more and more impatiently: ' Why does she talk like a bloomin' fool ?—one doesn't get married every day.' He is on the look-out for Jack Bartley now; only let him meet Jack, and it shall be seen who is the better man. Pennyloaf rejoices that the hostile party are nowhere discoverable. She is persuaded to join in a dance, though every moment it seems to her that she must sink to the ground in uttermost exhaustion. Naturally she does not dance with sufficient liveliness to please Bob; he seizes another girl, a stranger, and whirls round the six-foot circle with a laugh of triumph. Pennyloaf's misery is relieved by the beginning of the fireworks. Up shoot the rockets, and all the reeking multitude utters a huge ' Oh ' of idiot admiration.

Now at length must we think of tearing ourselves away from these delights. Already the more prudent people are hurrying to the railway, knowing by dire experience what it means to linger until the last cargoes. Pennyloaf has hard work to get her husband as far as the station; Bob is not quite steady upon his feet, and the hustling of the crowd perpetually excites him to bellicose challenges. They reach the platform somehow; they stand wedged amid a throng which roars persistently as a substitute for the activity of limb now become impossible. A train is drawing up slowly; the danger is lest people in the front row should be pushed over the edge of the platform, but porters exert themselves with success. A rush, a tumble, curses, blows, laughter, screams of pain—and we are in a carriage. Pennyloaf has to be dragged up from under the seat, and all her indignation cannot free her from the jovial embrace of a man who insists that there is plenty of room on his knee. Off we go! It is a long third-class coach, and already five or six musical instruments have struck up. We smoke and sing at the same time ; we quarrel and make love—the latter in somewhat primitive fashion ; we roll about with the rolling of the train ; we nod into hoggish sleep.

The platform at Holborn Viaduct; and there, to Pennyloaf's terror, it is seen that Clem Peckover and her satellites have come by the same train. She does her best to get Bob quickly away, but Clem keeps close in their neighbourhood. Just as they issue from the station Pennyloaf feels herself bespattered from head to foot with some kind of fluid ; turning, she is aware that all her enemies have squirts in their hands, and are preparing for a second discharge of filthy water. Anguish for the ruin of her dress overcomes all other fear ; she calls upon Bob to defend her.

But an immediate conflict was not Jack Bartley's intention. He and those with him made off at a run, Bob pursuing as closely as his unsteadiness would permit. In this way they all traversed the short distance to Clerkenwell Green, either party echoing the other's objurgations along the thinly-peopled streets. At length arrived the suitable moment. Near St. James's Church Jack Bartley made a stand, and defied his enemy to come on. Bob responded with furious eagerness ; amid a press of delighted spectators, swelled by people just turned out of the public-houses, the two lads fought like wild animals. Nor were they the only combatants. Exasperated by the certainty that her hat and dolman were ruined, Pennyloaf flew with erected nails at Clem Peckover. It was just what the latter desired. In an instant she had rent half Pennyloaf's garments off her back, and was tearing her face till the blood streamed. Inconsolable was the grief of the crowd when a couple of stalwart policemen came hustling forward, thrusting to left and right, irresistibly clearing the corner. There was no question of making arrests ; it was the night of Bank-holiday, and the capacity of police-cells is limited. Enough that the fight perforce came to an end. Amid frenzied blasphemy Bob and Jack went their several ways ; so did Clem and Pennyloaf.

Poor Pennyloaf! Arrived at Shooter's Gardens, and having groped her way blindly up to the black hole which was her wedding-chamber, she just managed to light a candle, then sank down upon the bare floor and wept. You could not have recognised her; her pretty face was all blood and dirt. She held in her hand the fragment of a hat, and her dolman had disappeared. Her husband was not in much better plight; his waistcoat and shirt were rent open, his coat was filth-smeared, and it seemed likely that he had lost the sight of one eye. Sitting there in drunken lassitude, he breathed nothing but threats of future vengeance.

An hour later noises of a familiar kind sounded beneath the window. A woman's voice was raised in the fury of mad drunkenness, and a man answered her with threats and blows.

'That's mother,' sobbed Pennyloaf. 'I knew she wouldn't get over to-day. She never did get over a Bank-holiday.'

Mrs. Candy had taken the pledge when her husband consented to return and live with her. Unfortunately she did not at the same time transfer herself to a country where there are no beer-shops and no Bank-holidays. Short of such decisive change, what hope for her?

Bob was already asleep, breathing stertorously. As for Pennyloaf, she was so overwearied that hours passed before oblivion fell upon her aching eyelids. She was thinking all the time that on the morrow it would be necessary to pawn her wedding-ring.

CHAPTER XIII

THE BRINGER OF ILL NEWS

KNOWING the likelihood that Clara Hewett would go from home for Bank-holiday, Sidney made it his request before he left Hanover Street on Sunday night that Jane might be despatched on her errand at an early hour next morning. At eight o'clock, accordingly, Snowdon went forth with his granddaughter, and, having discovered the street to which Sidney had directed him, he waited at a distance whilst Jane went to make her inquiries. In a few minutes the girl rejoined him.

'Miss Hewett has gone away,' she reported.

'To spend the day, do you mean?' was Snowdon's troubled question.

'No, she has left the house. She went yesterday, in the afternoon. It was very sudden, the landlady says, and she doesn't know where she's gone to.'

Jane had no understanding of what her information implied; seeing that it was received as grave news, she stood regarding her grandfather anxiously. Though Clara had passed out of her world since those first days of illness, Jane held her in a memory which knew no motive of retention so strong as gratitude. The thought of harm or sorrow coming upon her protector had a twofold painfulness. Instantly she divined that Clara was in some way the cause of Sidney Kirkwood's inability to go into the country to-day. For a long time the two had been closely linked in her reflections; Mrs. Peckover and Clem used constantly to exchange remarks which made this inevitable. But not until now had Jane really felt the significance of the bond. Of a sudden she had a throbbing at her heart, and a confusion of mind which would not allow her to pursue the direct train of thought naturally provoked by the visit she had just paid. A turbid flood of ideas, of vague surmises, of apprehensions, of forecasts, swept across her consciousness. The blood forsook her cheeks. But that the old man began to move away, she could have remained thus for many minutes, struggling with that new, half-understood thing which was taking possession of her life.

The disappointment of the day was no longer simple, and such as a child experiences. Nor ever from this hour onwards would Jane regard things as she had been wont to do, with the simple feelings of childhood.

Snowdon walked on in silence until the street they had visited was far behind them. Jane was accustomed to his long fits of musing, but now she with difficulty refrained from questioning him. He said at length:

'Jane, I'm afraid we shall have to give up our day in the country.'

She assented readily, gladly; all the joy had gone out of the proposed excursion, and she wished now to be by herself in quietness.

'I think I'll let you go home alone,' Snowdon continued. 'I want to see Mr. Kirkwood, and I dare say I shall find him in, if I walk on at once.'

They went in different directions, and Snowdon made what

speed he could to Tysoe Street. Sidney had already been out, walking restlessly and aimlessly for two or three hours. The news he now heard was the half-incredible fulfilment of a dread that had been torturing him through the night. No calamity is so difficult to realise when it befalls as one which has haunted us in imagination.

'That means nothing!' he exclaimed, as if resentfully. 'She was dissatisfied with the lodging, that's all. Perhaps she's already got a place. I dare say there's a note from her at home this morning.'

'Shall you go and see if there is?' asked Snowdon, allowing, as usual, a moment's silence to intervene.

Sidney hesitated, avoiding the other's look.

'I shall go to that house first of all, I think. Of course I shall hear no more than they told Jane; but——'

He took a deep breath.

'Yes, go there,' said Snowdon; 'but afterwards go to the Hewetts'. If she *hasn't* written to them, or let them have news of any kind, her father oughtn't to be kept in ignorance for another hour.'

'He ought to have been told before this,' replied Sidney in a thick under-voice. 'He ought to have been told on Saturday. And the blame'll be mine.'

It is an experience familiar to impulsive and self-confident men that a moment's crisis may render scarcely intelligible a mode of thought or course of action which till then one had deemed perfectly rational. Sidney, hopeless in spite of the pretences he made, stood aghast at the responsibility he had taken upon himself. It was so obvious to him now that he ought to have communicated to John Hewett without loss of time the news which Mrs. Hewett brought on Saturday morning. But could he be sure that John was still in ignorance of Clara's movements? Was it not all but certain that Mrs. Hewett must have broken the news before this? If not, there lay before him a terrible duty.

The two went forth together, and another visit was paid to the lodging-house. After that Sidney called upon Mrs. Tubbs, and made a simple inquiry for Clara, with the anticipated result.

'You won't find her in this part of London, it's my belief,' said the woman significantly. 'She's left the lodgings as she took—so much I know. Never meant to stay there, not she! You're a friend of her father's, mister?'

Sidney could not trust himself to make a reply. He rejoined Snowdon at a little distance, and expressed his intention
of going at once to Clerkenwell Close.

'Let me see you again to-day,' said the old man sadly.

Sidney promised, and they took leave of each other. It
was now nearing ten o'clock. In the Close an organ was
giving delight to a great crowd of children, some of them
wearing holiday garb, but most clad in the native rags which
served them for all seasons and all days. The volume of
clanging melody fell with torture upon Kirkwood's ear, and
when he saw that the instrument was immediately before
Mrs. Peckover's house, he stood aside in gloomy impatience,
waiting till it should move away. This happened in a few
minutes. The house door being open, he walked straight
upstairs.

On the landing he confronted Mrs. Hewett ; she started on
seeing him, and whispered a question. The exchange of a
few words apprised Sidney that Hewett did not even know of
Clara's having quitted Mrs. Tubbs'.

'Then I must tell him everything,' he said. To put the
task upon the poor woman would have been simple cowardice.
Merely in hearing his news she was blanched with dread.
She could only point to the door of the front room—the only
one rented by the family since Jane Snowdon's occupation of
the other had taught them to be as economical in this respect
as their neighbours were.

Sidney knocked and entered. Two months had passed
since his latest visit, and he observed that in the meantime
everything had become more squalid. The floor, the window,
the furniture, were not kept so clean as formerly—inevitable
result of the overcrowding of a room ; the air was bad, the
children looked untidy. The large bed had not been set in
order since last night ; in it lay the baby, crying as always,
ailing as it had done from the day of its birth. John Hewett
was engaged in mending one of the chairs, of which the legs
had become loose. He looked with surprise at the visitor,
and at once averted his face sullenly.

'Mr. Hewett,' Kirkwood began, without form of greeting,
'on Saturday morning I heard something that I believe I
ought to have let you know at once. I felt, though, that it
was hardly my business ; and somehow we haven't been quite
so open with each other just lately as we used to be.'

His voice sank. Hewett had risen from his crouching

attitude, and was looking him full in the face with eyes which grew momentarily darker and more hostile.

'Well? Why are you stopping? What have you got to say?'

The words came from a dry throat; the effort to pronounce them clearly made the last all but violent.

'On Friday night,' Sidney resumed, his own utterance uncertain, 'Clara left her place. She took a room not far from Upper Street, and I saw her, spoke to her. She'd quarrelled with Mrs. Tubbs. I urged her to come home, but she wouldn't listen to me. This morning I've been to try and see her again, but they tell me she went away yesterday afternoon. I can't find where she's living now.'

Hewett took a step forward. His face was so distorted, so fierce, that Sidney involuntarily raised an arm, as if to defend himself.

'An' it's you as comes tellin' me this!' John exclaimed, a note of anguish blending with his fury. 'You have the face to stand there an' speak like that to me, when you know it's all your own doing! Who was the cause as the girl went away from 'ome? Who was it, I say? Haven't been as friendly as we used to be, haven't we? An' why? Haven't I seen it plainer an' plainer what you was thinkin' when you told me to let her have her own way? I spoke the truth then —'cause I felt it; an' I was fool enough, for all that, to try an' believe I was in the wrong. Now you come an' stand before me—why, I couldn't a' thought there was a man had so little shame in him!'

Mrs. Hewett entered the room; the loud angry voice had reached her ears, and in spite of terror she came to interpose between the two men.

'Do you know what he's come to tell me?' cried her husband. 'Oh, you do! He's been tryin' to talk you over, has he? You just answer to me, an' tell the truth. Who was it persuaded me to let Clara go from 'ome? Who was it come here an' talked an' talked till he got his way? He knew what 'ud be the end of it—he knew, I tell you,—an' it's just what he wanted. Hasn't he been drawin' away from us ever since the girl left? I saw it all that night when he came here persuadin' me, an' I told it him plain. He wanted to 'a done with her, and to a' done with us. Am I speakin' the truth or not?'

'Why should he think that way, John?' pleaded the

woman faintly. 'You know very well as Clara 'ud never listen to him. What need had he to do such things?'

'Oh yes, I'm wrong! Of course I'm wrong! You always did go against me when there was anything to do with Clara. She'd never listen to him? No, of course she wouldn't, an' he couldn't rest until he saw her come to harm. What do *you* care either? She's no child of yours. But I tell you I'd see you an' all your children beg an' die in the streets rather than a hair of my own girl's head should be touched!'

Indulgence of his passion was making a madman of him. Never till now had he uttered an unfeeling word to his wife, but the look with which he accompanied this brutal speech was one of fiery hatred.

'Don't turn on *her*!' cried Sidney, with bitterness. 'Say what you like to me, and believe the worst you can of me; I shouldn't have come here if I hadn't been ready to bear everything. It's no good speaking reason to you now, but maybe you'll understand some day.'

'Who know's as she's come to harm?' urged Mrs. Hewett. 'Nobody can say it of her for certain, yet.'

'I'd have told him that, if he'd only listened to me and given me credit for honesty,' said Kirkwood. 'It is as likely as not she's gone away just because I angered her on Saturday. Perhaps she said to herself she'd have done with me once for all. It would be just her way.'

'Speak another word against my girl,' Hewett shouted, misinterpreting the last phrase, 'an' I'll do more than say what I think of you—old man though they call me! Take yourself out of this room; it was the worst day of my life that ever you came into it. Never let me an' you come across each other again. I hate the sight of you, an' I hate the sound of your voice!'

The animal in Sidney Kirkwood made it a terrible minute for him as he turned away in silence before this savage injustice. The veins upon his forehead were swollen; his clenched teeth gave an appearance of ferocity to his spirited features. With head bent, and shoulders quivering as if in supreme muscular exertion, he left the room without another word.

In a few minutes Hewett also quitted the house. He went to the luncheon-bar in Upper Street, and heard for the first time Mrs. Tubbs's rancorous surmises. He went to Clara's recent lodgings; a girl of ten was the only person in the house, and she could say nothing more than that Miss Hewett no longer lived there. Till midway in the afternoon John walked about the streets of Islington, Highbury, Hoxton, Clerken-well, impelled by the unreasoning hope that he might see Clara, but also because he could not rest in any place. He was half-conscious now of the madness of his behaviour to Kirkwood, but this only confirmed him in hostility to the young man; the thought of losing Clara was anguish intole-rable, yet with it mingled a bitter resentment of the girl's cruelty to him. And all these sources of misery swelled the current of rebellious feeling which had so often threatened to sweep his life into wreckage. He was Clara's father, and the same impulse of furious revolt which had driven the girl to recklessness now inflamed him with the rage of despair.

On a Bank-holiday only a few insignificant shops remain open even in the poor districts of London; sweets you can purchase, and tobacco, but not much else that is sold across an ordinary counter. The more noticeable becomes the brisk trade of public-houses. At the gin-shop centres the life of each street; here is a wide door and a noisy welcome, the more at-tractive by contrast with the stretch of closed shutters on either hand. At such a door, midway in the sultry afternoon, John Hewett paused. To look at his stooping shoulders, his uncertain swaying this way and that, his flushed, perspiring face, you might have taken him for one who had already been drinking. No; it was only a struggle between his despairing wretchedness and a lifelong habit of mind. Not difficult to foresee which would prevail; the public-house always has its doors open in expectation of such instances. With a gesture which made him yet more like a drunken man he turned from the pavement and entered. . . .

About nine o'clock in the evening, just when Mrs. Hewett had put the unwilling children to bed, and had given her baby a sleeping-dose—it had cried incessantly for eighteen hours,—the door of the room was pushed open. Her husband came in. She stood looking at him—unable to credit the evidence of her eyes.

'John!'

She laid her hand upon him and stared into his face. The man shook her off, without speaking, and moved staggeringly forward. Then he turned round, waved his arm, and shouted:

'Let her go to the devil! She cares nothing for her father.'

He threw himself upon the bed, and soon sank into drunken sleep.

CHAPTER XIV

A WELCOME GUEST

THE bells of St. James's, Clerkenwell, ring melodies in intervals of the pealing for service-time. One morning of spring their music, like the rain that fell intermittently, was flung westwards by the boisterous wind, away over Clerkenwell Close, until the notes failed one by one, or were clashed out of existence by the clamour of a less civilised steeple. Had the wind been under mortal control it would doubtless have blown thus violently and in this quarter in order that the inhabitants of the House of Detention might derive no solace from the melody. Yet I know not; just now the bells were playing 'There is a happy land, far, far away,' and that hymn makes too great a demand upon the imagination to soothe amid instant miseries.

In Mrs. Peckover's kitchen the music was audible in bursts. Clem and her mother, however, it neither summoned to prepare for church, nor lulled into a mood of restful reverie. The two were sitting very close together before the fire, and holding intimate converse; their voices kept a low murmur, as if, though the door was shut, they felt it necessary to use every precaution against being overheard. Three years have come and gone since we saw these persons. On the elder time has made little impression; but Clem has developed noticeably. The girl is now in the very prime of her ferocious beauty. She has grown taller and somewhat stouter; her shoulders spread like those of a caryatid;* the arm with which she props her head is as strong as a carter's and magnificently moulded. The head itself looks immense with its pile of glossy hair. Reddened by the rays of the fire, her features had a splendid savagery which seemed strangely at discord with the paltry surroundings amid which she sat; her eyes just now were gleaming with a crafty and cruel speculation which would have become those of a barbarian in ambush. I wonder how it came about that her strain, after passing through the basest conditions of modern life, had thus reverted to a type of ancestral exuberance.

'If only he doesn't hear about the old man or the girl from somebody!' said Mrs. Peckover. 'I've been afraid of it ever since he come into the 'ouse. There's so many people might tell him. You'll have to come round him sharp, Clem.'

The mother was dressed as her kind are wont to be on Sunday morning—that is to say, not dressed at all, but hung about with coarse garments, her hair in unbeautiful disarray. Clem, on the other hand, seemed to have devoted much attention to her morning toilet ; she wore a dark dress trimmed with velveteen, and a metal ornament of primitive taste gleamed amid her hair.

' There ain't no mistake ? ' she asked, after a pause. ' You're jolly sure of that ? '

' Mistake ? What a blessed fool you must be ! Didn't they advertise in the papers for him ? Didn't the lawyers themselves say as it was something to his advantage ? Don't you say yourself as Jane says her grandfather's often spoke about him and wished he could find him ? How can it be a mistake ? If it was only Bill's letter we had to go on, you might talk ; but—there, don't be a ijiot ! '

' If it turned out as he hadn't nothing,' remarked Clem resolutely, ' I'd leave him, if I was married fifty times.'

Her mother uttered a contemptuous sound. At the same time she moved her head as if listening ; some one was, in fact, descending the stairs.

' Here he comes,' she whispered. ' Get the eggs ready, an' I'll make the corffee.'

A tap at the door, then entered a tallish man of perhaps forty, though he might be a year or two younger. His face was clean-shaven, harsh-featured, unwholesome of complexion ; its chief peculiarity was the protuberance of the bone in front of each temple, which gave him a curiously animal aspect. His lower lip hung and jutted forward ; when he smiled, as now in advancing to the fire, it slightly overlapped the one above. His hair was very sparse ; he looked, indeed, like one who has received the tonsure.* The movement of his limbs betokened excessive indolence ; he dragged his feet rather than walked. His attire was equally suggestive ; not only had it fallen into the last degree of shabbiness (having originally been such as is worn by a man above the mechanic ranks), but it was patched with dirt of many kinds, and held together by a most inadequate supply of buttons. At present he wore no collar, and his waistcoat, half-open, exposed a red shirt.

' Why, you're all a-blowin' and a-growin' this morning, Miss Peckover,' was his first observation, as he dropped heavily into a wooden arm-chair. 'I shall begin to think that colour of yours ain't natural. Dare you let me rub it with a handkerchief?'

'Course I dare,' replied Clem, tossing her head. 'Don't be so forward, Mr. Snowdon.'

'Forward? Not I. I'm behind time if anything. I hope I haven't kept you from church.'

He chuckled at his double joke. Mother and daughter laughed appreciatively.

'Will you take your eggs boiled or fried?' inquired Mrs. Peckover.

'Going to give me eggs, are you? Well, I've no objection, I assure you. And I think I'll have them fried, Mrs. Peckover. But, I say, you mustn't be running up too big a bill. The Lord only knows when I shall get anything to do, and it ain't very likely to be a thousand a year when it does come.'

'Oh, that's all right,' replied the landlady, as if sordid calculation were a thing impossible to her. 'I can't say as you behaved quite straightforward years ago, Mr. Snowdon, but I ain't one to make a row about bygones, an' as you say you'll put it all straight as soon as you can, well, I won't refuse to trust you once more.'

Mr. Snowdon lay back in the chair, his hands in his waistcoat pockets, his legs outstretched upon the fender. He was smiling placidly, now at the preparing breakfast, now at Clem. The latter he plainly regarded with much admiration, and cared not to conceal it. When, in a few minutes, it was announced to him that the meal was ready, he dragged his chair up to the table and reseated himself with a sigh of satisfaction. A dish of excellent ham, and eggs as nearly fresh as can be obtained in Clerkenwell, invited him with appetising odour; a large cup of what is known to the generality of English people as coffee steamed at his right hand; slices of new bread lay ready cut upon a plate; a slab of the most expensive substitute for butter caught his eye with yellow promise;* vinegar and mustard appealed to the refinements of his taste.

'I've got a couple more eggs, if you'd like them doin',' said Mrs. Peckover, when she had watched the beginning of his attack upon the viands.

'I think I shall manage pretty well with this supply,' returned Mr. Snowdon.

As he ate he kept silence, partly because it was his habit,

partly in consequence of the activity of his mind. He was, in fact, musing upon a question which he found it very difficult to answer in any satisfactory way. 'What's the meaning of all this?' he asked himself, and not for the first time. 'What makes them treat me in this fashion? A week ago I came here to look up Mrs. Peckover, just because I'd run down to my last penny, and I didn't know where to find a night's lodging. I'd got an idea, too, that I should like to find out what had become of my child, whom I left here nine or ten years ago ; possibly she was still alive, and might welcome the duty of supporting her parent. The chance was, to be sure, that the girl had long since been in her grave, and that Mrs. Peckover no longer lived in the old quarters ; if I discovered the woman, on the other hand, she was not very likely to give me an affectionate reception, seeing that I found it inconvenient to keep sending her money for Jane's keep in the old days. The queer thing is, that everything turned out exactly the opposite of what I had expected. Mrs. Peckover had rather a sour face at first, but after a little talk she began to seem quite glad to see me. She put me into a room, undertook to board me for a while—till I find work, and I wonder when *that*'ll be ?—and blest if this strapping daughter of hers doesn't seem to have fallen in love with me from the first go off ! As for my girl, I'm told she was carried off by her grandfather, my old dad, three years ago, and where they went nobody knows. Very puzzling all this. How on earth came it that Mrs. Peckover kept the child so long, and didn't send her to the workhouse? If I'm to believe *her*, she took a motherly kindness for the poor brat. But that won't exactly go down with J. J. Snowdon ; he's seen a bit too much in his knocking about the world. Still, what if I'm making a mistake about the old woman ? There *are* some people do things of that sort; upon my soul, I've known people be kind even to me, without a chance of being paid back ! You may think you know a man or a woman, and then all at once they'll go and do something you'd have taken your davy couldn't possibly happen. I'd have sworn she was nothing but a skinflint and a lying old witch. And so she may be ; the chances are there's some game going on that I can't see through. Make inquiries? Why, so I have done, as far as I know how. I've only been able to hit on one person who knows anything about the matter, and he tells me it's true enough the girl was taken away about three years ago, but he's no idea where she went to. Surely the old man must be dead by now, though he *was* tough. Well, the fact of the matter is, I've got a good berth, and I'm a precious sight too lazy to go on the private detective job. Here's this girl Clem, the finest bit of flesh I've seen for a long time; I'm more than half a mind to see if she won't be fool enough to marry me. I'm not a bad-looking fellow, that's the truth, and she may have taken a real liking to me. Seems to me that I should have come in for a comfortable thing in my old age; if I haven't a daughter to provide for my needs, at all events I shall have a wife who can be persuaded into doing so. When the old woman gets out of the way I must have a little quiet talk with Clem.'

The opportunity he desired was not long in offering itself. Having made an excellent breakfast, he dragged his chair up to the fender again, and reached a pipe from the mantel-piece, where he had left it last night. Tobacco he carried loose in his waistcoat pocket; it came forth in the form of yellowish dust, intermingled with all sorts of alien scraps. When he had lit his pipe, he poised the chair on its hind-legs, clasped his hands over his bald crown, and continued his musing with an air of amiable calm. Smoke curled up from the corner of his loose lips, and occasionally, removing his pipe for an instant, he spat skilfully between the bars of the grate. Assured of his comfort, Mrs. Peckover said she must go and look after certain domestic duties. Her daughter had begun to clean some vegetables that would be cooked for dinner.

'How old may you be, Clem?' Mr. Snowdon inquired genially, when they had been alone together for a few minutes.

'What's that to you? Guess.'

'Why, let me see; you was not much more than a baby when I went away. You'll be eighteen or nineteen, I suppose.'

'Yes, I'm nineteen—last sixth of February. Pity you come too late to give me a birthday present, ain't it?'

'Ah! And who'd have thought you'd have grown up such a beauty! I say, Clem, how many of the young chaps about here have been wanting to marry you, eh?'

'A dozen or two, I dessay,' Clem replied, shrugging her shoulders scornfully.

Mr. Snowdon laughed, and then spat into the fire.

'Tell me about some o' them, will you? Who is it you're keeping company with now?'

'Who, indeed? Why, there isn't one I'd look at! Several

of 'em's took to drinking 'cause I won't have nothing to do with 'em.'

This excited Mr. Snowdon's mirth in a high degree; he rolled on his chair, and almost pitched backwards.

'I suppose you give one or other a bit of encouragement now and then, just to make a fool of him, eh?'

'Course I do. There was Bob Hewett; he used to lodge here, but that was after your time. I kep' him off an' on till he couldn't bear it no longer; then he went an' married a common slut of a thing, just because he thought it 'ud make me mad. Ha, ha! I believe he'd give her poison an' risk it any day, if only I promised to marry him afterwards. Then there was a feller called Jeck Bartley. I set him an' Bob fightin' one Bank-holiday—you should a' seen 'em go at it! Jack went an' got married a year ago to a girl called Suke Jollop; her mother forced him. How I did laugh! Last Christmas Day they smashed up their 'ome an' threw the bits out into the street. Jack got one of his eyes knocked out—I thought I should a' died o' laughin' when I saw him next mornin'.'

The hearer became uproarious in merriment.

'Tell you what it is, Clem,' he cried, 'you're something like a girl! Darn me if I don't like you! I say, I wonder what my daughter's grown up? Like her mother, I suppose. You an' she was sort of sisters, wasn't you?'

He observed her closely. Clem laughed and shrugged her shoulders.

'Queer sort o' sisters. She was a bit too quiet-like for me. There never was no fun in her.'

'Aye, like her mother. And where did you say she went to with the old man?'

'Where she went to?' repeated Clem, regarding him steadily with her big eyes, 'I never said nothing about it, 'cause I didn't know.'

'Well, I shan't cry about her, and I don't suppose she misses me much, wherever she is. All the same, Clem, I'm a domesticated sort of man; you can see that, can't you? I shouldn't wonder if I marry again one of these first days. Just tell me where to find a girl of the right sort. I dare say you know heaps.'

'Dessay I do. What sort do you want?'

'Oh, a littlish girl—yellow hair, you know—one of them that look as if they didn't weigh half-a-stone.'

'I'll throw this parsnip at you, Mr. Snowdon!'

'What's up now. You don't call yourself littlish, do you?'

Clem snapped the small end off the vegetable she was paring, and aimed it at his head. He ducked just in time. Then there was an outburst of laughter from both.

'Say, Clem, you haven't got a glass of beer in the house?'

'You'll have to wait till openin' time,' replied the girl sourly, going away to the far end of the room.

'Have I offended you, Clem?'

'Offended, indeed! As if I cared what you say!'

'Do you care what I think?'

'Not I!'

'That means you do. Say, Clem, just come here; I've something to tell you.'

'You're a nuisance. Let me get on with my work, can't you?'

'No, I can't. You just come here. You'd better not give me the trouble of fetching you!'

The girl obeyed him. Her cheeks were very hot, and the danger-signal was flashing in her eyes. Ten minutes later she went upstairs, and had a vivacious dialogue of whispers with Mrs. Peckover.

CHAPTER XV

SUNLIGHT IN DREARY PLACES

AMONG the by-ways of Clerkenwell you might, with some difficulty, have discovered an establishment known in its neighbourhood as 'Whitehead's.' It was an artificial-flower factory, and the rooms of which it consisted were only to be reached by traversing a timber-yard, and then mounting a wooden staircase outside a saw-mill. Here at busy seasons worked some threescore women and girls, who, owing to the nature of their occupation, were spoken of by the jocose youth of the locality as 'Whitehead's pastepots.'

Naturally they varied much in age and aspect. There was the child who had newly left school, and was now invited to consider the question of how to keep herself alive; there was the woman of uncertain age, who had spent long years of long days in the atmosphere of workrooms, and showed the re-

sult in her parchmenty cheek and lack-lustre eye; and between
these extremes came all the various types of the London crafts-
girl: she who is young enough to hope that disappointments
may yet be made up for by the future; she who is already
tasting such scanty good as life had in store for her; she who
has outlived her illusions and no longer cares to look beyond
the close of the week. If regularly engaged as time-workers,[*]
they made themselves easy in the prospect of wages that
allowed them to sleep under a roof and eat at certain intervals
of the day; if employed on piece-work they might at any
moment find themselves wageless, but this, being a familiar
state of things, did not trouble them. With few exceptions,
they were clad neatly; on the whole, they plied their task in
wonderful contentment. The general tone of conversation
among them was not high; moralists unfamiliar with the ways
of the nether world would probably have applied a term other
than negative to the laughing discussions which now and then
enlivened this or that group; but it was very seldom indeed
that a child newly arriving heard anything with which she
was not already perfectly familiar.

One afternoon at the end of May there penetrated into the
largest of the workrooms that rarest of visitants, a stray sunbeam. Only if the sun happened to shine at given moments
could any of its light fall directly into the room I speak of;
this afternoon, however, all circumstances were favourable,
and behold the floor chequered with uncertain gleam. The
workers were arranged in groups of three, called 'parties,'
consisting of a learner, an improver, and a hand. All sat
with sleeves pushed up to their elbows, and had a habit of
rocking to and fro as they plied their mechanical industry.
Owing to the movement of a cloud, the sunlight spread gradually towards one of these groups; it touched the skirt, the
arms, the head of one of the girls, who, as if gladdened by the
kindly warmth, looked round and smiled. A smile you would
have been pleased to observe—unconscious, gently thoughtful,
rich in possibilities of happiness. She was quite a young girl,
certainly not seventeen, and wore a smooth grey dress, with a
white linen collar; her brown hair was closely plaited, her
head well-shaped, the bend of her neck very graceful. From
her bare arms it could be seen that she was anything but
robustly made, yet her general appearance was not one of ill-
health, and she held herself, even thus late in the day, far
more uprightly than most of her companions. Had you

watched her for a while, you would have noticed that her eyes occasionally strayed beyond the work-table, and, perhaps unconsciously, fixed themselves for some moments on one or other of the girls near her; when she remembered herself and looked down again upon her task, there rose to her face a smile of the subtlest meaning, the outcome of busy reflection.

By her side was a little girl just beginning to learn the work, whose employment it was to paper wires and make 'centres.' This toil always results in blistered fingers, and frequent was the child's appeal to her neighbour for sympathy.

'It'll be easier soon,' said the latter, on one of these occasions, bending her head to speak in a low voice. 'You should have seen what blisters I had when I began.'

'It's all very well to say that. I can't do no more, so there! Oh, when'll it be five o'clock?'

'It's a quarter to. Try and go on, Annie.'

Five o'clock did come at length, and with it twenty minutes' rest for tea. The rule at Whitehead's was, that you could either bring your own tea, sugar, and eatables, or purchase them here from a forewoman; most of the workers chose to provide themselves. It was customary for each 'party' to club together, emptying their several contributions of tea out of little twists of newspaper into one teapot. Wholesome bustle and confusion succeeded to the former silence. One of the learners, whose turn it was to run on errands, was overwhelmed with commissions to a chandler's shop close by; a wry-faced, stupid little girl she was, and they called her, because of her slowness, the 'funeral horse.' She had strange habits, which made laughter for those who knew of them; for instance, it was her custom in the dinner-hour to go apart and eat her poor scraps on a doorstep close by a cook-shop; she confided to a companion that the odour of baked joints seemed to give her food a relish. From her present errand she returned with a strange variety of dainties—for it was early in the week, and the girls still had coppers in their pockets; for two or three she had purchased a farthing's-worth of jam, which she carried in paper. A bite of this and a taste of that rewarded her for her trouble.

The quiet-mannered girl whom we were observing took her cup of tea from the pot in which she had a share, and from her bag produced some folded pieces of bread and butter. She had begun her meal, when there came and sat down by her a young woman of very different appearance—our friend,

Miss Peckover. They were old acquaintances; but when we first saw them together it would have been difficult to imagine that they would ever sit and converse as at present, apparently in all friendliness. Strange to say, it was Clem who, during the past three years, had been the active one in seeking to obliterate disagreeable memories. The younger girl had never repelled her, but was long in overcoming the dread excited by Clem's proximity. Even now she never looked straight into Miss Peckover's face, as she did when speaking with others; there was reserve in her manner, reserve unmistakable, though clothed with her pleasant smile and amiable voice.

'I've got something to tell you, Jane,' Clem began, in a tone inaudible to those who were sitting near. 'Something as'll surprise you.'

'What is it, I wonder?'

'You must swear you won't tell nobody.'

Jane nodded. Then the other brought her head a little nearer, and whispered:

'I'm goin' to be married!'

'Are you really?'

'In a week. Who do you think it is? Somebody as you know of, but if you guessed till next Christmas you'd never come right.'

Nor had Clem any intention of revealing the name, but she laughed consumedly, as if her reticence covered the most amusing situation conceivable.

'It'll be the biggest surprise you ever had in your life. You've swore you won't speak about it. I don't think I shall come to work after this week—but you'll have to come an' see us. You'll promise to, won't you?'

Still convulsed with mirth, Clem went off to another part of the room. From Jane's countenance the look of amusement which she had perforce summoned soon passed; it was succeeded by a shadow almost of pain, and not till she had been at work again for nearly an hour was the former placidity restored to her.

When final release came, Jane was among the first to hasten down the wooden staircase and get clear of the timber-yard. By the direct way, it took her twenty minutes to walk from Whitehead's to her home in Hanover Street, but this evening she had an object in turning aside. The visit she wished to pay took her into a disagreeable quarter, a street of squalid houses, swarming with yet more squalid children. On all the doorsteps sat little girls, themselves only just out of infancy, nursing or neglecting bald, red-eyed, doughy-limbed abortions in every stage of babyhood, hapless spawn of diseased humanity, born to embitter and brutalise yet further the lot of those who unwillingly gave them life. With wide, pitiful eyes Jane looked at each group she passed. Three years ago she would have seen nothing but the ordinary and the inevitable in such spectacles, but since then her moral and intellectual being had grown on rare nourishment; there was indignation as well as heartache in the feeling with which she had learnt to regard the world of her familiarity. To enter the house at which she paused it was necessary to squeeze through a conglomerate of dirty little bodies. At the head of the first flight of stairs she came upon a girl sitting in a weary attitude on the top step and beating the wood listlessly with the last remnant of a hearth-brush; on her lap was one more specimen of the infinitely-multiplied baby, and a child of two years sprawled behind her on the landing.

'Waiting for him to come home, Pennyloaf?' said Jane.

'Oh, is that you, Miss Snowdon!' exclaimed the other, returning to consciousness and manifesting some shame at being discovered in this position. Hastily she drew together the front of her dress, which for the baby's sake had been wide open, and rose to her feet. Pennyloaf was not a bit more womanly in figure than on the day of her marriage; her voice was still an immature treble; the same rueful irresponsibility marked her features; but all her poor prettiness was wasted under the disfigurement of pains and cares. Incongruously enough, she wore a gown of bright-patterned calico, and about her neck had a collar of pretentious lace; her hair was dressed as if for a holiday, and a daub recently made on her cheeks by the baby's fingers lent emphasis to the fact that she had but a little while ago washed herself with much care.

'I can't stop,' said Jane, 'but I thought I'd just look in and speak a word. How have you been getting on?'

'Oh, do come in for just a minute!' pleaded Pennyloaf, moving backwards to an open door, whither Jane followed. They entered a room—much like other rooms that we have looked into from time to time. Following the nomadic custom of their kind, Bob Hewett and his wife had lived in six or seven different lodgings since their honeymoon in Shooter's Gardens. Mrs. Candy first of all made a change necessary, as might have been anticipated, and the restlessness of domestic ill-being subsequently drove them from place to place. 'Come in 'ere, Johnny,' she called to the child lying on the landing. 'What's the good o' washin' you, I'd like to know? Just see, Miss Snowdon, he's made his face all white with the milk as the boy spilt on the stairs! Take this brush an' play with it, do! I *can't* keep 'em clean, Miss Snowdon, so it's no use talkin'.'

'Are you going somewhere to-night?' Jane inquired, with a glance at the strange costume.

Pennyloaf looked up and down in a shamefaced way.

'I only did it just because I thought he might like to see me. He promised me faithful as he'd come 'ome to-night, and I thought—it's only somethink as got into my 'ed to-day, Miss Snowdon.'

'But hasn't he been coming home since I saw you last?'

'He did just once, an' then it was all the old ways again. I did what you told me; I did, as sure as I'm a-standin' 'ere! I made the room so clean you wouldn't have believed; I scrubbed the floor an' the table, an' I washed the winders —you can see they ain't dirty yet. An' he'd never a' paid a bit o' notice if I hadn't told him. He was jolly enough for one night, just like he can be when he likes. But I knew as it wouldn't last, an' the next night he was off with a lot o' fellers an' girls, same as ever. I didn't make no row when he came 'ome; I wish I may die if I said a word to set his back up! An' I've gone on just the same all the week; we haven't had not the least bit of a row; so you see I kep' my promise. But it's no good; he won't come 'ome; he's always got fellers an' girls to go round with. He took his hoath as he'd come back to-night, an' then it come into my 'ed as I'd put my best things on, just to—you know what I mean, Miss Snowdon. But he won't come before twelve o'clock : I know he won't. An' I get that low sittin' 'ere, you can't think! I can't go nowhere, because o' the children. If it wasn't for them I could go to work again, an' I'd be that glad; I feel as if my 'ed would drop off sometimes! I *ham* so glad you just come in!'

Jane had tried so many forms of encouragement, of consolation, on previous occasions that she knew not how to repeat herself. She was ashamed to speak words which sounded so hollow and profitless. This silence was only too signifi-

cant to Pennyloaf, and in a moment she exclaimed with
querulous energy :

'I know what'll be the hend of it! I'll go an' do like
mother does—I will! I will! I'll put my ring away, an' I'll go
an' sit all night in the public-'ouse! It's what all the others
does, an' I'll do the same. I often feel I'm a fool to go on
like this. I don't know what I live for. P'r'aps he'll be
sorry when I get run in like mother.'

'Don't talk like that, Pennyloaf!' cried Jane, stamping
her foot. (It was odd how completely difference of character
had reversed their natural relations to each other; Pennyloaf
was the child, Jane the mature woman.) 'You know better,
and you've no right to give way to such thoughts. I was
going to say I'd come and be with you all Saturday afternoon,
but I don't know whether I shall now. And I'd been thinking you might like to come and see me on Sunday, but I can't
have people that go to the public-house, so we won't say anything more about it. I shall have to be off; good-bye!'

She stepped to the door.

'Miss Snowdon!'

Jane turned, and after an instant of mock severity, broke
into a laugh which seemed to fill the wretched den with sunlight. Words, too, she found ; words of soothing influence
such as leap from the heart to the tongue in spite of the heavy
thoughts that try to check them. Pennyloaf was learning to
depend upon these words for strength in her desolation. They
did not excite her to much hopefulness, but there was a sustaining power in their sweet sincerity which made all the
difference between despair tending to evil and the sigh of
renewed effort. 'I don't care,' Pennyloaf had got into the
habit of thinking, after her friend's departure, 'I won't give
up as long as she looks in now and then.'

Out from the swarm of babies Jane hurried homewards.
She had a reason for wishing to be back in good time to-night;
it was Wednesday, and on Wednesday evening there was wont
to come a visitor, who sat for a couple of hours in her grandfather's room and talked, talked—the most interesting talk
Jane had ever heard or could imagine. A latch-key admitted
her; she ran up to the second floor. A voice from the front-
room caught her ear; certainly not *his* voice—it was too
early—but that of some unusual visitor. She was on the
point of entering her own chamber, when the other door
opened, and somebody exclaimed, 'Ah, here she is!'

The speaker was an old gentleman, dressed in black, bald, with small and rather rugged features; his voice was pleasant. A gold chain and a bunch of seals shone against his waistcoat, also a pair of eye-glasses. A professional man, obviously. Jane remembered that she had seen him once before, about a year ago, when he had talked with her for a few minutes, very kindly.

' Will you come in here, Jane ? ' her grandfather's voice called to her.

Snowdon had changed much. Old age was heavy upon his shoulders, and had even produced a slight tremulousness in his hands; his voice told the same story of enfeeblement. Even more noticeable was the ageing of his countenance. Something more, however, than the progress of time seemed to be here at work. He looked strangely careworn; his forehead was set in lines of anxiety; his mouth expressed a nervousness of which formerly there had been no trace. One would have said that some harassing preoccupation must have seized his mind. His eyes were no longer merely sad and absent, but restless with fatiguing thought. As Jane entered the room he fixed his gaze upon her—a gaze that appeared to reveal worrying apprehension.

' You remember Mr. Percival, Jane,' he said.

The old gentleman thus presented held out his hand with something of fatherly geniality.

' Miss Snowdon, I hope to have the pleasure of seeing you again before long, but just now I am carrying off your grandfather for a couple of hours, and indeed we mustn't linger that number of minutes. You look well, I think ? '

He stood and examined her intently, then cried :

' Come, my dear sir, come ! we shall be late.'

Snowdon was already prepared for walking. He spoke a few words to Jane, then followed Mr. Percival downstairs.

Flurried by the encounter, Jane stood looking about her. Then came a rush of disappointment as she reflected that the visitor of Wednesday evenings would call in vain. Hearing that her grandfather was absent, doubtless he would take his leave at once. Or, would he——

In a minute or two she ran downstairs to exchange a word with Mrs. Byass. On entering the kitchen she was surprised to see Bessie sitting idly by the fire. At this hour it was usual for Mr. Byass to have returned, and there was generally an uproar of laughing talk. This evening, dead silence, and a

noticeable something in the air which told of trouble. The
baby—of course a new baby—lay in a bassinette near its mother,
seemingly asleep ; the other child was sitting in a high chair
by the table, clattering ' bricks.'

Bessie did not even look round.

' Is Mr. Byass late ? ' inquired Jane, in an apprehensive
voice.

' He's somewhere in the house, I believe,' was the answer,
in monotone.

' Oh dear ! ' Jane recognised a situation which had already
come under her notice once or twice during the last six months.
She drew near, and asked in a low voice :

' What's happened, Mrs. Byass ? '

' He's a beast ! If he doesn't mind I shall go and leave
him. I mean it ! '

Bessie was in a genuine fit of sullenness. One of her
hands was clenched below her chin ; her pretty lips were not
pretty at all ; her brow was rumpled. Jane began to seek for
the cause of dissension, to put affectionate questions, to use
her voice soothingly.

' He's a beast ! ' was Bessie's reiterated observation ; but
by degrees she added phrases more explanatory. ' How can I
help it if he cuts himself when he's shaving ?—Serve him
right !—What for ? Why, for saying that babies was nothing
but a nuisance, and that *my* baby was the ugliest and noisiest ever
born ! '

' Did she cry in the night ? ' inquired Jane, with sympathy.

' Of course she did ! Hasn't she a right to ? '

' And then Mr. Byass cut himself with his razor ? '

' Yes. And he said it was because he was woke so often,
and it made him nervous, and his hand shook. And then I
told him he'd better cut himself on the other side, and it
wouldn't matter. And then he complained because he had to
wait for breakfast. And he said there'd been no comfort in
the house since we'd had children. And I cared nothing about
him, he said, and only about the baby and Ernest. And he
went on like a beast, as he is ! I hate him ! '

' Oh no, not a bit of it ! ' said Jane, seeing the opportunity
for a transition to jest.

' I do ! And you may go upstairs and tell him so.'

' All right ; I will.'

Jane ran upstairs and knocked at the door of the parlour.

A gruff voice bade her enter, but the room was nearly in darkness.

'Will you have a light, Mr. Byass?'

'No—thank you.'

Mr. Byass, Mrs. Byass says I'm to say she hates you.'

'All right. Tell her I've known it a long time. She needn't trouble about me; I'm going out to enjoy myself.'

Jane ran back to the kitchen.

'Mr. Byass says he's known it a long time,' she reported, with much gravity. 'And he's going out to enjoy himself.'

Bessie remained mute.

'What message shall I take back, Mrs. Byass?'

'Tell him if he dares to leave the house, I'll go to mother's the first thing to-morrow, and let them know how he's treating me.'

'Tell her,' was Mr. Byass's reply, 'that I don't see what it matters to her whether I'm at home or away. And tell her she's a cruel wife to me.'

Something like the sound of a snivel came out of the darkness as he concluded. Jane, in reporting his speech, added that she thought he was shedding tears. Thereupon Bessie gave a sob, quite in earnest.

'So am I,' she said chokingly. 'Go and tell him, Jane.'

'Mr. Byass, Mrs. Byass is crying,' whispered Jane at the parlour-door. 'Don't you think you'd better go downstairs?'

Hearing a movement, she ran to be out of the way. Samuel left the dark room, and with slow step descended to the kitchen. Then Jane knew that it was all right, and tripped up to her room humming a song of contentment.

Had she, then, wholly outgrown the bitter experiences of her childhood? Had the cruelty which tortured her during the years when the soul is being fashioned left upon her no brand of slavish vice, nor the baseness of those early associations affected her with any irremovable taint? As far as human observation could probe her, Jane Snowdon had no spot of uncleanness in her being; she had been rescued while it was yet time, and the subsequent period of fostering had enabled features of her character, which no one could have discerned in the helpless child, to expand with singular richness. Two effects of the time of her bondage were, however, clearly to be distinguished. Though nature had endowed her with a good intelligence, she could only with extreme labour acquire that elementary book-knowledge which vulgar children get easily enough; it seemed as if the bodily overstrain at a critical period of life had affected her memory, and her power of mental application generally. In spite of ceaseless endeavour, she could not yet spell words of the least difficulty; she could not do the easiest sums with accuracy; geographical names were her despair. The second point in which she had suffered harm was of more serious nature. She was subject to fits of hysteria, preceded and followed by the most painful collapse of that buoyant courage which was her supreme charm and the source of her influence. Without warning, an inexplicable terror would fall upon her; like the weakest child, she craved protection from a dread inspired solely by her imagination, and solace for an anguish of wretchedness to which she could give no form in words. Happily this illness afflicted her only at long intervals, and her steadily improving health gave warrant for hoping that in time it would altogether pass away.

Whenever an opportunity had offered for struggling successfully with some form of evil—were it poor Pennyloaf's dangerous despair, or the very human difficulties between Bessie and her husband—Jane lived at her highest reach of spiritual joy. For all that there was a disappointment on her mind, she felt this joy to-night, and went about her pursuits in happy self-absorption. So it befell that she did not hear a knock at the house-door. Mrs. Byass answered it, and not knowing that Mr. Snowdon was from home, bade his usual visitor go upstairs. The visitor did so, and announced his presence at the door of the room.

'Oh, Mr. Kirkwood,' said Jane, 'I'm so sorry, but grandfather had to go out with a gentleman.'

And she waited, looking at him, a gentle warmth on her face.

CHAPTER XVI

DIALOGUE AND COMMENT

'WILL it be late before he comes back?' asked Sidney, his smile of greeting shadowed with disappointment.

'Not later than half-past ten, he said.'

Sidney turned his face to the stairs. The homeward prospect was dreary after that glimpse of the familiar room through

the doorway. The breach of habit discomposed him, and
something more positive strengthened his reluctance to be
gone. It was not his custom to hang in hesitancy and court
chance by indirectness of speech; recognising and admitting
his motives, he said simply :

'I should like to stay a little, if you will let me—if I
shan't be in your way?'

'Oh no! Please come in. I'm only sewing.'

There were two round-backed wooden chairs in the room;
one stood on each side of the fireplace, and between them, beside the table, Jane always had her place on a small chair of
the ordinary comfortless kind. She seated herself as usual,
and Sidney took his familiar position, with the vacant chair
opposite. Snowdon and he were accustomed to smoke their
pipes whilst conversing, but this evening Sidney dispensed
with tobacco.

It was very quiet here. On the floor below dwelt at present two sisters who kept themselves alive (it is quite inac-
curate to use any other phrase in such instances) by doing all
manner of skilful needlework; they were middle-aged women,
gentle-natured, and so thoroughly subdued to the hopelessness
of their lot that scarcely ever could even their footfall be
heard as they went up and down stairs; their voices were
always sunk to a soft murmur. Just now no infant wailing
came from the Byasses' regions. Kirkwood enjoyed a sense
of restfulness, intenser, perhaps, for the momentary disappointment he had encountered. He had no desire to talk;
enough for a few minutes to sit and watch Jane's hand as it
moved backwards and forwards with the needle.

'I went to see Pennyloaf as I came back from work,' Jane
said at length, just looking up.

'Did you ? Do things seem to be any better?'

'Not much, I'm afraid. Mr. Kirkwood, don't you think you
might do something ? If you tried again with her husband ? '

'The fact is,' replied Sidney, 'I'm so afraid of doing more
harm than good.'

'You think—— But then perhaps that's just what *I'm*
doing?'

Jane let her hand fall on the sewing and regarded him
anxiously.

'No, no! I'm quite sure *you* can't do harm. Pennyloaf
can get nothing but good from having you as a friend. She
likes you; she misses you when you happen not to have seen her

for a few days. I'm sorry to say it's quite a different thing with Bob and me. We're friendly enough—as friendly as ever—but I haven't a scrap of influence with him like you have with his wife. It was all very well to get hold of him once, and try to make him understand, in a half-joking way, that he wasn't behaving as well as he might. He didn't take it amiss —just that once. But you can't think how difficult it is for one man to begin preaching to another. The natural thought is: Mind your own business. If I was the parson of the parish——'

He paused, and in the same instant their eyes met. The suggestion was irresistible; Jane began to laugh merrily.

What sweet laughter it was! How unlike the shrill discord whereby the ordinary workgirl expresses her foolish mirth! For years Sidney Kirkwood had been unused to utter any sound of merriment; even his smiling was done sadly. But of late he had grown conscious of the element of joy in Jane's character, had accustomed himself to look for its manifestations—to observe the brightening of her eyes which foretold a smile, the moving of her lips which suggested inward laughter—and he knew that herein, as in many another matter, a profound sympathy was transforming him. Sorrow such as he had suffered will leave its mark upon the countenance long after time has done its kindly healing, and in Sidney's case there was more than the mere personal affliction tending to confirm his life in sadness. With the ripening of his intellect, he saw only more and more reason to condemn and execrate those social disorders of which his own wretched experience was but an illustration. From the first, his friendship with Snowdon had exercised upon him a subduing influence; the old man was stern enough in his criticism of society, but he did not belong to the same school as John Hewett, and the sober authority of his character made appeal to much in Sidney that had found no satisfaction amid the uproar of Clerkenwell Green. For all that, Kirkwood could not become other than himself; his vehemence was moderated, but he never affected to be at one with Snowdon in that grave enthusiasm of far-off hope which at times made the old man's speech that of an exhorting prophet. Their natural parts were reversed; the young eyes declared that they could see nothing but an horizon of blackest cloud, whilst those enfeebled by years bore ceaseless witness to the raying forth of dawn.

And so it was with a sensation of surprise that Sidney first became aware of light-heartedness in the young girl who was a silent hearer of so many lugubrious discussions. Ridiculous as it may sound—as Sidney felt it to be—he almost resented this evidence of happiness; to him, only just recovering from a shock which would leave its mark upon his life to the end, his youth wronged by bitter necessities, forced into brooding over problems of ill when nature would have bidden him enjoy, it seemed for the moment a sign of shallowness that Jane could look and speak cheerfully. This extreme of morbid feeling proved its own cure; even in reflecting upon it, Sidney was constrained to laugh contemptuously at himself. And therewith opened for him a new world of thought. He began to study the girl. Of course he had already occupied himself much with the peculiarities of her position, but of Jane herself he knew very little; she was still, in his imagination, the fearful and miserable child over whose shoulders he had thrown his coat one bitter night; his impulse towards her was one of compassion merely, justified now by what he heard of her mental slowness, her bodily sufferings. It would take very long to analyse the process whereby this mode of feeling was changed, until it became the sense of ever-deepening sympathy which so possessed him this evening. Little by little Jane's happiness justified itself to him, and in so doing began subtly to modify his own temper. With wonder he recognised that the poor little serf of former days had been meant by nature for one of the most joyous among children. What must that heart have suffered, so scorned and trampled upon! But now that the days of misery were over, behold nature having its way after all. If the thousands are never rescued from oppression, if they perish abortive in their wretchedness, is that a reason for refusing to rejoice with the one whom fate has blest? Sidney knew too much of Jane by this time to judge her shallow-hearted. This instinct of gladness had a very different significance from the animal vitality which prompted the constant laughter of Bessie Byass; it was but one manifestation of a moral force which made itself nobly felt in many another way. In himself Sidney was experiencing its pure effects, and it was owing to his conviction of Jane's power for good that he had made her acquainted with Bob Hewett's wife. Snowdon warmly approved of this; the suggestion led him to speak expressly of Jane, a thing he very seldom did, and to utter a strong wish that she should begin to concern herself with the sorrows she might in some measure relieve.

Sidney joined in the laughter he had excited by picturing himself the parson of the parish. But the topic under discussion was a serious one, and Jane speedily recovered her gravity.

'Yes, I see how hard it is,' she said. 'But it's a cruel thing for him to neglect poor Pennyloaf as he does. She never gave him any cause.'

'Not knowingly, I quite believe,' replied Kirkwood. 'But what a miserable home it is!'

'Yes.' Jane shook her head. 'She doesn't seem to know how to keep things in order. She doesn't seem even to understand me when I try to show her how it might be different.'

'There's the root of the trouble, Jane. What chance had Pennyloaf of ever learning how to keep a decent home, and bring up her children properly? How was *she* brought up? The wonder is that there's so much downright good in her; I feel the same wonder about people every day. Suppose Pennyloaf behaved as badly as her mother does, who on earth would have the right to blame her? But we can't expect miracles; so long as she lives decently, it's the most that can be looked for. And there you are; that isn't enough to keep a fellow like Bob Hewett in order. I doubt whether any wife would manage it, but as for poor Pennyloaf——'

'I shall speak to him myself,' said Jane quietly.

'Do! There's much more hope in that than in anything I could say. Bob isn't a bad fellow; the worst thing I know of him is his conceit. He's good-looking, and he's clever in all sorts of ways, and unfortunately he can't think of anything but his own merits. Of course he'd no business to marry at all whilst he was nothing but a boy.'

Jane plied her needle, musing.

'Do you know whether he ever goes to see his father?' Sidney inquired presently.

'No, I don't,' Jane answered, looking at him, but immediately dropping her eyes.

'If he doesn't I should think worse of him. Nobody ever had a kinder father, and there's many a reason why he should be careful to pay the debt he owes.'

Jane waited a moment, then again raised her eyes to him. It seemed as though she would ask a question, and Sidney's grave attentiveness indicated a surmise of what she was about to say. But her thought remained unuttered, and there was a prolongation of silence.

Of course they were both thinking of Clara. That name had never been spoken by either of them in the other's presence, but as often as conversation turned upon the Hewetts, it was impossible for them not to supplement their spoken words by a silent colloquy of which Clara was the subject. From her grandfather Jane knew that, to this day, nothing had been heard of Hewett's daughter; what people said at the time of the girl's disappearance she had learned fully enough from Clem Peckover, who even yet found it pleasant to revive the scandal, and by contemptuous comments revenge herself for Clara's haughty usage in old days. Time had not impaired Jane's vivid recollection of that Bank-holiday morning when she herself was the first to make it known that Clara had gone away. Many a time since then she had visited the street whither Snowdon led her—had turned aside from her wonted paths in the thought that it was not impossible she might meet Clara, though whether with more hope or fear of such a meeting she could not have said. When two years had gone by, her grandfather one day led the talk to that subject; he was then beginning to change in certain respects the tone he had hitherto used with her, and to address her as one who had outgrown childhood. He explained to her how it came about that Sidney could no longer be even on terms of acquaintance with John Hewett. The conversation originated in Jane's bringing the news that Hewett and his family had at length left Mrs. Peckover's house. For two years things had gone miserably with them, their only piece of good fortune being the death of the youngest child. John was confirmed in a habit of drinking. Not that he had become a brutal sot ; sometimes for as much as a month he would keep sober, and even when he gave way to temptation he never behaved with violence to his wife and children. Still, the character of his life had once more suffered a degradation, and he possessed no friends who could be of the least use to him. Snowdon, for some reason of his own, maintained a slight intercourse with the Peckovers, and through them he endeavoured to establish an intimacy with Hewett; but the project utterly failed. Probably on Kirkwood's account, John met the old man's advances with something more than coldness. Sternly he had forbidden his wife and the little ones to exchange a word of any kind with Sidney, or with any friend of his.   He appeared to nourish incessantly the bitter resentment to which he gave expression when Sidney and he last met.

There was no topic on which Sidney was more desirous of speaking with Jane than this which now occupied both their minds. How far she understood Clara's story, and his part in it, he had no knowledge; for between Snowdon and himself there had long been absolute silence on that matter. It was not improbable that Jane had been instructed in the truth ; he hoped she had not been left to gather what she could from Clem Peckover's gossip. Yet the difficulty with which he found himself beset, now that an obvious opportunity offered for frank speech, was so great that, after a few struggles, he fell back on the reflection with which he was wont to soothe himself : Jane was still so young, and the progress of time, by confirming her knowledge of him, would make it all the simpler to explain the miserable past. Had he, in fact, any right to relate this story, to seek her sympathy in that direct way ? It was one aspect of a very grave question which occupied more and more of Sidney's thought.

With an effort, he turned the dialogue into quite a new direction, and Jane, though a little absent for some minutes, seemed at length to forget the abruptness of the change. Sidney had of late been resuming his old interest in pencil-work ; two or three of his drawings hung on these walls, and he spoke of making new sketches when he next went into the country. Years ago, one of his favourite excursions—of the longer ones which he now and then allowed himself—was to Danbury Hill, some five miles to the east of Chelmsford, one of the few pieces of rising ground in Essex, famous for its view over Maldon and the estuary of the Blackwater. Thither Snowdon and Jane accompanied him during the last summer but one, and the former found so much pleasure in the place that he took lodgings with certain old friends of Sidney's, and gave his granddaughter a week of healthful holiday. In the summer that followed, the lodgings were again taken for a week, and this year the same expedition was in view. Sidney had as good as promised that he would join his friends for the whole time of their absence, and now he talked with Jane of memories and anticipations. Neither was sensible how the quarters and the half-hours went by in such chatting. Sidney abandoned himself to the enjoyment of peace such as he had never known save in this room, to a delicious restfulness such as was always inspired in him by the girl's gentle voice, by her laughter, by her occasional quiet movements. The same influence was affecting his whole life. To Jane he owed the gradual transition from tumultuous politics and social bitterness to the mood which could find pleasure as of old in nature and art. This was his truer self, emancipated from the distorting effect of the evil amid which he perforce lived. He was recovering somewhat of his spontaneous boyhood; at the same time, reaching after a new ideal of existence which only ripened manhood could appreciate.

Snowdon returned at eleven; it alarmed Sidney to find how late he had allowed himself to remain, and he began shaping apologies. But the old man had nothing but the familiar smile and friendly words.

'Haven't you given Mr. Kirkwood any supper?' he asked of Jane, looking at the table.

'I really forgot all about it, grandfather,' was the laughing reply.

Then Snowdon laughed, and Sidney joined in the merriment; but he would not be persuaded to stay longer.

CHAPTER XVII

CLEM MAKES A DISCLOSURE

WHEN Miss Peckover suggested to her affianced that their wedding might as well take place at the registry-office, seeing that there would then be no need to go to expense in the article of costume, Mr. Snowdon readily assented; at the same time it gave him new matter for speculation. Clem was not exactly the kind of girl to relinquish without good reason that public ceremony which is the dearest of all possible ceremonies to women least capable of reverencing its significance. Every day made it more obvious that the Peckovers desired to keep this marriage a secret until it was accomplished. In one way only could Joseph James account for the mystery running through the whole affair; it must be that Miss Peckover had indiscretions to conceal, certain points in her history with which she feared lest her bridegroom should be made acquainted by envious neighbours. The thought had no effect upon Mr. Snowdon save to excite his mirth; his attitude with

regard to such possibilities was that of a philosopher. The
views with which he was entering upon this alliance were so
beautifully simple that he really did not find it worth while
to puzzle further as soon as the plausible solution of his difficulties had presented itself. Should he hereafter discover
that something unforeseen perturbed the smooth flow of life
to which he looked forward, nothing could be easier than his
remedy; the world is wide, and a cosmopolitan does not attach
undue importance to a marriage contracted in one of its somewhat numerous parishes. In any case he would have found
the temporary harbour of refuge which stress of weather
had made necessary. He surrendered himself to the pleasant
tickling of his vanity which was an immediate result of the
adventure. For, whatever Clem might be hiding, it seemed
to him beyond doubt that she was genuinely attracted by his
personal qualities. Her demonstrations were not extravagant,
but in one noteworthy respect she seemed to give evidence of
a sensibility so little in keeping with her general character
that it was only to be explained as the result of a strong
passion. In conversing with him she at times displayed a
singular timidity, a nervousness, a self-subdual surprisingly
unlike anything that could be expected from her. It was true
that at other moments her lover caught a gleam in her eyes,
a movement of her lips, expressive of anything rather than
diffidence, and tending to confirm his view of her as a cunning
as well as fierce animal, but the look and tone of subjugation
came often enough to make their impression predominant.
One would have said that she suffered from jealous fears which
for some reason she did not venture to utter. Now and then
he surprised her gazing at him as if in troubled apprehension,
the effect of which upon Mr. Snowdon was perhaps more
flattering than any other look.

'What's up, Clem?' he inquired, on one of these occasions.
'Are you wondering whether I shall cut and leave you when
we've had time to get tired of each other?'

Her face was transformed; she looked at him for an instant
with fierce suspicion, then laughed disagreeably.

'We'll see about that,' was her answer, with a movement
of the head and shoulders strongly reminding one of a lithe
beast about to spring.

The necessary delay passed without accident. As the morning of the marriage approached there was, however, a per-
ceptible increase of nervous restlessness in Clem. She had

given up her work at Whitehead's, and contrived to keep her future husband within sight nearly all day long. Joseph James found nothing particularly irksome in this, for beer and tobacco were supplied him *ad libitum*,* and a succession of appetising meals made the underground kitchen a place of the pleasantest associations. A loan from Mrs. Peckover had enabled him to renew his wardrobe. When the last night arrived, Clem and her mother sat conversing to a late hour, their voices again cautiously subdued. A point had been for some days at issue between them, and decision was now imperative.

'It's you as started the job,' Clem observed with emphasis, 'an' it's you as'll have to finish it.'

'And who gets most out of it, I'd like to know ?' replied her mother. 'Don't be such a fool! Can't you see as it'll come easier from you? A nice thing for his mother-in-law to tell him! If you don't like to do it the first day, then leave it to the second, or third. But if you take my advice, you'll get it over the next morning.'

'You'll have to do it yourself,' Clem repeated stubbornly, propping her chin upon her fists.

'Well, I never thought as you was such a frightened babby! Frightened of a feller like him! I'd be ashamed o' myself!'

'Who's frightened? Hold your row !'

'Why, you are; what else ?'

'I ain't!'

'You are !'

'I ain't! You'd better not make me mad, or I'll tell him before, just to spite you.'

'Spite *me*, you cat! What difference 'll it make to me ? I'll tell you what: I've a jolly good mind to tell him myself beforehand, and then we'll see who's spited.'

In the end Clem yielded, shrugging her shoulders defiantly.

'I'll have a kitchen-knife near by when I tell him,' she remarked with decision. 'If he lays a hand on me I'll cut his face open, an' chance it !'

Mrs. Peckover smiled with tender motherly deprecation of such extreme measures. But Clem repeated her threat, and there was something in her eyes which guaranteed the possibility of its fulfilment.

No personal acquaintance of either the Peckover or the

Snowdon family happened to glance over the list of names
which hung in the registrar's office during these weeks.   The
only interested person who had foreknowledge of Clem's wedding was Jane Snowdon, and Jane, though often puzzled in
thinking of the matter, kept her promise to speak of it to no
one.   It was imprudence in Clem to have run this risk, but
the joke was so rich that she could not deny herself its enjoyment ; she knew, moreover, that Jane was one of those
imbecile persons who scruple about breaking a pledge.   On
the eve of her wedding-day she met Jane as the latter came
from Whitehead's, and requested her to call in the Close next
Sunday morning at twelve o'clock.

' I want you to see my 'usband,' she said, grinning.   ' I'm
sure you'll like him.'

Jane promised to come.   On the next day, Saturday, Clem
entered the registry-office in a plain dress, and after a few
simple formalities came forth as Mrs. Snowdon ; her usual
high colour was a trifle diminished, and she kept glancing
at her husband from under nervously knitted brows.   Still
the great event was unknown to the inhabitants of the Close.
There was no feasting, and no wedding-journey ; for the present Mr. and Mrs. Snowdon would take possession of two
rooms on the first floor.

Twenty-four hours later, when the bells of St. James's
were ringing their melodies before service, Clem requested
her husband's attention to something of importance she had
to tell him.

Mr. Snowdon had just finished breakfast and was on the
point of lighting his pipe ; with the match burning down to
his fingers, he turned and regarded the speaker shrewdly.
Clem's face put it beyond question that at last she was about
to make a statement definitely bearing on the history of the
past month.   At this moment she was almost pale, and her
eyes avoided his.   She stood close to the table, and her right
hand rested near the bread-knife ; her left held a piece of
paper.

' What is it ? ' asked Joseph James mildly.   ' Go ahead,
Clem.'

' You ain't bad-tempered, are you ? You said you wasn't.'

' Not I ! Best-tempered feller you could have come across.
Look at me smiling.'

His grin was in a measure reassuring, but he had caught
sight of the piece of paper in her hand, and eyed it steadily.

'You know you played mother a trick a long time ago,' Clem pursued, 'when you went off an' left that child on her 'ands.'

'Hollo! What about that?'

'Well, it wouldn't be nothing but fair if someone was to go and play tricks with *you*—just to pay you off in a friendly sort o' way—see?'

Mr. Snowdon still smiled, but dubiously.

'Out with it!' he muttered. 'I'd have bet a trifle there was some game on. You're welcome, old girl. Out with it!'

'Did you know as I'd got a brother in 'Stralia—him as you used to know when you lived here before?'

'You said you didn't know where he was.'

'No more we do—not just now. But he wrote mother a letter about this time last year, an' there's something in it as I'd like you to see. You'd better read for yourself.'

Her husband laid down his pipe on the mantel-piece and began to cast his eye over the letter, which was much defaced by frequent foldings, and in any case would have been difficult to decipher, so vilely was it scrawled. But Mr. Snowdon's interest was strongly excited, and in a few moments he had made out the following communication:

'I don't begin with no deering, because it's a plaid out thing, and because I'm riting to too people at onse, both mother and Clem, and it's so long since I've had a pen in my hand I've harf forgot how to use it. If you think I'm making my pile, you think rong, so you've got no need to ask me when I'm going to send money home, like you did in the last letter. I jest keep myself and that's about all, because things ain't what they used to be in this busted up country. And that remminds me what it was as I ment to tell you when I cold get a bit of time to rite. Not so long ago, I met a chap as used to work for somebody called Snowdon, and from what I can make out it was Snowdon's brother at home, him as we use to ere so much about. He'd made his pile, this Snowdon, you bet, and Ned Williams says he died worth no end of thousands. Not so long before he died, his old farther from England came out to live with him; then Snowdon and a son as he had both got drownded going over a river at night. And Ned says as all the money went to the old bloak and to a brother in England, and that's what he herd when he was paid off. The old farther made traks very soon, and they sed he'd gone back to England. So it seams to me as you ouht to find Snowdon and make him pay up what he ose you. And I don't know as I've anything more to tell you both, ecsep I'm working at a place as I don't know how to spell, and it woldn't be no good if I did, because there's no saying were I shall be before you could rite back. So good luck to you both, from yours truly, W. P.'

In reading, Joseph James scratched his bald head thoughtfully. Before he had reached the end there were signs of emotion in his projecting lower lip. At length he regarded Clem, no longer smiling, but without any of the wrath she had anticipated.

'Ha, ha! This was your game, was it? Well, I don't object, old girl—so long as you tell me a bit more about it. Now there's no need for any more lies, perhaps you'll mention where the old fellow is.'

' He's livin' not so far away, an' Jane with him.'

Put somewhat at her ease, Clem drew her hand from the neighbourhood of the bread-knife, and detailed all she knew with regard to old Mr. Snowdon and his affairs. Her mother had from the first suspected that he possessed money, seeing that he paid, with very little demur, the sum she demanded for Jane's board and lodging. True, he went to live in poor lodgings, but that was doubtless a personal eccentricity. An important piece of evidence subsequently forthcoming was the fact that in sundry newspapers there appeared advertisements addressed to Joseph James Snowdon, requesting him to communicate with Messrs. Percival & Peel of Furnival's Inn, whereupon Mrs. Peckover made inquiries of the legal firm in question (by means of an anonymous letter), and received a simple assurance that Mr. Snowdon was being sought for his own advantage.

'You're cool hands, you and your mother,' observed Joseph James, with a certain involuntary admiration. 'This was not quite three years ago, you say; just when I was in America. Ha—hum! What I can't make out is, how the devil that brother of mine came to leave anything to me. We never did anything but curse each other from the time we were children to when we parted for good. And so the old man went out to Australia, did he? That's a rum affair, too; Mike and he could never get on together. Well, I suppose there's no mistake about it. I shouldn't much mind if there was, just to see the face *you'd* pull, young woman. On the whole, perhaps it's as well for you that I *am* fairly good-tempered—eh?'

Clem stood apart, smiling dubiously, now and then eyeing him askance. His last words once more put her on her guard; she moved towards the table again.

'Give me the address,' said her husband. 'I'll go and have a talk with my relations. What sort of a girl's Janey grown up—eh?'

'If you'll wait a bit, you can see for yourself. She's goin' to call here at twelve.'

'Oh, she is? I suppose you've arranged a pleasant little surprise for her? Well, I must say you're a cool hand, Clem. I shouldn't wonder if she's been in the house several times since I've been here?'

'No, she hasn't. It wouldn't have been safe, you see.'

'Give me the corkscrew, and I'll open this bottle of whisky. It takes it out of a fellow, this kind of thing. Here's to you, Mrs. Clem! Have a drink? All right; go downstairs and show your mother you're alive still; and let me know when Jane comes. I want to think a bit.'

When he had sat for a quarter of an hour in solitary reflection the door opened, and Clem led into the room a young girl, whose face expressed timid curiosity. Joseph James stood up, joined his hands under his coat-tail, and examined the stranger.

'Do you know who it is?' asked Clem of her companion.

'Your husband—but I don't know his name.'

'You ought to, it seems to me,' said Clem, giggling. 'Look at him.'

Jane tried to regard the man for a moment. Her cheeks flushed with confusion. Again she looked at him, and the colour rapidly faded. In her eyes was a strange light of painfully struggling recollection. She turned to Clem, and read her countenance with distress.

'Well, I'm quite sure I should never have known *you*, Janey,' said Snowdon, advancing. 'Don't you remember your father?'

Yes; as soon as consciousness could reconcile what seemed impossibilities Jane had remembered him. She was not seven years old when he forsook her, and a life of anything but orderly progress had told upon his features. Nevertheless Jane recognised the face she had never had cause to love, recognised yet more certainly the voice which carried her back

to childhood. But what did it all mean? The shock was
making her heart throb as it was wont to do before her fits of
illness. She looked about her with dazed eyes.

'Sit down, sit down,' said her father, not without a note
of genuine feeling. 'It's been a bit too much for you—like
something else was for me just now. Put some water in that
glass, Clem; a drop of this will do her good.'

The smell of what was offered her proved sufficient to
restore Jane; she shook her head and put the glass away.
After an uncomfortable silence, during which Joseph dragged
his feet about the floor, Clem remarked:

'He wants you to take him home to see your grandfather,
Jane. There's been reasons why he couldn't go before. Hadn't
you better go at once, Jo?'

Jane rose and waited whilst her father assumed his hat and
drew on a new pair of gloves. She could not look at either
husband or wife. Presently she found herself in the street,
walking without consciousness of things in the homeward
direction.

'You've grown up a very nice, modest girl, Jane,' was her
father's first observation. 'I can see your grandfather has
taken good care of you.'

He tried to speak as if the situation were perfectly simple.
Jane could find no reply.

'I thought it was better,' he continued, in the same matter-
of-fact voice, 'not to see either of you till this marriage of
mine was over. I've had a great deal of trouble in life—I'll
tell you all about it some day, my dear—and I wanted just to
settle myself before—I dare say you'll understand what I mean.
I suppose your grandfather has often spoken to you about
me?'

'Not very often, father,' was the murmured answer.

'Well, well; things'll soon be set right. I feel quite proud
of you, Janey; I do, indeed. And I suppose you just keep
house for him, eh?'

'I go to work as well.'

'What? You go to work? How's that, I wonder?'

'Didn't Miss Peckover tell you?'

Joseph laughed. The girl could not grasp all these astonishing facts at once, and the presence of her father made
her forget who Miss Peckover had become.

'You mean my wife, Janey! No, no; she didn't tell
me you went to work;—an accident. But I'm delighted you

and Clem are such good friends. Kind-hearted girl, isn't she?'

Jane whispered an assent.

'No doubt your grandfather often tells you about Australia, and your uncle that died there?'

'No, he never speaks of Australia. And I never heard of my uncle.'

'Indeed? Ha—hum!'

Joseph continued his examination all the way to Hanover Street, often expressing surprise, but never varying from the tone of affection and geniality. When they reached the door of the house he said:

'Just let me go into the room by myself. I think it'll be better. He's alone, isn't he?'

'Yes. I'll come up and show you the door.'

She did so, then turned aside into her own room, where she sat motionless for a long time.

CHAPTER XVIII

THE JOKE IS COMPLETED

MICHAEL SNOWDON—to distinguish the old man by name from the son who thus unexpectedly returned to him—professed no formal religion. He attended no Sunday service, nor had ever shown a wish that Jane should do so. We have seen that he used the Bible as a source of moral instruction; Jane and he still read passages together on a Sunday morning, but only such were chosen as had a purely human significance, and the comments to which they gave occasion never had any but a human bearing. Doubtless Jane reflected on these things; it was her grandfather's purpose to lead her to such reflection, without himself dogmatising on questions which from his own point of view were unimportant. That Jane should possess the religious spirit was a desire he never lost sight of; the single purpose of his life was involved therein; but formalism was against the bent of his nature. Born and bred amid the indifference of the London working classes, he was one of the very numerous thinking men who have never needed to cast aside a faith of childhood; from the dawn of rationality, they simply stand apart from all religious dogmas,

unable to understand the desire of such helps to conduct, untouched by spiritual trouble—as that phrase is commonly
interpreted. And it seemed that Jane closely resembled him
in this matter. Sensitive to every prompting of humanity,
instinct with moral earnestness, she betrayed no slightest
tendency to the religion of church, chapel, or street-corner.
A promenade of the Salvation Army half-puzzled, half-amused
her; she spoke of it altogether without intolerance, as did her
grandfather, but never dreamt that it was a phenomenon which
could gravely concern her. Prayers she had never said;
enough that her last thought before sleeping was one of kindness to those beings amid whom she lived her life, that on
awaking her mind turned most naturally to projects of duty
and helpfulness.

Excepting the Bible, Snowdon seldom made use of books
either for inquiry or amusement. Very imperfectly educated
in his youth, he had never found leisure for enriching his mind
in the ordinary way until it was too late; as an old man he
had so much occupation in his thoughts that the printed page
made little appeal to him. Till quite recently he had been in
the habit of walking for several hours daily, always choosing
poor districts; now that his bodily powers were sensibly failing
him, he passed more and more of his time in profound brooding,
so forgetful of external things that Jane, on her return from
work, had more than once been troubled by noticing that he
had taken no midday meal. It was in unconsciousness such
as this that he sat when his son Joseph, receiving no reply to
his knock, opened the door and entered; but that his eyes
were open, the posture of his body and the forward drooping
of his head would have made it appear that he slept. Joseph
stepped towards him, and at length the old man looked up.
He gazed at his visitor first unintelligently, then with wonder
and growing emotion.

'Jo?—Jo, at last? You were in my mind only a few
minutes ago, but I saw you as a boy.'

He rose from the chair and held out both his hands,
trembling more than they were wont to do.

'I almost wonder you knew me,' said Joseph. 'It's seventeen years since we saw each other. It was all Jane could do
to remember me.'

'Jane? Where have you seen her? At the house in the
Close?'

'Yes. It was me she went to see, but she didn't know it.

I've just been married to Miss Peckover. Sit down again, father, and let's talk over things quietly.'

'Married to Miss Peckover?' repeated the old man, as if making an effort to understand the words. 'Then why didn't you come here before?'

Joseph gave the explanation which he had already devised for the benefit of his daughter. His manner of speaking was meant to be very respectful, but it suggested that he looked upon the hearer as suffering from feebleness of mind, as well as of body. He supplemented his sentences with gestures and smiles, glancing about the room meantime with looks of much curiosity.

'So you've been living here a long time, father? It was uncommonly good of you to take care of my girl. I dare say you've got so used to having her by you, you wouldn't care for her to go away now?

'Do you wish to take Jane away?' Michael inquired gravely.

'No, no; not I! Why, it's nothing but her duty to keep you company and be what use she can. She's happy enough, that I can see. Well, well; I've gone through a good deal since the old days, father, and I'm not what you used to know me. I'm gladder than I can say to find you so easy in your old age. Neither Mike nor me did our duty by you, that's only too sure. I wish I could have the time back again; but what's the good of that? Can you tell me anything about Mike?'

'Yes. He died in Australia, about four years ago.'

'Did he now? Well, I've been in America, but I never got so far as Australia. So Mike's dead, is he? I hope he had better luck than me.'

The old man did not cease from examining his son's countenance.

'What is your position, at present?' he asked, after a pause. 'You don't look unprosperous.'

'Nothing to boast of, father. I've gone through all kinds of trades. In the States I both made and lost money. I invented a new method of nickel-plating, but it did me no good, and then I gave up that line altogether. Since I've been back in England—two years about—I've mostly gone in for canvassing, advertising agencies, and that kind of thing. I make an honest living, and that's about all. But I shouldn't wonder if things go a bit better now; I feel as if I was settled at last.

What with having a home of my own, and you and Janey near at hand—— You won't mind if I come and see you both now and then?'

'I shall hope to see you often,' replied the other, still keeping his grave face and tone. 'It's been my strong desire that we might come together again, and I've done the best I could to find you. But, as you said, we've been parted for a very long time, and it isn't in a day that we can come to understand each other. These seventeen years have made an old man of me, Jo; I think and speak and act slowly:—better for us all if I had learned to do so long ago! Your coming was unexpected; I shall need a little time to get used to the change it makes.'

'To be sure; that's true enough. Plenty of time to talk over things. As far as I'm concerned, father, the less said about bygones the better; it's the future that I care about now. I want to put things right between us—as they ought to be between father and son. You understand me, I hope?'

Michael nodded, keeping his eyes upon the ground. Again there was a silence, then Joseph said that if Jane would come in and speak a few words—so as to make things home-like— it would be time for him to take his leave for the present. At her grandfather's summons Jane entered the room. She was still oppressed by the strangeness of her position, and with difficulty took part in the colloquy. Joseph, still touching the note of humility in his talk, eyed his relatives alternately, and exhibited reluctance to quit them.

When he returned to the Close, it was with a face expressing dissatisfaction. Clem's eager inquiries he met at first with an ill-tempered phrase or two, which informed her of nothing; but when dinner was over he allowed himself to be drawn into a confidential talk, in which Mrs. Peckover took part. The old man, he remarked, was devilish close; it looked as if 'some game was on.' Mrs. Peckover ridiculed this remark; of course there was a game on; she spoke of Sidney Kirkwood, the influence he had obtained over Snowdon, the designs he was obviously pursuing. If Joseph thought he would recover his rights, at this time of day, save by direct measures, it only proved how needful it was for him to be instructed by shrewd people. The old man was a hard nut to crack; why he lived in Hanover Street, and sent Jane to work, when it was certain that he had wealth at command, Mrs. Peckover could not pretend to explain, but in all probability he found a pleasure in accumu-

lating money, and was abetted therein by Sidney Kirkwood.
Clem could bear witness that Jane always seemed to have
secrets to hide ; nevertheless a good deal of information had
been extracted from the girl during the last year or so, and it
all went to confirm the views which Mrs. Peckover now put
forth. After long discussion, it was resolved that Joseph
should call upon the lawyers whose names had appeared in
the advertisement addressed 'to himself. If he was met with
any shuffling, or if they merely referred him to his father, the
next step would be plain enough.

Clem began to exhibit sullenness ; her words were few,
and it was fortunate for Joseph that he could oppose a philo-
sophical indifference to the trouble with which his honeymoon
was threatened. As early as possible on Monday morning he
ascended the stairs of a building in Furnival's Inn and discovered the office of Messrs. Percival and Peel. He was hesitating whether to knock or simply turn the handle, when a
man came up to the same door, with the quick step of one at
home in the place.

'Business with us ? ' inquired the newcomer, as Joseph
drew back.

They looked at each other. He who had spoken was comparatively a young man, dressed with much propriety, gravely
polite in manner.

'Ha! How do you do ? ' exclaimed Snowdon, with embarrassment, and in an undertone. ' I wasn't expecting——'

The recognition was mutual, and whilst Joseph, though
disconcerted, expressed his feelings in a familiar smile, the
other cast a quick glance of uneasiness towards the stairs, his
mouth compressed, his eyebrows twitching a little.

'Business with Mr. Percival ? ' he inquired confidentially,
but without Joseph's familiar accentuation.

'Yes. That is—— Is he here ? '

'Won't be for another hour. Anything I could see about
for you ? '

Joseph moved in uncertainty, debating with himself. Their
eyes met again.

'Well, we might have a word or two about it,' he said.
'Better meet somewhere else, perhaps ? '

'Could you be at the top of Chancery Lane at six o'clock ? '

With a look of mutual understanding, they parted. Joseph
went home, and explained that, to his surprise, he had found
an old acquaintance at the lawyer's office, a man named

Scawthorne, whom he was going to see in private before
having an interview with the lawyer himself. At six o'clock
the appointed meeting took place, and from Chancery Lane
the pair walked to a quiet house of refreshment in the vicinity
of Lincoln's Inn Fields. On the way they exchanged a few
insignificant remarks, having reference to a former intimacy
and a period during which they had not come across each
other. Established in a semi-private room, with a modest
stimulant to aid conversation, they became more at ease; Mr.
Scawthorne allowed himself a discreet smile, and Joseph,
fingering his glass, broached the matter at issue with a cautious
question.

'Do you know anything of a man called Snowdon?'

'What Snowdon?'

'Joseph James Snowdon—a friend of mine. Your people
advertised for him about three years ago. Perhaps you haven't
been at the office as long as that?'

'Oh yes. I remember the name. What about him?'

'Your people wanted to find him—something to his advantage. Do you happen to know whether it's any use his
coming forward now?'

Mr. Scawthorne was not distinguished by directness of
gaze. He had handsome features, and a not unpleasant cast
of countenance, but something, possibly the habit of professional prudence, made his regard coldly, fitfully, absently observant. It was markedly so as he turned his face towards
Joseph whilst the latter was speaking. After a moment's
silence he remarked, without emphasis:

'A relative of yours, you said?'

'No, I said a friend—intimate friend. Polkenhorne knows
him too.'

'Does he? I haven't seen Polkenhorne for a long
time.'

'You don't care to talk about the business? Perhaps
you'd better introduce me to Mr. Percival.'

'By the name of Camden?'

'Hang it! I may as well tell you at once. Snowdon is
my own name.'

'Indeed? And how am I to be sure of that?'

'Come and see me where I'm living, in Clerkenwell Close,
and then make inquiries of my father, in Hanover Street,
Islington. There's no reason now for keeping up the old
name—a little affair—all put right. But the fact is, I'd as

soon find out what this business is with your office without my father knowing. I have reasons; shouldn't mind talking them over with you, if you can give me the information I want.'

'I can do that,' replied Scawthorne with a smile. 'If you are J. J. Snowdon, you are requested to communicate with Michael Snowdon—that's all.'

'Oh! but I *have* communicated with him, and he's nothing particular to say to me, as far as I can see.'

Scawthorne sipped at his glass, gave a stroke to each side of his moustache, and seemed to reflect.

'You were coming to ask Mr. Percival privately for information?'

'That's just it. Of course if you can't give me any, I must see him to-morrow.'

'He won't tell you anything more than I have.'

'And you don't *know* anything more?'

'I didn't say that, my dear fellow. Suppose you begin by telling me a little more about yourself?'

It was a matter of time, but at length the dialogue took another character. The glasses of stimulant were renewed, and as Joseph grew expansive Scawthorne laid aside something of his professional reserve, without, however, losing the discretion which led him to subdue his voice and express himself in uncompromising phrases. Their sitting lasted about an hour, and before taking leave of each other they arranged for a meeting at a different place in the course of a few days.

Joseph walked homewards with deliberation, in absent mood, his countenance alternating strangely between a look of mischievous jocoseness and irritable concern; occasionally he muttered to himself. Just before reaching the Close he turned into a public-house; when he came forth the malicious smile was on his face, and he walked with the air of a man who has business of moment before him. He admitted himself to the house.

'That you, Jo?' cried Clem's voice from upstairs.

'Me, sure enough,' was the reply, with a chuckle. 'Come up sharp, then.'

Humming a tune, Joseph ascended to the sitting-room on the first floor, and threw himself on a seat. His wife stood just in front of him, her sturdy arms a-kimbo; her look was fiercely expectant, answering in some degree to the smile with which he looked here and there.

'Well, can't you speak?'

'No hurry, Mrs. Clem; no hurry, my dear. It's all right. The old man's rolling in money.'

'And what about your share?'

Joseph laughed obstreperously, his wife's brow lowering the while.

'Just tell me, can't you?' she cried.

'Of course I will. The best joke you ever heard. You had yours yesterday, Mrs. Clem; my turn comes to-day. My share is—just nothing at all. Not a penny! Not a cent! Swallow that, old girl, and tell me how it tastes.'

'You're a liar!' shouted the other, her face flushing scarlet, her eyes aflame with rage.

'Never told a lie in my life,' replied her husband, still laughing noisily. But for that last glass of cordial on the way home he could scarcely have enjoyed so thoroughly the dramatic flavour of the situation. Joseph was neither a bully nor a man of courage; the joke with which he was delighting himself was certainly a rich one, but it had its element of danger, and only by abandoning himself to riotous mirth could he overcome the nervousness with which Clem's fury threatened to affect him. She, coming forward in the attitude of an enraged fishwife, for a few moments made the room ring with foul abuse, that vituperative vernacular of the nether world, which has never yet been exhibited by typography, and presumably never will be.

'Go it, Clem!' cried her husband, pushing his chair a little back. 'Go it, my angel! When you've eased your mind a little, I'll explain how it happens.'

She became silent, glaring at him with murderous eyes. But just at that moment Mrs. Peckover put her head in at the door, inquiring 'What's up?'

'Come in, if you want to know,' cried her daughter. 'See what you've let me in for! Didn't I tell you as it might be all a mistake? Oh yes, you may look!'

Mrs. Peckover was startled; her small, cunning eyes went rapidly from Clem to Joseph, and she fixed the latter with a gaze of angry suspicion.

'Got a bit of news for you, mother,' resumed Joseph, nodding. 'You and Clem were precious artful, weren't you now? It's my turn now. Thought I'd got money—ha, ha!'

'And so you have,' replied Mrs. Peckover. 'We know all about it, so you needn't try your little game.'

'Know all about it, do you? Well, see here. My brother Mike died out in Australia, and his son died at the same time —they was drowned. Mike left no will, and his wife was dead before him. What's the law, eh? Pity you didn't make sure of that. Why, all his money went to the old man, every cent of it. I've no claim on a penny. That's the law, my pretty dears!'

'He's a —— liar!' roared Clem, who at the best of times would have brought small understanding to a legal question. 'What did my brother say in his letter?'

'He was told wrong, that's all, or else he got the idea out of his own head.'

'Then why did they advertise for you?' inquired Mrs. Peckover, keeping perfect command of her temper.

'The old man thought he'd like to find his son again, that's all. Ha, ha! Why can't you take it good-humoured, Clem? You had your joke yesterday, and you can't say I cut up rough about it. I'm a good-natured fellow, I am. There's many a man would have broke every bone in your body, my angel, you just remember that!'

It rather seemed as if the merry proceeding would in this case be reversed; Joseph had risen, and was prepared to defend himself from an onslaught. But Mrs. Peckover came between the newly-wedded pair, and by degrees induced Clem to take a calmer view of the situation, or at all events to postpone her vengeance. It was absurd, she argued, to act as if the matter were hopeless. Michael Snowdon would certainly leave Joseph money in his will, if only the right steps were taken to secure his favour. Instead of quarrelling, they must put their heads together and scheme. She had her ideas; let them listen to her.

'Clem, you go and get a pot of old six* for supper, and don't be such a —— fool,' was her final remark.

CHAPTER XIX

A RETREAT

VISITING his friends as usual on Sunday evening, Sidney Kirkwood felt, before he had been many minutes in the room, that something unwonted was troubling the quiet he always found here. Michael Snowdon was unlike himself, nervously inattentive, moving frequently, indisposed to converse on any subject. Neither had Jane her accustomed brightness, and the frequent glances she cast at her grandfather seemed to show that the latter's condition was causing her anxiety. She withdrew very early, and, as at once appeared, in order that Sidney might hear in private what had that day happened. The story of Clem Peckover's marriage naturally occasioned no little astonishment in Sidney.

'And how will all this affect Jane?' he asked involuntarily.

'That is what I cannot tell,' replied Michael. 'It troubles me. My son is a stranger; all these years have made him quite a different man from what I remember; and the worst is, I can no longer trust myself to judge him. Yet I must know the truth—Sidney, I must know the truth. It's hard to speak ill of the only son left to me out of the four I once had, but if I think of him as he was seventeen years ago—no, no, he must have changed as he has grown older. But you must help me to know him, Sidney.'

And in a very few days Sidney had his first opportunity of observing Jane's father. At this meeting Joseph seemed to desire nothing so much as to recommend himself by an amiable bearing. Impossible to speak with more engaging frankness than he did whilst strolling away from Hanover Street in Sidney's company. Thereafter the two saw a great deal of each other. Joseph was soon a familiar visitor in Tysoe Street; he would come about nine o'clock of an evening, and sit till after midnight. The staple of his talk was at first the painfully unnatural relations existing between his father, his daughter, and himself. He had led a most unsatisfactory life; he owned it, deplored it. That the old man should distrust him was but natural; but would not Sidney, as a common friend, do his best to dispel this prejudice? On the subject of his brother Mike he kept absolute silence. The accident of meeting an intimate acquaintance at the office of Messrs. Percival and Peel had rendered it possible for him to pursue his inquiries in that direction without it becoming known to Michael Snowdon that he had done anything of the kind; and the policy he elaborated for himself demanded the appearance of absolute disinterestedness in all his dealings with his father. Aided by the shrewd Mrs. Peckover, he succeeded in reconciling Clem to a present disappointment, bitter as it was, by pointing out that there was every chance of his profiting largely upon

the old man's death, which could not be a very remote con-
tingency.   At present there was little that could be done save
to curry favour in Hanover Street, and keep an eye on what
went forward between Kirkwood and Jane.   This latter was,
of course, an issue of supreme importance.   A very little
observation convinced Joseph that his daughter had learned
to regard Sidney as more than a friend; whether there existed
any mutual understanding between them he could only discover
by direct inquiry, and for the present it seemed wiser to make
no reference to the subject.   He preserved the attitude of one
who has forfeited his natural rights, and only seeks with
humility the chance of proving that he is a reformed character.
Was, or was not, Kirkwood aware of the old man's wealth ?
That too must be left uncertain, though it was more than probable he had seen the advertisement in the newspapers, and,
like Mrs. Peckover, had based conclusions thereupon.   Another
possibility was, that Kirkwood had wormed himself into Michael's complete confidence.   From Joseph's point of view,
subtle machinations were naturally attributed to the young
man—whose appearance proved him anything but a commonplace person.   The situation was full of obscurities and
dangers.   From Scawthorne Joseph received an assurance
that the whole of the Australian property had been capitalised
and placed in English investments; also, that the income was
regularly drawn and in some way disposed of; the manner of
such disposal being kept private between old Mr. Percival and
his client.

In the meantime family discussions in the Close had
brought to Joseph's knowledge a circumstance regarding Kirkwood which interested him in a high degree.   When talking
of Sidney's character, it was natural that the Peckovers should
relate the story of his relations with Clara Hewett.

'Clara ?' exclaimed Mr. Snowdon, as if struck by the
name.   'Disappeared, has she ?   What sort of a girl to look
at ?'

Clem was ready with a malicious description, whereto her
husband attended very carefully.   He mused over it, and proceeded to make inquiries about Clara's family.   The Hewetts
were now living in another part of Clerkenwell, but there was
no hostility between them and the Peckovers.   Was anything
to be gained by keeping up intimacy with them ?   Joseph,
after further musing, decided that it would be just as well to
do so; suppose Clem called upon them and presented the

husband of whom she was so proud ? He would like, if possible, to hear a little more about their daughter; an idea he
had—never mind exactly what. So this call was paid, and in
a few weeks Joseph had established an acquaintance with John
Hewett.

Sidney, on his part, had a difficulty in coming to definite
conclusions respecting Jane's father. Of course he was pre-
judiced against the man, and though himself too little acquainted with the facts of the case to distinguish Joseph's
motives, he felt that the middle-aged prodigal's return was
anything but a fortunate event for Michael and his granddaughter. The secret marriage with Clem was not likely, in
any case, to have a respectable significance. True, there
were not lacking grounds for hesitation in refusing to accept
Joseph's account of himself. He had a fund of natural amia-
bility ; he had a good provision of intellect ; his talk was at
times very persuasive and much like that of one who has been
brought to a passable degree ot honesty by the slow development of his better instincts. But his face was against him ;
the worn, sallow features, the eyes which so obviously made a
struggle to look with frankness, the vicious lower lip, awoke
suspicion and told tales of base experience such as leaves its
stamp upon a man for ever. All the more repugnant was
this face to Sidney because it presented, in certain aspects, an
undeniable resemblance to Jane's ; impossible to say which
feature put forth this claim of kindred, but the impression
was there, and it made Sidney turn away his eyes in disgust
as often as he perceived it. He strove, however, to behave
with friendliness, for it was Michael's desire that he should do
so. That Joseph was using every opportunity of prying into
his thoughts, of learning the details of his history, he soon
became perfectly conscious ; but he knew of nothing that he
need conceal.

It was impossible that Sidney should not have reflected
many a time on Michael Snowdon's position, and have been
moved to curiosity by hints of the mysterious when he thought
of his friends in Hanover Street. As it happened, he never
saw those newspaper advertisements addressed to Joseph, and
his speculation had nothing whatever to support it save the
very few allusions to the past which Michael had permitted
himself in the course of talk. Plainly the old man had means
sufficient for his support, and in all likelihood this independence was connected with his visit to Australia ; but no act

or word of Michael's had ever suggested that he possessed more than a very modest competency. It was not, indeed, the circumstances, so much as the character and views, of his friend that set Kirkwood pondering. He did not yet know Michael Snowdon; of that he was convinced. He had not fathomed his mind, got at the prime motive of his being. Moreover, he felt that the old man was waiting for some moment, or some event, to make revelation of himself. Since Joseph's appearance, it had become more noticeable than ever that Snowdon suffered from some agitation of the mind; Sidney had met his eyes fixed upon him in a painful interrogation, and seemed to discern the importunity of a desire that was refused utterance. His own condition was affected by sympathy with this restlessness, and he could not overcome the feeling that some decisive change was at hand for him. Though nothing positive justified the idea, he began to connect this anticipation of change with the holiday that was approaching, the week to be spent in Essex at the end of July. It had been his fear that Joseph's presence might affect these arrangements, but Michael was evidently resolved to allow nothing of the kind. One evening, a fortnight before the day agreed upon for leaving town, and when Joseph had made a call in Hanover Street, the old man took occasion to speak of the matter. Joseph accepted the information with his usual pliancy.

' I only wish my wife and me could join you,' he remarked. But it wouldn't do to take a holiday so soon after settling to business. Better luck for me next year, father, let's hope.'

That he had settled to business was a fact of which Joseph made so much just now that one would have been tempted to suppose it almost a new experience for him. His engagement, he declared, was with a firm of advertising agents in the City; nothing to boast of, unfortunately, and remunerative only in the way of commission; but he saw his way to better things.

' Jane, my girl,' he continued, averting his eyes as if in emotion, ' I don't know how you and me are going to show our gratitude for all this kindness, I'm sure. I hope you haven't got so used to it that you think there's no need to thank your grandfather?'

The girl and the old man exchanged a look. Joseph sighed, and began to speak of another subject in a tone of cheery martyrdom.

Jane herself had not been quite so joyous as was her wont

since the occurrence that caused her to take a new view of her position in the world. She understood that her grandfather regarded the change very gravely, and in her own heart awoke all manner of tremulous apprehensions when she tried to look onward a little to the uncertainties of the future. Forecasts had not hitherto troubled her ; the present was so rich in satisfactions that she could follow the bent of her nature and live with no anxiety concerning the unknown. It was a great relief to her to be assured that the long-standing plans for the holiday would suffer no change. The last week was a time of impatience, resolutely suppressed. On the Saturday afternoon Sidney was to meet them at Liverpool Street.* Would any- thing happen these last few days—this last day—this last hour ? No ; all three stood together on the platform, and their holiday had already begun.

Over the pest-stricken regions of East London, sweltering in sunshine which served only to reveal the intimacies of abomination ; across miles of a city of the damned, such as thought never conceived before this age of ours ; above streets swarming with a nameless populace, cruelly exposed by the unwonted light of heaven ; stopping at stations which it crushes the heart to think should be the destination of any mortal ; the train made its way at length beyond the outmost limits of dread, and entered upon a land of level meadows, of hedges and trees, of crops and cattle. Michael Snowdon was anxious that Jane should not regard with the carelessness of familiarity those desolate tracts from which they were escaping. In Bethnal Green he directed her attention with a whispered word to the view from each window, and Jane had learnt well to understand him. But, the lesson over, it was none of his purpose to spoil her natural mood of holiday. Sidney sat opposite her, and as often as their eyes met a smile of con- tentment answered on either's face.

They alighted at Chelmsford, and were met by the farmer in whose house they were going to lodge, a stolid, good- natured fellow named Pammenter, with red, leathery cheeks, and a corkscrew curl of black hair coming forward on each temple. His trap was waiting, and in a few minutes they started on the drive to Danbury. The distance is about five miles, and, until Danbury Hill is reached, the countryside has no point of interest to distinguish it from any other represen- tative bit of rural Essex. It is merely one of those quiet corners of flat, homely England, where man and beast seem on good terms with each other, where all green things grow in abundance, where from of old tilth and pasture-land are humbly observant of seasons and alternations, where the brown roads are familiar only with the tread of the labourer, with the light wheel of the farmer's gig, or the rumbling of the solid wain. By the roadside you pass occasionally a mantled pool, where perchance ducks or geese are enjoying themselves; and at times there is a pleasant glimpse of farm-yard, with stacks and barns and stables. All things as simple as could be, but beautiful on this summer afternoon, and priceless when one has come forth from the streets of Clerkenwell.

Farmer Pammenter was talkative, and his honest chest-voice sounded pleasantly; but the matter of his discourse might have been more cheerful. Here, as elsewhere, the evil of the times was pressing upon men and disheartening them from labour. Farms lying barren, ill-will between proprietor and tenant, between tenant and hind, departure of the tillers of the soil to rot in towns that have no need of them—of such things did honest Pammenter speak, with many a sturdy male-diction of landlords and land-laws, whereat Sidney smiled, not unsympathetic.

Danbury Hill, rising thick-wooded to the village church, which is visible for miles around, with stretches of heath about its lower slopes, with its far prospects over the sunny country, was the pleasant end of a pleasant drive. Mrs. Pammenter and her children (seven of them, unhappily) gave the party a rough, warm-hearted welcome. Ha! how good it was to smell the rooms through which the pure air breathed freely! All the front of the house was draped with purple clematis; in the garden were sun-flowers and hollyhocks and lowly plants innumerable; on the red and lichened tiles pigeons were cooing themselves into a doze; the horse's hoofs rang with a pleasant clearness on the stones as he was led to his cool stable. Her heart throbbing with excess of delight, Jane pushed back the diamond-paned casement of her bedroom, the same room she had occupied last year and the year before, and buried her face in clematis. Then the tea that Mrs. Pammenter had made ready;—how delicious everything tasted! how white the cloth was! how fragrant the cut flowers in the brown jug!

But Michael had found the journey a greater tax upon his strength than he anticipated. Whilst Sidney and Jane talked merrily over the tea-table the old man was thinking. 'Another

year they will come without me,' and he smiled just to hide
his thoughts.   In the evening he smoked his pipe on a garden-
seat, for the most part silent, and at sunset he was glad to go
up to his chamber.

Jane was renewing her friendship with the Pammenters'
eldest girl, an apple-cheeked, red-haired, ungraceful, but
good-natured lass of sixteen.   Their voices sounded from all
parts of the garden and the farm-yard, Jane's clear-throated
laugh contrasting with the rougher utterance of her companion.
After supper, in the falling of the dusk, Sidney strolled away
from the gossiping circle within-doors, and found a corner of
the garden whence there was a view of wooded hillside against
the late glow of the heavens.   Presently he heard footsteps,
and through the leafage of a tree that shadowed him he saw
Jane looking this way and that, as if she sought some one.
Her dress was a light calico, and she held in her hand a rough
garden hat, the property of Miss Pammenter.   Sidney regarded
her for some moments, then called her by name.   She could
not see him at first, and looked about anxiously.   He moved
a branch of the tree and again called her ; whereupon she ran
forward.

'I thought perhaps you'd gone up the hill,' she said, resting
her arms on the wall by which he was standing.

Then they kept silence, enjoying the sweetness of the hour.
Differently, it is true ; for Kirkwood's natural sensitiveness
had been developed and refined by studies of which Jane had
no conception.   Imperfect as his instruction remained, the
sources of spiritual enjoyment were open to him, and with all
his feeling there blended that reflective bitterness which is the
sad privilege of such as he.   Jane's delight was as simple as
the language in which she was wont to express herself.   She
felt infinitely more than Pennyloaf, for instance, would have
done under the circumstances ; but her joy consisted, in the
main, of a satisfaction of pure instincts and a deep sense of
gratitude to those who made her life what it was.   She could
as little have understood Sidney's mind at this moment as she
could have given an analytic account of her own sensations.
For all that, the two were in profound sympathy ; how different soever the ways in which they were affected, the result,
as they stood side by side, was identical in the hearts of both.

Sidney began to speak of Michael Snowdon, keeping his
voice low, as if in fear of breaking those subtle harmonies
wherewith the night descended.

'We must be careful not to over-tire him. He looked very pale when he went upstairs. I've thought lately that he must suffer more than he tells us.'

'Yes, I'm afraid he often does,' Jane assented, as if relieved to speak of it. 'Yet he always says it's nothing to trouble about, nothing but what is natural at his age. He's altered a great deal since father came,' she added, regarding him diffidently.

'I hope it isn't because he thinks your father may be wanting to take you away?'

'Oh, it can't be that! Oh, he knows I wouldn't leave him! Mr. Kirkwood, you don't think my father will give us any trouble?'

She revealed an anxiety which delicacy of feeling had hitherto prevented her expressing. Sidney at once spoke reassuringly, though he had in fact no little suspicion of Joseph Snowdon's tactics.

'It's my grandfather that I ought to think most of,' pursued Jane earnestly. 'I can't feel to my father as I do to *him*. What should I have been now if——'

Something caused her to leave the speech unfinished, and for a few moments there was silence. From the ground exhaled a sweet fresh odour, soothing to the senses, and at times a breath of air brought subtler perfume from the alleys of the garden. In the branches above them rustled a bird's wing. At a distance on the country road sounded the trotting of a horse.

'I feel ashamed and angry with myself,' said Sidney, in a tone of emotion, 'when I think now of those times. I might have done something, Jane. I had no right to know what you were suffering and just go by as if it didn't matter!'

'Oh, but you didn't!' came eagerly from the girl's lips. 'You've forgotten, but I can't. You were very kind to me—you helped me more than you can think—you never saw me without speaking kindly. Don't you remember that night when I came to fetch you from the workshop, and you took off your coat and put it over me, because it was cold and raining?'

'Jane, what a long, long time ago that seems!'

'As long as I live I shall never forget it—never! You were the only friend I had then.'

'No; there was some one else who took thought for you,' said Sidney, regarding her gravely.

Jane met his look for an instant—they could just read each other's features in the pale light—then dropped her eyes.

'I don't think you've forgotten that either,' he added, in the same unusual voice.

'No,' said Jane, below her breath.

'Say who it is I mean.'

'You mean Miss Hewett,' was the reply, after a troubled moment.

'I wanted you to say her name. You remember one evening not long ago, when your grandfather was away? I had the same wish then. Why shouldn't we speak of her? She was a friend to you when you needed one badly, and it's right that you should remember her with gratitude. I think of her just like we do of people that are dead.'

Jane stood with one hand on the low wall, half-turned to him, but her face bent downwards. Regarding her for what seemed a long time, Sidney felt as though the fragrance of the earth and the flowers were mingling with his blood and confusing him with emotions. At the same his tongue was paralysed. Frequently of late he had known a timidity in Jane's presence, which prevented him from meeting her eyes, and now this tremor came upon him with painful intensity. He knew to what his last words had tended; it was with consciousness of a distinct purpose that he had led the conversation to Clara; but now he was powerless to speak the words his heart prompted. Of a sudden he experienced a kind of shame, the result of comparison between himself and the simple girl who stood before him; she was so young, and the memory of passions from which he had suffered years ago affected him with a sense of unworthiness, almost of impurity. Jane had come to be his ideal of maidenhood, but till this moment he had not understood the full significance of the feeling with which he regarded her. He could not transform with a word their relations to each other. The temptation of the hour had hurried him towards an end which he must approach with more thought, more preparation of himself.

It was scarcely for ten heart-beats. Then Jane raised her eyes and said in a voice that trembled:

'I've often wished I could see her again, and thank her for her kindness that night.'

'That will help me to think with less pain of things that are long since over and done with,' Sidney replied, forcing himself to speak firmly. 'We can't alter the past, Jane, but we can try to remember only the best part of it. You, I hope, very seldom look back at all.'

'Grandfather wishes me never to forget it. He often says that.'

'Does he? I think I understand.'

Jane drew down a branch and laid the broad cool leaves against her cheek; releasing it, she moved in the direction of the house. Her companion followed with slow step, his head bent. Before they came to the door Jane drew his attention to a bat that was sweeping duskily above their heads; she began to speak with her wonted cheerfulness.

'How I should like Pennyloaf to be here! I wonder what she'd think of it?'

At the door they bade each other good night. Sidney took yet a few turns in the garden before entering. But that it would have seemed to the Pammenters a crazy proceeding, he would have gladly struck away over the fields and walked for hours.

CHAPTER XX

A VISION OF NOBLE THINGS

HE slept but for an hour or two, and even then with such disturbance of fitful dreams that he could not be said to rest. At the earliest sound of movements in the house he rose and went out into the morning air. There had fallen a heavy shower just after sunrise, and the glory of the east was still partly veiled with uncertain clouds. Heedless of weather-signs, Sidney strode away at a great pace, urged by his ungovernable thoughts. His state was that miserable one in which a man repeats for the thousandth time something he has said, and torments himself with devising possible and impossible interpretations thereof. Through the night he had done nothing but imagine what significance Jane might have attached to his words about Clara Hewett. Why had he spoken of Clara at all? One moment he understood his reasons, and approved them; the next he was at a loss to account for such needless revival of a miserable story. How had Jane interpreted him? And was it right or wrong to have paused when on the point of confessing that he loved her?

Rain caught him at a distance from home, and he returned to breakfast in rather a cheerless plight. He found that Michael was not feeling quite himself, and would not rise till midday. Jane had a look of anxiety, and he fancied she behaved to him with a constraint hitherto unknown. The fancy was dispelled, however, when, later in the morning, she persuaded him to bring out his sketch-book, and suggested points of view for a drawing of the farm that had been promised to Mr. Pammenter. Himself unable to recover the tone of calm intimacy which till yesterday had been natural between them, Sidney found himself studying the girl, seeking to surprise some proof that she too was no longer the same, and only affected this unconsciousness of change. There was, perhaps, a little less readiness in her eyes to meet his, but she talked as naturally as ever, and the spontaneousness of her good-humour was assuredly not feigned.

On Monday the farmer had business in Maldon. Occasionally when he drove over to that town he took one or other of his children with him to visit a relative, and to-day he proposed that Jane should be of the party. They started after an early dinner. Michael and Sidney stood together in the road, watching the vehicle as it rolled away; then they walked in silence to a familiar spot where they could sit in shadow. Sidney was glad of Jane's departure for the afternoon. He found it impossible to escape the restlessness into which he had fallen, and was resolved to seek relief by opening his mind to the old man. There could be little doubt that Michael already understood his thoughts, and no better opportunity for such a conversation was likely to present itself. When they had been seated for a minute or two, neither speaking, Sidney turned to his companion with a grave look. At the same instant Michael also had raised his eyes and seemed on the point of saying something of importance. They regarded each other. The old man's face was set in an expression of profound feeling, and his lips moved tremulously before words rose to them.

'What were you going to say, Sidney?' he asked, reading the other's features.

'Something which I hope won't be displeasing to you. I was going to speak of Jane. Since she has been living with you she has grown from a child to a woman. When I was talking with her in the garden on Saturday night I felt this change more distinctly than I had ever done before. I understood that it had made a change in myself. I love her, Mr. Snowdon, and it's my dearest hope that she may come to feel the same for me.'

Michael was more agitated than the speaker; he raised a hand to his forehead and closed his eyes as if the light pained them. But the smile with which he speedily answered Sidney's look of trouble was full of reassurance.

'You couldn't have said anything that would give me more pleasure,' he replied, just above his breath. 'Does she know it? Did you speak to her?'

'We were talking of years ago, and I mentioned Clara Hewett. I said that I had forgotten all about her except that she'd befriended Jane. But nothing more than that. I couldn't say what I was feeling just then. Partly I thought that it was right to speak to you first; and then—it seemed to me almost as if I should be treating her unfairly. I'm so much older— she knows that it isn't the first time I——and she's always thought of me just as a friend.'

'So much older?' repeated Michael, with a grave smile. 'Why, you're both children to my sight. Wait and let me think a bit, Sidney. I too have something I want to say. I'm glad you've spoken this afternoon, when there's time for us to talk. Just wait a few minutes, and let me think.'

Sidney had as good as forgotten that there was anything unusual in his friend's circumstances; this last day or two he had thought of nothing but Jane and his love for her. Now he recalled the anticipation—originating he scarcely knew how —that some kind of disclosure would before long be made to him. The trouble of his mind was heightened; he waited with all but dread for the next words.

'I think I've told you,' Michael resumed at length, steadying his voice, 'that Joseph is my youngest son, and that I had three others. Three others: Michael, Edward, and Robert— all dead. Edward died when he was a boy of fifteen; Robert was killed on the railway—he was a porter—at three-and-twenty. The eldest went out to Australia; he took a wife there, and had one child; the wife died when they'd been married a year or two, and Michael and his boy were drowned, both together. I was living with them at the time, as you know. But what I've never spoken of, Sidney, is that my son had made his fortune. He left a deal of land, and many thousands of pounds, behind him. There was no finding any will; a lawyer in the nearest town, a man that had known

him a long time, said he felt sure there'd been no will made.
So, as things were, the law gave everything to his father.'

He related it with subdued voice, in a solemn and agitated
tone. The effect of the news upon Sidney was a painful con-
striction of the heart, a rush of confused thought, an involve-
ment of all his perceptions in a sense of fear. The pallor of
his cheeks and the pained parting of his lips bore witness to
how little he was prepared for such a story.

'I've begun with what ought by rights to have come last,'
pursued Michael, after drawing a deep sigh. 'But it does me
good to get it told; it's been burdening me this long while.
Now you must listen, Sidney, whilst I show you why I've kept
this a secret. I've no fear but *you*'ll understand me, though
most people wouldn't. It's a secret from everybody except a
lawyer in London, who does business for me ; a right-hearted
man he is, in most things, and I'm glad I met with him, but
he doesn't understand me as you will ; he thinks I'm making
a mistake. My son knows nothing about it ; at least, it's my
hope and belief he doesn't. He told me he hadn't heard of
his brother's death. I say I hope he doesn't know ; it isn't
selfishness, that ; I needn't tell you. I've never for a minute
thought of myself as a rich man, Sidney ; I've never thought
of the money as my own, never ; and if Joseph proves himself
honest, I'm ready to give up to him the share of his brother's
property that it seems to me ought to be rightly his, though
the law for some reason looks at it in a different way. I'm
ready, but I must know that he's an honest man ; I must
prove him first.'

The eagerness of his thought impelled him to repetitions
and emphasis. His voice fell upon a note of feebleness, and
with an effort he recovered the tone in which he had begun.

'As soon as I knew that all this wealth had fallen to me
I decided at once to come back to England. What could I do
out there ? I decided to come to England, but I couldn't see
further ahead than that. I sold all the land ; I had the business done for me by that lawyer I spoke of, that had known
my son, and he recommended me to a Mr. Percival in London.
I came back, and I found little Jane, and then bit by bit I
began to understand what my duty was. It got clear in my
mind ; I formed a purpose, a plan, and it's as strong in me
now as ever. Let me think again for a little, Sidney. I
want to make it as plain to you as it is to me. You'll understand me best if I go back and tell you more than I have

done yet about my life before I left England. Let me think a while.'

He was overcome with a fear that he might not be able to convey with sufficient force the design which had wholly possessed him. So painful was the struggle in him between enthusiasm and a consciousness of failing faculties, that Sidney grasped his hand and begged him to speak simply, without effort.

'Have no fear about my understanding you. We've talked a great deal together, and I know very well what your strongest motives are. Trust me to sympathise with you.'

'I do! If I hadn't that trust, Sidney, I couldn't have felt the joy I did when you spoke to me of my Jane. You'll help me to carry out my plan; you and Jane will; you and Jane! I've got to be such an old man all at once, as it seems, and I dursn't have waited much longer without telling you what I had in my mind. See now, I'll go back to when I was a boy, as far back as I can remember. You know I was born in Clerkenwell, and I've told you a little now and then of the hard times I went through. My poor father and mother came out of the country, thinking to better themselves; instead of that, they found nothing but cold and hunger, and toil and moil. They were both dead by when I was between thirteen and fourteen. They died in the same winter—a cruel winter. I used to go about begging bits of firewood from the neighbours. There was a man in our house who kept dogs, and I remember once catching hold of a bit of dirty meat—I can't call it meat—that one of them had gnawed and left on the stairs; and I ate it, as if I'd been a dog myself, I was that driven with hunger. Why, I feel the cold and the hunger at this minute! It was a cruel winter, that, and it left me alone. I had to get my own living as best I could.

'No teaching. I was nineteen before I could read the signs over shops, or write my own name. Between nineteen and twenty I got all the education I ever was to have, paying a man with what I could save out of my earnings. The blessing was I had health and strength, and with hard struggling I got into a regular employment. At five-and-twenty I could earn my pound a week, pretty certain. When it got to five shillings more, I must needs have a wife to share it with me. My poor girl came to live with me in a room in Hill Street.

'I've never spoken to you of her, but you shall hear it all now, cost me what it may in the telling. Of course she was out of a poor home, and she'd known as well as me what it was to go cold and hungry. I sometimes think, Sidney, I can see a look of her in Jane's face—but she was prettier than Jane; yes, yes, prettier than Jane. And to think a man could treat a poor little thing like her the way I did!—you don't know what sort of a man Michael Snowdon was then; no, you don't know what I was then. You're not to think I ill-used her in the common way; I never raised my hand, thank God! and I never spoke a word a man should be ashamed of. But I was a hard, self-willed, stubborn fool! How she came to like me and to marry me, I don't know; we were so different in every way. Well, it was partly my nature and partly what I'd gone through; we hadn't been married more than a month or two when I began to find fault with her, and from that day on she could never please me. I earned five-and-twenty shillings a week, and I'd made up my mind that we must save out of it. I wouldn't let *her* work; no, what *she* had to do was to keep the home on as little as possible, and always have everything clean and straight when I got back at night. But Jenny hadn't the same ideas about things as I had. She couldn't pinch and pare, and our plans of saving came to nothing. It grew worse as the children were born. The more need there was for carefulness, the more heedless Jenny seemed to get. And it was my fault, mine from beginning to end. Another man would have been gentle with her and showed her kindly when she was wrong, and have been thankful for the love she gave him, whatever her faults. That wasn't my way. I got angry, and made her life a burden to her. I must have things done exactly as I wished; if not, there was no end to my fault-finding. And yet, if you'll believe it, I loved my wife as truly as man ever did. Jenny couldn't understand that— and how should she? At last she began to deceive me in all sorts of little things; she got into debt with shop-people, she showed me false accounts, she pawned things without my knowing. Last of all, she began to drink. Our fourth child was born just at that time; Jenny had a bad illness, and I believe it set her mind wrong. I lost all control of her, and she used to say if it wasn't for the children she'd go and leave me. One morning we quarrelled very badly, and I did as I'd threatened to—I walked about the streets all the night that followed, never coming home. I went to work next day, but at dinner-time I got frightened and ran home just to speak a word. Little Mike, the eldest, was playing on the stairs, and he said his mother was asleep. I went into the room, and saw Jenny lying on the bed dressed. There was something queer in the way her arms were stretched out. When I got near I saw she was dead. She'd taken poison.

'And it was I had killed her, just as much as if I'd put the poison to her lips. All because I thought myself such a wise fellow, because I'd resolved to live more prudently than other men of my kind did. I wanted to save money for the future—out of five-and-twenty shillings a week. Many and many a day I starved myself to try and make up for expenses of the home. Sidney, you remember that man we once went to hear lecture, the man that talked of nothing but the thriftlessness of the poor, and how it was their own fault they suffered? I was very near telling you my story when we came away that night. Why, look; I myself was just the kind of poor man that would have suited that lecturer. And what came of it? If I'd let my poor Jenny go her own way from the first, we should have had hard times now and then, but there'd have been our love to help us, and we should have been happy enough. They talk about thriftiness, and it just means that poor people are expected to practise a self-denial that the rich can't even imagine, much less carry out! You know now why this kind of talk always angers me.'

Michael brooded for a few moments, his eyes straying sadly over the landscape before him.

'I was punished,' he continued, 'and in the fittest way. The two of my boys who showed most love for me, Edward and Robert, died young. The eldest and youngest were a constant trouble to me. Michael was quick-tempered and self-willed, like myself; I took the wrong way with him, just like I had with his mother, and there was no peace till he left home. Joseph was still harder to deal with; but he's the only one left alive, and there is no need to bring up things against him. With him I wasn't to blame, unless I treated him too kindly and spoilt him. He was my favourite, was Jo, and he repaid me cruelly. When he married, I only heard of it from other people; we'd been parted for a long time already. And just about then I had a letter from Michael, asking me if I was willing to go out and live with him in Australia. I

hadn't heard from him more than two or three times in twelve
years, and when this letter came to me I was living in
Sheffield; I'd been there about five years. He wrote to say
he was doing well, and that he didn't like to think of me
being left to spend my old age alone. It was a kind letter,
and it warmed my heart. Lonely I was; as lonely and sorrowful a man as any in England. I wrote back to say that I'd
come to him gladly if he could promise to put me in the way
of earning my own living. He agreed to that, and I left the
old country, little thinking I should ever see it again. I
didn't see Joseph before I went. All I knew of him was, that
he lived in Clerkenwell Close, married; and that was all I had
to guide me when I tried to find him a few years after. I
was bitter against him, and went without trying to say
good-bye.

'My son's fortune seems to have been made chiefly out of
horse-dealing and what they call "land-grabbing"—buying
sheep-runs over the heads of squatters, to be bought out again
at a high profit. Well, you know what my opinion is of
trading at the best, and as far as I could understand it, it
was trading at about its worst that had filled Michael's
pockets. He'd had a partner for a time, and very ugly stories
were told me about the man. However, Michael gave me as
kind a welcome as his letter promised; prosperity had done
him good, and he seemed only anxious to make up for the
years of unkindness that had gone by. Had I been willing, I
might have lived under his roof at my ease; but I held him
to his bargain, and worked like any other man who goes there
without money. It's a comfort to me to think of those few
years spent in quiet and goodwill with my eldest boy. His
own lad would have given trouble, I'm afraid, if he'd lived;
Michael used to talk to me uneasily about him, poor fellow!
But they both came to their end before the world had parted
them.

'If I'd been a young man, I dare say I should have felt
different when they told me how rich I was; it gave me no
pleasure at first, and when I'd had time to think about it I
only grew worried. I even thought once or twice of getting
rid of the burden by giving all the money to a hospital in
Sydney or Melbourne. But then I remembered that the poor
in the old country had more claim on me, and when I'd got
used to the idea of being a wealthy man, I found myself re-
calling all sorts of fancies and wishes that used to come into

my head when I was working hard for a poor living. It took some time to get all the lawyer's business finished, and by when it was done I began to see a way before me. First of all I must find my son in England, and see if he needed help. I hadn't made any change in my way of living, and I came back from Australia as a steerage passenger, wearing the same clothes that I'd worked in. The lawyer laughed at me, but I'm sure I should have laughed at myself if I'd dressed up as a gentleman and begun to play the fool in my old age. The money wasn't to be used in that way. I'd got my ideas, and they grew clearer during the voyage home.

'You know how I found Jane. Not long after, I put an advertisement in the papers, asking my son, if he saw it, to communicate with Mr. Percival—that's the lawyer I was recommended to in London. There was no answer; Joseph was in America at that time. I hadn't much reason to like Mrs. Peckover and her daughter, but I kept up acquaintance with them because I thought they might hear of Jo some day. And after a while I sent Jane to learn a business. Do you know why I did that? Can you think why I brought up the child as if I'd only had just enough to keep us both, and never gave a sign that I could have made a rich lady of her?'

In asking the question, he bent forward and laid his hand on Sidney's shoulder. His eyes gleamed with that light which betrays the enthusiast, the idealist. As he approached the explanation to which his story had tended, the signs of age and weakness disappeared before the intensity of his feeling. Sidney understood now why he had always been conscious of something in the man's mind that was not revealed to him, of a life-controlling purpose but vaguely indicated by the general tenor of Michael's opinions. The latter's fervour affected him, and he replied with emotion :

'You wish Jane to think of this money as you do yourself—not to regard it as wealth, but as the means of bringing help to the miserable.'

'That is my thought, Sidney. It came to me in that form whilst I was sitting by her bed, when she was ill at Mrs. Peckover's. I knew nothing of her character then, and the idea I had might have come to nothing through her turning out untrustworthy. But I thought to myself : Suppose she grows up to be a good woman—suppose I can teach her to look at things in the same way as I do myself, train her to feel that no happiness could be greater than the power to put an end

N

to ever so little of the want and wretchedness about her—
suppose when I die I could have the certainty that all this
money was going to be used for the good of the poor by a
woman who herself belonged to the poor ? You understand
me ? It would have been easy enough to leave it among
charities in the ordinary way; but my idea went beyond
that. I might have had Jane schooled and fashioned into
a lady, and still have hoped that she would use the money
well ; but my idea went beyond *that*. There's plenty of ladies
nowadays taking an interest in the miserable, and spending
their means unselfishly. What I hoped was to raise up for
the poor and the untaught a friend out of their own midst,
some one who had gone through all that *they* suffer, who was
accustomed to earn her own living by the work of her hands
as *they* do, who had never thought herself their better, who
saw the world as they see it and knew all their wants. A
lady may do good, we know that ; but she can't be the friend
of the poor as I understand it; there's too great a distance
between her world and theirs. Can you picture to yourself
how anxiously I've watched this child from the first day she
came to live with me ? I've scarcely had a thought but about
her. I saw very soon that she had good feelings, and I set
myself to encourage them. I wanted her to be able to read and
write, but there was no need of any more education than that;
it was the heart I cared about, not the mind. Besides, I had
always to keep saying to myself that perhaps, after all, she
wouldn't turn out the kind of woman I wished, and in that case
she mustn't be spoiled for an ordinary life. Sidney, it's this
money that has made me a weak old man when I might still
have been as strong as many at fifty; the care of it has worn me
out; I haven't slept quietly since it came into my hands. But
the worst is over. I shan't be disappointed. Jane will be the
woman I've hoped for, and however soon my own life comes
to an end, I shall die knowing that there's a true man by her
side to help her to make my idea a reality.

'I've mentioned Mr. Percival, the lawyer. He's an old
man like myself, and we've had many a long talk together.
About a year and a half ago I told him what I've told you
now. Since I came back to England he's been managing the
money for me; he's paid me the little we needed, and the
rest of the income has been used in charity by some people we
could trust. Well, Mr. Percival doesn't go with me in my
plans for Jane. He thinks I'm making a mistake, that I

ought to have had the child educated to fit her to live with rich people. It's no use; I can't get him to feel what a grand thing it'll be for Jane to go about among her own people and help them as nobody ever could. He said to me not long ago, " And isn't the girl ever to have a husband ? " It's my hope that she will, I told him. " And do you suppose," he went on, "that whoever marries her will let her live in the way you talk of ? Where are you going to find a working man that'll be content never to touch this money—to work on for his weekly wages, when he might be living at his ease ? " And I told him that it wasn't as impossible as he thought. What do you think, Sidney ? '

The communication of a noble idea has the same effect upon the brains of certain men—of one, let us say, in every hundred thousand—as a wine that exalts and enraptures. As Sidney listened to the old man telling of his wondrous vision, he became possessed with ardour such as he had known but once or twice in his life. Idealism such as Michael Snowdon had developed in these latter years is a form of genius ; given the susceptible hearer, it dazzles, inspires, raises to heroic contempt of the facts of life. Had this story been related to him of some unknown person, Sidney would have admired, but as one admires the nobly impracticable ; subject to the electric influence of a man who was great enough to conceive and direct his life by such a project, who could repose so supreme a faith in those he loved, all the primitive nobleness of his character asserted itself, and he could accept with a throbbing heart the superb challenge addressed to him.

' If Jane can think me worthy to be her husband,' he replied, ' your friend shall see that he has feared without cause.'

' I knew it, Sidney ; I knew it ! ' exclaimed the old man. ' How much younger I feel now that I have shared this burden with you ! '

' And shall you now tell Jane ? ' the other inquired.

' Not yet ; not just yet. She is very young ; we must wait a little. But there can be no reason why you shouldn't speak to her—of yourself.'

Sidney was descending from the clouds. As the flush of his humanitarian enthusiasm passed away, and he thought of his personal relations to Jane, a misgiving, a scruple began to make itself heard within him. Worldly and commonplace the thought, but—had he a right to ask the girl to pledge herself to him under circumstances such as these ? To be sure, it was not

as if Jane were an heiress in the ordinary way ; for all that,
would it not be a proceeding of doubtful justice to woo her
when as yet she was wholly ignorant of the most important
item in her situation ?   His sincerity was unassailable, but—
suppose, in fact, he had to judge the conduct of another man
thus placed?   Upon the heated pulsing of his blood succeeded
a coolness, almost a chill ; he felt as though he had been on
the verge of a precipice, and had been warned to draw back
only just in time.   Every second showed him more distinctly
what his duty was.   He experienced a sensation of thankful-
ness that he had not spoken definitely on Saturday evening.
His instinct had guided him aright ; Jane was still too young
to be called upon solemnly to decide her whole future.

'That, too, had better wait, Mr. Snowdon,' he said, after
a pause of a minute.   ' I should like her to know everything
before I speak to her in that way.   In a year it will be time
enough.'

Michael regarded him thoughtfully.

' Perhaps you are right.   I wish you knew Mr. Percival ;
but there is time, there is time.   He still thinks I shall be
persuaded to alter my plans.   That night you came to Hanover Street and found me away, he took me to see a lady who
works among the poor in Clerkenwell; she knew me by name,
because Mr. Percival had given her money from me to use,
but we'd never seen each other till then.   He wants me to ask
her opinion about Jane.'

' Has he spoken of her to the lady, do you think ? '

' Oh no ! ' replied the other, with perfect confidence.   ' He
has promised me to keep all that a secret as long as I wish.
The lady—her name is Miss Lant—seemed all that my friend
said she was, and perhaps Jane might do well to make her
acquaintance some day ; but that mustn't be till Jane knows
and approves the purpose of my life and hers.   The one thing
that troubles me still, Sidney, is—her father.   It's hard that
I can't be sure whether my son will be a help or a hindrance.
I must wait, and try to know him better.'

The conversation had so wearied Michael, that in returning to the house he had to lean on his companion's arm.
Sidney was silent, and yielded, he scarce knew why, to a
mood of depression.   When Jane returned from Maldon in
the evening, and he heard her happy voice as the children ran
out to welcome her, there was a heaviness at his heart.   Perhaps it came only of hope deferred.

CHAPTER XXI

DEATH THE RECONCILER

THERE is no accounting for tastes. Sidney Kirkwood, spending his Sunday evening in a garden away there in the chaw-
bacon regions of Essex, where it was so deadly quiet that you
could hear the flutter of a bird's wing or the rustle of a leaf,
not once only congratulated himself on his good fortune ; yet
at that hour he might have stood, as so often, listening to the
eloquence, the wit, the wisdom, that give proud distinction
to the name of Clerkenwell Green. Towards sundown, that
modern Agora* rang with the voices of orators, swarmed with
listeners, with disputants, with mockers, with indifferent
loungers. The circle closing about an agnostic lecturer inter-
sected with one gathered for a prayer-meeting; the roar of an
enthusiastic total-abstainer blended with the shriek of a Radical
politician. Innumerable were the little groups which had
broken away from the larger ones to hold semi-private debate
on matters which demanded calm consideration and the finer
intellect. From the doctrine of the Trinity to the question of
cabbage *versus* beef ; from Neo-Malthusianism to the griev-
ance of compulsory vaccination ;*not a subject which modernism
has thrown out to the multitude but here received its sufficient
mauling. Above the crowd floated wreaths of rank tobacco
smoke.

Straying from circle to circle might have been seen Mr.
Joseph Snowdon, the baldness of his crown hidden by a most
respectable silk hat, on one hand a glove, in the other his
walking-stick, a yellow waistcoat enhancing his appearance of
dignity, a white necktie spotted with blue and a geranium in
his button-hole correcting the suspicion of age suggested by
his countenance. As a listener to harangues of the most
various tendency, Mr. Snowdon exhibited an impartial spirit ;
he smiled occasionally, but was never moved to any expression of stronger feeling. His placid front revealed the philosopher.

Yet at length something stirred him to a more pronounced
interest. He was on the edge of a dense throng which had
just been delighted by the rhetoric of a well-known Clerkenwell
Radical ; the topic under discussion was Rent, and the last
speaker had, in truth, put before them certain noteworthy

views of the subject as it affected the poor of London. What attracted Mr. Snowdon's attention was the voice of the speaker who next rose. Pressing a little nearer, he got a glimpse of a lean, haggard, grey-headed man, shabbily dressed, no bad example of a sufferer from the hardships he was beginning to denounce. 'That's old Hewett,' remarked somebody close by. 'He's the feller to let 'em 'ave it!' Yes, it was John Hewett, much older, much more broken, yet much fiercer than when we last saw him. Though it was evident that he spoke often at these meetings, he had no command of his voice and no coherence of style; after the first few words he seemed to be overcome by rage that was little short of frenzy. Inarticulate screams and yells interrupted the torrent of his invective; he raised both hands above his head and clenched them in a gesture of frantic passion; his visage was frightfully distorted, and in a few minutes there actually fell drops of blood from his bitten lip. Rent!—it was a subject on which the poor fellow could speak to some purpose. What was the root of the difficulty a London workman found in making both ends meet? Wasn't it that accursed law by which the owner of property can make him pay a half, and often more, of his earnings for permission to put his wife and children under a roof? And what sort of dwellings were they, these in which the men who made the wealth of the country were born and lived and died? What would happen to the landlords of Clerkenwell if they got their due? Ay, what *shall* happen, my boys, and that before so very long? For fifteen or twenty minutes John expended his fury, until, in fact, he was speechless. It was terrible to look at him when at length he made his way out of the crowd; his face was livid, his eyes bloodshot, a red slaver covered his lips and beard; you might have taken him for a drunken man, so feebly did his limbs support him, so shattered was he by the fit through which he had passed.

Joseph followed him, and presently walked along at his side.

'That was about as good a speech as I've heard for a long time, Mr. Hewett,' he began by observing. 'I like to hear a man speak as if he meant it.'

John looked up with a leaden, rheumy eye, but the compliment pleased him, and in a moment he smiled vacantly.

'I haven't said my last word yet,' he replied, with difficulty making himself audible through his hoarseness.

'It takes it out of you, I'm afraid. Suppose we have a drop of something at the corner here?'

'I don't mind, Mr. Snowdon. I thought of looking in at my club for a quarter of an hour; perhaps you'd come round with me afterwards?'

They drank at the public-house, then Hewett led the way by back streets to the quarters of the club of which he had been for many years a member. The locality was not cheerful, and the house itself stood in much need of repair. As they entered, John requested his companion to sign his name in the visitors' book; Mr. Snowdon did so with a flourish. They ascended to the first floor and passed into a room where little could be seen but the gas-jets, and those dimly, owing to the fume of pipes. The rattle of bones, the strumming of a banjo, and a voice raised at intervals in a kind of whoop announced that a nigger entertainment was in progress. Recreation of this kind is not uncommon on Sunday evening at the workmen's clubs; you will find it announced in the remarkable list of lectures, &c., printed in certain Sunday newspapers. The company which was exerting itself in the present instance had at all events an appreciative audience; laughter and applause broke forth very frequently.

'I'd forgot it was this kind o' thing to-night,' said Hewett, when he could discover no vacant seat. 'Do you care about it? No more don't I; let's go down into the readin'-room.'

Downstairs they established themselves at their ease. John ordered two half-pints of ale—the club supplied refreshment for the body as well as for the mind—and presently he was more himself.

'How's your wife?' inquired Joseph. 'Better, I hope?'

'I wish I could say so,' answered the other, shaking his head. 'She hasn't been up since Thursday. She's bad, poor woman! she's bad.'

Joseph murmured his sympathy between two draughts of ale.

'Seen young Kirkwood lately?' Hewett asked, averting his eyes and assuming a tone of half-absent indifference.

'He's gone away for his holiday; gone into Essex somewhere. When was it he was speaking of you? Why, one day last week, to be sure.'

'Speakin' about me, eh?' said John, turning his glass round and round on the table. And as the other remained

silent, he added, 'You can tell him, if you like, that my
wife's been very bad for a long time. Him an' me don't have
nothing to say to each other—but you can tell him that, if
you like.'

'So I will,' replied Mr. Snowdon, nodding with a confidential air.

He had noticed from the beginning of his acquaintance
with Hewett that the latter showed no disinclination to receive
news of Kirkwood. As Clem's husband, Joseph was understood to be perfectly aware of the state of things between the
Hewetts and their former friend, and in a recent conversation
with Mrs. Hewett he had assured himself that she, at all
events, would be glad if the estrangement could come to an
end. For reasons of his own, Joseph gave narrow attention
to these signs.

The talk was turning to other matters, when a man who
had just entered the room and stood looking about him with
an uneasy expression caught sight of Hewett and approached
him. He was middle-aged, coarse of feature, clad in the creased
black which a certain type of artisan wears on Sunday.

'I'd like a word with you, John,' he said, 'if your friend'll
excuse.'

Hewett rose from the table, and they walked together to
an unoccupied spot.

'Have you heard any talk about the Burial Club?'
inquired the man, in a low voice of suspicion, knitting his
eyebrows.

'Heard anything? No. What?'

'Why, Dick Smales says he can't get the money for his
boy, as died last week.'

'Can't get it? Why not?'

'That's just what I want to know. Some o' the chaps is
talkin' about it upstairs. M'Cosh ain't been seen for four or
five days. Somebody had news as he was ill in bed, and now
there's no findin' him. I've got a notion there's something
wrong, my boy.'

Hewett's eyes grew large and the muscles of his mouth
contracted.

'Where's Jenkins?' he asked abruptly. 'I suppose he
can explain it?'

'No, by God, he can't! He won't say nothing, but he's
been runnin' about all yesterday and to-day, lookin' precious
queer.'

Without paying any further attention to Snowdon, John left the room with his companion, and they went upstairs. Most of the men present were members of the Burial Club in question, an institution of some fifteen years' standing and in connection with the club which met here for social and political purposes; they were in the habit, like John Hewett, of depositing their coppers weekly, thus insuring themselves or their relatives for a sum payable at death. The rumour that something was wrong, that the secretary M'Cosh could not be found, began to create a disturbance; presently the nigger entertainment came to an end, and the Burial Club was the sole topic of conversation.

On the morrow it was an ascertained fact that one of the catastrophes which occasionally befall the provident among wage-earners had come to pass. Investigation showed that for a long time there had been carelessness and mismanagement of funds, and that fraud had completed the disaster. M'Cosh was wanted by the police.

To John Hewett the blow was a terrible one. In spite of his poverty, he had never fallen behind with those weekly payments. The thing he dreaded supremely was, that his wife or one of the children should die and he be unable to provide a decent burial. At the death of the last child born to him the club had of course paid, and the confidence he felt in it for the future was a sensible support under the many miseries of his life, a support of which no idea can be formed by one who has never foreseen the possibility of those dear to him being carried to a pauper's grave. It was a touching fact that he still kept up the payment for Clara; who could say but his daughter might yet come back to him to die? To know that he had lost that one stronghold against fate was a stroke that left him scarcely strength to go about his daily work.

And he could not breathe a word of it to his wife. Oh that better curse of poverty, which puts corrupting poison into the wounds inflicted by nature, which outrages the spirit's tenderness, which profanes with unutterable defilement the secret places of the mourning heart! He could not, durst not, speak a word of this misery to her whose gratitude and love had resisted every trial, who had shared uncomplainingly all the evil of his lot, and had borne with supreme patience those added sufferings of which he had no conception. For she lay on her deathbed. The doctor told him so on the very day when he

learnt that it would be out of his power to discharge the
fitting pieties at her grave. So far from looking to her for
sympathy, it behoved him to keep from her as much as a suspicion of what had happened.

Their home at this time was a kitchen* in King's Cross
Road. The eldest child, Amy, was now between ten and
eleven; Annie was nine; Tom seven. These, of course, went
to school every day, and were being taught to appreciate the
woefulness of their inheritance. Amy was, on the whole, a
good girl; she could make purchases as well as her mother,
and when in the mood, look carefully after her little brother
and sister; but already she had begun to display restiveness
under the hard discipline to which the domestic poverty subjected her. Once she had played truant from school, and told
falsehoods to the teachers to explain her absence. It was
discovered that she had been tempted by other girls to go and
see the Lord Mayor's show. Annie and Tom threatened to
be troublesome when they got a little older; the boy could
not be taught to speak the truth, and his sister was constantly
committing petty thefts of jam, sugar, even coppers; and
during the past year their mother was seldom able to exert
herself in correcting these faults. Only by dint of struggle
which cost her agonies could she discharge the simplest duties
of home. She made a brave fight against disease and penury
and incessant dread of the coming day, but month after month
her strength failed. Now at length she tried vainly to leave
her bed. The last reserve of energy was exhausted, and the
end near.

After her death, what then? Through the nights of this
week after her doom had been spoken she lay questioning the
future. She knew that but for her unremitting efforts Hewett
would have yielded to the despair of a drunkard; the crucial
moment was when he found himself forsaken by his daughter,
and no one but this poor woman could know what force of
loving will, what entreaties, what tears, had drawn him back
a little way from the edge of the gulf. Throughout his life
until that day of Clara's disappearance he had seemed in no
danger from the deadliest enemy of the poor; one taste of the
oblivion that could be bought at any street-corner, and it was
as though drinking had been a recognised habit with him. A
year, two years, and he still drank himself into forgetfulness
as often as his mental suffering waxed unendurable. On the
morrow of every such crime—interpret the word rightly—he

hated himself for his cruelty to that pale sufferer whose reproaches were only the utterances of love. The third year saw an improvement, whether owing to conscious self-control or to the fact that time was blunting his affliction. Instead of the public-house, he frequented all places where the woes of the nether world found fierce expression. He became a constant speaker at the meetings on Clerkenwell Green and at the Radical clubs. The effect upon him of this excitement was evil enough, yet not so evil as the malady of drink. Mrs. Hewett was thankful for the alternative. But when she was no longer at his side—what then?

His employment was irregular, but for the most part at cabinet-making. The workshop where he was generally to be found was owned by two brothers, who invariably spent the first half of each week in steady drinking. Their money gone, they set to work and made articles of furniture, which on Saturday they took round to the shops of small dealers and sold for what they could get. When once they took up their tools, these men worked with incredible persistency, and they expected the same exertion from those they employed. ' I wouldn't give a —— for the chap as can't do his six-and-thirty hours at the bench ! ' remarked one of them on the occasion of a workman falling into a fainting-fit, caused by utter exhaustion. Hewett was anything but strong, and he earned little.

Late on Saturday afternoon, Sidney Kirkwood and his friends were back in London. As he drew near to Tysoe Street, carrying the bag which was all the luggage he had needed, Sidney by chance encountered Joseph Snowdon, who, after inquiring about his relatives, said that he had just come from visiting the Hewetts. Mrs. Hewett was very ill indeed ; and it was scarcely to be expected she would live more than a few days.

' You mean that ? ' exclaimed Kirkwood, upon whom, after his week of holiday and of mental experiences which seemed to have changed the face of the world for him, this sudden announcement came with a painful shock, reviving all the miserable past. ' She is dying ? '

' There's no doubt of it.'

And Joseph added his belief that John Hewett would certainly not take it ill if the other went there before it was too late.

Sidney had no appetite now for the meal he would have purchased on reaching home. A profound pity for the poor woman who had given him so many proofs of her affection made his heart heavy almost to tears. The perplexities of the present vanished in a revival of old tenderness, of bygone sympathies and sorrows. He could not doubt but that it was his duty to go to his former friends at a time such as this. Perhaps, if he had overcome his pride, he might have sooner brought the estrangement to an end.

He did not know, and had forgotten to ask of Snowdon, the number of the house in King's Cross Road where the Hewetts lived. He could find it, however, by visiting Penny-loaf. Conquering his hesitation, he was on the point of going forth, when his landlady came up and told him that a young girl wished to see him. It was Amy Hewett, and her face told him on what errand she had come.

' Mr. Kirkwood,' she began, looking up with embarrass-ment, for he was all but a stranger to her now, ' mother wants to know if you'd come and see her. She's very bad ; they're afraid she's——'

The word was choked. Amy had been crying, and the tears again rose to her eyes.

' I was just coming,' Sidney answered, as he took her hand and pressed it kindly.

They crossed Wilmington Square and descended by the streets that slope to Coldbath Fields Prison. The cellar in which John Hewett and his family were housed was underneath a milk-shop ; Amy led the way down stone steps from the pave-ment of the street into an area, where more than two people would have had difficulty in standing together. Sidney saw that the window which looked upon this space was draped with a sheet. By an open door they entered a passage, then came to the door of the room. Amy pushed it open, and showed that a lamp gave light within.

To poor homes Sidney Kirkwood was no stranger, but a poorer than this now disclosed to him he had never seen. The first view of it made him draw in his breath, as though a pang went through him. Hewett was not here. The two younger children were sitting upon a mattress, eating bread. Amy stepped up to the bedside and bent to examine her mother's face.

' I think she's asleep,' she whispered, turning round to Sidney.

Sleep, or death? It might well be the latter, for anything Sidney could determine to the contrary. The face he could not recognise, or only when he had gazed at it for several minutes. Oh, pitiless world, that pursues its business and its pleasure, that takes its fill of life from the rising to the going down of the sun, and within sound of its clamour is this hiding-place of anguish and desolation!

'Mother, here's Mr. Kirkwood.'

Repeated several times, the words at length awoke consciousness. The dying woman could not move her head from the pillow; her eyes wandered, but in the end rested upon Sidney. He saw an expression of surprise, of anxiety, then a smile of deep contentment.

'I knew you'd come. I did so want to see you. Don't go just yet, will you?'

The lump in his throat hindered Sidney from replying. Hot tears, an agony in the shedding, began to stream down his cheeks.

'Where's John?' she continued, trying to look about the room. 'Amy, where's your father? He'll come soon, Sidney. I want you and him to be friends again. He knows he'd never ought to a' said what he did. Don't take on so, Sidney! There'll be Amy to look after the others. She'll be a good girl. She's promised me. It's John I'm afraid for. If only he can keep from drink. Will you try and help him, Sidney?'

There was a terrible earnestness of appeal in the look she fixed upon him. Sidney replied that he would hold nothing more sacred than the charge she gave him.

'It'll be easier for them to live,' continued the feeble voice. 'I've been ill so long, and there's been so much expense. Amy'll be earning something before long.'

'Don't trouble,' Sidney answered. 'They shall never want as long as I live—never!'

'Sidney, come a bit nearer. Do you know anything about *her*?'

He shook his head.

'If ever—if ever she comes back, don't turn away from her—will you?'

'I would welcome her as I would a sister of my own.'

'There's such hard things in a woman's life. What would a' become of me, if John hadn't took pity on me! The world's a hard place; I should be glad to leave it, if it wasn't

for them as has to go on in their trouble. I knew you'd come
when I sent Amy. Oh, I feel that easier in my mind!'
    'Why didn't you send long before? No, it's my fault.
Why didn't I come ?   Why didn't I come ?'
    There was a footstep in the passage, a slow, uncertain
step; then the door moved a little. With blurred vision
Sidney saw Hewett enter and come forward. They grasped
each other's hands without speaking, and John, as though his
strength were at an end, dropped upon the chair by the bedside. For the last four or five nights he had sat there; if he
got half an hour's painful slumber now and then it was the
utmost. His face was like that of some prisoner, whom the
long torture of a foul dungeon has brought to the point of
madness. He uttered only a few words during the half-hour
that Sidney still remained in the room. The latter, when
Mrs. Hewett's relapse into unconsciousness made it useless
for him to stay, beckoned Amy to follow him out into the area
and put money in her hand, begging her to get whatever was
needed without troubling her father. He would come again
in the morning.
    Mrs. Hewett died just before daybreak without a pang, as
though death had compassion on her. When Sidney came,
about nine o'clock, he found Amy standing at the door of the
milk-shop; the people who kept it had brought the children
up into their room. Hewett still sat by the bed; seeing Kirkwood, he pointed to the hidden face.
    'How am I to bury her?' he whispered hoarsely. 'Haven't
you heard about it ?   They've stole the club-money; they've
robbed me of it; I haven't as much as'll pay for her coffin.'
    Sidney fancied at first that the man's mind was wandering,
but Hewett took out of his pocket a scrap of newspaper in
which the matter was briefly reported.
    'See, it's there. I've known since last Sunday, and I had
to keep it from her. No need to be afraid of speakin' now.
They've robbed me, and I haven't as much as'll pay for her
coffin. It's a nice blasted world, this is, where they won't let
you live, and then make you pay if you don't want to be buried
like a dog ! She's had nothing but pain and poverty all her
life, and now they'll pitch her out of the way in a parish box.
Do you remember what hopes I used to have when we were
first married ?   See the end of 'em—look at this underground
hole—look at this bed as she lays on ! Is it my fault ? By
God, I wonder I haven't killed myself before this ! I've been

drove mad, I tell you—mad! It's well if I don't do murder yet; every man as I see go by with a good coat on his back and a face fat with good feeding, it's all I can do to keep from catchin' his throat an tearin' the life out of him!'

'Let's talk about the burial,' interposed Sidney. 'Make your mind at ease. I've got enough to pay for all that, and you must let me lend you what you want.'

'Lend me money? You as I haven't spoke to for years?'

'The more fault mine. I ought to have come back again long since; you wouldn't have refused an old friend that never meant an unkindness to you.'

'No, it was me as was to blame,' said the other, with choking voice. 'She always told me so, and she always said what was right. But I can't take it of you, Sidney; I can't! Lend it? An' where am I goin' to get it from to pay you back? It won't be so long before I lie like she does there. It's getting too much for me.'

The first tears he had shed rose at this generosity of the man he had so little claim upon. His passionate grief and the spirit of rebellion, which grew more frenzied as he grew older, were subdued to a sobbing gratitude for the kindness which visited him in his need. Nerveless, voiceless, he fell back again upon the chair and let his head lie by that of the dead woman.

CHAPTER XXII

WATCHING FROM AMBUSH

MR. JOSEPH SNOWDON, though presenting a calm countenance to the world and seeming to enjoy comparative prosperity, was in truth much harassed by the difficulties of his position. Domestic troubles he had anticipated, but the unforeseen sequel of his marriage resulted in a martyrdom at the hands of Clem and her mother such as he had never dreamed of. His faults and weaknesses distinctly those of the civilised man, he found himself in disastrous alliance with two savages, whose characters so supplemented each other as to constitute in unison a formidable engine of tyranny. Clem—suspicious, revengeful, fierce, watching with cruel eyes every opportunity of taking payment on account for the ridicule to which she had exposed herself; Mrs. Peckover—ceaselessly occupied with

the basest scheming, keen as an Indian on any trail she happened to strike, excited by the scent of money as a jackal by
that of carrion; for this pair Joseph was no match. Not only
did they compel him to earn his daily bread by dint of metho-
dical effort such as was torture to his indolent disposition, but,
moreover, in pursuance of Mrs. Peckover's crafty projects, he
was constrained to an assiduous hypocrisy in his relations with
Michael and Jane which wearied him beyond measure. Joseph
did not belong to the most desperate class of hungry mortals;
he had neither the large ambitions and the passionate sensual
desires which make life an unending fever, nor was he possessed with that foul itch of covetousness which is the explanation of the greater part of the world's activity. He understood
quite sufficiently the advantages of wealth, and was prepared
to go considerable lengths for the sake of enjoying them, but
his character lacked persistence. This defect explained the
rogueries and calamities of his life. He had brains in abundance, and a somewhat better education would have made of
him either a successful honest man or a rascal of superior
scope—it is always a toss-up between these two results where
a character such as his is in question. Ever since he abandoned the craft to which his father had had him trained, he
had lived on his wits; there would be matter for a volume in
the history of his experiences at home and abroad, a volume
infinitely more valuable considered as a treatise on modern
civilisation than any professed work on that subject in existence. With one episode only in his past can we here concern
ourselves; the retrospect is needful to make clear his relations
with Mr. Scawthorne.

On his return from America, Joseph possessed a matter of
a hundred pounds; the money was not quite legally earned
(pray let us reserve the word honesty for a truer use than the
common one), and on the whole he preferred to recommence
life in the old country under a pseudonym—that little affair
of the desertion of his child would perhaps, in any case, have
made this advisable. A hundred pounds will not go very far,
but Joseph took care to be well dressed, and allowed it to be
surmised by those with whom he came in contact that the resources at his command were considerable. In early days, as
we know, he had worked at electroplating, and the natural
bent of his intellect was towards mechanical and physical
science; by dint of experimenting at his old pursuit, he persuaded himself, or at all events attained plausibility for the

persuading of others, that he had discovered a new and valuable method of plating with nickel. He gave it out that he was in search of a partner to join him in putting this method into practice. Gentlemen thus situated naturally avail themselves of the advertisement columns of the newspaper, and Joseph by this means had the happiness to form an acquaintance with one Mr. Polkenhorne, who, like himself, had sundry schemes for obtaining money without toiling for it in the usual vulgar way. Polkenhorne was a man of thirty-five, much of a black-guard, but keen-witted, handsome, and tolerably educated; the son of a Clerkenwell clockmaker, he had run through an inheritance of a few thousand pounds, and made no secret of his history—spoke of his experiences, indeed, with a certain pride. Between these two a close intimacy sprang up, one of those partnerships, beginning with mutual deception, which are so common in the border-land of enterprise just skirting the criminal courts. Polkenhorne resided at this time in Kennington; he was married—or said that he was—to a young lady in the theatrical profession, known to the public as Miss Grace Danver. To Mrs. Polkenhorne, or Miss Danver, Joseph soon had the honour of being presented, for she was just then playing at a London theatre; he found her a pretty but con-sumptive-looking girl, not at all likely to achieve great suc-cesses, earning enough, however, to support Mr. Polkenhorne during this time of his misfortunes—a most pleasant and natural arrangement.

Polkenhorne's acquaintances were numerous, but, as he informed Joseph, most of them were 'played out,' that is to say, no further use could be made of them from Polkenhorne's point of view. One, however, as yet imperfectly known, pro-mised to be useful, perchance as a victim, more probably as an ally; his name was Scawthorne, and Polkenhorne had come across him in consequence of a friendship existing between Grace Danver and Mrs. Scawthorne—at all events, a young lady thus known—who was preparing herself for the stage. This gentleman was 'something in the City;' he had rather a close look, but proved genial enough, and was very ready to discuss things in general with Mr. Polkenhorne and his capi-talist friend Mr. Camden, just from the United States.

A word or two about Charles Henry Scawthorne, of the circumstances which made him what you know, or what you conjecture. His father had a small business as a dyer in Islington, and the boy, leaving school at fourteen, was sent to

become a copying-clerk in a solicitor's office; his tastes were
so strongly intellectual that it seemed a pity to put him to
work he hated, and the clerkship was the best opening that
could be procured for him. Two years after, Mr. Scawthorne
died; his wife tried to keep on the business, but soon failed,
and thenceforth her son had to support her as well as himself.
From sixteen to three-and-twenty was the period of young
Scawthorne's life which assured his future advancement—and
his moral ruin. A grave, gentle, somewhat effeminate boy,
with a great love of books and a wonderful power of application to study, he suffered so much during those years of early
maturity, that, as in almost all such cases, his nature was
corrupted. Pity that some self-made intellectual man of our
time has not flung in the world's teeth a truthful autobiography.
Scawthorne worked himself up to a position which had at first
seemed unattainable; what he paid for the success was loss of
all his pure ideals, of his sincerity, of his disinterestedness, of
the fine perceptions to which he was born. Probably no one
who is half-starved and overworked during those critical years
comes out of the trial with his moral nature uninjured; to
certain characters it is a wrong irreparable. To stab the root
of a young tree, to hang crushing burdens upon it, to rend off
its early branches—that is not the treatment likely to result in
growth such as nature purposed. There will come of it a
vicious formation, and the principle applies also to the youth
of men.

Scawthorne was fond of the theatre; as soon as his time
of incessant toil was over, he not only attended performances
frequently, but managed to make personal acquaintance with
sundry theatrical people. Opportunity for this was afforded
by his becoming member of a club, consisting chiefly of solicitors' clerks, which was frequently honoured by visits from
former associates who had taken to the stage; these happy
beings would condescend to recite at times, to give help in
getting up a dramatic entertainment, and soon, in this way,
Scawthorne came to know an old actor named Drake, who
supported himself by instructing novices, male and female, in
his own profession; one of Mr. Drake's old pupils was Miss
Grace Danver, in whom, as soon as he met her, Scawthorne
recognised the Grace Rudd of earlier days. And it was not
long after this that he brought to Mr. Drake a young girl of
interesting appearance, but very imperfect education, who
fancied she had a turn for acting; he succeeded in arranging

for her instruction, and a year and a half later she obtained
her first engagement at a theatre in Scotland. The name she
adopted was Clara Vale. Joseph Snowdon saw her once or
twice before she left London, and from Grace Danver he heard
that Grace and she had been schoolfellows in Clerkenwell.
These facts revived in his memory when he afterwards heard
Clem speak of Clara Hewett.

Nothing came of the alliance between Polkenhorne and
Joseph; when the latter's money was exhausted, they naturally
fell apart. Joseph made a living in sundry precarious ways,
but at length sank into such straits that he risked the step of
going to Clerkenwell Close. Personal interest in his child he
had then none whatever; his short married life seemed an episode in the remote past, recalled with indifference. But in spite
of his profound selfishness, it was not solely from the specu-
lative point of view that he regarded Jane, when he had had
time to realise that she was his daughter, and in a measure to
appreciate her character. With the merely base motives which
led him to seek her affection and put him at secret hostility
with Sidney Kirkwood, there mingled before long a strain of
feeling which was natural and pure; he became a little jealous
of his father and of Sidney on other grounds than those of
self-interest. Intolerable as his home was, no wonder that he
found it a pleasant relief to spend an evening in Hanover
Street; he never came away without railing at himself for his
imbecility in having married Clem. For the present he had
to plot with his wife and Mrs. Peckover, but only let the chance
for plotting *against* them offer itself! The opportunity might
come. In the meantime, the great thing was to postpone the
marriage—he had no doubt it was contemplated—between
Jane and Sidney. That would be little less than a fatality.

The week that Jane spent in Essex was of course a time
of desperate anxiety with Joseph; immediately on her return
he hastened to assure himself that things remained as before.
It seemed to him that Jane's greeting had more warmth than
she was wont to display when they met; sundry other little
changes in her demeanour struck him at the same interview,
and he was rather surprised that she had not so much blitheness
as before she went away. But his speculation on minutiæ such
as these was suddenly interrupted a day or two later by news
which threw him into a state of excitement; Jane sent word
that her grandfather was very unwell, that he appeared to have
caught a chill in the journey home, and could not at present

leave his bed.   For a week the old man suffered from feverish
symptoms, and, though he threw off the ailment, it was in a
state of much feebleness that he at length resumed the ordinary
tenor of his way. Jane had of course stayed at home to nurse
him ; a fortnight, a month passed, and Michael still kept her
from work.   Then it happened that, on Joseph's looking in
one evening, the old man said quietly, 'I think I'd rather
Jane stayed at home in future.   We've had a long talk about
it this afternoon.'

Joseph glanced at his daughter, who met the look very
gravely. He had a feeling that the girl was of a sudden grown
older ; when she spoke it was in brief phrases, and with but
little of her natural spontaneity ; noiseless as always in her
movements, she walked with a staider gait, held herself less
girlishly, and on saying good-night she let her cheek rest for a
moment against her father's, a thing she had never yet done.

The explanation of it all came a few minutes after Jane's
retirement. Michael, warned by his illness how unstable was
the tenure on which he henceforth held his life, had resolved
to have an end of mystery and explain to his son all that he had
already made known to Sidney Kirkwood. With Jane he had
spoken a few hours ago, revealing to her the power that was
in his hands, the solemn significance he attached to it, the
responsibility with which her future was to be invested. To
make the same things known to Joseph was a task of more
difficulty. He could not here count on sympathetic intelligence ; it was but too certain that his son would listen with
disappointment, if not with bitterness. In order to mitigate
the worst results, he began by making known the fact of his
wealth and asking if Joseph had any practical views which
could be furthered by a moderate sum put at his disposal.

' At my death,' he added, ' you'll find that I haven't dealt
unkindly by you. But you're a man of middle age, and I
should like to see you in some fixed way of life before I go.'

Having heard all, Joseph promised to think over the proposal which concerned himself. It was in a strange state of
mind that he returned to the Close ; one thing only he was
clear upon, that to Clem and her mother he would breathe no
word of what had been told him. After a night passed without a wink of sleep, struggling with the amazement, the
incredulity, the confusion of understanding caused by his
father's words, he betook himself to a familiar public-house,
and there penned a note to Scawthorne, requesting an inter-

view as soon as possible. The meeting took place that evening at the retreat behind Lincoln's Inn Fields where the two had held colloquies on several occasions during the last half-year. Scawthorne received with gravity what his acquaintance had to communicate. Then he observed :

'The will was executed ten days ago.'

'It was? And what's he left me?'

'Seven thousand pounds—less legacy duty.'

'And thirty thousand to Jane?'

'Just so.'

Joseph drew in his breath; his teeth ground together for a moment; his eyes grew very wide. With a smile Scawthorne proceeded to explain that Jane's trustees were Mr. Percival, senior, and his son. Should she die unmarried before attaining her twenty-first birthday, the money bequeathed to her was to be distributed among certain charities.

'It's my belief there's a crank in the old fellow,' exclaimed Joseph. 'Is he really such a fool as to think Jane won't use the money for herself? And what about Kirkwood? I tell you what it is; he's a deep fellow, is Kirkwood. I wish you knew him.'

Scawthorne confessed that he had the same wish, but added that there was no chance of its being realised; prudence forbade any move in that direction.

'If he marries her,' questioned Joseph, 'will the money be his?'

'No; it will be settled on her. But it comes to very much the same thing; there's to be no restraint on her discretion in using it.'

'She might give her affectionate parent a hundred or so now and then, if she chose?'

'If she chose.'

Scawthorne began a detailed inquiry into the humanitarian projects of which Joseph had given but a rude and contemptuous explanation. The finer qualities of his mind enabled him to see the matter in quite a different light from that in which it presented itself to Jane's father; he had once or twice had an opportunity of observing Michael Snowdon at the office, and could realise in a measure the character which directed its energies to such an ideal aim. Concerning Jane he asked many questions; then the conversation turned once more to Sidney Kirkwood.

'I wish he'd married his old sweetheart,' observed Joseph, watching the other's face.

'Who was that?'

'A girl called Clara Hewett.'

Their looks met. Scawthorne, in spite of habitual self-command, betrayed an extreme surprise.

'I wonder what's become of her?' continued Joseph, still observing his companion, and speaking with unmistakable significance.

'Just tell me something about this,' said Scawthorne peremptorily.

Joseph complied, and ended his story with a few more hints.

'I never saw her myself—at least I can't be sure that I did. There was somebody of the same name—Clara—a friend of Polkenhorne's wife.'

Scawthorne appeared to pay no attention; he mused with a wrinkled brow.

'If only I could put something between Kirkwood and the girl,' remarked Joseph, as if absently. 'I shouldn't wonder if it could be made worth some one's while to give a bit of help that way. Don't you think so?'

In the tone of one turning to a different subject, Scawthorne asked suddenly:

'What use are you going to make of your father's offer?'

'Well, I'm not quite sure, Shouldn't wonder if I go in for filters.'

'Filters?'

Joseph explained. In the capacity of 'commission agent' —denomination which includes and apologises for such a vast variety of casual pursuits—he had of late been helping to make known to the public a new filter, which promised to be a commercial success. The owner of the patent lacked capital, and a judicious investment might secure a share in the business; Joseph thought of broaching the subject with him next day.

'You won't make a fool of yourself?' remarked Scawthorne.

'Trust me; I think I know my way about.'

For the present these gentlemen had nothing more to say to each other; they emptied their glasses with deliberation, exchanged a look which might mean either much or nothing, and so went their several ways.

The filter project was put into execution. When Joseph had communicated it in detail to his father, the latter took the professional advice of his friend Mr. Percival, and in the course of a few weeks Joseph found himself regularly established in a business which had the—for him—novel characteristic of serving the purposes of purity. The manufactory was situated in a by-street on the north of Euston Road : a small concern, but at all events a genuine one. On the window of the office you read, ' Lake, Snowdon, & Co.' As it was necessary to account for this achievement to Clem and Mrs. Peckover, Joseph made known to them a part of the truth ; of the will he said nothing, and, for reasons of his own, he allowed these tender relatives to believe that he was in a fair way to inherit the greater part of Michael's possessions. There was jubilation in Clerkenwell Close, but mother and daughter kept stern watch upon Joseph's proceedings.

Another acquaintance of ours benefited by this event. Michael made it a stipulation that some kind of work should be found at the factory for John Hewett, who, since his wife's death, had been making a wretched struggle to establish a more decent home for the children. The firm of Lake, Snowdon, & Co. took Hewett into their employment as a porter, and paid him twenty-five shillings a week—of which sum, however, the odd five shillings were privately made up by Michael. On receiving this appointment, John drew the sigh of a man who finds himself in haven after perilous beating about a lee shore. The kitchen in King's Cross Road was abandoned, and with Sidney Kirkwood's aid the family found much more satisfactory quarters. Friends of Sidney's, a man and wife of middle age without children, happened to be looking for lodgings : it was decided that they and John Hewett should join in the tenancy of a flat, up on the fifth storey of the huge block of tenements called Farringdon Road Buildings. By this arrangement the children would be looked after, and the weekly twenty-five shillings could be made to go much further than on the ordinary system. As soon as everything had been settled, and when Mr. and Mrs. Eagles had already housed themselves in the one room which was all they needed for their private accommodation, Hewett and the children began to pack together their miserable sticks and rags for removal. Just then Sidney Kirkwood looked in.

' Eagles wants to see you for a minute about something,' he said. ' Just walk round with me, will you ? '

John obeyed, in the silent, spiritless way now usual with him. It was but a short distance to the buildings : they went up the winding stone staircase, and Sidney gave a hollow-sounding knock at one of the two doors that faced each other on the fifth storey. Mrs. Eagles opened, a decent, motherly woman, with a pleasant and rather curious smile on her face. She led the way into one of the rooms which John had seen empty only a few hours ago. How was this? Oil-cloth on the floor, a blind at the window, a bedstead, a table, a chest of drawers——

Mrs. Eagles withdrew, discreetly. Hewett stood with a look of uneasy wonderment, and at length turned to his companion.

' Now, look here,' he growled, in an unsteady voice, ' what's all this about ? '

' Somebody seems to have got here before you,' replied Sidney, smiling.

' How the devil am I to keep any self-respect if you go on treatin' me in this fashion ? ' blustered John, hanging his head.

' It isn't my doing, Mr. Hewett.'

' Whose, then ? '

' A friend's. Don't make a fuss. You shall know the person some day.'

CHAPTER XXIII

ON THE EVE OF TRIUMPH

' I HAVE got your letter, but it tells me no more than the last did. Why don't you say plainly what you mean ? I suppose it's something you are ashamed of. You say that there's a chance for me of earning a large sum of money, and if you are in earnest, I shall be only too glad to hear how it's to be done. This life is no better than what I used to lead years ago ; I'm no nearer to getting a good part than I was when I first began acting, and unless I can get money to buy dresses and all the rest of it, I may go on for ever at this hateful drudgery. I shall take nothing more from you: I say it, and I mean it ; but as you tell me that this chance has nothing to do with yourself, let me know what it really is. For a large sum of money there are few things I wouldn't do. Of course it's something disgraceful, but you needn't be afraid on that account ; I haven't lost all my pride yet, but I know what I'm fighting for, and I won't be beaten. Cost what it may, I'll make people hear of me and talk of me, and I'll pay myself back for all I've gone through. So write in plain words, or come and see me.   C. V.'

She wrote at a round table, shaky on its central support, in the parlour of an indifferent lodging-house ; the October afternoon drew towards dusk ; the sky hung low and murky, or, rather, was itself invisible, veiled by the fume of factory chimneys ; a wailing wind rattled the sash and the door. A newly lighted fire refused to flame cheerfully, half smothered in its own smoke, which every now and then was blown downwards and out into the room. The letter finished—scribbled angrily with a bad pen and in pale ink—she put it into its envelope—' C. H. Scawthorne, Esq.'

Then a long reverie, such as she always fell into when alone and unoccupied. The face was older, but not greatly changed from that of the girl who fought her dread fight with temptation, and lost it, in the lodging at Islington, who, then as now, brooded over the wild passions in her heart and defied the world that was her enemy. Still a beautiful face, its haughty characteristics strengthened, the lips a little more sensual, a little coarser ; still the same stamp of intellect upon the forehead, the same impatient scorn and misery in her eyes. She asked no one's pity, but not many women breathed at that moment who knew more of suffering.

For three weeks she had belonged to a company on tour in the northern counties. In accordance with the modern custom—so beneficial to actors and the public—their repertory consisted of one play, the famous melodrama, ' A Secret of the Thames,' recommended to provincial audiences by its run of four hundred and thirty-seven nights at a London theatre. These, to be sure, were not the London actors, but advertisements in local newspapers gave it to be understood that they ' made an *ensemble* in no respect inferior to that which was so long the delight of the metropolis.' Starred on the placards was the name of Mr. Samuel Peel, renowned in the North of England ; his was the company, and his the main glory in the piece. As leading lady he had the distinguished Miss Erminia Walcott ; her part was a trying one, for she had to be half-strangled by ruffians and flung—most decorously—

over the parapet of London Bridge. In the long list of sub-
ordinate performers occurred two names with which we are
familiar, Miss Grace Danver and Miss Clara Vale. The present evening would be the third and last in a certain town of
Lancashire, one of those remarkable centres of industry which
pollute heaven and earth, and on that account are spoken of
with somewhat more of pride than stirred the Athenian when
he named his Acropolis.

Clara had just risen to stir the fire, compelled to move by
the smoke that was annoying her, when, after a tap at the
door, there came in a young woman of about five-and-twenty,
in a plain walking costume, tall, very slender, pretty, but
looking ill. At this moment there was a slight flush on her
cheeks and a brightness in her eyes which obviously came of
some excitement. She paused just after entering and said in
an eager voice, which had a touch of huskiness :

'What do you think? Miss Walcott's taken her hook!'

Clara did not allow herself to be moved at this announcement. For several days what is called unpleasantness had
existed between the leading lady and the manager : in other
words, they had been quarrelling violently on certain professional matters, and Miss Walcott had threatened to ruin the
tour by withdrawing her invaluable services. The menace
was at last executed, in good earnest, and the cause of Grace
Danver's excitement was that she, as Miss Walcott's under-
study, would to-night, in all probability, be called upon to
take the leading part.

'I'm glad to hear it,' Clara replied, very soberly.

'You don't look as if you cared much,' rejoined the other,
with a little irritation.

'What do you want me to do? An I to scream with joy
because the greatest actress in the world has got her chance
at last?'

There was bitterness in the irony. Whatever their friendship in days gone by, these two were clearly not on the most
amiable terms at present. This was their first engagement
in the same company, and it had needed but a week of association to put a jealousy and ill-feeling between them which proved
fatal to such mutual kindness as they had previously cherished.
Grace, now no less than in her schooldays, was fond of patronising : as the elder in years and in experience, she adopted a
tone which Clara speedily resented. To heighten the danger of
a conflict between natures essentially incompatible, both were

in a morbid and nervous state, consumed with discontent, sensitive to the most trifling injury, abandoned to a fierce egoism, which the course of their lives and the circumstances of their profession kept constantly inflamed. Grace was of acrid and violent temper; when stung with words such as Clara was only too apt at using, she speedily lost command of herself and spoke, or even acted, frantically. Except that she had not Clara's sensibilities, her lot was the harder of the two; for she knew herself stricken with a malady which would hunt her unsparingly to the grave. On her story I have no time to dwell; it was full of wretchedness, which had caused her, about a year ago, to make an attempt at suicide. A little generosity, and Clara might have helped to soothe the pains of one so much weaker than herself; but noble feeling was extinct in the girl, or so nearly extinct that a breath of petty rivalry could make her base, cruel, remorseless.

'At all events I *have* got my chance!' exclaimed Grace, with a harsh laugh. 'When you get yours, ask me to congratulate you.'

And she swept her skirts out of the room. In a few minutes Clara put a stamp on her letter and went out to the post. Her presence at the theatre would not be necessary for another two hours, but as the distance was slight, and nervousness would not let her remain at home, she walked on to make inquiry concerning Grace's news. Rain had just begun to fall, and with it descended the smut and grime that darkened above the houses; the pavement was speedily oversmeared with sticky mud, and passing vehicles flung splashes in every direction. Odours of oil and shoddy, and all such things as characterised the town, grew more pungent under the heavy shower. On reaching the stage-door, Clara found two or three of her companions just within; the sudden departure of Miss Walcott had become known to everyone, and at this moment Mr. Peel was holding a council, to which, as the doorkeeper testified, Miss Danver had been summoned.

The manager decided to make no public announcement of what had happened before the hour came for drawing up the curtain. A scrappy rehearsal for the benefit of Grace Danver and the two or three other ladies who were affected by the necessary rearrangement went on until the last possible moment, then Mr. Peel presented himself before the drop and made a little speech. The gallery was full of mill-hands; in the pit was a sprinkling of people; the circles and boxes pre-

sented half a dozen occupants. 'Sudden domestic calamity
. . . . enforced absence of the lady who played . . . . efficient
substitution . . . . deep regret, but confidence in the friendly
feeling of audience on this last evening.'

They growled, but in the end applauded the actor-manager,
who had succeeded in delicately hinting that, after all, the
great attraction was still present in his own person. The
play went very much as usual, but those behind the scenes
were not allowed to forget that Mr. Peel was in a furious
temper : the ladies noticed with satisfaction that more than
once he glared ominously at Miss Danver, who naturally could
not aid him to make his 'points' as Miss Walcott had accustomed herself to do. At his final exit, it was observed that he
shrugged his shoulders and muttered a few oaths.

Clara had her familiar part ; it was a poor one from every
point of view, and the imbecility of the words she had to speak
affected her to-night with exceptional irritation. Clara always
acted in ill-humour. She despised her audience for their
acceptance of the playwright's claptrap ; she felt that she
could do better than any of the actresses entrusted with the
more important characters ; her imagination was for ever
turning to powerful scenes in plays she had studied privately,
and despair possessed her at the thought that she would perhaps never have a chance of putting forth her strength. To-
night her mood was one of sullen carelessness ; she did little
more than 'walk through' her part, feeling a pleasure in thus
insulting the house. One scrap of dialogue she had with
Grace, and her eyes answered with a flash of hatred to the
arrogance of the other's regard. At another point she all but
missed her cue, for her thoughts were busy with that letter to
which she had replied this afternoon. Mr. Peel looked at her
savagely, and she met his silent rebuke with an air of indifference. After that the manager appeared to pay peculiar attention to her as often as they were together before the footlights. It was not the first time that Mr. Peel had allowed
her to see that she was an object of interest to him.

There was an after-piece, but Clara was not engaged in it.
When, at the fall of the curtain on the melodrama, she went
to the shabby dressing-room which she shared with two companions, a message delivered by the call boy bade her repair
as soon as possible to the manager's office. What might this
mean ? She was startled on the instant, but speedily recovered
her self-control ; most likely she was to receive a rating—let

it come! Without unusual hurry, she washed, changed her dress, and obeyed the summons.

Mr. Peel was still a young man, of tall and robust stature, sanguine, with much sham refinement in his manner; he prided himself on the civility with which he behaved to all who had business relations with him, but every now and then the veneer gave an awkward crack, and, as in his debate with Miss Walcott, the man himself was discovered to be of coarse grain. His aspect was singular when, on Clara's entrance into the private room, he laid down his cigarette and scrutinised her. There was a fiery hue on his visage, and the scowl of his black eyebrows had a peculiar ugliness.

'Miss Vale,' he began, after hesitation, 'do you consider that you played your part this evening with the conscientiousness that may fairly be expected of you?'

'Perhaps not,' replied the girl, averting her eyes, and resting her hand on the table.

'And may I ask *why* not?'

'I didn't feel in the humour. The house saw no difference.'

'Indeed? The house saw no difference? Do you mean to imply that you always play badly?'

'I mean that the part isn't worth any attention—even if they were able to judge.'

There was a perfection of insolence in her tone that in itself spoke strongly for the abilities she could display if occasion offered.

'This is rather an offhand way of treating the subject, madam,' cried Mr. Peel. 'If you disparage our audiences, I beg you to observe that it is much the same thing as telling me that my own successes are worthless!'

'I intended nothing of the kind.'

'Perhaps not.' He thrust his hands into his pockets, and looked down at his boots for an instant. 'So you are discontented with your part?'

'It's only natural that I should be.'

'I presume you think yourself equal to Juliet, or perhaps Lady Macbeth?'

'I could play either a good deal better than most women do.'

The manager laughed, by no means ill-humouredly.

'I'm sorry I can't bring you out in Shakespeare just at present, Miss Vale; but—should you think it a condescension to play Laura Denton?'

This was Miss Walcott's part, now Grace Danver's. Clara looked at him with mistrust; her breath did not come quite naturally.

'How long would it take you, do you think,' pursued the other, ' to get the words ? '

'An hour or two; I all but know them.'

The manager took a few paces this way and that.

'We go on to Bolton to-morrow morning. Could you undertake to be perfect for the afternoon rehearsal ? '

' Yes.'

' Then I'll try you. Here's a copy you can take. I make no terms, you understand; it's an experiment. We'll have another talk to-morrow. Good-night.'

She left the room. Near the door stood Grace Danver and another actress, both of whom were bidden to wait upon the manager before leaving. Clara passed under the fire of their eyes, but scarcely observed them.

Rain drenched her between the theatre and her lodgings, for she did not think of putting up an umbrella ; she thought indeed of nothing; there was fire and tumult in her brain. On the round table in her sitting-room supper was made ready, but she did not heed it. Excitement compelled her to walk incessantly round and round the scanty space of floor. Already she had begun to rehearse the chief scenes of Laura Denton; she spoke the words with all appropriate loudness and emphasis; her gestures were those of the stage, as though an audience sat before her ; she seemed to have grown taller. There came a double knock at the house-door, but it did not attract her attention; a knock at her own room, and only when some one entered was she recalled to the present. It was Grace again; her lodging was elsewhere, and this late visit could have but one motive.

They stood face to face. The elder woman was so incensed that her lips moved fruitlessly, like those of a paralytic.

'I suppose you're going to make a scene,' Clara addressed her. ' Please remember how late it is, and don't let all the house hear you.'

'You mean to tell me you accepted that offer of Peel's— without saying a word—without as much as telling him that he ought to speak to me first ? '

' Certainly I did. I've waited long enough; I'm not going to beat about the bush when my chance comes.'

' And you called yourself my friend ? '

'I'm nobody's friend but my own in an affair of this kind. If you'd been in my place you'd have done just the same.'

'I wouldn't! I *couldn't* have been such a mean creature! Every man and woman in the company'll cry shame on you.'

'Don't deafen me with your nonsense! If you played the part badly, I suppose some one else must take it. You were only on trial, like I shall be.'

Grace was livid with fury.

'Played badly! As if we didn't all know how you've managed it! Much it has to do with good or bad acting! We know how creatures of your kind get what they want.'

Before the last word was uttered she was seized with a violent fit of coughing; her cheeks flamed, and spots of blood reddened on the handkerchief she put to her mouth. Half-stifled, she lay back in the angle of the wall by the door. Clara regarded her with a contemptuous pity, and when the cough had nearly ceased, said coldly:

'I'm not going to try and match you in insulting language; I dare say you'd beat me at that. If you take my advice, you'll go home and take care of yourself; you look ill enough to be in bed. I don't care what you or anyone else thinks of me; what you said just now was a lie, but it doesn't matter. I've got the part, and I'll take good care that I keep it. You talk about us being friends; I should have thought you knew by this time that there's no such thing as friendship or generosity or feeling for women who have to make their way in the world. You've had your hard times as well as I, and what's the use of pretending what you don't believe? You wouldn't give up a chance for me; I'm sure I should never expect you to. We have to fight, to fight for everything, and the weak get beaten. That's what life has taught me.'

'You're right,' was the other's reply, given with a strangely sudden calmness. 'And we'll see who wins.'

Clara gave no thought to the words, nor to the look of deadly enmity that accompanied them. Alone again, she speedily became absorbed in a vision of the triumph which she never doubted was near at hand. A long, long time it seemed since she had sold herself to degradation with this one hope. You see that she had formulated her philosophy of life since then; a child of the nether world whom fate had endowed with intellect, she gave articulate utterance to what is seething in the brains of thousands who fight and perish in the obscure depths. The bitter bargain was issuing to her profit at last;, she would yet attain that end which had shone through all her misery—to be known as a successful actress by those she had abandoned, whose faces were growing dim to her memory, but of whom, in truth, she still thought more than of all the multitudinous unknown public. A great success during the remainder of this tour, and she might hope for an engagement in London. Her portraits would at length be in the windows; some would recognise her.

Yet she was not so pitiless as she boasted. The next morning, when she met Grace, there came a pain at her heart in seeing the ghastly, bloodless countenance which refused to turn towards her. Would Grace be able to act at all at the next town? Yes, one more scene.

They reached Bolton. In the afternoon the rehearsal took place, but the first representation was not until to-morrow. Clara saw her name attached to the leading female character on bills rapidly printed and distributed through the town. She went about in a dream, rather a delirium. Mr. Peel used his most affable manner to her; his compliments after the rehearsal were an augury of great things. And the eventful evening approached.

To give herself plenty of time to dress (the costumes needed for the part were fortunately simple, and Mr. Peel had advanced her money to make needful purchases) she left her lodgings at half-past six. It was a fine evening, but very dark in the two or three by-streets along which she had to pass to reach the theatre. She waited a minute on the doorstep to let a troop of female mill-hands go by; their shoes clanked on the pavement, and they were singing in chorus, a common habit of their kind in leaving work. Then she started and walked quickly. . . .

Close by the stage-door, which was in a dark, narrow passage, stood a woman with veiled face, a shawl muffling the upper part of her body. Since six o'clock she had been waiting about the spot, occasionally walking to a short distance, but always keeping her face turned towards the door. One or two persons came up and entered; she observed them, but held aloof. Another drew near. The woman advanced, and, as she did so, freed one of her arms from the shawl.

'That you, Grace?' said Clara, almost kindly, for in her victorious joy she was ready to be at peace with all the world.

The answer was something dashed violently in her face— something fluid and fiery—something that ate into her flesh, that frenzied her with pain, that drove her shrieking she knew not whither.

Late in the same night, a pointsman, walking along the railway a little distance out of the town, came upon the body of a woman, train-crushed, horrible to view. She wore the dress of a lady ; a shawl was still partly wrapped about her, and her hands were gloved. Nothing discoverable upon her would have helped strangers in the task of identification, and as for her face—— But a missing woman was already sought by the police, and when certain persons were taken to view this body, they had no difficulty in pronouncing it that of Grace Danver.

CHAPTER XXIV

THE FAMILY HISTORY PROGRESSES

WHAT could possess John Hewett that, after resting from the day's work, he often left his comfortable room late in the evening and rambled about the streets of that part of London which had surely least interest for him, the streets which are thronged with idlers, with carriages going homeward from the theatres, with those who can only come forth to ply their business when darkness has fallen ? Did he seek food for his antagonism in observing the characteristics of the world in which he was a stranger, the world which has its garners full and takes its ease amid superfluity? It could scarcely be that, for since his wife's death an indifference seemed to be settling upon him ; he no longer cared to visit the Green or his club on Sunday, and seldom spoke on the subjects which formerly goaded him to madness. He appeared to be drawn forth against his will, in spite of weariness, and his look as he walked on was that of a man who is in search of some one. Yet whom could he expect to meet in these highways of the West End ?

Oxford Street, Regent Street, Piccadilly, the Strand, the ways about St. James's Park ; John Hewett was not the only father who has come forth after nightfall from an obscure home to look darkly at the faces passing on these broad pavements. At times he would shrink into a shadowed corner,

and peer thence at those who went by under the gaslight.
When he moved forward, it was with the uneasy gait of one
who shuns observation ; you would have thought, perchance,
that he watched an opportunity of begging and was shamefaced : it happened now and then that he was regarded suspiciously. A rough-looking man, with grizzled beard, with
eyes generally bloodshot, his shoulders stooping—naturally
the miserable are always suspected where law is conscious of
its injustice.

Two years ago he was beset for a time with the same
restlessness, and took night-walks in the same directions ; the
habit wore away, however. Now it possessed him even more
strongly. Between ten and eleven o'clock, when the children
were in bed, he fell into abstraction, and presently, with an
unexpected movement, looked up as if some one had spoken
to him—just the look of one who hears a familiar voice ; then
he sighed, and took his hat and went forth. It happened
sometimes when he was sitting with his friends Mr. and Mrs.
Eagles ; in that case he would make some kind of excuse.
The couple suspected that his business would take him to the
public-house, but John never came back with a sign about
him of having drunk ; of that failing he had broken himself.
He went cautiously down the stone stairs, averting his face if
anyone met him ; then by cross-ways he reached Gray's Inn
Road, and so westwards.

He had a well-ordered home, and his children were about
him, but these things did not compensate him for the greatest
loss his life had suffered. The children, in truth, had no very
strong hold upon his affections. Sometimes, when Amy sat
and talked to him, he showed a growing nervousness, an impatience, and at length turned away from her as if to occupy
himself in some manner. The voice was not that which had
ever power to soothe him when it spoke playfully. Memory
brought back the tones which had been so dear to him, and at
times something more than memory ; he seemed really to hear
them, as if from a distance. And then it was that he went
out to wander in the streets.

Of Bob in the meantime he saw scarcely anything. That
young man presented himself one Sunday shortly after his
father had become settled in the new home, but practically
he was a stranger. John and he had no interests in common ;
there even existed a slight antipathy on the father's part of
late years. Strangely enough this feeling expressed itself one

day in the form of a rebuke to Bob for neglecting Pennyloaf —Pennyloaf, whom John had always declined to recognise.

'I hear no good of your goin's on,' remarked Hewett, on a casual encounter in the street. 'A married man ought to give up the kind of company as you keep.'

'I do no harm,' replied Bob bluntly. 'Has my wife been complaining to you?'

'I've nothing to do with her; it's what I'm told.'

'By Kirkwood, I suppose? You'd better not have made up with him again, if he's only making mischief.'

'No, I didn't mean Kirkwood.'

And John went his way. Odd thing, was it not, that this embittered leveller should himself practise the very intolerance which he reviled in people of the upper world. For his refusal to recognise Pennyloaf he had absolutely no grounds, save—I use the words advisedly—an aristocratic prejudice. Bob had married deplorably beneath him; it was unpardonable, let the character of the girl be what it might. Of course you recognise the item in John Hewett's personality which serves to explain this singular attitude. But, viewed generally, it was one of those bits of human inconsistency over which the observer smiles, and which should be recommended to good people in search of arguments for the equality of men.

After that little dialogue, Bob went home in a disagreeable temper. To begin with, his mood had been ruffled, for the landlady at his lodgings—the fourth to which he had removed this year—was 'nasty' about a week or two of unpaid rent, and a man on whom he had counted this evening for the payment of a debt was keeping out of his way. He found Pennyloaf sitting on the stairs with her two children, as usual; poor Pennyloaf had not originality enough to discover new expressions of misery, and that one bright idea of donning her best dress was a single instance of ingenuity. In obedience to Jane Snowdon, she kept herself and the babies and the room tolerably clean, but everything was done in the most dispirited way.

'What are you kicking about here for?' asked Bob impatiently. 'That's how that kid gets its cold—of course it is!—Ger out!'

The last remark was addressed to the elder child, who caught at his legs as he strode past. Bob was not actively unkind to the little wretches for whose being he was responsible; he simply occupied the natural position of unsophisticated man to children of that age, one of indifference, or impatience. The infants were a nuisance; no one desired their coming, and the older they grew the more expensive they were.

It was a cold evening of October; Pennyloaf had allowed the fire to get very low (she knew not exactly where the next supply of coals was to come from), and her husband growled as he made a vain endeavour to warm his hands.

'Why haven't you got tea ready?' he asked.

'I couldn't be sure as you was comin', Bob; how could I? But I'll soon get the kettle boilin'.'

'Couldn't be sure as I was coming? Why, I've been back every night this week—except two or three.'

It was Thursday, but Bob meant nothing jocose.

'Look here!' he continued, fixing a surly eye upon her. 'What do you mean by complaining about me to people? Just mind your own business. When was that girl Jane Snowdon here last?'

'Yesterday, Bob.'

'I thought as much. Did she give you anything?' He made this inquiry in rather a shamefaced way.

'No, she didn't.'

'Well, I tell you what it is. I'm not going to have her coming about the place, so understand that. When she comes next, you'll just tell her she needn't come again.'

Pennyloaf looked at him with dismay. For the delivery of this command Bob had seated himself on the corner of the table and crossed his arms. But for the touch of black-guardism in his appearance, Bob would have been a very good-looking fellow; his face was healthy, by no means commonplace in its mould, and had the peculiar vividness which indicates ability—so impressive, because so rarely seen, in men of his level. Unfortunately his hair was cropped all but to the scalp, in the fashionable manner; it was greased, too, and curled up on one side of his forehead with a peculiarly offensive perkishness. Poor Pennyloaf was in a great degree responsible for the ills of her married life; not only did she believe Bob to be the handsomest man who walked the earth, but in her weakness she could not refrain from telling him as much. At the present moment he was intensely self-conscious; with Pennyloaf's eye upon him, he posed for effect. The idea of forbidding future intercourse with Jane had come to him quite suddenly; it was by no means his intention to make his order permanent, for Jane had now and then brought little

presents which were useful, but just now he felt a satisfaction
in asserting authority. Jane should understand that he regarded her censure of him with high displeasure.

' You don't mean that, Bob ? ' murmured Pennyloaf.

' Of course I do. And let me catch you disobeying me !
I should think you might find better friends than a girl as
used to be the Peckovers' dirty little servant.'

Bob turned up his nose and sniffed the air. And Pennyloaf, in spite of the keenest distress, actually felt that there
was something in the objection, thus framed ! She herself
had never been a servant—never ; she had never sunk below
working with the needle for sixteen hours a day for a payment
of ninepence. The work-girl regards a domestic slave as very
distinctly her inferior.

' But that's a long while ago,' she ventured to urge, after
reflection.

' That makes no difference. Do as I tell you, and don't
argue.'

It was not often that visitors sought Bob at his home of
an evening, but whilst this dialogue was still going on an
acquaintance made his arrival known by a knock at the door.
It was a lank and hungry individual, grimy of face and hands,
his clothing such as in the country would serve well for a
scarecrow. Who could have recognised in him the once spruce
and spirited Mr. Jack Bartley, distinguished by his chimney-
pot hat at the Crystal Palace on Bob's wedding-day ? At the
close of that same day, as you remember, he and Bob engaged
in terrific combat, the outcome of earlier rivalry for the favour
of Clem Peckover. Notwithstanding that memory, the two
were now on very friendly terms. You have heard from
Clem's lips that Jack Bartley, failing to win herself, ended by
espousing Miss Susan Jollop ; also what was the result of that
alliance. Mr. Bartley was an unhappy man. His wife had
a ferocious temper, was reckless with money, and now drank
steadily ; the consequence was, that Jack had lost all regular
employment, and only earned occasional pence in the most
various ways. Broken in spirit, he himself first made advances to his companion of former days, and Bob, flattered
by the other's humility, encouraged him as a hanger-on.—
Really, we shall soon be coming to a conclusion that the differences between the nether and the upper world are purely
superficial.

Whenever Jack came to spend an hour with Mr. and Mrs.

Hewett, he was sure sooner or later to indulge the misery that preyed upon him and give way to sheer weeping. He did so this evening, almost as soon as he entered.

'I ain't had a mouthful past my lips since last night, I ain't!' he sobbed. 'It's 'ard on a feller as used to have his meals regular. I'll murder Suke yet, see if I don't! I'll have her life! She met me last night and gave me this black eye as you see—she did! It's 'ard on a feller.'

'You mean to say as she *it* you?' cried Pennyloaf.

Bob chuckled, thrust his hands into his pockets, spread himself out. His own superiority was so gloriously manifest.

'Suppose *you* try it on with *me*, Penny!' he cried.

'You'd give me something as I should remember,' she answered, smirking, the good little slavey.

'Shouldn't wonder if I did,' assented Bob.

Mr. Bartley's pressing hunger was satisfied with some bread and butter and a cup of tea. Whilst taking a share of the meal, Bob brought a small box on to the table; it had a sliding lid, and inside were certain specimens of artistic work with which he was wont to amuse himself when tired of roaming the streets in jovial company. Do you recollect that, when we first made Bob's acquaintance, he showed Sidney Kirkwood a medal of his own design and casting? His daily work at die-sinking had of course supplied him with this suggestion, and he still found pleasure in work of the same kind. In days before commercialism had divorced art and the handicrafts, a man with Bob's distinct faculty would have found encouragement to exercise it for serious ends; as it was, he remained at the semi-conscious stage with regard to his own aptitudes, and cast leaden medals just as a way of occupying his hands when a couple of hours hung heavy on them. Partly with the thought of amusing the dolorous Jack, yet more to win laudation, he brought forth now a variety of casts and moulds and spread them on the table. His latest piece of work was a medal in high relief bearing the heads of the Prince and Princess of Wales surrounded with a wreath. Bob had no political convictions; with complacency he drew these royal features, the sight of which would have made his father foam at the mouth. True, he might have found subjects artistically more satisfying, but he belonged to the people, and the English people.

Jack Bartley, having dried his eyes and swallowed his bread and butter, considered the medal with much attention.

'I say,' he remarked at length, 'will you give me this, Bob?'

'I don't mind.   You can take it if you like.'

'Thanks!'

Jack wrapped it up and put it in his waistcoat pocket, and before long rose to take leave of his friends.

'I only wish I'd got a wife like you,' he observed at the door, as he saw Pennyloaf bending over the two children, recently put to bed.

Pennyloaf's eyes gleamed at the compliment, and she turned them to her husband.

'She's nothing to boast of,' said Bob, judicially and masculinely.   'All women are pretty much alike.'

And Pennyloaf tried to smile at the snub.

Having devoted one evening to domestic quietude, Bob naturally felt himself free to dispose of the next in a manner more to his taste.   The pleasures which sufficed to keep him from home had the same sordid monotony which characterises life in general for the lower strata of society.   If he had money, there was the music-hall; if he had none, there were the streets.   Being in the latter condition to-night, he joined a company of male and female intimates, and with them strolled aimlessly from one familiar rendezvous to another.   Would that it were possible to set down a literal report of the conversation which passed during hours thus spent!   Much of it, of course, would be merely revolting, but for the most part it would consist of such wearying, such incredible imbecilities as no human patience could endure through five minutes' perusal.   Realise it, however, and you grasp the conditions of what is called the social problem.   As regards Robert Hewett in particular, it would help you to understand the momentous change in his life which was just coming to pass.

On his reaching home at eleven o'clock, Pennyloaf met him with the news that Jack Bartley had looked in twice and seemed very anxious to see him.   To-morrow being Saturday, Jack would call again early in the afternoon.   When the time came, he presented himself, hungry and dirty as ever, but with an unwonted liveliness in his eye.

'I've got something to say to you,' be began, in a low voice, nodding significantly towards Pennyloaf.

'Go and buy what you want for to-morrow,' said Bob to his wife, giving her some money out of his wages.   'Take the kids.'

Disappointed in being thus excluded from confidence, but obedient as ever, Pennyloaf speedily prepared herself and the children, the younger of whom she still had to carry. When she was gone Mr. Bartley assumed a peculiar attitude and began to speak in an undertone.

'You know that medal as you gave me the other night?'

'What about it?'

'I sold it for fourpence to a chap I know. It got me a bed at the lodgings in Pentonville Road.'

'Oh, you did! Well, what else?'

Jack was writhing in the most unaccountable way, peering hither and thither out of the corners of his eyes, seeming to have an obstruction in his throat.

'It was in a public-house as I sold it—a chap I know. There was another chap as I didn't know standing just by—see? He kep' looking at the medal, and he kep' looking at me. When I went out the chap as I didn't know followed behind me. I didn't see him at first, but he come up with me just at the top of Rosoman Street—a red-haired chap, looked like a corster. "Hollo!" says he. "Hollo!" says I. "Got any more o' them medals?" he says, in a quiet way like. "What do you want to know for?" I says—'cos you see he was a bloke as I didn't know nothing about, and there's no good being over-free with your talk. He got me to walk on a bit with him, and kept talking. "You didn't buy that nowhere," he says, with a sort of wink. "What if I didn't?" I says. "There's no harm as I know." Well, he kept on with his sort o' winks, and then he says, "Got any *queer* to put round?"'

At this point Jack lowered his voice to a whisper and looked timorously towards the door.

'You know what he meant, Bob?'

Bob nodded and became reflective.

'Well, I didn't say nothing,' pursued Bartley, 'but the chap stuck to me. "A fair price for a fair article," he says. "You'll always find me there of a Thursday night, if you've got any business going. Give me a look round," he says. "It ain't in my line," I says. So he gave a grin like, and kep' on talking. "If you want a *four-half shiner*," he says, "you know where to come. Reasonable with them as is reasonable. Thursday night," he says, and then he slung his hook round the corner.'

'What's a four-half shiner?' inquired Bob, looking from under his eyebrows.

'Well, I didn't know myself, just then: but I've found out. It's a public-house pewter—see?'

A flash of intelligence shot across Bob's face. . . .

When Pennyloaf returned she found her husband with his box of moulds and medals on the table. He was turning over its contents, meditatively. On the table there also lay a half-crown and a florin,* as though Bob had been examining these products of the Royal Mint with a view to improving the artistic quality of his amateur workmanship. He took up the coins quietly as his wife entered and put them in his pocket.

'Mrs. Rendal's been at me again, Bob,' Pennyloaf said, as she set down her market-basket. 'You'll have to give her something to-day.'

He paid no attention, and Pennyloaf had a difficulty in bringing him to discuss the subject of the landlady's demands. Ultimately, however, he admitted with discontent the advisability of letting Mrs. Rendal have something on account. Though it was Saturday night, he let hour after hour go by and showed no disposition to leave home; to Pennyloaf's surprise, he sat almost without moving by the fire, absorbed in thought.

Genuine respect for law is the result of possessing something which the law exerts itself to guard. Should it happen that you possess nothing, and that your education in metaphysics has been grievously neglected, the strong probability is, that your mind will reduce the principle of society to its naked formula: Get, by whatever means, so long as with impunity. On that formula Bob Hewett was brooding; in the hours of this Saturday evening he exerted his mind more strenuously than ever before in the course of his life. And to a foregone result. Here is a man with no moral convictions, with no conscious relations to society save those which are hostile, with no personal affections; at the same time, vaguely aware of certain faculties in himself for which life affords no scope and encouraged in various kinds of conceit by the crass stupidity of all with whom he associates. It is suggested to him all at once that there is a very easy way of improving his circumstances, and that by exercise of a certain craft with which he is perfectly familiar; only, the method happens to be criminal. 'Men who do this kind of thing are

constantly being caught and severely punished. Yes; men of
a certain kind; not Robert Hewett. Robert Hewett is altogether an exceptional being; he is head and shoulders above
the men with whom he mixes; he is clever, he is remarkably
good-looking. If anyone in this world, of a truth Robert
Hewett may reckon on impunity when he sets his wits against
the law. Why, his arrest and punishment is an altogether
inconceivable thing; he never in his life had a charge brought
against him.'

Again and again it came back to that. Every novice in
unimpassioned crime has that thought, and the more self-
conscious the man, the more impressed with a sense of his
own importance, so much the weightier is its effect with him.

We know in what spirit John Hewett regarded rebels
against the law. Do not imagine that any impulse of that
nature actuated his son. Clara alone had inherited her father's
instinct of revolt. Bob's temperament was, in a certain
measure, that of the artist; he felt without reasoning; he let
himself go whither his moods propelled him. Not a man of
evil propensities; entertain no such thought for a moment.
Society produces many a monster, but the mass of those
whom, after creating them, it pronounces bad are merely bad
from the conventional point of view; they are guilty of weaknesses, not of crimes. Bob was not incapable of generosity;
his marriage had, in fact, implied more of that quality than
you in the upper world can at all appreciate. He neglected
his wife, of course, for he had never loved her, and the burden
of her support was too great a trial for his selfishness. Weakness, vanity, a sense that he has not satisfactions proportionate
to his desert, a strong temptation—here are the data which,
in ordinary cases, explain a man's deliberate attempt to profit
by criminality.

In a short time Pennyloaf began to be aware of peculiarities of behaviour in her husband for which she could not
account. Though there appeared no necessity for the step,
he insisted on their once more seeking new lodgings, and,
before the removal, he destroyed all his medals and moulds.

'What's that for, Bob?' Pennyloaf inquired.

'I'll tell you, and mind you hold your tongue about it.
Somebody's been saying as these things might get me into
trouble. Just you be careful not to mention to people that I
used to make these kind of things.'

'But why should it get you into trouble?'

'Mind what I tell you, and don't ask questions. You're always too ready at talking.'

His absences of an evening were nothing new, but his manner on returning was such as Pennyloaf had never seen in him. He appeared to be suffering from some intense excitement; his hands were unsteady; he showed the strangest nervousness if there were any unusual sounds in the house. Then he certainly obtained money of which his wife did not know the source; he bought new articles of clothing, and in explanation said that he had won bets. Pennyloaf remarked these things with uneasiness; she had a fear during her lonely evenings for which she could give no reason. Poor slow-witted mortal though she was, a devoted fidelity attached her to her husband, and quickened wonderfully her apprehension in everything that concerned him.

'Miss Snowdon came to-day, Bob,' she had said, about a week after his order with regard to Jane.

'Oh, she did? And did you tell her she'd better keep away?'

'Yes,' was the dispirited answer.

'Glad to hear it.'

As for Jack Bartley, he never showed himself at the new lodgings.

Bob shortly became less regular in his attendance at the workshop. An occasional Monday he had, to be sure, been in the habit of allowing himself, but as the winter wore on he was more than once found straying about the streets in mid-week. One morning towards the end of November, as he strolled along High Holborn, a hand checked his progress; he gave almost a leap, and turned a face of terror upon the person who stopped him. It was Clem—Mrs. Snowdon. They had, of course, met casually since Bob's marriage, and in progress of time the ferocious glances they were wont to exchange had softened into a grin of half-friendly recognition; Clem's behaviour at present was an unexpected revival of familiarity. When he had got over his shock Bob felt surprised, and expressed the feeling in a—'Well, what have *you* got to say for yourself?'

'You jumped as if I'd stuck a pin in you,' replied Clem. 'Did you think it was a copper?'

Bob looked at her with a surly smile. Though no one could have mistaken the class she belonged to, Clem was dressed in a way which made her companionship with Bob in his workman's clothing somewhat incongruous; she wore a heavily trimmed brown hat, a long velveteen jacket, and carried a little bag of imitation fur.

'Why ain't you at work?' she added. 'Does Mrs. Penny-loaf Hewett know how you spend your time?'

'Hasn't your husband taught you to mind your own business?'

Clem took the retort good-humouredly, and they walked on conversing. Not altogether at his ease thus companioned, Bob turned out of the main street, and presently they came within sight of the British Museum.

'Ever been in that place?' Clem asked.

'Of course I have,' he replied, with his air of superiority.

'I haven't. Is there anything to pay? Let's go in for half an hour.'

It was an odd freak, but Bob began to have a pleasure in this renewal of intimacy; he wished he had been wearing his best suit. Years ago his father had brought him on a public holiday to the Museum, and his interest was chiefly excited by the collection of the Royal Seals. To that quarter he first led his companion, and thence directed her towards objects more likely to supply her with amusement; he talked freely, and was himself surprised at the show of information his memory allowed him to make—desperately vague and often ludicrously wide of the mark, but still a something of know-ledge, retained from all sorts of chance encounters by his capable mind. Had the British Museum been open to visitors in the hours of the evening, or on Sundays, Bob Hewitt would possibly have been employing his leisure nowadays in more profitable pursuits. Possibly; one cannot say more than that; for the world to which he belonged is above all a world of frustration, and only the one man in half a million has fate for his friend.

Much Clem cared for antiquities; when she had wearied herself in pretending interest, a seat in an unvisited corner gave her an opportunity for more congenial dialogue.

'How's Mrs. Pennyloaf?' she asked, with a smile of malice.

'How's Mr. What's-his-name Snowdon?' was the reply.

'My husband's a gentleman. Good thing for me I had the sense to wait.'

'And for me too, I dare say.'

'Why ain't you at work? Got the sack?'

'I can take a day off if I like, can't I?'

'And you'll go 'ome and tell your wife as you've been working. I know what you men are. What 'ud Mrs. Pennyloaf say if she knew you was here with me? You daren't tell her; you daren't!'

'I'm not doing any harm as I know of. I shall tell her if I choose, and if I choose I shan't. I don't ask *her* what I'm to do.'

'I dare say. And how does that mother of hers get on? And her brother at the public? Nice relations for Mr. Bob Hewett. Do they come to tea on a Sunday?'

Bob glared at her, and Clem laughed, showing all her teeth. From this exchange of pleasantries the talk passed to various subjects—the affairs of Jack Bartley and his precious wife, changes in Clerkenwell Close, then to Clem's own circumstances; she threw out hints of brilliant things in store for her.

'Do you come here often?' she asked at length.

'Can't say I do.'

'Thought p'r'aps you brought Mrs. Pennyloaf. When'll you be here again?'

'Don't know,' Bob replied, fidgeting and looking to a distance.

'I shouldn't wonder if I'm here this day next week,' said Clem, after a pause. 'You can bring Pennyloaf if you like.'

It was dinner-time, and they left the building together. At the end of Museum Street they exchanged a careless nod and went their several ways.

CHAPTER XXV

A DOUBLE CONSECRATION

BESSIE BYASS and her husband had, as you may suppose, devoted many an hour to intimate gossip on the affairs of their top-floor lodgers. Having no relations with Clerkenwell Close, they did not even hear the rumours which spread from Mrs. Peckover's house at the time of Jane's departure thence; their curiosity, which only grew keener as time went on, found no appeasement save in conjecture. That Sidney Kirkwood was in the secret from the first they had no doubt;

Bessie made a sly attempt now and then to get a hint from
him, but without the least result. The appearance on the
scene of Jane's father revived their speculation, and just after
the old man's illness in the month of August occurred something which gave them still fresh matter for argument. The
rooms on the first floor having become vacant, Michael proposed certain new arrangements. His own chamber was too
much that of an invalid to serve any longer as sitting-room
for Jane ; he desired to take the front room below for that
purpose, to make the other on the same floor Jane's bed-room,
and then to share with the Byasses the expense of keeping
a servant, whose lodging would be in the chamber thus set
free. Hitherto Bessie and Jane and an occasional char-
woman had done all the work of the house ; it was a day of
jubilation for Mrs. Byass when she found herself ruling over
a capped and aproned maid. All these things set it beyond
doubt that Michael Snowdon had means greater than one
would have supposed from his way of living hitherto. Jane's
removal from work could, of course, be explained by her grandfather's growing infirmities, but Bessie saw more than this in
the new order of things; she began to look upon the girl with
a certain awe, as one whose future might reveal marvels.

For Jane, as we know, the marvels had already begun.
She came back from Danbury not altogether like herself;
unsettled a little, as it appeared ; and Michael's illness, befalling so soon, brought her into a nervous state such as she
had not known for a long time. The immediate effect of the
disclosure made to her by Michael whilst he was recovering
was to overwhelm her with a sense of responsibilities, to
throw her mind into painful tumult. Slow of thought, habi-
tuated to the simplest views of her own existence, very ignorant
of the world beyond the little circle in which her life had
been passed, she could not at once bring into the control of
her reflection this wondrous future to which her eyes had
been opened. The way in which she had been made acquainted with the facts was unfortunate. Michael Snowdon,
in spite of his deep affection for her, and of the trust he had
come to repose in her character, did not understand Jane
well enough to bring about this revelation with the needful
prudence. Between him, a man burdened with the sorrowful
memories of a long life, originally of stern temperament, and
now, in the feebleness of his age, possessed by an enthusiasm
which in several respects disturbed his judgment, which made

him desperately eager to secure his end now that he felt life
slipping away from him—between him and such a girl as
Jane there was a wider gulf than either of them could be
aware of. Little as he desired it, he could not help using a
tone which seemed severe rather than tenderly trustful.
Absorbed in his great idea, conscious that it had regulated
every detail in his treatment of Jane since she came to live
with him, he forgot that the girl herself was by no means
adequately prepared to receive the solemn injunctions which
he now delivered to her. His language was as general as
were the ideas of beneficent activity which he desired to em-
body in Jane's future; but instead of inspiring her with his
own zeal, he afflicted her with grievous spiritual trouble. For
a time she could only feel that something great and hard and
high was suddenly required of her; the old man's look seemed
to keep repeating, 'Are you worthy?' The tremor of bygone days came back upon her as she listened, the anguish of
timidity, the heart-sinking, with which she had been wont to
strain her attention when Mrs. Peckover or Clem imposed a
harsh task.

One thing alone had she grasped as soon as it was uttered;
one word of reassurance she could recall when she sat down
in solitude to collect her thoughts. Her grandfather had
mentioned that Sidney Kirkwood already knew this secret.
To Sidney her whole being turned in this hour of distress;
he was the friend who would help her with counsel and teach
her to be strong. But hereupon there revived in her a trouble
which for the moment she had forgotten, and it became so
acute that she was driven to speak to Michael in a way
which had till now seemed impossible. When she entered his
room—it was the morning after their grave conversation—
Michael welcomed her with a face of joy, which, however,
she still felt to be somewhat stern and searching in its look.
When they had talked for a few moments, Jane said:

'I may speak about this to Mr. Kirkwood, grandfather?'

'I hope you will, Jane. Strangers needn't know of it yet,
but we can speak freely to him.'

After many endeavours to find words that would veil her
thought, she constrained herself to ask:

'Does he think I can be all you wish?'

Michael looked at her with a smile.

'Sidney has no less faith in you than I have, be sure of
that.'

'I've been thinking—that perhaps he distrusted me a little.'

'Why, my child?'

'I don't quite know. But there's been a little difference in him, I think, since we came back.'

Michael's countenance fell.

'Difference? How?'

But Jane could not go further. She wished she had not spoken. Her face began to grow hot, and she moved away.

'It's only your fancy,' continued Michael. 'But may be that—— You think he isn't quite so easy in his talking to you as he was?'

'I've fancied it. But it was only——'

'Well, you may be partly right,' said her grandfather, softening his voice. 'See, Jane, I'll tell you something. I think there's no harm; perhaps I ought to. You must know that I hadn't meant to speak to Sidney of these things just when I did. It came about, because *he* had something to tell *me*, and something I was well pleased to hear. It was about you, Jane, and in that way I got talking—something about you, my child. Afterwards, I asked him whether he wouldn't speak to you yourself, but he said no—not till you'd heard all that was before you. I think I understood him, and I dare say you will, if you think it over.'

Matter enough for thinking over, in these words. Did she understand them aright? Before leaving the room she had not dared to look her grandfather in the face, but she knew well that he was regarding her still with the same smile. Did she understand him aright?

Try to read her mind. The world had all at once grown very large, a distress to her imagination ; worse still, she had herself become a person of magnified importance, irrecognisable in her own sight, moving, thinking so unnaturally. Jane, I assure you, had thought very little of herself hitherto —in both senses of the phrase. Joyous because she could not help it, full of gratitude, admiration, generosity, she occupied her thoughts very much with other people, but knew not self-seeking, knew not self-esteem. The one thing affecting herself over which she mused frequently was her suffering as a little thrall in Clerkenwell Close, and the result was to make her very humble. She had been an ill-used, ragged, work-worn child, and something of that degradation seemed, in her feeling, still to cling to her. Could she have known Bob

Hewett's view of her position, she would have felt its injustice, but at the same time would have bowed her head. And in this spirit had she looked up to Sidney Kirkwood, regarding him as when she was a child, save for that subtle modification which began on the day when she brought news of Clara Hewett's disappearance. Perfect in kindness, Sidney had never addressed a word to her which implied more than friendship— never until that evening at the farm; then for the first time had he struck a new note. His words seemed spoken with the express purpose of altering his and her relations to each other. So much Jane had felt, and his change since then was all the more painful to her, all the more confusing. Now that of a sudden she had to regard herself in an entirely new way, the dearest interest of her life necessarily entered upon another phase. Struggling to understand how her grandfather could think her worthy of such high trust, she inevitably searched her mind for testimony as to the account in which Sidney held her. A fearful hope had already flushed her cheeks before Michael spoke the words which surely could have but one meaning.

On one point Sidney had left her no doubts; that his love for Clara Hewett was a thing of the past he had told her distinctly. And why did he wish her to be assured of that? Oh, had her grandfather been mistaken in those words he reported? Durst she put faith in them, coming thus to her by another's voice?

Doubts and dreads and self-reproofs might still visit her from hour to hour, but the instinct of joy would not allow her to refuse admission to this supreme hope. As if in spite of herself, the former gladness—nay, a gladness multiplied beyond conception—reigned once more in her heart. Her grandfather would not speak lightly in such a matter as this; the meaning of his words was confessed, to all eternity immutable. Had it, then, come to this? The friend to whom she looked up with such reverence, with voiceless gratitude, when he condescended to speak kindly to *her*, the Peckovers' miserable little servant—he, after all these changes and chances of life, sought her now that she was a woman, and had it on his lips to say that he loved her. Hitherto the impossible, the silly thought to be laughed out of her head, the desire for which she would have chid herself durst she have faced it seriously —was it become a very truth? 'Keep a good heart, Jane; things'll be better some day.' How many years since the

rainy and windy night when he threw his coat over her and
spoke those words? Yet she could hear them now, and the
tears that rushed to her eyes as she blessed him for his manly
goodness were as much those of the desolate child as of the
full-hearted woman.

And the change that she had observed in him since that
evening at Danbury? A real change, but only of manner.
He would not say to her what he had meant to say until she
knew the truth about her own circumstances. In simple
words, she being rich and he having only what he earned by
his daily work, Sidney did not think it right to speak whilst
she was still in ignorance. The delicacy of her instincts, and
the sympathies awakened by her affection, made this perfectly
clear to her, strange and difficult to grasp as the situation was
at first. When she understood, how her soul laughed with
exulting merriment! Consecration to a great idea, endowment with the means of wide beneficence—this not only left
her cold, but weighed upon her, afflicted her beyond her
strength. What was it, in truth, that restored her to herself
and made her heart beat joyously? Knit your brows against
her; shake your head and raze her name from that catalogue
of saints whereon you have inscribed it in anticipation. Jane
rejoiced simply because she loved a poor man, and had riches
that she could lay at his feet.

Great sums of money, vague and disturbing to her imagination when she was bidden hold them in trust for unknown
people, gleamed and made music now that she could think of
them as a gift of love. By this way of thought she could
escape from the confusion in which Michael's solemn appeal
had left her. Exalted by her great hope, calmed by the
assurance of aid that would never fail her, she began to feel
the beauty of the task to which she was summoned; the
appalling responsibility became a high privilege now that it
was to be shared with one in whose wisdom and strength she
had measureless confidence. She knew now what wealth
meant; it was a great and glorious power, a source of blessings
incalculable. This power it would be hers to bestow, and no
man more worthy than he who should receive it at her hands.

It was not without result that Jane had been so long a
listener to the conversations between Michael and Kirkwood.
Defective as was her instruction in the ordinary sense, those
evenings spent in the company of the two men had done much
to refine her modes of thought. In spite of the humble powers

of her mind and her narrow experience, she had learned to
think on matters which are wholly strange to girls of her
station, to regard the life of the world and the individual in a
light of idealism and with a freedom from ignoble association
rare enough in any class. Her forecast of the future to be
spent with Sidney was pathetic in its simplicity, but had the
stamp of nobleness. Thinking of the past years, she made
clear to herself all the significance of her training. In her
general view of things, wealth was naturally allied with education, but she understood why Michael had had her taught so
little. A wealthy woman is called a lady; yes, but that was
exactly what she was not to become. On that account she
had gone to work, when in reality there was no need for her
to do so. Never must she remove herself from the poor and
the laborious, her kin, her care; never must she forget those
bitter sufferings of her childhood, precious as enabling her
to comprehend the misery of others for whom had come no
rescue. She saw, moreover, what was meant by Michael's
religious teaching, why he chose for her study such parts of
the Bible as taught the beauty of compassion, of service rendered to those whom the world casts forth and leaves to perish.
All this grew upon her, when once the gladness of her heart
was revived. It was of the essence of her being to exercise all
human and self-forgetful virtues, and the consecration to a
life of beneficence moved her profoundly now that it followed
upon consecration to the warmer love. . . .

When Sidney paid his next visit Jane was alone in the
new sitting-room; her grandfather said he did not feel well
enough to come down this evening. It was the first time that
Kirkwood had seen the new room. After making his inquiries about Michael he surveyed the arrangements, which
were as simple as they could be, and spoke a few words regarding the comfort Jane would find in them. He had his
hand on a chair, but did not sit down, nor lay aside his hat.
Jane suffered from a constraint which she had never before
felt in his presence.

'You know what grandfather has been telling me?' she
said at length, regarding him with grave eyes.

'Yes. He told me of his intention.'

'I asked him if I might speak to you about it. It was
hard to understand at first.'

'It would be, I've no doubt.'

Jane moved a little, took up some sewing, and seated herself. Sidney let his hat drop on to the chair, but remained standing, his arms resting on the back.

'It's a very short time since I myself knew of it,' he continued. 'Till then, I as little imagined as you did that ——' He paused, then resumed more quickly, 'But it explains many things which I had always understood in a simpler way.'

'I feel, too, that I know grandfather much better than I did,' Jane said. 'He's always been thinking about the time when I should be old enough to hear what plans he'd made for me. I do so hope he really trusts me, Mr. Kirkwood! I don't know whether I speak about it as he wishes. It isn't easy to say all I think, but I mean to do my best to be what he——'

'He knows that very well. Don't be anxious; he feels that all his hopes have been realised in you.'

There was silence. Jane made a pretence of using her needle, and Sidney watched her hands.

'He spoke to you of a lady called Miss Lant?' were his next words.

'Yes. He just mentioned her.'

'Are you going to see her soon?'

'I don't know. Have *you* seen her?'

'No. But I believe she's a woman you could soon be friendly with. I hope your grandfather will ask her to come here before long.'

'I'm rather afraid of strangers.'

'No doubt,' said the other, smiling. 'But you'll get over that. I shall do my best to persuade Mr. Snowdon to make you acquainted with her.'

Jane drew in her breath uneasily.

'She won't want me to know other people, I hope?'

'Oh, if she does, they'll be kind and nice and easy to talk to.'

Jane raised her eyes and said half-laughingly:

'I feel as if I was very childish, and that makes me feel it still more. Of course, if it's necessary, I'll do my best to talk to strangers. But they won't expect too much of me, at first? I mean, if they find me a little slow, they won't be impatient?'

'You mustn't think that hard things are going to be asked of you. You'll never be required to say or do anything that you haven't already said and done many a time, quite naturally.

Why, it's some time since you began the kind of work of which your grandfather has been speaking.'

'I have begun it? How?'

'Who has been such a good friend to Pennyloaf, and helped her as nobody else could have done?'

'Oh, but that's nothing!'

Sidney was on the point of replying, but suddenly altered his intention. He raised himself from the leaning attitude, and took his hat.

'Well, we'll talk about it another time,' he said carelessly. 'I can't stop long to-night, so I'll go up and see your grandfather.'

Jane rose silently.

'I'll just look in and say good-night before I go,' Sidney added, as he left the room.

He did so, twenty minutes after. When he opened the door Jane was sewing busily, but it was only on hearing his footsteps that she had so applied herself. He gave a friendly nod, and departed.

Still the same change in his manner. A little while ago he would have chatted freely and forgotten the time.

Another week, and Jane made the acquaintance of the lady whose name we have once or twice heard, Miss Lant, the friend of old Mr. Percival. Of middle age and with very plain features, Miss Lant had devoted herself to philanthropic work; she had an income of a few hundred pounds, and lived almost as simply as the Snowdons in order to save money for charitable expenditure. Unfortunately the earlier years of her life had been joyless, and in the energy which she brought to this self-denying enterprise there was just a touch of excess, common enough in those who have been defrauded of their natural satisfactions and find a resource in altruism. She was no pietist, but there is nowadays coming into existence a class of persons who substitute for the old religious acerbity a narrow and oppressive zeal for good works of purely human sanction, and to this order Miss Lant might be said to belong. However, nothing but what was agreeable manifested itself in her intercourse with Michael and Jane; the former found her ardent spirit very congenial, and the latter was soon at ease in her company.

It was a keen distress to Jane when she heard from Pennyloaf that Bob would allow no future meetings between them. In vain she sought an explanation; Pennyloaf professed to know nothing of her husband's motives, but implored her friend to keep away for a time, as any disregard of Bob's injunction would only result in worse troubles than she yet had to endure. Jane sought the aid of Kirkwood, begging him to interfere with young Hewett; the attempt was made, but proved fruitless. ' *Sic volo, sic jubeo,*'*was Bob's standpoint, and he as good as bade Sidney mind his own affairs.

Jane suffered, and more than she herself would have anticipated. She had conceived a liking, almost an affection, for poor, shiftless Pennyloaf, strengthened, of course, by the devotion with which the latter repaid her. But something more than this injury to her feelings was involved in her distress on being excluded from those sorry lodgings. Pennyloaf was comparatively an old friend ; she represented the past, its contented work, its familiar associations, its abundant happiness. And now, though Jane did not acknowledge to herself that she regretted the old state of things, still less that she feared the future, it was undeniable that the past seemed very bright in her memory, and that something weighed upon her heart, forbidding such gladsomeness as she had known.

CHAPTER XXVI

SIDNEY'S STRUGGLE

IN the dreary days when autumn is being choked by the first fogs, Sidney Kirkwood had to bestir himself and to find new lodgings. The cheerless task came upon him just when he had already more than sufficient trouble, and to tear himself out of the abode in which he had spent eight years caused him more than regret ; he felt superstitiously about it, and questioned fate as to what sorrows might be lurking for him behind this corner in life's journey. Move he must; his landlady was dead, and the house would perhaps be vacant for a long time. After making search about Islington one rainy evening, he found himself at the end of Hanover Street, and was drawn to the familiar house ; not, however, to visit the Snowdons, but to redeem a promise recently made to Bessie Byass, who declared herself vastly indignant at the neglect with which he treated her. So, instead of going up the steps to the front door, he descended into the area. Bessie herself opened to him, and after a shrewd glance, made as though she would close the door again. ' Nothing for you ! The idea of beggars coming down the area-steps ! Be off ! '

' I'm worse than a beggar,' replied Sidney. ' Housebreaking's more in my line.'

And he attempted to force an entrance. Bessie struggled, but had to give in, overcome with laughter. Samuel was enjoying a pipe in the front kitchen ; in spite of the dignity of keeping a servant (to whom the back kitchen was sacred), Mr. and Mrs. Byass frequently spent their evenings below stairs in the same manner as of old.

The talk began with Sidney's immediate difficulties.

' Now if it had only happened half a year ago,' said Bessie, ' I should have got you into our first-floor rooms.'

' Shouldn't wonder if we have him there yet, some day,' remarked Sam, winking at his wife.

' Not him,' was Bessie's rejoinder, with a meaning smile. ' He's a cool hand, is Mr. Kirkwood. He knows how to wait. When *something* happens, we shall have him taking a house out at Highbury,* you see if he don't.'

Sidney turned upon her with anything but a jesting look.

' What do you mean by that, Mrs. Byass ? ' he asked, sharply. ' When *what* happens ? What are you hinting at ? '

' Bless us and save us ! ' cried Bessie. ' Here, Sam, he's going to swallow me. What harm have I done ? '

' Please tell me what you meant ? ' Sidney urged, his face expressing strong annoyance. ' Why do you call me a " cool hand," and say that " I know how to wait " ? What did you mean ? I'm serious ; I want you to explain.'

Whilst he was speaking there came a knock at the kitchen door. Bessie cried, ' Come in,' and Jane showed herself ; she glanced in a startled way at Sidney, murmured a ' good-evening ' to him, and made a request of Bessie for some trifle she needed. Sidney, after just looking round, kept his seat and paid no further attention to Jane, who speedily retired.

Silence followed, and in the midst of it Kirkwood pushed his chair impatiently.

' Bess,' cried Samuel, with an affected jocoseness, ' you're called upon to apologise. Don't make a fool of yourself again.'

' I don't see why he need be so snappish with me,' replied his wife. ' I beg his pardon, if he wants me.'

But Sidney was laughing now, though not in a very natural way. He put an end to the incident, and led off into talk of quite a different kind. When supper-time was at hand he declared that it was impossible for him to stay. The hour had been anything but a lively one, and when he was gone his friends discussed at length this novel display of ill-humour on Sidney's part.

He went home muttering to himself, and passed as bad a night as he had ever known. Two days later his removal to new lodgings was effected; notwithstanding his desire to get into a cleaner region, he had taken a room at the top of a house in Red Lion Street, in the densest part of Clerkenwell, where his neighbours under the same roof were craftsmen, carrying on their business at home.

'It'll do well enough just for a time,' he said to himself. 'Who can say when I shall be really settled again, or whether I ever shall?'

Midway in an attempt to put his things in order, to nail his pictures on the walls and bring forth his books again, he was seized with such utter discouragement that he let a volume drop from his hand and threw himself into a seat. A moan escaped his lips—'That cursed money!'

Ever since the disclosure made to him by Michael Snowdon at Danbury he had been sensible of a grave uneasiness respecting his relations with Jane. At the moment he might imagine himself to share the old man's enthusiasm, or dream, or craze—whichever name were the most appropriate—but not an hour had passed before he began to lament that such a romance as this should envelop the life which had so linked itself with his own. Immediately there arose in him a struggle between the idealist tendency, of which he had his share, and stubborn everyday sense, supported by his knowledge of the world and of his own being—a struggle to continue for months, thwarting the natural current of his life, racking his intellect, embittering his heart's truest emotions. Conscious of mystery in Snowdon's affairs, he had never dreamed of such a solution as this; the probability was—so he had thought—that Michael received an annuity under the will of his son who died in Australia. No word of the old man's had ever hinted at wealth in his possession; the complaints he frequently made of the ill use to which wealthy people put their means seemed to imply a regret that he, with his purer purposes, had no power of doing anything. There was no explaining the manner of Jane's bringing-up if it were not necessary that she should be able to support herself; the idea on which Michael acted was not such as would suggest itself, even to Sidney's mind. Deliberately to withhold education from a girl who was to inherit any property worth speaking of would be acting with such boldness of originality that Sidney could not seriously have attributed it to his friend. In fact, he did not know Michael until the revelation was made; the depths of the man's character escaped him.

The struggle went all against idealism. It was a noble vision, that of Michael's, but too certainly Jane Snowdon was not the person to make it a reality; the fearful danger was, that all the possibilities of her life might be sacrificed to a vain conscientiousness. Her character was full of purity and sweetness and self-forgetful warmth, but it had not the strength necessary for the carrying out of a purpose beset with difficulties and perils. Michael, it was true, appeared to be aware of this; it did not, however, gravely disturb him, and for the simple reason that not to Jane alone did he look for the completion of his design; destiny had brought him aid such as he could never have anticipated; Jane's helpmate was at hand, in whom his trust was unbounded.

What was in his way, that Sidney should not accept the responsibility? Conscience from the first whispered against his doing so, and the whisper was grown to so loud a voice that not an adverse argument could get effective hearing. Temptations lurked for him and sprang out in moments of his weakness, but as temptations they were at once recognised. ' He had gone too far to retire; he would be guilty of sheer treachery to Jane; he would break the old man's heart.' All which meant merely that he loved the girl, and that it would be like death to part from her. But why part? What had conscience got hold of, that it made all this clamour? Oh, it was simple enough; Sidney not only had no faith in the practicability of such a life's work as Michael visioned, but he had the profoundest distrust of his own moral strength if he should allow himself to be committed to lifelong renunciation. ' I am no hero,' he said, ' no enthusiast. The time when my whole being could be stirred by social questions has gone by. I am a man in love, and in proportion as my love has strengthened, so has my old artist-self revived in me, until now I can imagine no bliss so perfect as to marry Jane Snowdon and go off to live with her amid fields and trees, where no echo of the suffering world should ever reach us.' To confess this was to make it terribly certain that sooner or

later the burden of conscientiousness would become intolerable. Not from Jane would support come in that event; she,
poor child! would fall into miserable perplexity, in conflict
between love and duty, and her life would be ruined.

Of course a man might have said, 'What matter how
things arrange themselves when Michael is past knowledge of
them? I will marry the woman I honestly desire, and together we will carry out this humanitarian project so long as
it be possible. When it ceases to be so, well——.' But
Sidney could not take that view. It shamed him beyond
endurance to think that he must ever avoid Jane's look,
because he had proved himself dishonest, and, what were
worse, had tempted her to become so.

The conflict between desire and scruple made every day a
weariness. Instead of looking forward eagerly to the evening
in the week which he spent with Michael and Jane, he dreaded
its approach. Scarcely had he met Jane's look since this
trouble began; he knew that her voice when she spoke to
him expressed consciousness of something new in their relations, and even whilst continuing to act his part he suffered
ceaselessly. Had Michael ever repeated to his granddaughter
the confession which Sidney would now have given anything
to recall? It was more than possible. Of Jane's feeling
Sidney could not entertain a serious doubt, and he knew that
for a long time he had done his best to encourage it. It was
unpardonable to draw aloof from her just because these circumstances had declared themselves, circumstances which
brought perplexity into her life and doubtless made her long
for another kind of support than Michael could afford her.
The old man himself appeared to be waiting anxiously; he
had fallen back into his habit of long silences, and often
regarded Sidney in a way which the latter only too well
understood.

He tried to help himself through the time of indecision
by saying that there was no hurry. Jane was very young,
and with the new order of things her life had in truth only
just begun. She must have a space to look about her; all
the better if she could form various acquaintances. On that
account he urged so strongly that she should be brought into
relation with Miss Lant, and, if possible, with certain of Miss
Lant's friends. All very well, had not the reasoning been
utterly insincere. It might have applied to another person;
in Jane's case it was mere sophistry. Her nature was home-

keeping; to force her into alliance with conscious philan-
thropists was to set her in the falsest position conceivable;
striving to mould herself to the desires of those she loved, she
would suffer patiently and in secret mourn for the time when
she had been obscure and happy. These things Sidney knew
with a certainty only less than that wherewith he judged his
own sensations; between Jane and himself the sympathy was
perfect. And in despite of scruple he would before long
have obeyed the natural impulse of his heart, had it not been
that still graver complications declared themselves, and by
exasperating his over-sensitive pride made him reckless of the
pain he gave to others so long as his own self-torture was
made sufficiently acute.

With Joseph Snowdon he was doing his best to be on
genial terms, but the task was a hard one. The more he
saw of Joseph, the less he liked him. Of late the filter manufacturer had begun to strike notes in his conversation which
jarred on Sidney's sensibilities, and made him disagreeably
suspicious that something more was meant than Joseph cared
to put into plain speech. Since his establishment in business
Joseph had become remarkably attentive to his father; he
appeared to enter with much zeal into all that concerned
Jane; he conversed privately with the old man for a couple
of hours at a time, and these dialogues, for some reason or
other, he made a point of reporting to Sidney. According to
these reports—and Sidney did not wholly discredit them—
Michael was coming to have a far better opinion of his son
than formerly, was even disposed to speak with him gravely
of his dearest interests.

'We talked no end about you, Sidney, last night,' said
Joseph on one occasion, with the smile whereby he meant to
express the last degree of friendly intelligence.

And Sidney, though anxiously desiring to know the gist of
the conversation, in this instance was not gratified. He could
not bring himself to put questions, and went away in a mood
of vague annoyance which Joseph had the especial power of
exciting.

With the Byasses, Joseph was forming an intimacy; of
this too Sidney became aware, and it irritated him. The
exact source of this irritation he did not at first recognise, but
it was disclosed at length unmistakably enough, and that on
the occasion of the visit recently described. Bessie's pleasantry,
which roused him in so unwonted a manner, could bear, of

course, but one meaning; as soon as he heard it, Sidney saw
as in a flash that one remaining aspect of his position which
had not as yet attracted his concern. The Byasses had learnt,
or had been put in the way of surmising, that Michael Snowdon was wealthy; instantly they passed to the reflection that
in marrying Jane their old acquaintance would be doing an
excellent stroke of business. They were coarse-minded, and
Bessie could even venture to jest with him on this detestable
view of his projects. But was it not very likely that they
derived their information from Joseph Snowdon? And if so,
was it not all but certain that Joseph had suggested to them
this way of regarding Sidney himself?

So when Jane's face appeared at the door he held himself
in stubborn disregard of her. A thing impossible to him, he
would have said a few minutes ago. He revenged himself
upon Jane. Good; in this way he was likely to make noble
advances.

The next evening he was due at the Snowdons', and for
the very first time he voluntarily kept away. He posted a
note to say that the business of his removal had made him
irregular; he would come next week, when things were
settled once more.

Thus it came to pass that he sat wretchedly in his unfamiliar room and groaned about ' that accursed money.' His
only relief was in bursts of anger. Why had he not the
courage to go to Michael and say plainly what he thought?
' You have formed a wild scheme, the project of a fanatic.
Its realisation would be a miracle, and in your heart you
must know that Jane's character contains no miraculous
possibilities. You are playing with people's lives, as fanatics
always do. For Heaven's sake, bestow your money on the
practical folks who make a solid business of relieving distress!
Jane, I know, will bless you for making her as poor as ever.
Things are going on about you which you do not suspect.
Your son is plotting, plotting; I can see it. This money will
be the cause of endless suffering to those you really love, and
will never be of as much benefit to the unknown as if practical people dealt with it. Jane is a simple girl, of infinite
goodness; what possesses you that you want to make her an
impossible sort of social saint?' Too hard to speak thus
frankly. Michael had no longer the mental pliancy of even
six months ago; his *idea* was everything to him; as he became weaker, it would gain the dire force of an hallucination.

And in the meantime he, Sidney, must submit to be slandered by that fellow who had his own ends to gain.

To marry Jane, and, at the old man's death, resign every farthing of the money to her trustees, for charitable uses ?— But the old pang of conscience ; the life-long wound to Jane's tender heart.

A day of headache and incapacity, during which it was all he could do to attend to his mechanical work, and again the miserable loneliness of his attic. It rained, it rained. He had half a mind to seek refuge at some theatre, but the energy to walk so far was lacking. And whilst he stood stupidly abstracted there came a knock at his door.

'I thought I'd just see if you'd got straight,' said Joseph Snowdon, entering with his genial smile.

Sidney made no reply, but turned as if to stir the fire. Hands in pockets, Joseph sauntered to a seat.

'Think you'll be comfortable here ? ' he went on. ' Well, well ; of course it's only temporary.'

'I don't know about that,' returned Sidney. I may stay here as long as I was at the last place—eight years.'

Joseph laughed, with exceeding good-nature.

' Oh yes ; I shouldn't wonder,' he said, entering into the joke. ' Still '—becoming serious—' I wish you'd found a pleasanter place. With the winter coming on, you see—— '

Sidney broke in with splenetic perversity.

'I don't know that I shall pass the winter here. My arrangements are all temporary—all of them.'

After glancing at him the other crossed his legs and seemed to dispose himself for a stay of some duration.

' You didn't turn up the other night—in Hanover Street.'

' No.'

' I was there. We talked about you. My father has a notion you haven't been quite well lately. I dare say you're worrying a little, eh ? '

Sidney remained standing by the fireplace, turned so that his face was in shadow.

' Worry ? Oh, I don't know,' he replied, idly.

Well, *I'm* worried a good deal, Sidney, and that's the fact.'

' What about ? '

' All sorts of things. I've meant to have a long talk with you ; but then I don't quite know how to begin. Well, see, it's chiefly about Jane.'

Sidney neither moved nor spoke.

'After all, Sidney,' resumed the other, softening his voice, 'I *am* her father, you see. A precious bad one I've been, that there's no denying, and dash it if I don't sometimes feel ashamed of myself. I do when she speaks to me in that pleasant way she has—you know what I mean. For all that, I am her father, and I think it's only right I should do my best to make her happy. You agree with that, I know.'

'Certainly I do.'

'You won't take it ill if I ask whether—in fact, whether you've ever asked her—you know what I mean.'

'I have not,' Sidney replied, in a clear, unmoved tone, changing his position at the same time so as to look his interlocutor in the face.

Joseph seemed relieved.

'Still,' he continued, 'you've given her to understand—eh? I suppose there's no secret about that?'

'I've often spoken to her very intimately, but I have used no words such as you are thinking of. It's quite true that my way of behaving has meant more than ordinary friendship.'

'Yes, yes; you're not offended at me bringing this subject up, old man? You see, I'm her father, after all, and I think we ought to understand each other.'

'You are quite right.'

'Well, now, see.' He fidgeted a little. 'Has my father ever told you that his friend the lawyer, Percival, altogether went against that way of bringing up Jane?'

'Yes, I know that.'

'You do?' Joseph paused before proceeding. 'To tell you the truth, I don't much care about Percival. I had a talk with him, you know, when my business was being settled. No, I don't quite take to him, so to say. Now, you won't be offended? The fact of the matter is, he asked some rather queer questions about you—or, at all events, if they weren't exactly questions, they—they came to the same thing.'

Sidney was beginning to glare under his brows. Commonsense told him how very unlikely it was that a respectable solicitor should compromise himself in talk with a stranger, and that such a man as J. J. Snowdon; yet, whether the story were true or not, it meant that Joseph was plotting in some vile way, and thus confirmed his suspicions. He inquired, briefly and indifferently, what Mr. Percival's insinuations had been.

'Well, I told you I don't much care for the fellow. He didn't say as much, mind, but he seemed to be hinting-like that, as Jane's father, I should do well to—to keep an eye on you—ha, ha ! It came to that, I thought—though, of course, I may have been mistaken. It shows how little he knows about you and father. I fancy he'd got it into his head that it was *you* set father on those plans about Jane—though *why* I'd like to know.'

He paused. Sidney kept his eyes down, and said nothing.

'Well, there's quite enough of that; too much. Still I thought I'd tell you, you see. It's well to know when we've got enemies behind our backs. But see, Sidney; to speak seriously, between ourselves.' He leaned forward in the confidential attitude. 'You say you've gone just a bit further than friendship with our Janey. Well, I don't know a better man, and that's the truth—but don't you think we might put this off for a year or two ? Look now, here's this lady, Miss Lant, taking up the girl, and it's an advantage to her; you won't deny that. I sympathise with my good old dad; I do, honestly; but I can't help thinking that Janey, in her position, ought to see a little of the world. There's no secrets between *us*; you know what she'll have as well as I do. I should be a brute if I grudged it her, after all she's suffered from my neglect. But don't you think we might leave her free for a year or two ? '

'Yes, I agree with you.'

'You do ? I thought you and I could understand each other, if we only got really talking. Look here, Sidney; I don't mind just whispering to you. For anything I know, Percival is saying disagreeable things to the old man ; but don't you worry about that. It don't matter a scrap, you see, so long as you and I keep friendly, eh ? I'm talking very open to you, but it's all for Janey's sake. If you went and told father I'd been saying anything against Percival—well, it would make things nasty for me. I've put myself in your hands, but I know the kind of man you are. It's only right you should hear of what's said. Don't worry; we'll just wait a little, that's all. I mean it all for the little girl's sake. It wouldn't be nice if you married her and then she was told—eh ? '

Sidney looked at the speaker steadily, then stirred the fire and moved about for a few moments. As he kept absolute silence, Joseph, after throwing out a few vague assurances of goodwill and trust, rose to take his leave. Kirkwood shook hands with him, but spoke not a word. Late the same night Sidney penned a letter to Michael Snowdon. In the morning he read it over, and instead of putting it into an envelope, locked it away in one of his drawers.

When the evening for his visit to Hanover Street again came round he again absented himself, this time just calling to leave word with the servant that business kept him away. The business was that of walking aimlessly about Clerkenwell, in mud and fog. About ten o'clock he came to Farringdon Road Buildings, and with a glance up towards the Hewetts' window he was passing by when a hand clutched at him. Turning, he saw the face of John Hewett, painfully disturbed, strained in some wild emotion.

'Sidney! Come this way; I want to speak to you.'

'Why, what's wrong?'

'Come over here. Sidney—I've found my girl—I've found Clara!

CHAPTER XXVII

CLARA'S RETURN

MRS. EAGLES, a middle-aged woman of something more than average girth, always took her time in ascending to that fifth storey where she and her husband shared a tenement with the Hewett family. This afternoon her pause on each landing was longer than usual, for a yellow fog, which mocked the pale glimmer of gas-jets on the staircase, made her gasp asthmatically. She carried, too, a heavy market-bag, having done her Saturday purchasing earlier than of wont on account of the intolerable weather. She reached the door at length, and being too much exhausted to search her pocket for the latchkey, knocked for admission. Amy Hewett opened to her, and she sank on a chair in the first room, where the other two Hewett children were bending over 'home-lessons' with a studiousness not altogether natural. Mrs. Eagles had a shrewd eye; having glanced at Annie and Tom with a discreet smile, she turned her look towards the elder girl, who was standing full in the lamplight.

'Come here, Amy,' she said after a moment's scrutiny. 'So you *will* keep doin' that foolish thing! Very well, then,

I shall have to speak to your father about it; I'm not goin' to see you make yourself ill and do nothing to prevent you.'

Amy, now a girl of eleven, affected much indignation.

' Why, I haven't touched a drop, Mrs. Eagles ! '

' Now, now, now, now, now ! Why, your lips are shrivelled up like a bit of o' dried orange-peel ! You're a silly girl, that's what you are ! '

Of late Amy Hewett had become the victim of a singular propensity; whenever she could obtain vinegar, she drank it as a toper does spirits. Inadequate nourishment, and especially an unsatisfied palate, frequently have this result in female children among the poor; it is an anticipation of what will befall them as soon as they find their way to the public-house.

Having administered a scolding, Mrs. Eagles went into the room which she and her husband occupied. It was so encumbered with furniture that not more than eight or ten square feet of floor can have been available for movement. On the bed sat Mr. Eagles, a spare, large-headed, ugly, but very thoughtful-looking man ; he and Sidney Kirkwood had been acquaintances and fellow-workmen for some years, but no close intimacy had arisen between them, owing to the difference of their tastes and views. Eagles was absorbed in the study of a certain branch of political statistics; the enthusiasm of his life was Financial Reform. Every budget presented to Parliament he criticised with extraordinary thoroughness, and, in fact, with an acumen which would have made him no inefficient auxiliary of the Chancellor himself. Of course he took the view that the nation's resources were iniquitously wasted, and of course had little difficulty in illustrating a truth so obvious ; what distinguished him from the ordinary mal-content of Clerkenwell Green was his logical faculty and the surprising extent of the information with which he had fur-nished himself. Long before there existed a 'Financial Reform Almanack,'* Eagles practically represented that work in his own person. Disinterested, ardent, with thoughts for but one subject in the scope of human inquiry, he lived contentedly on his two pounds a week, and was for ever engaged in the theoretic manipulation of millions. Utopian budgets multiplied them-selves in his brain and his note-books. He devised imposts such as Minister never dreamt of, yet which, he declared, could not fail of vast success. ' You just look at these figures ! ' he would exclaim to Sidney, in his low, intense voice. 'There

it is in black and white!' But Sidney's faculties were quite
unequal to calculations of this kind, and Eagles could never
summon resolve to explain his schemes before an audience.
Indefatigably he worked on, and the work had to be its own
reward.

He was busy in the usual way this afternoon, as he sat on
the bed, coatless, a trade journal open on his knees. His
wife never disturbed him; she was a placid, ruminative woman,
generally finding the details of her own weekly budget quite a
sufficient occupation. When she had taken off her bonnet
and was turning out the contents of her bag, Eagles remarked
quietly:

'They'll have a bad journey.'

'What a day for her to be travelling all that distance, poor
thing! But perhaps it ain't so bad out o' London.'

Lowering their voices, they began to talk of John Hewett
and the daughter he was bringing from Lancashire, where she
had lain in hospital for some weeks. Of the girl and her past
they knew next to nothing, but Hewett's restricted confidences
suggested disagreeable things. The truth of the situation was,
that John had received by post, from he knew not whom, a
newspaper report of the inquest held on the body of Grace
Danver, wherein, of course, was an account of what had happened to Clara Vale; in the margin was pencilled, 'Clara
Vale's real name is Clara Hewett.' An hour after receiving
this John encountered Sidney Kirkwood. They read the report
together. Before the coroner it had been made public that
the dead woman was in truth named Rudd; she who was
injured refused to give any details concerning herself, and her
history escaped the reporters. Harbouring no doubt of the
information thus mysteriously sent him—the handwriting
seemed to be that of a man, but gave no further hint as to its
origin—Hewett the next day journeyed down into Lancashire,
Sidney supplying him with money. He found Clara in a
perilous condition; her face was horribly burnt with vitriol,
and the doctors could not as yet answer for the results of the
shock she had suffered. One consolation alone offered itself
in the course of Hewett's inquiries; Clara, if she recovered,
would not have lost her eyesight. The fluid had been thrown
too low to effect the worst injury; the accident of a trembling
hand, of a movement on her part, had kept her eyes untouched.

Necessity brought the father back to London almost at

once, but the news sent him at brief intervals continued to be favourable. Now that the girl could be removed from the infirmary, there was no retreat for her but her father's home. Mr. Peel, the manager, had made her a present of 20*l.*—it was all he could do; the members of the company had subscribed another 5*l.*, generously enough, seeing that their tour was come perforce to an abrupt close. Clara's career as an actress had ended. . . .

When the fog's artificial night deepened at the close of the winter evening, Mrs. Eagles made the Hewetts' two rooms as cheerful as might be, expecting every moment the arrival of John and his companion. The children were aware that an all but forgotten sister was returning to them, and that she had been very ill; they promised quietude. Amy set the tea-table in order, and kept the kettle ready. . . . The knock for which they were waiting! Mrs. Eagles withdrew into her own room; Amy went to the door.

A tall figure, so wrapped and veiled that nothing but the womanly outline could be discerned, entered, supported by John Hewett.

'Is there a light in the other room, Amy?' John inquired in a thick voice.

'Yes, father.'

He led the muffled form into the chamber where Amy and Annie slept. The door closed, and for several minutes the three children stood regarding each other, alarmed, mute. Then their father joined them. He looked about in an absent way, slowly drew off his overcoat, and when Amy offered to take it, bent and kissed her cheek. The girl was startled to hear him sob and to see tears starting from his eyes. Turning suddenly away, he stood before the fire and made a pretence of warming himself; but his sobs overmastered him. He leaned his arms on the mantel-piece.

'Shall I pour out the tea, father?' Amy ventured to ask, when there was again perfect silence.

'Haven't you had yours?' he replied, half-facing her.

'Not yet.'

'Get it, then—all of you. Yes, you can pour me out a cup —and put another on the little tray. Is this stuff in the saucepan ready?'

'Mrs. Eagles said it would be in five minutes.'

'All right. Get on with your eatin', all of you.'

He went to Mrs. Eagles' room and talked there for a short

time. Presently Mrs. Eagles herself came out and silently
removed from the saucepan a mixture of broth and meat.
Having already taken the cup of tea to Clara, Hewett now
returned to her with this food. She was sitting by the fire,
her face resting upon her hands. The lamp was extinguished;
she had said that the firelight was enough. John deposited
his burden on the table, then touched her shoulder gently and
spoke in so soft a voice that one would not have recognised it
as his.

'You'll try an' eat a little, my dear? Here's somethin' as
has been made particular. After travellin'—just a spoonful
or two.'

Clara expressed reluctance.

'I don't feel hungry, father. Presently, perhaps.'

'Well, well; it do want to cool a bit. Do you feel able
to sit up?'

'Yes. Don't take so much trouble, father. I'd rather
you left me alone.'

The tone was not exactly impatient; it spoke a weary
indifference to everything and every person.

'Yes, I'll go away, dear. But you'll eat just a bit? If
you don't like this, you must tell me, and I'll get something
you could fancy.'

'It'll do well enough. I'll eat it presently; I promise
you.'

John hesitated before going.

'Clara—shall you mind Amy and Annie comin' to sleep
here? If you'd rather, we'll manage it somehow else.'

'No. What does it matter? They can come when they
like, only they mustn't want me to talk to them.'

He went softly from the room, and joined the children at
their tea. His mood had grown brighter. Though in talking
he kept his tone much softened, there was a smile upon his
face, and he answered freely the questions put to him about
his journey. Overcome at first by the dark aspect of this
home-coming, he now began to taste the joy of having Clara
under his roof, rescued alike from those vague dangers of the
past and from the recent peril. Impossible to separate the
sorrow he felt for her blighted life, her broken spirit, and the
solace lurking in the thought that henceforth she could not
abandon him. Never a word to reproach her for the unalter-
able; it should be as though there were no gap between the
old love and its renewal in the present. For Clara used to

love him, and already she had shown that his tenderness did not appeal to her in vain; during the journey she had once or twice pressed his hand in gratitude. How well it was that he had this home in which to receive her! Half a year ago, and what should he have done? He would not admit to himself that there were any difficulties ahead; if it came to that, he would manage to get some extra work in the evening and on Saturday afternoons. He would take Sidney into council. But thereupon his face darkened again, and he lost himself in troubled musing.

Midway in the Sunday morning Amy told him that Clara had risen and would like him to go and sit with her. She would not leave her room; Amy had put it in order, and the blind was drawn low. Clara sat by the fireside, in her attitude of last night, hiding her face as far as she was able. The beauty of her form would have impressed anyone who approached her, the grace of her bent head; but the countenance was no longer that of Clara Hewett; none must now look at her, unless to pity. Feeling herself thus utterly changed, she could not speak in her former natural voice; her utterance was oppressed, unmusical, monotonous.

When her father had taken a place near her she asked him, ' Have you got that piece of newspaper still? '

He had, and at her wish produced it. Clara held it in the light of the fire, and regarded the pencilled words closely. Then she inquired if he wished to keep it, and on his answering in the negative threw it to be burnt. Hewett took her hand, and for a while they kept silence.

' Do you live comfortably here, father? ' she said presently.

' We do, Clara. It's a bit high up, but that don't matter much.'

' You've got new furniture.'

' Yes, some new things. The old was all done for, you know.'

' And where did you live before you came here? '

' Oh, we had a place in King's Cross Road—it wasn't much of a place, but I suppose it might a' been worse.'

' And that was where—— ? '

' Yes—yes—it was there.'

' And how did you manage to buy this furniture? ' Clara asked, after a pause.

' Well, my dear, to tell you the truth—it was a friend as— an old friend helped us a bit.'

'You wouldn't care to say who it was?'

John was gravely embarrassed. Clara moved her head a little, so as to regard him, but at once turned away, shrinkingly, when she met his eyes.

'Why don't you like to tell me, father? Was it Mr. Kirkwood?'

'Yes, my dear, it was.'

'I suppose he's altered in some ways?'

Neither spoke for a long time. Clara's head sank lower; she drew her hand away from her father's, and used it to shield her face. When she spoke, it was as if to herself.

'I suppose he's altered in some ways?'

'Not much; I don't see much change, myself, but then of course—— No, he's pretty much the same.'

'He's married, isn't he?'

'Married? Why, what made you think that, Clara? No, not he. He had to move not long ago; his lodgin's is in Red Lion Street now.'

'And does he ever come here?'

'He has been—just now an' then.'

'Have you told him?'

'Why—yes, dear—I felt I had to.'

'There's no harm. You couldn't keep it a secret. But he mustn't come whilst I'm here; you understand that, father?'

'No, no, he shan't. He shall never come, if you don't wish it.'

'Only whilst I'm here.'

'But—Clara—you'll *always* be here.'

'Oh no! Do you think I'm going to burden you all the rest of my life? I shall find some way of earning a living, and then I shall go and get a room for myself.'

'Now don't—now don't talk like that!' exclaimed her father, putting his hand on her. 'You shall do what else you like, my girl, but don't talk about goin' away from me. That's the one thing as I couldn't bear. I ain't so young as I was, and I've had things as was hard to go through—I mean when the mother died and—and other things at that time. Let you an' me stay by each other whilst we may, my girl. You know it was always you as I thought most of, and I want to keep you by me—I do, Clara. You won't speak about goin' away?'

She remained mute. Shadows from the firelight rose and fell upon the walls of the half-darkened room. It was a cloudy morning; every now and then a gust flung rain against the window.

'If you went,' he continued, huskily, 'I should be afraid o' myself. I haven't told you. I didn't behave as I'd ought to have done to the poor mother, Clara; I got into drinkin' too much; yes, I did. I've broke myself off that; but if you was to leave me—— I've had hard things to go through. Do you know the Burial Club broke up just before she died? I couldn't get not a ha'penny! A lot o' the money was stolen. You may think how I felt, Clara, with her lyin' there, and I hadn't got as much as would pay for a coffin. It was Sidney Kirkwood found the money—he did! There was never man had as good a friend as he's been to me; I shall never have a chance of payin' what I owe him. Things is better with me now, but I'd rather beg my bread in the streets than you should go away. Don't be afraid, my dearest. I promise you nobody shan't come near. You won't mind Mrs. Eagles; she's very good to the children. But I must keep you near to me, my poor girl!'

Perhaps it was that word of pity—though the man's shaken voice was throughout deeply moving. For the first time since the exultant hope of her life was blasted, Clara shed tears.

CHAPTER XXVIII

THE SOUP-KITCHEN

WITH the first breath of winter there passes a voice half-menacing, half-mournful, through all the barren ways and phantom-haunted refuges of the nether world. Too quickly has vanished the brief season when the sky is clement, when a little food suffices, and the chances of earning that little are more numerous than at other times; this wind that gives utterance to its familiar warning is the vaunt-courier of cold and hunger and solicitude that knows not sleep. Will the winter be a hard one? It is the question that concerns this world before all others, that occupies alike the patient work-folk who have yet their home unbroken, the strugglers foredoomed to loss of such scant needments as the summer gifted them withal, the hopeless and the self-abandoned and the lurking creatures of prey. To all of them the first chill breath from a lowering sky has its voice of admonition; they set their faces; they sigh, or whisper a prayer, or fling out a curse, each according to his nature.

And as though the strife here were not already hard enough, behold from many corners of the land come needy emigrants, prospectless among their own people, fearing the dark season which has so often meant for them the end of wages and of food, tempted hither by thought that in the shadow of palaces work and charity are both more plentiful. Vagabonds, too, no longer able to lie about the country roads, creep back to their remembered lairs and join the combat for crusts flung forth by casual hands. Day after day the stress becomes more grim. One would think that hosts of the weaker combatants might surely find it seasonable to let themselves be trodden out of existence, and so make room for those of more useful sinew ; somehow they cling to life ; so few in comparison yield utterly. The thoughtful in the world above look about them with contentment when carriage-ways are deep with new-fallen snow. 'Good; here is work for the unemployed.' Ah, if the winter did but last a few months longer, if the wonted bounds of endurance were but, by some freak of nature, sensibly overpassed, the carriage-ways would find another kind of sweeping ! . . .

This winter was the last that Shooter's Gardens were destined to know. The leases had all but run out; the middle-men were garnering their latest profits ; in the spring there would come a wholesale demolition, and model-lodgings would thereafter occupy the site. Meanwhile the Gardens looked their surliest; the walls stood in a perpetual black sweat ; a mouldy reek came from the open doorways ; the beings that passed in and out seemed soaked with grimy moisture, puffed into distortions, hung about with rotting garments. One such was Mrs. Candy, Pennyloaf's mother. Her clothing consisted of a single gown and a shawl made out of the fragments of an old counterpane ; her clothing—with exception of the shoes on her feet, those two articles were literally all that covered her bare body. Rage for drink was with her reaching the final mania. Useless to bestow anything upon her ; straightway it or its value passed over the counter of the beershop in Rosoman Street. She cared only for beer, the brave, thick, medicated draught, that was so cheap and frenzied her so speedily.

Her husband was gone for good. One choking night of November he beat her to such purpose that she was carried off to the police-station as dead ; the man effected his escape, and was not likely to show himself in the Gardens again. With her still lived her son Stephen, the potman. His payment was ten shillings a week (with a daily allowance of three pints), and he saw to it that there was always a loaf of bread in the room they occupied together. Stephen took things with much philosophy; his mother would, of course, drink herself to death—what was there astonishing in that? He himself had heart disease, and surely enough would drop down dead one of these days; the one doom was no more to be quarrelled with than the other. Pennyloaf came to see them at very long intervals; what was the use of making her visits more frequent? She, too, viewed with a certain equanimity the progress of her mother's fate. Vain every kind of interposition; worse than imprudence to give the poor creature money or money's worth. It could only be hoped that the end would come before very long.

An interesting house, this in which Mrs. Candy resided. It contained in all seven rooms, and each room was the home of a family; under the roof slept twenty-five persons, men, women, and children; the lowest rent paid by one of these domestic groups was four-and-sixpence.* You would have enjoyed a peep into the rear chamber on the ground floor. There dwelt a family named Hope—Mr. and Mrs. Hope, Sarah Hope, aged fifteen, Dick Hope, aged twelve, Betsy Hope, aged three. The father was a cripple; he and his wife occupied themselves in the picking of rags—of course at home*—and I can assure you that the atmosphere of their abode was worthy of its aspect. Mr. Hope drank, but not desperately. His forte was the use of language so peculiarly violent that even in Shooter's Gardens it gained him a proud reputation. On the slightest excuse he would threaten to brain one of his children, to disembowel another, to gouge out the eyes of the third. He showed much ingenuity in varying the forms of menaced punishment. Not a child in the Gardens but was constantly threatened by its parents with a violent death; this was so familiar that it had lost its effect; where the nurse or mother in the upper world cries, 'I shall scold you!' in the nether the phrase is, 'I'll knock yer 'ed orff!' To 'I shall be very angry with you' in the one sphere, corresponds in the other, 'I'll murder you!' These are conventions—matters of no importance. But Mr. Hope was a man of individuality; he could make his family tremble; he could bring lodgers about the door to listen and admire his resources.

In another room abode a mother with four children. This woman drank moderately, but was very conscientious in despatching her three younger children to school. True, there was just a little inconvenience in this punctuality of hers, at all events from the youngsters' point of view, for only on the first three days of the week had they the slightest chance of a mouthful of breakfast before they departed. 'Never mind, I'll have some dinner for you,' their parent was wont to say. Common enough in the Board schools, this pursuit of knowledge on an empty stomach. But then the end is so inestimable!

Yet another home. It was tenanted by two persons only; they appeared to be man and wife, but in the legal sense were not so, nor did they for a moment seek to deceive their neighbours. With the female you are slightly acquainted; christened Sukey Jollop, she first became Mrs. Jack Bartley, and now, for courtesy's sake, was styled Mrs. Higgs. Sukey had strayed on to a downward path; conscious of it, she abandoned herself to her taste for strong drink, and braved out her degradation. Jealousy of Clem Peckover was the first cause of discord between her and Jack Bartley; a robust young woman, she finally sent Jack about his business by literal force of arms, and entered into an alliance with Ned Higgs, a notorious swashbuckler, the captain of a gang of young ruffians who at this date were giving much trouble to the Clerkenwell police. Their speciality was the skilful use, as an offensive weapon, of a stout leathern belt heavily buckled; Mr. Higgs boasted that with one stroke of his belt he could, if it seemed good to him, kill his man, but the fitting opportunity for this display of prowess had not yet offered. . . .

Now it happened that, at the time of her making Jane Snowdon's acquaintance, Miss Lant was particularly interested in Shooter's Gardens and the immediate vicinity. She had associated herself with certain ladies who undertook the control of a soup-kitchen in the neighbourhood, and as the winter advanced she engaged Jane in this work of charity. It was a good means, as Michael Snowdon agreed, of enabling the girl to form acquaintances among the very poorest, those whom she hoped to serve effectively—not with aid of money alone, but by her personal influence. And I think it will be worth while to dwell a little on the story of this same soup-kitchen; it is significant, and shall take the place of abstract comment on Miss Lant's philanthropic enterprises.

The kitchen had been doing successful work for some

years; the society which established it entrusted its practical conduct to very practical people, a man and wife who were themselves of the nether world, and knew the ways thereof. The 'stock' which formed the basis of the soup was wholesome and nutritious; the peas were of excellent quality; twopence a quart was the price at which this fluid could be purchased (one penny if a ticket from a member of the committee were presented), and sometimes as much as five hundred quarts would be sold in a day. Satisfactory enough this. When the people came with complaints, saying that they were tired of this particular soup, and would like another kind for a change, Mr. and Mrs. Batterby, with perfect understanding of the situation, bade their customers ' take it or leave it—an' none o' your cheek here, or you won't get nothing at all!' The result was much good-humour all round.

But the present year saw a change in the constitution of the committee: two or three philanthropic ladies of great conscientiousness began to inquire busily into the working of the soup-kitchen, and they soon found reason to be altogether dissatisfied with Mr. and Mrs. Batterby. No, no; these managers were of too coarse a type; they spoke grossly; what possibility of their exerting a humanising influence on the people to whom they dispensed soup? Soup and refinement must be disseminated at one and the same time, over the same counter. Mr. and Mrs. Batterby were dismissed, and quite a new order of things began. Not only were the ladies zealous for a high ideal in the matter of soup-distributing, they also aimed at practical economy in the use of funds. Having engaged a cook after their own hearts, and acting upon the advice of competent physiologists, they proceeded to make a ' stock' out of sheep's and bullocks' heads; moreover, they ordered their peas from the City, thus getting them at two shillings a sack less than the price formerly paid by the Batterbys to a dealer in Clerkenwell. But, alas! these things could not be done secretly; the story leaked out; Shooter's Gardens and vicinity broke into the most excited feeling. I need not tell you that the nether world will consume—when others supply it—nothing but the very finest quality of food, that the heads of sheep and bullocks are peculiarly offensive to its stomach, that a saving effected on sacks of peas outrages its dearest sensibilities. What was the result? Shooter's Gardens, convinced of the

fraud practised upon them, nobly brought back their quarts
of soup to the kitchen, and with proud independence of language demanded to have their money returned. On being
met with a refusal, they—what think you?—emptied the soup
on to the floor, and went away with heads exalted.

Vast was the indignation of Miss Lant and the other ladies.
' This is their gratitude!' Now if you or I had been there,
what an opportunity for easing our minds! ' Gratitude,
mesdames? You have entered upon this work with expectation of gratitude?—And can you not perceive that these
people of Shooter's Gardens are poor, besotted, disease-struck
creatures, of whom—in the mass—scarcely a human quality
is to be expected? Have you still to learn what this nether
world has been made by those who belong to the sphere above
it?—Gratitude, quotha?—Nay, do *you* be grateful that these
hapless, half-starved women do not turn and rend you. At
present they satisfy themselves with insolence. Take it
silently, you who at all events hold some count of their dire
state; and endeavour to feed them without arousing their
animosity!'

Well, the kitchen threatened to be a failure. It turned
out that the cheaper peas were, in fact, of inferior quality, and
the ladies hastened to go back to the dealer in Clerkenwell.
This was something, but now came a new trouble; the complaint with which Mr. and Mrs. Batterby had known so well
how to deal revived in view of the concessions made by the
new managers. Shooter's Gardens would have no more
peas; let some other vegetable be used. Again the point was
conceded; a trial was made of barley soup. Shooter's Gardens came, looked, smelt, and shook their heads. ' It don't
look nice,' was their comment; they would none of it.

For two or three weeks, just at this crisis in the kitchen's
fate, Jane Snowdon attended with Miss Lant to help in the dis-
pensing of the decoction. Jane was made very nervous by the
disturbances that went on, but she was able to review the matter
at issue in a far more fruitful way than Miss Lant and the other
ladies. Her opinion was not asked, however. In the homely
grey dress, with her modest, retiring manner, her gentle,
diffident countenance, she was taken by the customers for a
paid servant, and if ever it happened that she could not supply
a can of soup quickly enough sharp words reached her ear.
' Now then, you gyurl there! Are you goin' to keep me all
d'y? I've got somethink else to do but stand 'ere.' And

Jane, by her timid hastening, confirmed the original impression, with the result that she was treated yet more unceremoniously next time. Of all forms of insolence there is none more flagrant than that of the degraded poor receiving charity which they have come to regard as a right.

Jane did speak at length. Miss Lant had called to see her in Hanover Street; seated quietly in her own parlour, with Michael Snowdon to approve—with him she had already discussed the matter—Jane ventured softly to compare the present state of things and that of former winters, as described to her by various people.

'Wasn't it rather a pity,' she suggested, 'that the old people were sent away?'

'You think so?' returned Miss Lant, with the air of one to whom a novel thought is presented. 'You really think so, Miss Snowdon?'

'They got on so well with everybody,' Jane continued. 'And don't you think it's better, Miss Lant, for everybody to feel satisfied?'

'But really, Mr. Batterby used to speak so very harshly. He destroyed their self-respect.'

'I don't think they minded it,' said Jane, with simple good faith. 'And I'm always hearing them wish he was back, instead of the new managers.'

'I think we shall have to consider this,' remarked the lady, thoughtfully.

Considered it was, and with the result that the Batterbys before long found themselves in their old position, uproariously welcomed by Shooter's Gardens. In a few weeks the soup was once more concocted of familiar ingredients, and customers, as often as they grumbled, had the pleasure of being rebuked in their native tongue.

It was with anything but a cheerful heart that Jane went through this initiation into the philanthropic life. Her brief period of joy and confidence was followed by a return of anxiety, which no resolve could suppress. It was not only that the ideals to which she strove to form herself made no genuine appeal to her nature; the imperative hunger of her heart remained unsatisfied. At first, when the assurance received from Michael began to lose a little of its sustaining force, she could say to herself, 'Patience, patience; be faithful, be trustful, and your reward will soon come.' Nor would patience have failed her had but the current of life flowed on in the old way. It was the introduction of new and disturbing things that proved so great a test of fortitude. Those two successive absences of Sidney on the appointed evening were strangely unlike him, but perhaps could be explained by the unsettlement of his removal; his manner when at length he did come proved that the change in himself was still proceeding. Moreover, the change affected Michael, who manifested increase of mental trouble at the same time that he yielded more and more to physical infirmity.

The letter which Sidney wrote after receiving Joseph Snowdon's confidential communications was despatched two days later. He expressed himself in carefully chosen words, but the purport of the letter was to make known that he no longer thought of Jane save as a friend; that the change in her position had compelled him to take another view of his relations to her than that he had confided to Michael at Danbury. Most fortunately—he added—no utterance of his feelings had ever escaped him to Jane herself, and henceforth he should be still more careful to avoid any suggestion of more than brotherly interest. In very deed nothing was altered; he was still her steadfast friend, and would always aid her to his utmost in the work of her life.

That Sidney could send this letter, after keeping it in reserve for a couple of days, proved how profoundly his instincts were revolted by the difficulties and the ambiguity of his position. It had been bad enough when only his own conscience was in play; the dialogue with Joseph, following upon Bessie Byass's indiscretion, threw him wholly off his balance, and he could give no weight to any consideration but the necessity of recovering self-respect. Even the sophistry of that repeated statement that he had never approached Jane as a lover did not trouble him in face of the injury to his pride. Every word of Joseph Snowdon's transparently artful hints was a sting to his sensitiveness; the sum excited him to loathing. It was as though the corner of a curtain had been raised, giving him a glimpse of all the vile greed, the base machination, hovering about this fortune that Jane was to inherit. Of Scawthorne he knew nothing, but his recollection of the Peckovers was vivid enough to suggest what part Mrs. Joseph Snowdon was playing in the present intrigues, and he felt convinced that in the background were other beasts of prey, watching with keen, envious eyes. The sudden revelation was a shock from which he would not soon recover; he seemed to himself to be in a degree contaminated; he questioned his most secret thoughts again and again, recognising with torment the fears which had already bidden him draw back; he desired to purify himself by some unmistakable action.

That which happened he had anticipated. On receipt of the letter Michael came to see him; he found the old man waiting in front of the house when he returned to Red Lion Street after his work. The conversation that followed was a severe test of Sidney's resolve. Had Michael disclosed the fact of his private understanding with Jane, Sidney would probably have yielded; but the old man gave no hint of what he had done—partly because he found it difficult to make the admission, partly in consequence of an indecision in his own mind with regard to the very point at issue. Though agitated by the consciousness of suffering in store for Jane, his thoughts disturbed by the derangement of a part of his plan, he did not feel that Sidney's change of mind gravely affected the plan itself. Age had cooled his blood; enthusiasm had made personal interests of comparatively small account to him; he recognised his granddaughter's feeling, but could not appreciate its intensity, its surpreme significance. When Kirkwood made a show of explaining himself, saying that he shrank from that form of responsibility, that such a marriage suggested to him many and insuperable embarrassments, Michael began to reflect that perchance this was the just view. With household and family cares, could Jane devote herself to the great work after the manner of his ideal? Had he not been tempted by his friendship for Sidney to introduce into his scheme what was really an incompatible element? Was it not decidedly, infinitely better that Jane should be unmarried?

Michael had taken the last step in that process of dehumanisation which threatens idealists of his type. He had reached at length the pass of those frenzied votaries of a supernatural creed who exact from their disciples the sacrifice of every human piety. Returning home, he murmured to himself again and again, 'She must not marry. She must overcome this desire of a happiness such as ordinary women may enjoy. For my sake, and for the sake of her suffering fellow-creatures, Jane must win this victory over herself.'

He purposed speaking to her, but put it off from day to

day. Sidney paid his visits as usual, and tried desperately to behave as though he had no trouble. Could he have divined why it was that Michael had ended by accepting his vague pretences with apparent calm, indignation, wrath, would have possessed him; he believed, however, that the old man out of kindness subdued what he really felt. Sidney's state was pitiable. He knew not whether he more shrank from the thought of being infected with Joseph Snowdon's baseness or despised himself for his attitude to Jane. Despicable entirely had been his explanations to Michael, but how could he make them more sincere? To tell the whole truth, to reveal Joseph's tactics would be equivalent to taking a part in the dirty contest; Michael would probably do him justice, but who could say how far Joseph's machinations were becoming effectual? The slightest tinct of uncertainty in the old man's thought, and he, Kirkwood, became a plotter, like the others, meeting mine with countermine.

'There will be no possibility of perfect faith between men until there is no such thing as money! H'm, and when is that likely to come to pass?'

Thus he epigrammatised to himself one evening, savagely enough, as with head bent forward he plodded to Red Lion Street. Some one addressed him; he looked up and saw Jane. Seemingly it was a chance meeting, but she put a question at once almost as though she had been waiting for him. 'Have you seen Pennyloaf lately, Mr. Kirkwood?'

Pennyloaf? The name suggested Bob Hewett, who again suggested John Hewett, and so Sidney fell upon thoughts of some one who two days ago had found a refuge in John's home. To Michael he had said nothing of what he knew concerning Clara; a fresh occasion of uneasy thought. Bob Hewett—so John said—had no knowledge of his sister's situation, otherwise Pennyloaf might have come to know about it, and in that case, perchance, Jane herself. Why not? Into what a wretched muddle of concealments and inconsistencies and insincerities had he fallen!

'It's far too long since I saw her,' he replied, in that softened tone which he found it impossible to avoid when his eyes met Jane's.

She was on her way home from the soup-kitchen, where certain occupations had kept her much later than usual; this, however, was far out of her way, and Sidney remarked on the fact, perversely, when she had offered this explanation of her meeting him. Jane did not reply. They walked on together, towards Islington.

'Are you going to help at that place all the winter?' he inquired.

'Yes; I think so.'

If he had spoken his thought, he would have railed against the soup-kitchen and all that was connected with it. So far had he got in his revolt against circumstances; Jane's 'mission' was hateful to him; he could not bear to think of her handing soup over a counter to ragged wretches.

'You're nothing like as cheerful as you used to be, he said, suddenly, and all but roughly. 'Why is it?'

What a question! Jane reddened as she tried to look at him with a smile; no words would come to her tongue.

'Do you go anywhere else, besides to—to that place?'

Not often. She had accompanied Miss Lant on a visit to some people in Shooter's Gardens.

Sidney bent his brows. A nice spot, Shooter's Gardens.

'The houses are going to be pulled down, I'm glad to say,' continued Jane. 'Miss Lant thinks it'll be a good opportunity for helping a few of the families into better lodgings. We're going to buy furniture for them—so many have as good as none at all, you know. It'll be a good start for them, won't it?'

Sidney nodded. He was thinking of another family who already owed their furniture to Jane's beneficence, though they did not know it.

'Mind you don't throw away kindness on worthless people,' he said presently.

'We can only do our best, and hope they'll keep comfortable for their own sakes.'

'Yes, yes. Well, I'll say good-night to you here. Go home and rest; you look tired.'

He no longer called her by her name. Tearing himself away, with a last look, he raged inwardly that so sweet and gentle a creature should be condemned to such a waste of her young life.

Jane had obtained what she came for. At times the longing to see him grew insupportable, and this evening she had yielded to it, going out of her way in the hope of encountering him as he came from work. He spoke very strangely. What did it all mean, and when would this winter of suspense give sign of vanishing before sunlight?

CHAPTER XXIX

PHANTOMS

MR. and Mrs. Joseph Snowdon were now established in rooms in Burton Crescent, which is not far from King's Cross. Joseph had urged that Clerkenwell Close was scarcely a suitable quarter for a man of his standing, and, though with difficulty, he had achieved thus much deliverance. Of Clem he could not get rid—just yet; but it was something to escape Mrs. Peckover's superintendence. Clem herself favoured the removal, naturally for private reasons. Thus far working in alliance with her shrewd mother, she was now forming independent projects. Mrs. Peckover's zeal was assuredly not disinterested, and why, Clem mused with herself, should the fruits of strategy be shared? Her husband's father could not, she saw every reason to believe, be much longer for this world. How his property was to be divided she had no means of discovering; Joseph professed to have no accurate information, but as a matter of course he was deceiving her. Should he inherit a considerable sum, it was more than probable he would think of again quitting his native land—and without encumbrances. That movement must somehow be guarded against; how, it was difficult as yet to determine. In the next place, Jane was sure to take a large share of the fortune. To that Clem strongly objected, both on abstract grounds and because she regarded Jane with a savage hatred—a hatred which had its roots in the time of Jane's childhood, and which had grown in proportion as the girl reaped happiness from life. The necessity of cloaking this sentiment had not, you may be sure, tended to mitigate it. Joseph said that there was no longer any fear of a speedy marriage between Jane and Kirkwood, but that such a marriage would come off some day, —if not prevented—Clem held to be a matter of certainty. Sidney Kirkwood was a wide-awake young man; of course he had his satisfactory reasons for delay. Now Clem's hatred of Sidney was, from of old, only less than that wherewith she regarded Jane. To frustrate the hopes of that couple would be a gratification worth a good deal of risk.

She heard nothing of what had befallen Clara Hewett until the latter's return home, and then not from her husband.

Joseph and Scawthorne, foiled by that event in an ingenious
scheme which you have doubtless understood (they little
knowing how easily the severance between Jane and Kirkwood
might be effected), agreed that it was well to get Clara restored to her father's household—for, though it seemed unlikely, it was not impossible that she might in one way or
another aid their schemes—and on that account the anonymous letter was despatched which informed John Hewett of
his daughter's position. Between John and Snowdon, now
that they stood in the relations of master and servant, there
was naturally no longer familiar intercourse, and, in begging
leave of absence for his journey northwards, Hewett only said
that a near relative had met with a bad accident. But it
would be easy, Joseph decided, to win the man's confidence
again, and thus be apprised of all that went on. With Clem
he kept silence on the subject; not improbably she would
learn sooner or later what had happened, and indeed, as things
now stood, it did not matter much; but on principle he excluded her as much as possible from his confidence. He knew
she hated him, and he was not backward in returning the
sentiment, though constantly affecting a cheerful friendliness
in his manner to her; after all, their union was but temporary.
In Hanover Street he was also silent regarding the Hewetts, for
there his *rôle* was that of a good, simple-minded fellow, incapable of intrigue, living for the domestic affections. If Kirkwood chose to speak to Michael or Jane of the matter, well,
one way or another, that would advance things a stage, and
there was nothing for it but to watch the progress.

Alone all through the day, and very often in the evening
Clem was not at all disposed to occupy herself in domestic
activity. The lodgings were taken furnished, and a bondmaid
of the house did such work as was indispensable. Dirt and
disorder were matters of indifference to the pair, who represented therein the large class occupying cheap London
lodgings; an impure atmosphere, surroundings more or less
squalid, constant bickering with the landlady, coarse usage of
the servant—these things Clem understood as necessaries of
independent life, and it would have cost her much discomfort
had she been required to live in a more civilised manner.
Her ambitions were essentially gross. In the way of social
advancement she appreciated nothing but an increased power
of spending money, and consequently of asserting herself over
others. She had no desire whatever to enter a higher class

than that in which she was born ; to be of importance in her
familiar circle was the most she aimed at. In visiting the
theatre, she did not so much care to occupy a superior place
—indeed, such a position made her ill at ease—as to astonish
her neighbours in the pit by a lavish style of costume, by
loud remarks implying a free command of cash, by purchase
between the acts of something expensive to eat or drink.
Needless to say that she never read anything but police news ;
in the fiction of her world she found no charm, so sluggishly
unimaginative was her nature. Till of late she had either
abandoned herself all day long to a brutal indolence, eating
rather too much, and finding quite sufficient occupation for
her slow brain in the thought of how pleasant it was not to be
obliged to work, and occasionally in reviewing the chances that
she might eventually have plenty of money and no Joseph
Snowdon as a restraint upon her ; or else, her physical robust-
ness demanding exercise, she walked considerable distances
about the localities she knew, calling now and then upon an
acquaintance.

Till of late ; but a change had come upon her life. It was
now seldom that she kept the house all day ; when within-
doors she was restless, quarrelsome. Joseph became aware
with surprise that she no longer tried to conceal her enmity
against him ; on a slight provocation she broke into a fierceness which reminded him of the day when he undeceived her
as to his position, and her look at such times was murderous.
It might come, he imagined, of her being released from the
prudent control of her mother. However, again a few weeks
and things were somewhat improved ; she eyed him like a wild
beast, but was less frequent in her outbreaks. Here, too, it
might be that Mrs. Peckover's influence was at work, for Clara
spent at least four evenings of the seven away from home, and
always said she had been at the Close. As indifferent as it
was possible to be, Joseph made no attempt to restrain her
independence ; indeed he was glad to have her out of his
way.

We must follow her on one of these evenings os ensibly
passed at Mrs. Peckover's—no, not follow, but discover her
at nine o'clock.

In Old Street, not far from Shoreditch Station, was a
shabby little place of refreshment, kept by an Italian ; pastry
and sweet-stuff filled the window ; at the back of the shop,
through a doorway on each side of which was looped a pink

curtain, a room, furnished with three marble-topped tables, invited those who wished to eat and drink more at ease than was possible before the counter. Except on Sunday evening this room was very little used, and there, on the occasion of which I speak, Clem was sitting with Bob Hewett. They had been having supper together—French pastry and a cup of cocoa.

She leaned forward on her elbows, and said imperatively, 'Tell Pennyloaf to make it up with her again.'

'Why?'

'Because I want to know what goes on in Hanover Street. You was a fool to send her away, and you'd ought to have told me about it before now. If they was such friends, I suppose the girl told her lots o' things. But I expect they see each other just the same. You don't suppose she does all *you* tell her?'

'I'll bet you what you like she does!' cried Bob.

Clem glared at him.

'Oh, you an' your Pennyloaf! Likely she tells you the truth. You're so fond of each other, ain't you! Tells you everything, does she?—and the way you treat her!"

'Who's always at me to make me treat her worse still?' Bob retorted half angrily, half in expostulation.

'Well, and so I am, 'cause I hate the name of her! I'd like to hear as you starve her and her brats half to death. How much money did you give her last week? Now you just tell me the truth. How much was it?'

'How can I remember? Three or four bob, I s'pose.'

'Three or four bob!' she repeated, snarling. 'Give her one, and make her live all the week on it. Wear her down! Make her pawn all she has, and go cold!'

Her cheeks were on fire; her eyes started in the fury of jealousy; she set her teeth together.

'I'd better do for her altogether,' said Bob, with an evil grin.

Clem looked at him, without speaking; kept her gaze on him; then she said in a thick voice:

'There's many a true word said in joke.'

Bob moved uncomfortably. There was a brief silence, then the other, putting her face nearer his:

'Not just yet. I want to use her to get all I can about that girl and her old beast of a grandfather. Mind you do as I tell you. Pennyloaf's to have her back again, and she's to

make her talk, and you're to get all you can from Pennyloaf
—understand ? '

There came noises from the shop. Three work-girls had
just entered and were buying cakes, which they began to eat
at the counter. They were loud in gossip and laughter, and
their voices rang like brass against brass. Clem amused
herself in listening to them for a few minutes; then she
became absent, moving a finger round and round on her
plate. A disagreeable flush still lingered under her eyes.

' Have you told her about Clara ? '

' Told who ? '

' Who? Pennyloaf, of course.'

' No, I haven't. Why should I ? '

' Oh, you're such a affectionate couple! See, you're only
to give her two shillin's next week. Let her go hungry this
nice weather.'

' She won't do that if Jane Snowdon comes back, so there
you're out of it! '

Clem bit her lip.

' What's the odds? Make it up with a hit in the mouth
now and then.'

' What do you expect to know from that girl ? ' inquired
Bob.

' Lots o' things. I want to know what the old bloke's
goin' to do with his money, don't I ? And I want to know
what my beast of a 'usband's got out of him. And I want to
know what that feller Kirkwood's goin' to do. He'd ought to
marry your sister by rights.'

' Not much fear of that now.'

' Trust him! He'll stick where there's money. See, Bob;
if that Jane was to kick the bucket, do you think the old bloke
'ud leave it all to Jo ? '

' How can I tell ? '

' Well, look here. Supposin' he died an' left most to her;
an' then supposin' *she* was to go off; would Jo have all her
tin ? '

' Course he would.'

Clem mused, eating her lower lip.

' But supposin' Jo was to go off first, after the old bloke ?
Should I have all he left ? '

' I think so, but I'm not sure.'

' You think so? And then should I have all *hers* ? If
she had a accident, you know.'

'I suppose you would. But then that's only if they didn't make wills, and leave it away from you.'

Clem started. Intent as she had been for a long time on the possibilities hinted at, the thought of unfavourable disposition by will had never occurred to her. She shook it away.

'Why should they make wills? They ain't old enough for that, neither of them.'

'And you might as well say they ain't old enough to be likely to take their hook, either,' suggested Bob, with a certain uneasiness in his tone.

Clem looked about her, as if her fierce eyes sought something. Her brows twitched a little. She glanced at Bob, but he did not meet her look. 'I don't care so much about the money,' she said, in a lower and altered voice. 'I'd be content with a bit of it, if only I could get rid of him at the same time.'

Bob looked gloomy.

'Well, it's no use talking,' he muttered.

'It's all your fault.'

'How do you make that out? It was you quarrelled first.'

'You're a liar!'

'Oh, there's no talking to you!'

He shuffled with his feet, then rose.

'Where can I see you on Wednesday morning?' asked Clem. 'I want to hear about that girl.'

'It can't be Wednesday morning. I tell you I shall be getting the sack next thing; they've promised it. Two days last week I wasn't at the shop, and one day this. It can't go on.'

His companion retorted angrily, and for five minutes they stood in embittered colloquy. It ended in Bob's turning away and going out into the street. Clem followed, and they walked westwards in silence. Reaching City Road, and crossing to the corner where lowers St. Luke's Hospital—grim abode of the insane, here in the midst of London's squalor and uproar—they halted to take leave. The last words they exchanged, after making an appointment, were of brutal violence.

This was two days after Clara Hewett's arrival in London, and the same fog still hung about the streets, allowing little to be seen save the blurred glimmer of gas. Bob sauntered

through it, his hands in his pockets, observant of nothing;
now and then a word escaped his lips, generally an oath.
Out of Old Street he turned into Whitecross Street, whence
by black and all but deserted ways—Barbican and Long
Lane—he emerged into West Smithfield. An alley in the
shadow of Bartholomew's Hospital brought him to a certain
house: just as he was about to knock at the door it opened,
and Jack Bartley appeared on the threshold. They exchanged
a 'Hollo!' of surprise, and after a whispered word or two on
the pavement, went in. They mounted the stairs to a bedroom which Jack occupied. When the door was closed:

'Bill's got copped!' whispered Bartley.

'Copped? Any of it on him?'

'Only the half-crown as he was pitchin', thank God!
They let him go again after he'd been to the station. It was
a conductor. I'd never try them blokes myself; they're too
downy.'*

'Let's have a look at 'em,' said Bob, after musing. 'I
thought myself as they wasn't quite the reg'lar.''

As he spoke he softly turned the key in the door. Jack
then put his arm up the chimney and brought down a small
tin box, soot-blackened; he opened it, and showed about a
dozen pieces of money—in appearance half-crowns and
florins. One of the commonest of offences against the law in
London, this to which our young friends were not unsuccess-
fully directing their attention; one of the easiest to commit,
moreover, for a man with Bob's craft at his finger-ends. A
mere question of a mould and a pewter-pot, if one be content
with the simpler branches of the industry. 'The snyde' or
'the queer' is the technical name by which such products
are known. Distribution is, of course, the main difficulty; it
necessitates mutual trust between various confederates. Bob
Hewett still kept to his daily work, but gradually he was
being drawn into alliance with an increasing number of men
who scorned the yoke of a recognised occupation. His face,
his clothing, his speech, all told whither he was tending, had
one but the experience necessary for the noting of such points.
Bob did not find his life particularly pleasant; he was in
perpetual fear; many a time he said to himself that he would
turn back. Impossible to do so; for a thousand reasons impossible; yet he still believed that the choice lay with him.

His colloquy with Jack only lasted a few minutes, then
he walked homewards, crossing the Metropolitan Meat-market,

going up St. John's Lane, beneath St. John's Arch, thence to Rosoman Street and Merlin Place, where at present he lived. All the way he pondered Clem's words. Already their import had become familiar enough to lose that first terribleness. Of course he should never take up the proposal seriously; no, no, that was going a bit too far; but suppose Clem's husband were really contriving this plot on his own account? Likely, very likely; but he'd be a clever fellow if he managed such a thing in a way that did not immediately subject him to suspicion. How could it be done? No harm in thinking over an affair of that kind when you have no intention of being drawn into it yourself. There was that man at Peckham who poisoned his sister not long ago; he was a fool to get found out in the way he did; he might have——

The room in which he found Pennyloaf sitting was so full of fog that the lamp seemed very dim; the fire had all but died out. One of the children lay asleep; the other Pennyloaf was nursing, for it had a bad cough and looked much like a wax doll that has gone through a great deal of ill-usage. A few more weeks and Pennyloaf would be again a mother; she felt very miserable as often as she thought of it, and Bob had several times spoken with harsh impatience on the subject.

At present he was in no mood for conversation; to Pennyloaf's remarks and questions he gave not the slightest heed, but in a few minutes tumbled himself into bed.

'Get that light put out,' he exclaimed, after lying still for a while.

Pennyloaf said she was uneasy about the child; its cough seemed to be better, but it moved about restlessly and showed no sign of getting to sleep.

'Give it some of the mixture, then. Be sharp and put the light out.'

Pennyloaf obeyed the second injunction, and she too lay down, keeping the child in her arms; of the 'mixture' she was afraid, for a few days since the child of a neighbour had died in consequence of an overdose of this same anodyne. For a long time there was silence in the room. Outside, voices kept sounding with that peculiar muffled distinctness which they have on a night of dense fog, when there is little or no wheel-traffic to make the wonted rumbling.

'Are y'asleep?' Bob asked suddenly.

'No.'

'There's something I wanted to tell you. You can have
Jane Snowdon here again, if you like.'

'I can? Really?'

'You may as well make use of her. That'll do; shut up
and go to sleep.'

In the morning Pennyloaf was obliged to ask for money;
she wished to take the child to the hospital again, and as the
weather was very bad she would have to pay an omnibus fare.
Bob growled at the demand, as was nowadays his custom.
Since he had found a way of keeping his own pocket tolerably
well supplied from time to time, he was becoming so penurious
at home that Pennyloaf had to beg for what she needed copper
by copper. Excepting breakfast, he seldom took a meal with
her. The easy good-nature which in the beginning made
him an indulgent husband had turned in other directions
since his marriage was grown a weariness to him. He did
not, in truth, spend much upon himself, but in his leisure
time was always surrounded by companions whom he had a
pleasure in treating with the generosity of the public-house.
A word of flattery was always sure of payment if Bob had a
coin in his pocket. Ever hungry for admiration, for prominence, he found new opportunities of gratifying his taste
now that he had a resource when his wages ran out. So far
from becoming freer-handed again with his wife and children,
he grudged every coin that he was obliged to expend on them.
Pennyloaf's submissiveness encouraged him in this habit;
where other wives would have 'made a row,' she yielded at
once to his grumbling and made shift with the paltriest
allowance. You should have seen the kind of diet on which
she habitually lived. Like all the women of her class, utterly
ignorant and helpless in the matter of preparing food, she
abandoned the attempt to cook anything, and expended her
few pence daily on whatever happened to tempt her in a shop,
when meal-time came round. In the present state of her
health she often suffered from a morbid appetite and fed on
things of incredible unwholesomeness. Thus, there was a
kind of cake exposed in a window in Rosoman Street, two
layers of pastry with half an inch of something like very coarse
mincemeat between; it cost a halfpenny a square, and not
seldom she ate four, or even six, of these squares, as heavy as
lead, making this her dinner. A cookshop within her range
exhibited at midday great dough-puddings, kept hot by jets of
steam that came up through the zinc on which they lay; this

food was cheap and satisfying, and Pennyloaf often regaled both herself and the children on thick slabs of it. Pease-pudding also attracted her; she fetched it from the pork-butcher's in a little basin, which enabled her to bring away at the same time a spoonful or two of gravy from the joints of which she was not rich enough to purchase a cut. Her drink was tea; she had the pot on the table all day, and kept adding hot water. Treacle she purchased now and then, but only as a treat when her dinner had cost even less than usual; she did not venture to buy more than a couple of ounces at a time, knowing by experience that she could not resist this form of temptation, and must eat and eat till all was finished.

Bob flung sixpence on the table. He was ashamed of himself—you will not understand him if you fail to recognise that—but the shame only served to make him fret under his bondage. Was he going to be tied to Pennyloaf all his life, with a family constantly increasing? Practically he had already made a resolve to be free before very long; the way was not quite clear to him as yet. But he went to work still brooding over Clem's words of the night before.

Pennyloaf let the fire go out, locked the elder child into the room for safety against accidents, and set forth for the hospital. It rained heavily, and the wind rendered her umbrella useless. She had to stand for a long time at a street-corner before the omnibus came; the water soaked into her leaky shoes, but that didn't matter; it was the child on whose account she was anxious. Having reached her destination, she sat for a long time waiting her turn among the numerous out-patients. Just as the opportunity for pass-ing into the doctor's room arrived, a movement in the bundle she held made her look closely at the child's face; at that instant it had ceased to live.

The medical man behaved kindly to her, but she gave way to no outburst of grief; with tearless eyes she stared at the unmoving body in a sort of astonishment. The questions addressed to her she could not answer with any intelligence; several times she asked stupidly, 'Is she really dead?' There was nothing to wonder at, however; the doctor glanced at the paper on which he had written prescriptions twice or thrice during the past few weeks, and found the event natural enough. . . .

Towards the close of the afternoon Pennyloaf was in Hanover Street. She wished to see Jane Snowdon, but had a fear of going up to the door and knocking. Jane might not be at home, and, if she were, Pennyloaf did not know in what words to explain her coming and say what had happened. She was in a dazed, heavy, tongue-tied state ; indeed she did not clearly remember how she had come thus far, or what she had done since leaving the hospital at midday. However, her steps drew nearer to the house, and at last she had raised the knocker—just raised it and let it fall.

Mrs. Byass opened ; she did not know Pennyloaf by sight. The latter tried to say something, but only stammered a meaningless sound; thereupon Bessie concluded she was a beggar, and with a shake of the head shut the door upon her.

Pennyloaf turned away in confusion and dull misery. She walked to the end of the street and stood there. On leaving home she had forgotten her umbrella, and now it was raining heavily again. Of a sudden her need became powerful enough to overcome all obstacles; she knew that she *must* see Jane Snowdon, that she could not go home till she had done so. Jane was the only friend she had ; the only creature who would speak the kind of words to her for which she longed.

Again the knocker fell, and again Mrs. Byass appeared.

' What do you want ? I've got nothing for you,' she cried impatiently.

' I want to see Miss Snowdon, please, mum—Miss Snowdon, please——'

' Miss Snowdon ? Then why didn't you say so ? Step inside.'

A few moments and Jane came running downstairs.

' Pennyloaf ! '

Ah ! that was the voice that did good. How it comforted and blessed, after the hospital, and the miserable room in which the dead child was left lying, and the rainy street !

CHAPTER XXX

ON A BARREN SHORE

ABOUT this time Mr. Scawthorne received one morning a letter which, though not unexpected, caused him some annoyance, and even anxiety. It was signed ' C. V.,' and made brief request for an interview on the evening of the next day at Waterloo Station.

The room in which our friend sat at breakfast was of such very modest appearance that it seemed to argue but poor remuneration for the services rendered by him in the office of Messrs. Percival & Peel. It was a parlour on the second floor of a lodging-house in Chelsea; Scawthorne's graceful person and professional bearing were out of place amid the trivial appointments. He lived here for the simple reason that in order to enjoy a few of the luxuries of civilisation he had to spend as little as possible on bare necessaries. His habits away from home were those of a man to whom a few pounds are no serious consideration; his pleasant dinner at the restaurant, his occasional stall at a theatre, his easy acquaintance with easy livers of various kinds, had become indispensable to him, and as a matter of course his expenditure increased although his income kept at the same figure. That figure was not contemptible, regard had to the path by which he had come thus far; Mr. Percival esteemed his abilities highly, and behaved to him with generosity. Ten years ago Scawthorne would have lost his senses with joy at the prospect of such a salary; to-day he found it miserably insufficient to the demands he made upon life. Paltry debts harassed him; inabilities fretted his temperament and his pride; it irked him to have no better abode than this musty corner to which he could never invite an acquaintance. And then, notwithstanding his mental endowments, his keen social sense, his native tact, in all London not one refined home was open to him, not one domestic circle of educated people could he approach and find a welcome.

Scawthorne was passing out of the stage when a man seeks only the gratification of his propensities; he began to focus his outlook upon the world, and to feel the significance of maturity. The double existence he was compelled to lead —that of a laborious and clear-brained man of business in office hours, that of a hungry rascal in the time which was his own—not only impressed him with a sense of danger, but made him profoundly dissatisfied with the unreality of what he called his enjoyments. What, he asked himself, had condemned him to this kind of career? Simply the weight under which he started, his poor origin, his miserable youth. However carefully regulated his private life had been, his position to-day could not have been other than it was; no degree of purity would have opened to him the door of a civilised house. Suppose he had wished to marry; where,

pray, was he to find his wife? A barmaid? Why, yes, other
men of his standing wedded barmaids and girls from the
houses of business, and so on; but they had neither his
tastes nor his brains. Never had it been his lot to exchange
a word with an educated woman—save in the office on rare
occasions. There is such a thing as self-martyrdom in the
cause of personal integrity; another man might have said to
himself, 'Providence forbids me the gratification of my higher
instincts, and I must be content to live a life of barrenness,
that I may at least be above reproach.' True, but Scawthorne
happened not to be so made. He was of the rebels of the
earth. Formerly he revolted because he could not indulge
his senses to their full; at present his ideal was changed, and
the past burdened him.

Yesterday he had had an interview with old Mr. Percival
which, for the first time in his life, opened to him a prospect
of the only kind of advancement conformable with his higher
needs. The firm of Percival & Peel was, in truth, Percival &
Son, Mr. Peel having been dead for many years; and the son
in question lacked a good deal of being the capable lawyer
whose exertions could supplement the failing energy of the
senior partner. Mr. Percival having pondered the matter for
some time, now proposed that Scawthorne should qualify
himself for admission as a solicitor (the circumstances required
his being under articles for three years only), and then, if
everything were still favourable, accept a junior partnership
in the firm. Such an offer was a testimony of the high regard
in which Scawthorne was held by his employer; it stirred
him with hope he had never dared to entertain since his eyes
were opened to the realities of the world, and in a single day
did more for the ripening of his prudence than years would
have effected had his position remained unaltered. Scawthorne
realised more distinctly what a hazardous game he had been
playing.

And here was this brief note, signed 'C. V.' An ugly
affair to look back upon, all that connected itself with those
initials. The worst of it was, that it could not be regarded
as done with. Had he anything to fear from 'C. V.' directly?
The meeting must decide that. He felt now what a fortunate
thing it was that his elaborate plot to put an end to the
engagement between Kirkwood and Jane Snowdon had been
accidentally frustrated—a plot which *might* have availed
himself nothing, even had it succeeded. But was he, in his

abandonment of rascality in general, to think no more of the fortune which had so long kept his imagination uneasy? Had he not, rather, a vastly better chance of getting some of that money into his own pocket? It really seemed as if Kirkwood—though he might be only artful—had relinquished his claim on the girl, at all events for the present; possibly he was an honest man, which would explain his behaviour. Michael Snowdon could not live much longer; Jane would be the ward of the Percivals, and certainly would be aided to a position more correspondent with her wealth. Why should it then be impossible for *him* to become Jane's husband? Joseph, beyond a doubt, could be brought to favour that arrangement, by means of a private understanding more advantageous to him than anything he could reasonably hope from the girl's merely remaining unmarried. This change in his relations to the Percivals would so far improve his social claims that many of the difficulties hitherto besieging such a scheme as this might easily be set aside. Come, come; the atmosphere was clearing. Joseph himself, now established in a decent business, would become less a fellow-intriguer than an ordinary friend bound to him, in the way of the world, by mutual interests. Things must be put in order; by some device the need of secrecy in his intercourse with Joseph must come to an end. In fact, there remained but two hazardous points. Could the connection between Jane and Kirkwood be brought definitely to an end. And was anything to be feared from poor ' C. V.' ?

Waterloo Station is a convenient rendezvous; its irregular form provides many corners of retirement, out-of-the-way recesses where talk can be carried on in something like privacy. To one of these secluded spots Scawthorne drew aside with the veiled woman who met him at the entrance from Waterloo Road. So closely was her face shrouded, that he had at first a difficulty in catching the words she addressed to him. The noise of an engine getting up steam, the rattle of cabs and porters' barrows, the tread and voices of a multitude of people made fitting accompaniment to a dialogue which in every word presupposed the corruptions and miseries of a centre of modern life.

' Why did you send that letter to my father? ' was Clara's first question.

' Letter? What letter? '

' Wasn't it you who let him know about me ? '

'Certainly not. How should I have known his address? When I saw the newspapers, I went down to Bolton and made inquiries. When I heard your father had been, I concluded you had yourself sent for him. Otherwise, I should, of course, have tried to be useful to you in some way. As it was, I supposed you would scarcely thank me for coming forward.'

It might or might not be the truth, as far as Clara was able to decide. Possibly the information had come from some one else. She knew him well enough to be assured by his tone that nothing more could be elicited from him on that point.

'You are quite recovered, I hope?' Scawthorne added, surveying her as she stood in the obscurity. 'In your general health?'

He was courteous, somewhat distant.

'I suppose I'm as well as I shall ever be,' she answered coldly. 'I asked you to meet me because I wanted to know what it was you spoke of in your last letters. You got my answer, I suppose.'

'Yes, I received your answer. But—in fact, it's too late. The time has gone by; and perhaps I was a little hasty in the hopes I held out. I had partly deceived myself.'

'Never mind. I wish to know what it was,' she said impatiently.

'It can't matter now. Well, there's no harm in mentioning it. Naturally you went out of your way to suppose it was something dishonourable. Nothing of the kind; I had an idea that you might come to terms with an Australian who was looking out for actresses for a theatre in Melbourne— that was all. But he wasn't quite the man I took him for. I doubt whether it could have been made as profitable as I thought at first.'

'You expect me to believe that story?'

'Not unless you like. It's some time since you put any faith in my goodwill. The only reason I didn't speak plainly was because I felt sure that the mention of a foreign country would excite your suspicions. You have always attributed evil motives to me rather than good. However, this is not the time to speak of such things. I sympathise with you— deeply. Will you tell me if I can—can help you at all?'

'No, you can't. I wanted to make quite sure that you were what I thought you, that's all.'

'I don't think, on the whole, you have any reason to complain of ill-faith on my part. I secured you the opportunities that are so hard to find.'

'Yes, you did. We don't owe each other anything—that's one comfort. I'll just say that you needn't have any fear I shall trouble you in future ; I know that's what you're chiefly thinking about.'

'You misjudge me ; but that can't be helped. I wish very much it were in my power to be of use to you.'

'Thank you.'

On that last note of irony they parted. True enough, in one sense, that there remained debt on neither side. But Clara, for all the fierce ambition which had brought her life to this point, could not divest herself of a woman's instincts. That simple fact explained various inconsistencies in her behaviour to Scawthorne since she had made herself independent of him ; it explained also why this final interview became the bitterest charge her memory preserved against him.

Her existence for some three weeks kept so gloomy a monotony that it was impossible she should endure it much longer. The little room which she shared at night with Annie and Amy was her cell throughout the day. Of necessity she had made the acquaintance of Mrs. Eagles, but they scarcely saw more of each other than if they had lived in different tenements on the same staircase ; she had offered to undertake a share of the housework, but her father knew that everything of the kind was distasteful to her, and Mrs. Eagles continued to assist Amy as hitherto. To save trouble, she came into the middle room for her meals, at these times always keeping as much of her face as possible hidden. The children could not overcome a repulsion, a fear, excited by her veil and the muteness she preserved in their presence ; several nights passed before little Annie got to sleep with any comfort. Only with her father did Clara hold converse ; in the evening he always sat alone with her for an hour. She went out perhaps every third day, after dark, stealing silently down the long staircase, and walking rapidly until she had escaped the neighbourhood—like John Hewett when formerly he wandered forth in search of her. Her strength was slight ; after half-an-hour's absence she came back so wearied that the ascent of stairs cost her much suffering.

The economy prevailing in to-day's architecture takes good

care that no depressing circumstance shall be absent from
the dwellings in which the poor find shelter. What terrible
barracks, those Farringdon Road Buildings !* Vast, sheer
walls, unbroken by even an attempt at ornament; row above
row of windows in the mud-coloured surface, upwards, upwards, lifeless eyes, murky openings that tell of bareness, disorder, comfortlessness within. One is tempted to say that
Shooter's Gardens are a preferable abode. An inner courtyard, asphalted, swept clean—looking up to the sky as from a
prison. Acres of these edifices, the tinge of grime declaring
the relative dates of their erection; millions of tons of brute
brick and mortar, crushing the spirit as you gaze. Barracks,
in truth; housing for the army of industrialism, an army
fighting with itself, rank against rank, man against man, that
the survivors may have whereon to feed. Pass by in the
night, and strain imagination to picture the weltering mass
of human weariness, of bestiality, of unmerited dolour, of
hopeless hope, of crushed surrender, tumbled together within
those forbidding walls.

Clara hated the place from her first hour in it. It seemed
to her that the air was poisoned with the odour of an unclean
crowd. The yells of children at play in the courtyard tortured
her nerves; the regular sounds on the staircase, day after day
repeated at the same hours, incidents of the life of poverty,
irritated her sick brain and filled her with despair to think
that as long as she lived she could never hope to rise again
above this world to which she was born. Gone for ever, for
ever, the promise that always gleamed before her whilst she
had youth and beauty and talent. With the one, she felt as
though she had been robbed of all three blessings; her twenty
years were now a meaningless figure; the energies of her
mind could avail no more than an idiot's mummery. For the
author of her calamity she nourished no memory of hatred:
her resentment was against the fate which had cursed her
existence from its beginning.

For this she had dared everything, had made the supreme
sacrifice. Conscience had nothing to say to her, but she felt
herself an outcast even among these wretched toilers whose
swarming aroused her disgust. Given the success which had
been all but in her grasp, and triumphant pride would have
scored out every misgiving as to the cost at which the victory
had been won. Her pride was unbroken; under the stress of
anguish it became a scorn for goodness and humility; but in

the desolation of her future she read a punishment equal to
the daring wherewith she had aspired. Excepting her poor
old father, not a living soul that held account of her. She
might live for years and years. Her father would die, and
then no smallest tribute of love or admiration would be hers
for ever. More than that; perforce she must gain her own
living, and in doing so she must expose herself to all manner
of insulting wonder and pity. Was it a life that could be
lived?

Hour after hour she sat with her face buried in her hands.
She did not weep; tears were trivial before a destiny such as
this. But groans and smothered cries often broke the silence
of her solitude—cries of frenzied revolt, wordless curses.
Once she rose up suddenly, passed through the middle room,
and out on to the staircase; there a gap in the wall, guarded by
iron railings breast-high, looked down upon the courtyard.
She leaned forward over the bar and measured the distance
that separated her from the ground; a ghastly height! Surely
one would not feel much after such a fall? In any case, the
crashing agony of but an instant. Had not this place tempted
other people before now?

Some one coming upstairs made her shrink back into her
room. She had felt the horrible fascination of that sheer
depth, and thought of it for days, thought of it until she
dreaded to quit the tenement, lest a power distinct from will
should seize and hurl her to destruction. She knew that that
must not happen here; for all her self-absorption, she could
not visit with such cruelty the one heart that loved her. And
thinking of him, she understood that her father's tenderness
was not wholly the idle thing that it had been to her at first;
her love could never equal his, had never done so in her
childhood, but she grew conscious of a soothing power in the
gentle and timid devotion with which he tended her. His
appearance of an evening was something more than a relief
after the waste of hours which made her day. The rough,
passionate man made himself as quiet and sympathetic as a
girl when he took his place by her. Compared with her, his
other children were as nothing to him. Impossible that
Clara should not be touched by the sense that he who had
everything to forgive, whom she had despised and abandoned,
behaved now as one whose part it is to beseech forgiveness.
She became less impatient when he tried to draw her into
conversation; when he held her thin soft hand in those rude

ones of his, she knew a solace in which there was something of gratitude.

Yet it was John who revived her misery in its worst form. Pitying her unoccupied loneliness, he brought home one day a book that he had purchased from a stall in Farringdon Street; it was a novel (with a picture on the cover which seemed designed to repel any person not wholly without taste), and might perhaps serve the end of averting her thoughts from their one subject. Clara viewed it contemptuously, but made a show of being thankful, and on the next day she did glance at its pages. The story was better than its illustration; it took a hold upon her; she read all day long. But when she returned to herself, it was to find that she had been exasperating her heart's malady. The book dealt with people of wealth and refinement, with the world to which she had all her life been aspiring, and to which she might have attained. The meanness of her surroundings became in comparison more mean, the bitterness of her fate more bitter. You must not lose sight of the fact that since abandoning her work-girl existence Clara had been constantly educating herself, not only by direct study of books, but through her association with people, her growth in experience. Where in the old days of rebellion she had only an instinct, a divination to guide her, there was now just enough of knowledge to give occupation to her developed intellect and taste. Far keener was her sense of the loss she had suffered than her former longing for what she knew only in dream. The activity of her mind received a new impulse when she broke free from Scawthorne and began her upward struggle in independence. Whatever books were obtainable she read greedily; she purchased numbers of plays in the acting-editions, and studied with the utmost earnestness such parts as she knew by repute; no actress entertained a more superb ambition, none was more vividly conscious of power. But it was not only at stage-triumph that Clara aimed; glorious in itself, this was also to serve her as a means of becoming nationalised among that race of beings whom birth and breeding exalt above the multitude. A notable illusion; pathetic to dwell upon. As a work-girl, she nourished envious hatred of those the world taught her to call superiors; they were then as remote and unknown to her as gods on Olympus. From her place behind the footlights she surveyed the occupants of boxes and stalls in a changed spirit; the distance was no longer insuperable; she heard of fortunate players who mingled on equal terms with men and women of refinement. There, she imagined, was her ultimate goal. 'It is to *them* that I belong! Be my origin what it may, I have the intelligence and the desires of one born to freedom. Nothing in me, nothing, is akin to that gross world from which I have escaped!' So she thought—with every drop of her heart's blood crying its source from that red fountain of revolt whereon never yet did the upper daylight gleam! Brain and pulses such as hers belong not to the mild breed of mortals fostered in sunshine. But for the stroke of fate, she might have won that reception which was in her dream, and with what self-mockery when experience had matured itself! Never yet did true rebel, who has burst the barriers of social limitation, find aught but *ennui* in the trim gardens beyond.

When John asked if the book had given her amusement, she said that reading made her eyes ache. He noticed that her hand felt feverish, and that the dark mood had fallen upon her as badly as ever to-night.

'It's just what I said,' she exclaimed with abruptness, after long refusal to speak. 'I knew your friend would never come as long as I was here.'

John regarded her anxiously. The phrase 'your friend' had a peculiar sound that disturbed him. It made him aware that she had been thinking often of Sidney Kirkwood since his name had been dismissed from their conversation. He, too, had often turned his mind uneasily in the same direction, wondering whether he ought to have spoken of Sidney so freely. At the time it seemed best, indeed almost inevitable; but habit and the force of affection were changing his view of Clara in several respects. He recognised the impossibility of her continuing to live as now, yet it was as difficult as ever to conceive a means of aiding her. Unavoidably he kept glancing towards Kirkwood. He knew that Sidney was no longer a free man; he knew that, even had it been otherwise, Clara could be nothing to him. In spite of facts, the father kept brooding on what might have been. His own love was perdurable; how could it other than intensify when its object was so unhappy? His hot, illogical mood all but brought about a revival of the old resentment against Sidney.

'I haven't seen him for a week or two,' he replied, in an embarrassed way.

'Did he tell you he shouldn't come?'

'No. After we'd talked about it, you know—when you told me you didn't mind—I just said a word or two; and he nodded, that was all.'

She became silent. John, racked by doubts as to whether he should say more of Sidney or still hold his peace, sat rubbing the back of one hand with the other and looking about the room.

'Father,' Clara resumed presently, 'what became of that child at Mrs. Peckover's, that her grandfather came and took away? Snowdon; yes, that was her name; Jane Snowdon.'

'You remember they went to live with somebody you used to know,' John replied, with hesitation. 'They're still in the same house.'

'So she's grown up. Did you ever hear about that old man having a lot of money?'

'Why, my dear, I never heard nothing but what them Peckovers talked at the time. But there was a son of his turned up as seemed to have some money. He married Mrs. Peckover's daughter.'

Clara expressed surprise.

'A son of his? Not the girl's father?'

'Yes; her father. I don't know nothing about his history. It's for him, or partly for him, as I'm workin' now, Clara. The firm's Lake, Snowdon & Co.'

'Why didn't you mention it before?'

'I don't hardly know, my dear.'

She looked at him, aware that something was being kept back.

'Tell me about the girl. What does she do?'

'She goes to work, I believe; but I haven't heard much about her since a good time. Sidney Kirkwood's a friend of her grandfather. He often goes there, I believe.'

'What is she like?' Clara asked, after a pause. 'She used to be such a weak, ailing thing, I never thought she'd grow up. What's she like to look at?'

'I can't tell you, my dear. I don't know as ever I see her since those times.'

Again a silence.

'Then it's Mr. Kirkwood that has told you what you know of her?'

'Why, no. It was chiefly Mrs. Peckover told me. She did say, Clara—but then I can't tell whether it's true or not—she did say something about Sidney and her.'

He spoke with difficulty, feeling constrained to make the disclosure, but anxious as to its result. Clara made no movement, seemed to have heard with indifference.

'It's maybe partly 'cause of that,' added John, in a low voice, 'that he doesn't like to come here.'

'Yes; I understand.'

They spoke no more on the subject.

<hr />

CHAPTER XXXI

WOMAN AND ACTRESS

In a tenement on the same staircase, two floors below, lived a family with whom John Hewett was on friendly terms. Necessity calling these people out of London for a few days, they had left with John the key of their front door; a letter of some moment might arrive in their absence, and John undertook to re-post it to them. The key was hung on a nail in Clara's room.

'I'll just go down and see if the postman's left anything at Mrs. Holland's this morning,' said Amy Hewett, coming in between breakfast and the time of starting for school.

She reached up to the key, but Clara, who sat by the fire with a cup of tea on her lap, the only breakfast she ever took, surprised her by saying, 'You needn't trouble, Amy. I shall be going out soon, and I'll look in as I pass.'

The girl was disappointed, for she liked this private incursion into the abode of other people, but the expression of a purpose by her sister was so unusual that, after a moment's hesitating, she said, 'Very well,' and left the room again.

When silence informed Clara that the children were gone, Mrs. Eagles being the only person besides herself who remained in the tenement, she put on her hat, drew down the veil which was always attached to it, and with the key in her hand descended to the Hollands' rooms. Had a letter been delivered that morning, it would have been—in default of box —just inside the door; there was none, but Clara seemed to have another purpose in view. She closed the door and walked forward into the nearest room; the blind was down, but the dusk thus produced was familiar to her in consequence of her own habit, and, her veil thrown back, she examined

the chamber thoughtfully. It was a sitting-room, ugly,
orderly; the air felt damp, and even in semi-darkness she
was conscious of the layers of London dust which had softly
deposited themselves since the family went away forty-eight
hours ago. A fire was laid ready for lighting, and the smell
of moist soot spread from the grate. Having stood on one
spot for nearly ten minutes, Clara made a quick movement and
withdrew; she latched the front door with as little noise as
possible, ran upstairs and shut herself again in her own room.

Presently she was standing at her window, the blind partly
raised. On a clear day the view from this room was of wide
extent, embracing a great part of the City; seen under a low,
blurred, dripping sky, through the ragged patches of smoke
from chimneys innumerable, it had a gloomy impressiveness
well in keeping with the mind of her who brooded over it.
Directly in front, rising mist-detached from the lower masses
of building, stood in black majesty the dome of St. Paul's; its
vastness suffered no diminution from this high outlook, rather
was exaggerated by the flying scraps of mirky vapour which
softened its outline and at times gave it the appearance of
floating on a vague troubled sea. Somewhat nearer, amid
many spires and steeples, lay the surly bulk of Newgate, the
lines of its construction shown plan-wise; its little windows
multiplied for points of torment to the vision. Nearer again,
the markets of Smithfield, Bartholomew's Hospital, the tract
of modern deformity, cleft by a gulf of railway, which spreads
between Clerkenwell Road and Charterhouse Street. Down
in Farringdon Street the carts, waggons, vans, cabs, omni-
buses, crossed and intermingled in a steaming splash-bath of
mud; human beings, reduced to their due paltriness, seemed
to toil in exasperation along the strips of pavement, bound on
errands, which were a mockery, driven automaton-like by
forces they neither understood nor could resist.

'Can I go out into a world like that—alone?' was the
thought which made Clara's spirit fail as she stood gazing.
'Can I face life as it is for women who grow old in earning
bare daily bread among those terrible streets? Year after
year to go in and out from some wretched garret that I call
home, with my face hidden, my heart stabbed with misery till
it is cold and bloodless!'

Then her eye fell upon the spire of St. James's Church, on
Clerkenwell Green, whose bells used to be so familiar to her.

The memory was only of discontent and futile aspiration, but
—Oh, if it were possible to be again as she was then, and yet
keep the experience with which life had since endowed her!
With no moral condemnation did she view the records of her
rebellion; but how easy to see now that ignorance had been
one of the worst obstacles in her path, and that, like all
unadvised purchasers, she had paid a price that might well
have been spared. A little more craft, a little more patience—
it is with these that the world is conquered. The world was
her enemy, and had proved too strong; woman though she
was—only a girl striving to attain the place for which birth
adapted her—pursuing only her irrepressible instincts—fate
flung her to the ground pitilessly, and bade her live out the
rest of her time in wretchedness.

No! There remained one more endeavour that was possible to her, one bare hope of saving herself from the extremity which only now she estimated at its full horror. If that
failed, why, then, there was a way to cure all ills.

From her box, that in which were hidden away many
heart-breaking mementoes of her life as an actress, she took
out a sheet of notepaper and an envelope. Without much
thought, she wrote nearly three pages, folded the letter,
addressed it with a name only: 'Mr. Kirkwood.' Sidney's
address she did not know; her father had mentioned Red
Lion Street, that was all. She did not even know whether
he still worked at the old place, but in that way she must try
to find him. She cloaked herself, took her umbrella, and
went out.

At a corner of St. John's Square she soon found an urchin
who would run an errand for her. He was to take this note
to a house that she indicated, and to ask if Mr. Kirkwood was
working there. She scarcely durst hope to see the messenger
returning with empty hands, but he did so. A terrible
throbbing at her heart, she went home again.

In the evening, when her father returned, she surprised
him by saying that she expected a visitor.

'Do you want me to go out of the way?' he asked, eager
to submit to her in everything.

'No. I've asked my friend to come to Mrs. Holland's. I
thought there would be no great harm. I shall go down just
before nine o'clock.'

'Oh no, there's no harm,' conceded her father. 'It's only

if the neighbours opposite got talkin' to them when they come back.'

'I can't help it. They won't mind. I can't help it.'

John noticed her agitated repetition, the impatience with which she flung aside difficulties.

'Clara—it ain't anything about work, my dear ? '

'No, father. I wouldn't do anything without telling you; I've promised.'

'Then I don't care ; it's all right.'

She had begun to speak immediately on his entering the room, and so it happened that he had not kissed her as he always did at home-coming. When she had sat down, he came with awkwardness and timidity and bent his face to hers.

'What a hot cheek it is to-night, my little girl ! ' he murmured. 'I don't like it; you've got a bit of fever hangin' about you.'

She wished to be alone ; the children must not come into the room until she had gone downstairs. When her father had left her, she seated herself before the looking-glass, abhorrent as it was to her to look thus in her own face, and began dressing her hair with quite unusual attention. This beauty at least remained to her ; arranged as she had learned to do it for the stage, the dark abundance of her tresses crowned nobly the head which once held itself with such defiant grace. She did not change her dress, which, though it had suffered from wear, was well-fitting and of better material than Farringdon Road Buildings were wont to see ; a sober draping which became her tall elegance as she moved. At a quarter to nine she arranged the veil upon her head so that she could throw her hat aside without disturbing it ; then, taking the lamp in her hand, and the key of the Hollands' door, she went forth.

No one met her on the stairs. She was safe in the cold deserted parlour where she had stood this morning. Cold, doubtless, but she could not be conscious of it ; in her veins there seemed rather to be fire than blood. Her brain was clear, but in an unnatural way ; the throbbing at her temples ought to have been painful, but only excited her with a strange intensity of thought. And she felt, amid it all, a dread of what was before her ; only the fever, to which she abandoned herself with a sort of reckless confidence, a faith that it would continue till this interview was over, overcame an impulse to rush back into her hiding-place, to bury herself in shame, or desperately whelm her wretchedness in the final oblivion. . . .

He was very punctual. The heavy bell of St. Paul's had not reached its ninth stroke when she heard his knock at the door.

He came in without speaking, and stood as if afraid to look at her. The lamp, placed on a side-table, barely disclosed all the objects within the four walls ; it illumined Sidney's face, but Clara moved so that she was in shadow. She began to speak.

'You understood my note ? The people who live here are away, and I have ventured to borrow their room. They are friends of my father's.'

At the first word, he was surprised by the change in her voice and accentuation. Her speech was that of an educated woman; the melody which always had such a charm for him had gained wonderfully in richness. Yet it was with difficulty that she commanded utterance, and her agitation touched him in a way quite other than he was prepared for. In truth, he knew not what experience he had anticipated, but the reality, now that it came, this unimaginable blending of memory with the unfamiliar, this refinement of something that he had loved, this note of pity struck within him by such subtle means, affected his inmost self. Immediately he laid stern control upon his feelings, but all the words which he had designed to speak were driven from memory. He could say nothing, could only glance at her veiled face and await what she had to ask of him.

'Will you sit down ? I shall feel grateful if you can spare me a few minutes. I have asked you to see me because— indeed, because I am sadly in want of the kind of help a friend might give me. I don't venture to call you that, but I thought of you ; I hoped you wouldn't refuse to let me speak to you. I am in such difficulties—such a hard position——'

'You may be very sure I will do anything I can to be of use to you,' Sidney replied, his thick voice contrasting so strongly with that which had just failed into silence that he coughed and lowered his tone after the first few syllables. He meant to express himself without a hint of emotion, but it was beyond his power. The words in which she spoke of her calamity seemed so pathetically simple that they went to his heart. Clara had recovered all her faculties. The fever and the anguish and the dread were no whit diminished, but they helped instead of checking her. An actress improvising her part, she regulated every tone with perfect skill, with inspiration; the very attitude in which she seated herself was a triumph of the artist's felicity.

'I just said a word or two in my note,' she resumed, 'that you might have replied if you thought nothing could be gained by my speaking to you. I couldn't explain fully what I had in mind. I don't know that I've anything very clear to say even now, but—you know what has happened to me; you know that I have nothing to look forward to, that I can only hope to keep from being a burden to my father. I am getting stronger; it's time I tried to find something to do. But I——'

Her voice failed again. Sidney gazed at her, and saw the dull lamplight just glisten on her hair. She was bending forward a little, her hands joined and resting on her knee.

'Have you thought what kind of—of work would be best for you?' Sidney asked. The 'work' stuck in his throat, and he seemed to himself brutal in his way of uttering it. But he was glad when he had put the question thus directly; one at least of his resolves was carried out.

'I know I've no right to choose, when there's necessity,' she answered, in a very low tone. 'Most women would naturally think of needlework; but I know so little of it; I scarcely ever did any. If I could—I might perhaps do that at home, and I feel—if I could only avoid—if I could only be spared going among strangers——'

Her faltering voice sank lower and lower; she seemed as if she would have hidden her face even under its veil.

'I feel sure you will have no difficulty,' Sidney hastened to reply, his own voice unsteady. 'Certainly you can get work at home. Why do you trouble yourself with the thought of going among strangers? There'll never be the least need for that; I'm sure there won't. Haven't you spoken about it to your father?'

'Yes. But he is so kind to me that he won't hear of work at all. It was partly on that account that I took the step of appealing to you. He doesn't know who I am meeting here to-night. Would you—I don't know whether I ought to ask—but perhaps if you spoke to him in a day or two, and made him understand how strong my wish is. He dreads lest we should be parted, but I hope I shall never have to leave him. And then, of course, father is not very well able to advise me—about work, I mean. You have more experience. I am so helpless. Oh, if you knew how helpless I feel!'

'If you really wish it, I will talk with your father——'

'Indeed, I do wish it. My coming to live here has made everything so uncomfortable for him and the children. Even his friends can't visit him as they would; I feel that, though he won't admit that it's made any difference.'

Sidney looked to the ground. He heard her voice falter as it continued.

'If I'm to live here still, it mustn't be at the cost of all his comfort. I keep almost always in the one room. I shouldn't be in the way if anyone came. I've been afraid, Mr. Kirkwood, that perhaps you feared to come lest, whilst I was not very well, it might have been an inconvenience to us. Please don't think that. I shall never—see either friends or strangers unless it is absolutely needful.'

There was silence.

'You do feel much better, I hope?' fell from Sidney's lips.

'Much stronger. It's only my mind; everything is so dark to me. You know how little patience I always had. It was enough if any one said, 'You *must* do this,' or 'You *must* put up with that'—at once I resisted. It was my nature; I couldn't bear the feeling of control. That's what I've had to struggle with since I recovered from my delirium at the hospital, and hadn't even the hope of dying. Can you put yourself in my place, and imagine what I have suffered?'

Sidney was silent. His own life had not been without its passionate miseries, but the modulations of this voice which had no light of countenance to aid it raised him above the plane of common experience and made actual to him the feelings he knew only in romantic story. He could not stir, lest the slightest sound should jar on her speaking. His breath rose visibly upon the chill air, but the discomfort of the room was as indifferent to him as to his companion. Clara rose, as if impelled by mental anguish; she stretched out her hand to the mantel-piece, and so stood, between him and the light, her admirable figure designed on a glimmering background.

'I know why you say nothing,' she continued, abruptly but without resentment. 'You cannot use words of sympathy which would be anything but formal, and you prefer to let me understand that. It is like you. Oh, you mustn't think I mean the phrase as a reproach. Anything but that. I mean

that you were always honest, and time hasn't changed you—
in that.' A slight, very slight, tremor on the close. 'I'd
rather you behaved to me like your old self. A sham sympathy
would drive me mad.'

'I said nothing,' he replied, 'only because words seemed
meaningless.'

'Not only that. You feel for me, I know, because you are
not heartless; but at the same time you obey your reason,
which tells you that all I suffer comes of my own self-will.'

'I should like you to think better of me than that. I'm
not one of those people, I hope, who use every accident to
point a moral, and begin by inventing the moral to suit
their own convictions. I know all the details of your misfortune.'

'Oh, wasn't it cruel that she should take such revenge
upon me!' Her voice rose in unrestrained emotion. 'Just
because she envied me that poor bit of advantage over her!
How could I be expected to refuse the chance that was
offered? It would have been no use; she couldn't have kept
the part. And I was so near success. I had never had a
chance of showing what I could do. It wasn't much of a
part, really, but it was the lead, at all events, and it would
have made people pay attention to me. You don't know how
strongly I was always drawn to the stage; there I found the
work for which I was meant. And I strove so hard to make
my way. I had no friends, no money. I earned only just
enough to supply my needs. I know what people think about
actresses. Mr. Kirkwood, do you imagine I have been living
at my ease, congratulating myself that I had escaped from all
hardships ?'

He could not raise his eyes. As she still awaited his
answer, he said in rather a hard voice :

'As I have told you, I read all the details that were published.

'Then you know that I was working hard and honestly—
working far, far harder than when I lived in Clerkenwell
Close. But I don't know why I am talking to you about it.
It's all over. I went my own way, and I all but won what I
fought for. You may very well say, what's the use of mourning over one's fate ?'

Sidney had risen.

'You were strong in your resolve to succeed,' he said
gravely, 'and you will find strength to meet even this trial.'

'A weaker woman would suffer far less. One with a little more strength of character would kill herself.'

'No. In that you mistake. You have not yourself only to think of. It would be an easy thing to put an end to your life. You have a duty to your father.'

She bent her head.

'I think of him. He is goodness itself to me. There are fathers who would have shut the door in my face. I know better now than I could when I was only a child how hard his life has been; he and I are like each other in so many ways; he has always been fighting against cruel circumstances. It's right that you, who have been his true and helpful friend, should remind me of my duty to him.'

A pause; then Sidney asked:

'Do you wish me to speak to him very soon about your finding occupation?'

'If you will. If you could think of anything.'

He moved, but still delayed his offer to take leave.

'You said just now,' Clara continued, falteringly, 'that you did not try to express sympathy, because words seemed of no use. How am I to find words of thanks to you for coming here and listening to what I had to say?'

'But surely so simple an act of friendship——'

'Have I so many friends? And what right have I to look to you for an act of kindness? Did I merit it by my words when I last——'

There came a marvellous change—a change such as it needed either exquisite feeling or the genius of simulation to express by means so simple. Unable to show him by a smile, by a light in her eyes, what mood had come upon her, what subtle shifting in the direction of her thought had checked her words—by her mere movement as she stepped lightly towards him, by the carriage of her head, by her hands half held out and half drawn back again, she prepared him for what she was about to say. No piece of acting was ever more delicately finished. He knew that she smiled, though nothing of her face was visible; he knew that her look was one of diffident, half-blushing pleasure. And then came the sweetness of her accents, timorous, joyful, scarcely to be recognised as the voice which an instant ago had trembled sadly in self-reproach.

'But that seems to you so long ago, doesn't it? You can forgive me now. Father has told me what happiness you have found, and I—I am so glad!'

Sidney drew back a step, involuntarily; the movement came of the shock with which he heard her make such confident reference to the supposed relations between himself and Jane Snowdon. He reddened—stood mute. For a few seconds his mind was in the most painful whirl and conflict; a hundred impressions, arguments, apprehensions, crowded upon him, each with its puncturing torment. And Clara stood there waiting for his reply, in the attitude of consummate grace.

'Of course I know what you speak of,' he said at length, with the bluntness of confusion. 'But your father was mistaken. I don't know who can have led him to believe that—— It's a mistake, altogether.'

Sidney would not have believed that anyone could so completely rob him of self-possession, least of all Clara Hewett. His face grew still more heated. He was angry with he knew not whom, he knew not why—perhaps with himself in the first instance.

'A mistake ?' Clara murmured, under her breath. 'Oh, you mean people have been too hasty in speaking about it. Do pardon me. I ought never to have taken such a liberty— but I felt——'

She hesitated.

'It was no liberty at all. I dare say the mistake is natural enough to those who know nothing of Miss Snowdon's circumstances. I myself, however, have no right to talk about her. But what you have been told is absolute error.'

Clara walked a few paces aside.

'Again I ask you to forgive me.' Her tones had not the same clearness as hitherto. 'In any case, I had no right to approach such a subject in speaking with you.'

'Let us put it aside,' said Sidney, mastering himself. 'We were just agreeing that I should see your father, and make known your wish to him.'

'Thank you. I shall tell him, when I go upstairs, that you were the friend whom I had asked to come here. I felt it to be so uncertain whether you would come.'

'I hope you couldn't seriously doubt it.'

'You teach me to tell the truth. No. I knew too well your kindness. I knew that even to me——'

Sidney could converse no longer. He felt the need of being alone, to put his thoughts in order, to resume his experiences during this strange hour. An extreme weariness was possessing him, as though he had been straining his intellect in attention to some difficult subject. And all at once the dank, cold atmosphere of the room struck into his blood; he had a fit of trembling.

'Let us say good-bye for the present.'

Clara gave her hand silently. He touched it for the first time, and could not but notice its delicacy; it was very warm, too, and moist. Without speaking she went with him to the outer door. His footsteps sounded along the stone staircase; Clara listened until the last echo was silent.

She too had begun to feel the chilly air. Hastily putting on her hat, she took up the lamp, glanced round the room to see that nothing was left in disorder, and hastened up to the fifth storey.

In the middle room, through which she had to pass, her father and Mr. Eagles were talking together. The latter gave her a 'good-evening,' respectful, almost as to a social superior. Within, Amy and Annie were just going to bed. She sat with them in her usual silence for a quarter of an hour, then, having ascertained that Eagles was gone into his own chamber, went out to speak to her father.

'My friend came,' she said. 'Do you suspect who it was?'

'Why, no, I can't guess, Clara.'

'Haven't you thought of Mr. Kirkwood?'

'You don't mean that?'

'Father, you are quite mistaken about Jane Snowdon—quite.'

John started up from his seat.

'Has he told you so, himself?'

'Yes. But listen; you are not to say a word on that subject to him. You will be very careful, father?'

John gazed at her wonderingly. She kissed his forehead, and withdrew to the other room.

CHAPTER XXXII

A HAVEN

John Hewett no longer had membership in club or society. The loss of his insurance-money made him for the future regard all such institutions with angry suspicion. ' Workin' men ain't satisfied with bein' robbed by the upper classes; they must go and rob one another.' He had said good-bye to Clerkenwell Green ; the lounging crowd no longer found amusement in listening to his frenzied voice and in watching the contortions of his rugged features. He discussed the old subjects with Eagles, but the latter's computative mind was out of sympathy with zeal of the tumid description ; though quite capable of working himself into madness on the details of the Budget, John was easily soothed by his friend's calmer habits of debate. Kirkwood's influence, moreover, was again exerting itself upon him—an influence less than ever likely to encourage violence of thought or speech. In Sidney's company the worn rebel became almost placid ; his rude, fretted face fell into a singular humility and mildness. Having ended by accepting what he would formerly have called charity, and that from a man whom he had wronged with obstinate perverseness, John neither committed the error of obtruding his gratitude, nor yet suffered it to be imagined that obligation sat upon him too lightly. He put no faith in Sidney's assertion that some unknown benefactor was to be thanked for the new furniture ; one and the same pocket had supplied that and the money for Mrs. Hewett's burial. Gratitude was all very well, but he could not have rested without taking some measures towards a literal repayment of his debt. The weekly coppers which had previously gone for club subscriptions were now put away in a money-box ; they would be long enough in making an appreciable sum, but yet, if he himself could never discharge the obligation, his children must take it up after him, and this he frequently impressed upon Amy, Annie, and Tom.

Nothing, however, could have detached John's mind so completely from its habits of tumult, nor have fixed it so firmly upon the interests of home, as his recovery of his daughter. From the day of Clara's establishment under his roof he thought of her, and of her only. Whilst working at

the filter-factory he remained in imagination by her side,
ceaselessly repeating her words of the night before, eagerly
looking for the hour that would allow him to return to her.
Joy and trouble mingled in an indescribable way to constitute
his ordinary mood; one moment he would laugh at a thought,
and before a companion could glance at him his gladness
would be overshadowed as if with the heaviest anxiety. Men
who saw him day after day said at this time that he seemed
to be growing childish; he muttered to himself a good deal,
and looked blankly at you when you addressed him. In the
course of a fortnight his state became more settled, but it was
not the cheerful impulse that predominated. Out of the multitude of thoughts concerning Clara, one had fixed itself as the
main controller of his reflection. Characteristically, John hit
upon what seemed an irremediable misfortune, and brooded
over it with all his might. If only Sidney Kirkwood were in
the same mind as four years ago!

And now was he to believe that what he had been told
about Sidney and Jane Snowdon was misleading? Was the
impossible no longer so? He almost leapt from his chair
when he heard that Sidney was the visitor with whom his
daughter had been having her private conversation. How
came they to make this appointment? There was something
in Clara's voice that set his nerves a-tremble. That night he
could not sleep, and next morning he went to work with a
senile quiver in his body. For the first time for more than
two months he turned into a public-house on his way, just to
give himself a little 'tone.' The natural result of such a
tonic was to heighten the fever of his imagination; goodness
knows how far he had got in a drama of happiness before he
threw off his coat and settled to his day's labour.

Clara, in the meanwhile, suffered a corresponding agitation,
more penetrative in proportion to the finer substance of her
nature. She did not know until the scene was over how much
vital force it had cost her; when she took off the veil a fire
danced before her eyes, and her limbs ached and trembled as
she lay down in the darkness. All night long she was acting
her part over and over; when she woke up, it was always at
the point where Sidney replied to her, 'But you are mistaken!'

Acting her part; yes, but a few hours had turned the
make-believe into something earnest enough. She could not
now have met Kirkwood with the self-possession of last evening. The fever that then sustained her was much the same

as she used to know before she had thoroughly accustomed
herself to appearing in front of an audience; it exalted all her
faculties, gifted her with a remarkable self-consciousness. It
was all very well as long as there was need of it, but why did
it afflict her in this torturing form now that she desired to rest,
to think of what she had gained, of what hope she might
reasonably nourish? The purely selfish project which, in her
desperation, had seemed the only resource remaining to her
against a life of intolerable desolateness, was taking hold
upon her in a way she could not understand. Had she not
already made a discovery that surpassed all expectation?
Sidney Kirkwood was not bound to another woman; why
could she not accept that as so much clear gain, and deliberate
as to her next step? She had been fully prepared for the
opposite state of things, prepared to strive against any odds,
to defy all probabilities, all restraints; why not thank her
fortune and plot collectedly now that the chances were so
much improved?

But from the beginning of her interview with him, Clara
knew that something more entered into her designs on Sidney
than a cold self-interest. She had never loved him; she
never loved any one; yet the inclinations of her early girlhood
had been drawn by the force of the love he offered her, and to
this day she thought of him with a respect and liking such as
she had for no other man. When she heard from her father
that Sidney had forgotten her, had found some one by whom
his love was prized, her instant emotion was so like a pang of
jealousy that she marvelled at it. Suppose fate had prospered
her, and she had heard in the midst of triumphs that Sidney
Kirkwood, the working man in Clerkenwell, was going to
marry a girl he loved, would any feeling of this kind have
come to her? Her indifference would have been complete.
It was calamity that made her so sensitive. Self-pity longs
for the compassion of others. That Sidney, who was once
her slave, should stand aloof in freedom now that she wanted
sympathy so sorely, this was a wound to her heart. That
other woman had robbed her of something she could not
spare.

Jane Snowdon, too! She found it scarcely conceivable
that the wretched little starveling of Mrs. Peckover's kitchen
should have grown into anything that a man like Sidney could
love. To be sure, there was a mystery in her lot. Clara remembered perfectly how Scawthorne pointed out of the cab

at the old man Snowdon, and said that he was very rich. A miser, or what? More she had never tried to discover. Now Sidney himself had hinted at something in Jane's circumstances which, he professed, put it out of the question that he could contemplate marrying her. Had he told her the truth? Could she in fact consider him free? Might there not be some reason for his wishing to keep a secret?

With burning temples, with feverish lips, she moved about her little room like an animal in a cage, finding the length of the day intolerable. She was constrained to inaction, when it seemed to her that every moment in which she did not do something to keep Sidney in mind of her was worse than lost. Could she not see that girl, Jane Snowdon? But was not Sidney's denial as emphatic as it could be? She recalled his words, and tried numberless interpretations. Would anything that he had said bear being interpreted as a sign that something of the old tenderness still lived in him? And the strange thing was, that she interrogated herself on these points not at all like a coldly scheming woman, who aims at something that is to be won, if at all, by the subtlest practising on another's emotions, whilst she remains unaffected. Rather like a woman who loves passionately, whose ardour and jealous dread wax moment by moment.

For what was she scheming? For food, clothing, assured comfort during her life? Twenty-four hours ago Clara would most likely have believed that she had indeed fallen to this; but the meeting with Sidney enlightened her. Least of all women could *she* live by bread alone; there was the hunger of her brain, the hunger of her heart. I spoke once, you remember, of her ' defect of tenderness; ' the fault remained, but her heart was no longer so sterile of the tender emotions as when revolt and ambition absorbed all her energies. She had begun to feel gently towards her father; it was an intimation of the need which would presently bring all the forces of her nature into play. She dreaded a life of drudgery; she dreaded humiliation among her inferiors; but that which she feared most of all was the barrenness of a lot into which would enter none of the passionate joys of existence. Speak to Clara of renunciation, of saintly glories, of the stony way of perfectness, and you addressed her in an unknown tongue; nothing in her responded to these ideas. Hopelessly defeated in the one way of aspiration which promised a large life, her being, rebellious against the martyrdom it had suffered, went

forth eagerly towards the only happiness which was any longer
attainable. Her beauty was a dead thing; never by that
means could she command homage. But there is love, ay, and
passionate love, which can be independent of mere charm of
face. In one man only could she hope to inspire it; successful in that, she would taste victory, and even in this fallen
estate could make for herself a dominion.

In these few hours she so wrought upon her imagination
as to believe that the one love of her life had declared itself.
She revived every memory she possibly could of those years
on the far side of the gulf, and convinced herself that even
then she had loved Sidney. Other love of a certainty she had
not known. In standing face to face with him after so long
an interval, she recognised the qualities which used to impress
her, and appraised them as formerly she could not. His
features had gained in attractiveness; the refinement which
made them an index to his character was more noticeable at
the first glance, or perhaps she was better able to distinguish
it. The slight bluntness in his manner reminded her of the
moral force which she had known only as something to be resisted; it was now one of the influences that drew her to him.
Had she not always admitted that he stood far above the other
men of his class whom she used to know? Between his mind
and hers there was distinct kinship; the sense that he had
both power and right to judge her explained in a great
measure her attitude of defiance towards him when she was
determined to break away from her humble conditions. All
along, had not one of her main incentives to work and strive
been the resolve to justify herself in *his* view, to prove to *him*
that she possessed talent, to show herself to *him* as one whom
the world admired? The repugnance with which she thought
of meeting him, when she came home with her father, meant
in truth that she dreaded to be assured that he could only
shrink from her.

All her vital force setting in this wild current, her self-
deception complete, she experienced the humility of supreme
egoism—that state wherein self multiplies its claims to pity
in passionate support of its demand for the object of desire.
She felt capable of throwing herself at Sidney's feet, and im-
ploring him not to withdraw from her the love of which he
had given her so many assurances. She gazed at her scarred
face until the image was blurred with tears; then, as though
there were luxury in weeping, sobbed for an hour, crouching

down in a corner of her room. Even though his love were as
dead as her beauty, must he not be struck to the heart with
compassion, realising her woeful lot? She asked nothing
more eagerly than to humiliate herself before him, to confess
that her pride was broken. Not a charge he could bring
against her but she would admit its truth. Had she been
humble enough last night? When he came again—and he
must soon—she would throw aside every vestige of dignity,
lest he should think that she was strong enough to bear her
misery alone. No matter how poor-spirited she seemed, if
only she could move his sympathies.

Poor rebel heart! Beat for beat, in these moments it
matched itself with that of the purest woman who surrenders
to a despairing love. Had one charged her with insincerity,
how vehemently would her conscience have declared against
the outrage! Natures such as hers are as little to be judged
by that which is conventionally the highest standard as by
that which is the lowest. The tendencies which we agree to
call good and bad became in her merely directions of a native
force which was at all times in revolt against circumstance.
Characters thus moulded may go far in achievement, but can
never pass beyond the bounds of suffering. Never is the world
their friend, nor the world's law. As often as our conventions
give us the opportunity, we crush them out of being; they
are noxious; they threaten the frame of society. Oftenest the
crushing is done in such a way that the hapless creatures
seem to have brought about their own destruction. Let us
congratulate ourselves; in one way or other it is assured that
they shall not trouble us long.

Her father was somewhat later than usual in returning
from work. When he entered her room she looked at him
anxiously, and as he seemed to have nothing particular to say,
she asked if he had seen Mr. Kirkwood.

'No, my dear, I ain't seen him.'

Their eyes met for an instant. Clara was in anguish at
the thought that another night and day must pass and nothing
be altered.

'When did you see him last? A week or more ago,
wasn't it?'

'About that.'

'Couldn't you go round to his lodgings to-night? I know
he's got something he wants to speak to you about.'

He assented. But on his going into the other room Eagles

met him with a message from Sidney, anticipating his design, and requesting him to step over to Red Lion Street in the course of the evening. John instantly announced this to his daughter. She nodded, but said nothing.

In a few minutes John went on his way. The day's work had tired him exceptionally, doubtless owing to his nervousness, and again on the way to Sidney's he had recourse to a dose of the familiar stimulant. With our eyes on a man of Hewett's station we note these little things; we set them down as a point scored against him; yet if our business were with a man of leisure, who, owing to worry, found his glass of wine at luncheon and again at dinner an acceptable support, we certainly should not think of paying attention to the matter. Poverty makes a crime of every indulgence. John himself came out of the public-house in a slinking way, and hoped Kirkwood might not scent the twopenny-worth of gin.

Sidney was in anything but a mood to detect this little lapse in his visitor. He gave John a chair, but could not sit still himself. The garret was a spacious one, and whilst talking he moved from wall to wall.

'You know that I saw Clara last night? She told me she should mention it to you.'

'Yes, yes. I was afraid she'd never have made up her mind to it. It was the best way for you to see her alone first, poor girl! You won't mind comin' to us now, like you used?'

'Did she tell you what she wished to speak to me about?'

'Why, no, she hasn't. Was there—anything particular?'

'She feels the time very heavy on her hands. It seems you don't like the thought of her looking for employment?'

John rose from his chair and grasped the back of it.

'You ain't a-goin' to encourage her to leave us? It ain't that you was talkin' about, Sidney?'

'Leave you? Why, where should she go?'

'No, no; it's all right; so long as you wasn't thinkin' of her goin' away again. See, Sidney, I ain't got nothing to say against it, if she can find some kind of job for home. I know as the time must hang heavy. There she sit, poor thing! from mornin' to night, an' can't get her thoughts away from herself. It's easy enough to understand, ain't it? I took a book home for her the other day, but she didn't seem to care about it. There she sit, with her poor face on her hands, thinkin' and thinkin'. It breaks my heart to see her. I'd rather she had some work, but she mustn't go away from home for it.'

Sidney took a few steps in silence.

'You don't misunderstand me,' resumed the other, with suddenness. 'You don't think as I won't trust her away from me. If she went, it 'ud be because she thinks herself a burden—as if I wouldn't gladly live on a crust for my day's food an' spare her goin' among strangers! You can think yourself what it 'ud be to her, Sidney. No, no, it mustn't be nothing o' that kind. But I can't bear to see her livin' as she does; it's no life at all. I sit with her when I get back home at night, an' I'm glad to say she seems to find it a pleasure to have me by her; but it's the only bit o' pleasure she gets, an' there's all the hours whilst I'm away. You see she don't take much to Mrs. Eagles; that ain't her sort of friend. Not as she's got any pride left about her, poor girl! don't think that. I tell you, Sidney, she's a dear good girl to her old father. If I could only see her a bit happier, I'd never grumble again as long as I lived, I wouldn't!'

Is there such a thing in this world as speech that has but one simple interpretation, one for him who utters it and for him who hears? Honester words were never spoken than these in which Hewett strove to represent Clara in a favourable light, and to show the pitifulness of her situation; yet he himself was conscious that they implied a second meaning, and Sidney was driven restlessly about the room by his perception of the same lurking motive in their pathos. John felt half-ashamed of himself when he ceased; it was a new thing for him to be practising subtleties with a view to his own ends. But had he said a word more than the truth?

I suppose it was the association of contrast that turned Sidney's thoughts to Joseph Snowdon. At all events it was of him he was thinking in the silence that followed. Which silence having been broken by a tap at the door, oddly enough there stood Joseph himself. Hewett, taken by surprise, showed embarrassment and awkwardness; it was always hard for him to reconcile his present subordination to Mr. Snowdon with the familiar terms on which they had been not long ago.

'Ah, you here, Hewett!' exclaimed Joseph, in a genial tone, designed to put the other at his ease. 'I just wanted a word with our friend. Never mind; some other time.'

For all that, he did not seem disposed to withdraw, but stood with a hand on the door, smiling. Sidney, having nodded to him, walked the length of the room, his head bent and his hands behind him.

'Suppose I look in a bit later,' said Hewett. 'Or to-morrow night, Sidney?'

'Very well, to-morrow night.'

John took his leave, and on the visitor who remained Sidney turned a face almost of anger. Mr. Snowdon seated himself, supremely indifferent to the inconvenience he had probably caused. He seemed in excellent humour.

'Decent fellow, Hewett,' he observed, putting up one leg against the fireplace. 'Very decent fellow. He's getting old, unfortunately. Had a good deal of trouble, I understand; it breaks a man up.'

Sidney scowled, and said nothing.

'I thought I'd stay, as I *was* here,' continued Joseph, unbuttoning his respectable overcoat and throwing it open. 'There was something rather particular I had in mind. Won't you sit down?'

'No, thank you.'

Joseph glanced at him, and smiled all the more.

'I've had a little talk with the old man about Jane. By-the-by, I'm sorry to say he's very shaky; doesn't look himself at all. I didn't know you had spoken to him quite so —you know what I mean. It seems to be his idea that everything's at an end between you.'

'Perhaps so.'

'Well, now, look here. You won't mind me just—— Do you think it was wise to put it in that way to him? I'm afraid you're making him feel just a little uncertain about you. I'm speaking as a friend, you know. In your own interest, Kirkwood. Old men get queer ideas into their heads. You know, he *might* begin to think that you had some sort of—eh?'

It was not the second, nor yet the third, time that Joseph had looked in and begun to speak in this scrappy way, continuing the tone of that dialogue in which he had assumed a sort of community of interest between Kirkwood and himself. But the limit of Sidney's endurance was reached.

'There's no knowing,' he exclaimed, 'what anyone may think of me, if people who have their own ends to serve go spreading calumnies. Let us understand each other, and have done with it. I told Mr. Snowdon that I could never be anything but a friend to Jane. I said it, and I meant it.

If you've any doubt remaining, in a few days I hope it'll be removed. What your real wishes may be I don't know, and I shall never after this have any need to know. I can't help speaking in this way, and I want to tell you once for all that there shall never again be a word about Jane between us. Wait a day or two, and you'll know the reason.'

Joseph affected an air of gravity—of offended dignity.

'That's rather a queer sort of way to back out of your engagements, Kirkwood. I won't say anything about myself, but with regard to my daughter——'

'What do you mean by speaking like that?' cried the young man, sternly. 'You know very well that it's what you wish most of all, to put an end to everything between your daughter and me! You've succeeded; be satisfied. If you've anything to say to me on any other subject, say it. If not, please let's have done for the present. I don't feel in a mood for beating about the bush any longer.'

'You've misunderstood me altogether, Kirkwood,' said Joseph, unable to conceal a twinkle of satisfaction in his eyes.

'No; I've understood you perfectly well—too well. I don't want to hear another word on the subject, and I won't. It's over; understand that.'

'Well, well; you're a bit out of sorts. I'll say good-bye for the present.'

He retired, and for a long time Sidney sat in black brooding.

John Hewett did not fail to present himself next evening. As he entered the room he was somewhat surprised at the cheerful aspect with which Sidney met him; the grasp which his hand received seemed to have a significance. Sidney, after looking at him steadily, asked if he had not been home.

'Yes, I've been home. Why do you want to know?'

'Hadn't Clara anything to tell you?'

'No. What is it?'

'Did she know you were coming here?'

'Why, yes; I mentioned it.'

Sidney again regarded him fixedly, with a smile.

'I suppose she preferred that I should tell you. I looked in at the Buildings this afternoon, and had a talk with Clara.'

John hung upon his words, with lips slightly parted, with a trembling in the hairs of his grey beard.

'You did?'

'I had something to ask her, so I went when she was likely to be alone. It's a long while ago since I asked her the question for the first time—but I've got the right answer at last.'

John stared at him in pathetic agitation.

'You mean to tell me you've asked Clara to marry you?'

'There's nothing very dreadful in that, I should think.'

'Give us your hand again! Sidney Kirkwood, give us your hand again! If there's a good-hearted man in this world, if there's a faithful, honest man, as only lives to do kindness—— What am I to say to you? It's too much for me. I can't find a word as I'd wish to speak. Stand out and let's look at you. You make me as I can't neither speak nor see—I'm just like a child——'

He broke down utterly, and shook with the choking struggle of laughter and sobs. His emotion affected Sidney, who looked pale and troubled in spite of the smile still clinging feebly about his lips.

'If it makes you glad to hear it,' said the young man, in an uncertain voice, 'I'm all the more glad myself, on that account.'

'Makes me glad? That's no word for it, boy; that's no word for it! Give us your hand again. I feel as if I'd ought to go down on my old knees and crave your pardon. If only she could have lived to see this, the poor woman as died when things was at their worst! If I'd only listened to her there'd never have been them years of unfriendliness between us. You've gone on with one kindness after another, but this is more than I could ever a' thought possible. Why, I took it for certain as you was goin' to marry that other young girl; they told me as it was all settled.'

'A mistake.'

'I'd never have dared to hope it, Sidney. The one thing as I wished more than anything else on earth, and I couldn't think ever to see it. Glad's no word for what I feel. And to think as my girl kep' it from me! Yes, yes; there was something on her face; I remember it now. "I'm just goin' round to have a word with Sidney," I says. "Are you, father?" she says. "Don't stay too long." And she had a sort o' smile I couldn't quite understand. She'll be a good wife to you, Sidney. Her heart's softened to all as she used to care for. She'll be a good and faithful wife to you as long as she lives. But I must go back home and speak to her. There ain't a man livin', let him be as rich as he may, that feels such happiness as you've given me to-night.'

He went stumbling down the stairs, and walked homewards at a great speed, so that when he reached the Buildings he had to wipe his face and stand for a moment before beginning the ascent. The children were at their home lessons; he astonished them by flinging his hat mirthfully on to the table.

'Now then, father!' cried young Tom, the eight-year-old, whose pen was knocked out of his hand.

With a chuckle John advanced to Clara's room. As he closed the door behind him she rose. His face was mottled; there were tear-stains about his eyes, and he had a wild, breathless look.

'An' you never told me! You let me go without half a word!'

Clara put her hands upon his shoulders and kissed him. 'I didn't quite know whether it was true or not, father.'

'My darling! My dear girl! Come an' sit on my knee, like you used to when you was a little 'un. I'm a rough old father for such as you, but nobody'll never love you better than I do, an' always have done. So he's been faithful to you, for all they said. There ain't a better man livin'! "It's a long time since I first asked the question," he says, "but she's give me the right answer at last." And he looks that glad of it.'

'He does? You're sure he does?'

'Sure? Why, you should a' seen him when I went into the room! There's nothing more as I wish for now. I only hope I may live a while longer, to see you forget all your troubles, my dear. He'll make you happy, will Sidney; he's got a deal more education than anyone else I ever knew, and you'll suit each other. But you won't forget all about your old father? You'll let me come an' have a talk with you now and then, my dear, just you an' me together, you know?'

'I shall love you and be grateful to you always, father. You've kept a warm heart for me all this time.'

'I couldn't do nothing else, Clara; you've always been what I loved most, and you always will be.'

'If I hadn't had you to come back to, what would have become of me?'

'We'll never think of that. We'll never speak another word of that.'

'Father—— Oh, if I had my face again ! If I had my own face ! '

A great anguish shook her; she lay in his arms and sobbed. It was the farewell, even in her fulness of heart and deep sense of consolation, to all she had most vehemently desired. Gratitude and self-pity being indivisible in her emotions, she knew not herself whether the ache of regret or the soothing restfulness of deliverance made her tears flow. But at least there was no conscious duplicity, and for the moment no doubt that she had found her haven. It is a virtuous world, and our frequent condemnations are invariably based on justice ; will it be greatly harmful if for once we temper our righteous judgment with ever so little mercy ?

CHAPTER XXXIII

A FALL FROM THE IDEAL

JOSEPH SNOWDON waxed daily in respectability. He was, for one thing, clothing himself in flesh, and, though still any-thing but a portly man, bore himself as becomes one who can indulge a taste for eating and drinking ; his step was more deliberate, he no longer presented the suppleness of limb that so often accompanies a needy condition in the man of wits, he grew attentive to his personal equipment; he was always well combed and well shaven, and generally, in hours of leisure, you perceived a fragrance breathing from his handkerchief. Nor was this refinement addressed only to the public. To Clem he behaved with a correctness which kept that lady in a state of acute suspicion ; not seldom he brought her a trifling gift, which he would offer with compliments, and he made a point of consulting her pleasure or convenience in all matters that affected them in common. A similar dignity of bearing marked his relations with Hanover Street. When he entered Jane's parlour it was with a beautiful blending of familiarity and courtesy ; he took his daughter's hand with an air of graceful affection, retaining it for a moment between his own, and regarding her with a gentle smile which hinted the pride of a parent. In speaking with the old man he habitually subdued his voice, respectfully bending forward, solicitously watching the opportunity of a service. Michael had pleasure in his company and conversation. Without overdoing it, Joseph accustomed himself to speak of philanthropic interests. He propounded a scheme for supplying the poor with a certain excellent filter at a price all but nominal; who did not know the benefit to humble homes of pure water for use as a beverage? The filter was not made yet, but Lake, Snowdon, & Co., had it under their consideration.

Michael kept his room a good deal in these wretched days of winter, so that Joseph had no difficulty in obtaining private interviews with his daughter. Every such occasion he used assiduously, his great end being to possess himself of Jane's confidence. He did not succeed quite so well with the girl as with her grandfather; there was always a reserve in her behaviour which as yet he found it impossible to overcome. Observation led him to conclude that much of this arose from the view she took of his relations with Sidney Kirkwood. Jane was in love with Sidney; on that point he could have no doubt; and in all likelihood she regarded him as unfriendly to Sidney's suit—women are so shrewd in these affairs. Accordingly, Joseph made it his business by artful degrees to remove this prepossession from her mind. In the course of this endeavour he naturally pressed into his service the gradually discovered fact that Sidney had scruples of conscience regarding Jane's fortune. Marvellous as it appeared to him, he had all but come to the conclusion that this *was* a fact. Now, given Jane's character, which he believed he had sounded; given her love for Kirkwood, which was obviously causing her anxiety and unhappiness; Joseph saw his way to an admirable piece of strategy. What could be easier, if he played his cards well and patiently enough, than to lead Jane to regard the fortune as her most threatening enemy? Valuable results might come of that, whether before or after the death of the old man.

The conversation in which he first ventured to strike this note undisguisedly took place on the same evening as that unpleasant scene when Sidney as good as quarrelled with him —the evening before the day on which Sidney asked Clara Hewett to be his wife. Having found Jane alone, he began to talk in his most paternal manner, his chair very near hers, his eyes fixed on her sewing. And presently, when the ground was prepared:

'Jane, there's something I've been wanting to say to you for a long time. My dear, I'm uneasy about you.'

' Uneasy, father ? ' and she glanced at him nervously.

' Yes, I'm uneasy. But whether I ought to tell you why, I'm sure I don't know. You're my own child, Janey, and you become dearer to me every day; but—it's hard to say it—there naturally isn't all the confidence between us that there might have been if—well, well, I won't speak of that.'

' But won't you tell me what makes you anxious ? '

He laid the tips of his fingers on her head. ' Janey, shall you be offended if I speak about Mr. Kirkwood ? '

' No, father.'

She tried in vain to continue sewing.

' My dear—I believe there's no actual engagement between you ? '

' Oh no, father,' she replied, faintly.

' And yet—don't be angry with me, my child—I think you are something more than friends ? '

She made no answer.

' And I can't help thinking, Janey—I think about you very often indeed—that Mr. Kirkwood has rather exaggerated views about the necessity of—of altering things between you.'

Quite recently Joseph had become aware of the understanding between Michael and Kirkwood. The old man still hesitated to break the news to Jane, saying to himself that it was better for Sidney to prepare her by the change in his behaviour.

' Of altering things ? ' Jane repeated, under her breath.

' It seems to me wrong—wrong to both of you,' Joseph pursued, in a pathetic voice. ' I can't help noticing my child's looks. I know she isn't what she used to be, poor little girl ! And I know Kirkwood isn't what he used to be. It's very hard, and I feel for you—for both of you.'

Jane sat motionless, not daring to lift her eyes, scarcely daring to breathe.

' Janey.'

' Yes, father.'

' I wonder whether I'm doing wrong to your grandfather in speaking to you confidentially like this ? I can't believe he notices things as I do ; he'd never wish you to be unhappy.'

' But I don't quite understand, father. What do you mean about Mr. Kirkwood ? Why should he——— '

The impulse failed her. A fear which she had harboured for many weary days was being confirmed and she could not ask directly for the word that would kill hope.

'Have I a right to tell you? I thought perhaps you understood.'

'As you have gone so far, I think you must explain. I don't see how you can be doing wrong.'

'Poor Kirkwood! You see, he's in such a delicate position, my dear. I think myself that he's acting rather strangely, after everything; but it's—it's your money, Jane. He doesn't think he ought to ask you to marry him, under the circumstances.'

She trembled.

'Now who should stand by you, in a case like this, if not your own father? Of course he can't say a word to you himself; and of course you can't say a word to him; and altogether it's a pitiful business.'

Jane shrank from discussing such a topic with her father. Her next words were uttered with difficulty.

'But the money isn't my own—it'll never be my own. He —Mr. Kirkwood knows that.'

'He does, to be sure. But it makes no difference. He has told your grandfather, my love, that—that the responsibility would be too great. He has told him distinctly that everything's at an end—everything that *might* have happened.'

She just looked at him, then dropped her eyes on her sewing.

'Now, as your father, Janey, I know it's right that you should be told of this. I feel you're being very cruelly treated, my child. And I wish to goodness I could only see any way out of it for you both. Of course I'm powerless either for acting or speaking: you can understand that. But I want you to think of me as your truest friend, my love.'

More still he said, but Jane had no ears for it. When he left her, she bade him good-bye mechanically, and stood on the same spot by the door, without thought, stunned by what she had learnt.

That Sidney would be impelled to such a decision as this she had never imagined. His reserve whilst yet she was in ignorance of her true position she could understand: also his delaying for a while even after everything had been explained to her. But that he should draw away from her altogether seemed inexplicable, for it implied a change in him which nothing had prepared her to think possible. Unaltered in his love, he refused to share the task of her life, to aid in the work which he regarded with such fervent sympathy. Her mind was not subtle enough to conceive those objections to

Michael's idea which had weighed with Sidney almost from
the first, for though she had herself shrunk from the great
undertaking, it was merely in weakness—a reason she never
dreamt of attributing to him.   Nor had she caught as much
as a glimpse of those base, scheming interests, contact with
which had aroused Sidney's vehement disgust.   Was her
father to be trusted?   This was the first question that shaped
itself in her mind.   He did not like Sidney; that she had felt
all along, as well as the reciprocal coldness on Sidney's part.
But did his unfriendliness go so far as to prompt him to
intervene with untruths?   'Of course you can't say a word to
him '—that remark would bear an evil interpretation, which her
tormented mind did not fail to suggest.   Moreover, he had
seemed so anxious that she should not broach the subject with
her grandfather.   But what constrained her to silence?   If,
indeed, he had nothing but her happiness at heart, he could
not take it ill that she should seek to understand the whole
truth, and Michael must tell her whether Sidney had indeed
thus spoken to him.

Before she had obtained any show of control over her
agitation Michael came into the room.   Evening was the old
man's best time, and when he had kept his own chamber
through the day he liked to come and sit with Jane as she had
her supper.

'Didn't I hear your father's voice?' he asked, as he
moved slowly to his accustomed chair.

'Yes.   He couldn't stay.'

Jane stood in an attitude of indecision.   Having seated
himself, Michael glanced at her.   His regard had not its old
directness; it seemed apprehensive, as if seeking to probe her
thought.

'Has Miss Lant sent you the book she promised?'

'Yes, grandfather.'

This was a recently published volume dealing with charitable enterprise in some part of London.   Michael noticed
with surprise the uninterested tone of Jane's reply.   Again
he looked at her, and more searchingly.

'Would you like to read me a little of it?'

She reached the book from a side-table, drew near, and
stood turning the pages.   The confusion of her mind was
such that she could not have read a word with understanding.
Then she spoke, involuntarily.

'Grandfather, has Mr. Kirkwood said anything more—
about me?'

The words made painful discord in her ears, but instead of showing heightened colour she grew pallid. Holding the book partly open, she felt all her nerves and muscles strained as if in some physical effort; her feet were rooted to the spot.

'Have you heard anything from him?' returned the old man, resting his hands on the sides of the easy-chair.

'Father has been speaking about him. He says Mr. Kirkwood has told you something.'

'Yes. Come and sit down by me, Jane.'

She could not move nearer. Though unable to form a distinct conception, she felt a foreboding of what must come to pass. The dread failure of strength was more than threatening her; ker heart was sinking, and by no effort of will could she summon the thoughts that should aid her against herself.

'What has your father told you?' Michael asked, when he perceived her distress. He spoke with a revival of energy, clearly, commandingly.

'He says that Mr. Kirkwood wishes you to forget what ho told you, and what you repeated to me.'

'Did he give you any reason?'

'Yes. I don't understand, though.'

'Come here by me, Jane. Let's talk about it quietly. Sidney doesn't feel able to help you as he thought he could. We mustn't blame him for that; he must judge for himself. He thinks it'll be better if you continue to be only friends.'

Jane averted her face, his steady look being more than she could bear. For an instant a sense of uttermost shame thrilled through her, and without knowing what she did, she moved a little and laid the book down.

'Come here, my child,' he repeated, in a gentler voice.

She approached him.

'You feel it hard. But when you've thought about it a little you won't grieve; I'm sure you won't. Remember, your life is not to be like that of ordinary women. You've higher objects before you, and you'll find a higher reward. You know that, don't you? There's no need for me to remind you of what we've talked about so often, is there? If it's a sacrifice, you're strong enough to face it; yes, yes, strong enough to face more than this, my Jane is! Only fix your thoughts on the work you're going to do. It'll take up all your life, Jane, won't it? You'll have no time to give to such things as occupy other women—no mind for them.'

His grey eyes searched her countenance with that horrible intensity of fanaticism which is so like the look of cruelty, of greed, of any passion originating in the baser self. Unlike too, of course, but it is the pitilessness common to both extremes that shows most strongly in an old, wrinkled visage. He had laid his hand upon her. Every word was a stab in the girl's heart, and so dreadful became her torture, so intolerable the sense of being drawn by a fierce will away from all she desired, that at length a cry escaped her lips. She fell on her knees by him, and pleaded in a choking voice.

'I can't! Grandfather, don't ask it of me! Give it all to some one else—to some one else! I'm not strong enough to make such a sacrifice. Let me be as I was before!'

Michael's face darkened. He drew his hand away and rose from the seat; with more than surprise, with anger and even bitterness, he looked down at the crouching girl. She did not sob; her face buried in her arms, she lay against the chair, quivering, silent.

'Jane, stand up and speak to me!'

She did not move.

'Jane!'

He laid his hand on her. Jane raised her head, and endeavoured to obey him; in the act she moaned and fell insensible.

Michael strode to the door and called twice or thrice for Mrs. Byass; then he stooped by the lifeless girl and supported her head. Bessie was immediately at hand, with a cry of consternation, but also with helpful activity.

'Why, I thought she'd got over this; it's a long time since she was took last isn't it? Sam's downstairs, Mr. Snowdon; do just shout out to him to go for some brandy. Tell him to bring my smelling-bottle first, if he knows where it is—I'm blest if I do! Poor thing! She ain't been at all well lately, and that's the truth.'

The truth, beyond a doubt. Pale face, showing now the thinness which it had not wholly outgrown, the inheritance from miserable childhood; no face of a stern heroine, counting as idle all the natural longings of the heart, consecrated to a lifelong combat with giant wrongs. Nothing better nor worse than the face of one who can love and must be loved in turn.

She came to herself, and at the same moment Michael went from the room.

'There now; there now,' crooned Bessie, with much patting of the hands and stroking of the cheeks. 'Why, what's come to you, Jane? Cry away; don't try to prevent yourself; it'll do you good to cry a bit. Of course, here comes Sam with all sorts of things, when there's no need of him. He's always either too soon or too late, is Sam. Just look at him, Jane; now if *he* don't make you laugh, nothing will!'

Mr. Byass retired, shamefaced. Leaning against Bessie's shoulder, Jane sobbed for a long time, sobbed in the misery of shame. She saw that her grandfather had gone away. How should she ever face him after this? It was precious comfort to feel Bessie's sturdy arms about her, and to hear the foolish affectionate words, which asked nothing but that she should take them kindly and have done with her trouble.

'Did grandfather tell you how it was?' she asked, with a sudden fear lest Bessie should have learnt her pitiful weakness.

'Why, no; how did it come?'

'I don't know. We were talking. I can stand up now, Mrs. Byass, thank you. I'll go up to my room. I've forgotten the time; is it late?'

It was only nine o'clock. Bessie would have gone upstairs with her, but Jane insisted that she was quite herself. On the stairs she trod as lightly as possible, and she closed her door without a sound. Alone, she again gave way to tears. Michael's face was angry in her memory; he had never looked at her in that way before, and now he would never look with the old kindness. What a change had been wrought in these few minutes!

And Sidney never anything but her friend—cold, meaningless word! If he knew how she had fallen, would that be likely to bring him nearer to her? She had lost both things, that was all.

CHAPTER XXXIV

THE DEBT REPAID

SHE rose early, in the murky cold of the winter morning. When, at eight o'clock, she knocked as usual at her grandfather's door his answer made her tremble.

'I shall be down in a few minutes, Jane; I'll have breakfast with you.'

It was long since he had risen at this hour. His voice sounded less like that of an old man, and, in spite of his calling her by her name, she felt the tone to be severe. When he reached the parlour he did not offer to take her hand, and she feared to approach him. She saw that his features bore the mark of sleeplessness. Hers, poor girl! were yet more woeful in their pallor.

Through the meal he affected to occupy himself with the book Miss Lant had sent—the sight of which was intolerable to Jane. And not for a full hour did he speak anything but casual words. Jane had taken her sewing; unexpectedly he addressed her.

'Let's have a word or two together, Jane. I think we ought to, oughtn't we?'

She forced herself to regard him.

'I think you meant what you said last night?'

'Grandfather, I will do whatever you bid me. I'll do it faithfully. I was ungrateful. I feel ashamed to have spoken so.'

'That's nothing to do with it, Jane. You're not ungrateful; anything but that. But I've had a night to think over your words. You couldn't speak like that if you weren't driven to it by the strongest feeling you ever knew or will know. I hadn't thought of it in that way; I hadn't thought of you in that way.'

He began gently, but in the last words was a touch of reproof, almost of scorn. He gazed at her from under his grey eyebrows, perhaps hoping to elicit some resistance of her spirit, some sign of strength that would help him to reconstruct his shattered ideal.

'Grandfather, I'll try with all my strength to be what you wish—I will!'

'And suppose the strength isn't sufficient, child?'

Even in her humility she could not but feel that this was unjust. Had she ever boasted? Had she ever done more than promise tremblingly what he demanded? But the fear was legitimate. A weak thing, all but heart-broken, could she hope to tread firmly in any difficult path? She hung her head, making no answer.

He examined her, seeming to measure the slightness of her frame. Sad, unutterably sad, was the deep breath he drew as he turned his eyes away again.

'Do you feel well this morning, Jane?'

'Yes, grandfather.'

'Have you slept?'

'I couldn't. You were grieving about me. I hoped never to have disappointed you.'

He fell into reverie. Was he thinking of that poor wife of his, dead long, long ago, the well-meaning girl of whom he had expected impossible things? A second time had he thus erred, no longer with the excuse of inexperience and hot blood. That cry of Jane's had made its way to his heart. An enthusiast, he was yet capable of seeing by the common light of day, when his affections were deeply stirred. And in the night he had pondered much over his son's behaviour. Was he being deceived in that quarter also, and there intentionally? Did Joseph know this child better than he had done, and calculate upon her weakness? The shock, instead of disabling him, had caused a revival of his strength. He could walk more firmly this morning than at any time since his accident. His brain was clear and active; he knew that it behoved him to reconsider all he had been doing, and that quickly, ere it was too late. He must even forget that aching of the heart until he had leisure to indulge it.

'You shan't disappoint me, my dear,' he said gravely. 'It's my own fault if I don't take your kindness as you mean it. I have to go out, Jane, but I shall be back to dinner. Perhaps we'll talk again afterwards.'

Of late, on the rare occasions of his leaving the house, he had always told her where he was going, and for what purpose; Jane understood that this confidence was at an end. When he was gone she found occupation for a short time, but presently could only sit over the fire, nursing her many griefs. She was no longer deemed worthy of confidence; worse than that, she had no more faith in herself. If Sidney learnt what had happened he could not even retain his respect for her. In this way she thought of it, judging Kirkwood by the ideal standard, which fortunately is so unlike human nature; taking it for granted—so oppressed was her mind by the habit of dwelling on artificial motives—that he only liked her because he had believed her strong in purpose, forgetting altogether that his love had grown before he was aware that anything unusual was required of her. She did remember, indeed, that it was only the depth of her love for him which had caused her disgrace; but, even if he came to understand that, it would not, she feared, weigh in her favour against his judgment.

It was the natural result of the influences to which she
had been subjected. Her mind, overwrought by resolute
contemplation of ideas beyond its scope, her gentle nature
bent beneath a burden of duty to which it was unequal, and
taught to consider with painful solemnity those impulses of
kindness which would otherwise have been merely the simple
joys of life, she had come to distrust every instinct which did
not subserve the supreme purpose. Even of Sidney's conduct
she could not reason in a natural way. Instinct would have
bidden her reproach him, though ever so gently; was it well
done to draw away when he must have known how she looked
for his aid? Her artificial self urged, on the other hand, that
he had not acted thus without some gravely considered
motive. What it was she could not pretend to divine; her
faith in his nobleness overcame every perplexity. Of the
persons constituting this little group and playing their several
parts, she alone had fallen altogether below what was expected
of her. As humble now as in the days of her serfdom, Jane
was incapable of revolting against the tyranny of circumstances. Life had grown very hard for her again, but she
believed that this was to a great extent her own fault, the
outcome of her own unworthy weakness.

At Michael's return she did her best to betray no idle
despondency. Their midday meal was almost as silent as
breakfast had been; his eyes avoided her, and frequently he
lost himself in thought. As he was rising from the table Jane
observed an unsteadiness in his movement; he shook his
head mechanically and leaned forward on both his hands, as
if feeling giddy. She approached him, but did not venture to
speak.

'I'll go upstairs,' he said, having sighed slightly.

'May I come and read to you, grandfather?'

'Not just now, Jane. Go out whilst it's a bit fine.'

He went from the room, still with an unsteady walk.
Reaching his own room, where there was a cheerful fire, he
sat down, and remained for a long time unoccupied, save with
his reflections. This chamber had scarcely changed in a detail
of its arrangement since he first came to inhabit it. There
was the chair which Sidney always used, and that on which
Jane had sat since she was the silent, frail child of thirteen.
Here had his vision taken form, growing more definite with
the growth of his granddaughter, seeming to become at length
a splendid reality. What talk had been held here between

Kirkwood and himself whilst Jane listened! All gone into silence; gone, too, the hope it had encouraged.

He was weary after the morning's absence from home, and fell into a light slumber. Dreams troubled him. First he found himself in Australia; he heard again the sudden news of his son's death; the shock awoke him. Another dozing fit, and he was a young man with a wife and children to support; haunted with the fear of coming to want; harsh, unreasonable in his exactions at home. Something like a large black coffin came into his dream, and in dread of it he again returned to consciousness.

All night he had been thinking of the dark story of long ago—his wife's form motionless on the bed—the bottle which told him what had happened. Why must that memory revive to trouble his last days? Part of his zeal for the great project had come of a feeling that he might thus in some degree repair his former ill-doing; Jane would be a providence to many hapless women whose burden was as heavy as his own wife's had been. Must he abandon that solace? In any case he could bestow his money for charitable purposes, but it would not be the same, it would not effect what he had aimed at.

Late in the afternoon he drew from the inner pocket of his coat a long envelope and took thence a folded paper. It was covered with clerkly writing, which he perused several times. At length he tore the paper slowly across the middle, again tore the fragments, and threw them on to the fire. . . .

Jane obeyed her grandfather's word and went out for an hour. She wished for news of Pennyloaf, who had been ill, and was now very near the time of her confinement. At the door of the house in Merlin Place she was surprised to encounter Bob Hewett, who stood in a lounging attitude; he had never appeared to her so disreputable—not that his clothes were worse than usual, but his face and hands were dirty, and the former was set in a hang-dog look.

'Is your wife upstairs, Mr. Hewett?' Jane asked, when he had nodded sullenly in reply to her greeting.

'Yes; and somebody else too as could have been dispensed with. There's another mouth to feed.'

'No, there ain't,' cried a woman's voice just behind him.

Jane recognised the speaker, a Mrs. Griffin, who lived in the house and was neighbourly to Pennyloaf.

'There ain't?' inquired Bob, gruffly.

'The child's dead.'

'Thank goodness for that, any way!'

Mrs. Griffin explained to Jane that the birth had taken place twelve hours ago. Pennyloaf was 'very low,' but not in a state to cause anxiety; perhaps it would be better for Jane to wait until to-morrow before seeing her.

'She didn't say "thank goodness," added the woman, with a scornful glance at Bob, 'but I don't think she's over sorry as it's gone, an' small blame to her. There's some people as doesn't care much what sort o' times she has—not meanin' *you*, Miss, but them as had *ought* to care.'

Bob looked more disreputable than ever. His eyes were fixed on Jane, and with such a singular expression that the latter, meeting their gaze, felt startled, she did not know why. At the same moment he stepped down from the threshold and walked away without speaking.

'I shouldn't care to have *him* for a 'usband,' pursued Mrs. Griffin. 'Of course he must go an' lose his work, just when his wife's wantin' a few little extries, as you may say.'

'Lost his work?'

'Day 'fore yes'day. I don't like him, an' I don't like his ways; he'll be gettin' into trouble before long, you mind what I say. His family's a queer lot, 'cordin' to what they tell. Do you know them, Miss?'

'I used to, a long time ago.'

'You knew his sister—her as is come 'ome?'

'His sister?'

'Her as was a actress. Mrs. Bannister was tellin' me only last night; she had it from Mrs. Horrocks, as heard from a friend of hers as lives in the Farrin'don Buildin's, where the Hewetts lives too. They tell me it was in the Sunday paper, though I don't remember nothing about it at the time. It seems as how a woman threw vitrol over her an' burnt her face so as there's no knowin' her, an' she goes about with a veil, an' 'cause she can't get her own livin' no more, of course she's come back 'ome, for all she ran away an' disgraced herself shameful.'

Jane gazed fixedly at the speaker, scarcely able to gather the sense of what was said.

'Miss Hewett, you mean? Mr. Hewett's eldest daughter?'

'So I understand.'

'She has come home? When?'

'I can't just say; but a few weeks ago, I believe. They say it's nearly two months since it was in the paper.'

'Does Mrs. Hewett know about it?'

'I can't say. She's never spoke to me as if she did. And, as I tell you, I only heard yes'day myself. If you're a friend of theirs, p'r'aps I hadn't oughtn't to a' mentioned it. It just come to my lips in the way o' talkin'. Of course I don't know nothin' about the young woman myself; it's only what you comes to 'ear in the way o' talkin', you know.'

This apology was doubtless produced by the listener's troubled countenance. Jane asked no further question, but said she would come to see Pennyloaf on the morrow, and so took her leave.

At ten o'clock next morning, just when Jane was preparing for her visit to Merlin Place, so possessed with anxiety to ascertain if Pennyloaf knew anything about Clara Hewett that all her troubles were for the moment in the back ground, Bessie Byass came running upstairs with a strange announcement. Sidney Kirkwood had called, and wished to see Miss Snowdon in private for a few minutes.

'Something must have happened,' said Jane, her heart standing still.

Bessie had a significant smile, but suppressed it when she noticed the agitation into which her friend was fallen.

'Shall I ask him up into the front room?'

Michael was in his own chamber, which he had not left this morning. On going to the parlour Jane found her visitor standing in expectancy. Yes, something had happened; it needed but to look at him to be convinced of that. And before a word was spoken Jane knew that his coming had reference to Clara Hewett, knew it with the strangest certainty.

'I didn't go to work this morning,' Sidney began, 'because I was very anxious to see you—alone. I have something to speak about—to tell you.'

'Let us sit down.'

Sidney waited till he met her look; she regarded him without self-consciousness, without any effort to conceal her agitated interest.

'You see young Hewett and his wife sometimes. Have you heard from either of them that Clara Hewett is living with her father again?'

'Not from them. A person in their house spoke about it yesterday. It was the first I had heard.'

'Spoke of Miss Hewett? In a gossiping way, do you mean?'

'Yes.'

'Then you know what has happened to her?'

'If the woman told the truth.'

There was silence.

'Miss Snowdon——'

'Oh, I don't like you to speak so. You used to call me Jane.'

He looked at her in distress. She had spoken impulsively, but not with the kind of emotion the words seem to imply. It was for his sake, not for hers, that she broke that formal speech.

'You called me so when I was a child, Mr. Kirkwood,' she continued, smiling for all she was so pale. 'It sounds as if something had altered. You're my oldest friend, and won't you always be so? Whatever you're going to tell me, surely it doesn't prevent us from being friends, just the same as always?'

He had not seen her in her weakness, the night before last. As little as he could imagine that, was he able to estimate the strength with which she now redeemed her womanly dignity. His face told her what he had to disclose. No question now of proving herself superior to common feelings; it was Sidney who made appeal to her, and her heart went forth to grant him all he desired.

'Jane—dear, good Jane—you remember what I said to you in the garden at Danbury—that I had forgotten her. I thought it was true. But you know what a terrible thing has befallen her. I should be less than a man if I could say that she is nothing to me.'

'Have you spoken to her?'

'I have asked her to be my wife. Jane, if I had come to you yesterday, before going to her, and had told you what I meant to do, and explained all I felt, how the love of years ago had grown in me again, wouldn't you have given me a friendly hand?'

'Just like I do now. Do you think I have forgotten one night when she stood by me and saved me from cruel treatment, and then nursed me when I fell ill?'

Neither of them had the habit of making long speeches. They understood each other—very nearly; sufficiently, at all events, to make the bond of sympathy between them stronger than ever. Jane was misled a little, for she thought that here was the explanation of Sidney's withdrawing his word to her grandfather; doubtless he heard of the calamity when it happened. But on a more essential point she fell into no misconception. Did Sidney desire that she should?

He held her hand until she gently drew it away.

'You will go up and tell grandfather,' she said, gravely; then added, before he could speak, 'But I'll just see him first for a minute. He hasn't been out of his room this morning yet. Please wait here.'

She left him, and Sidney fell back on his chair, woebegone, distracted.

Michael, brooding sorrowfully, at first paid no heed to Jane when she entered his room. It was not long since he had risen, and his simple breakfast, scarcely touched, was still on the table.

'Grandfather, Mr. Kirkwood is here, and wishes to speak to you.'

He collected himself, and, regarding her, became aware that she was strongly moved.

'Wishes to see me, Jane? Then I suppose he came to see you first?'

Prepared now for anything unexpected, feeling that the links between himself and these young people were artificial, and that he could but watch, as if from a distance, the course of their lives, his first supposition was, that Sidney had again altered his mind. He spoke coldly, and had little inclination for the interview.

'Yes,' Jane replied, 'he came to see me, but only to tell me that he is going to be married.'

His wrinkled face slowly gathered an expression of surprise.

'He will tell you who it is; he will explain. But I wanted to speak to you first. Grandfather, I was afraid you might say something about me. Will you—will you forget my foolishness? Will you think of me as you did before? When he has spoken to you, you will understand why I am content to put everything out of my mind, everything you and I talked of. But I couldn't bear for him to know how I have disappointed you. Will you let me be all I was to you before? Will you trust me again, grandfather? You haven't spoken to him yet about me, have you?'

Michael shook his head.

'Then you will let it be as if nothing had happened?
Grandfather——'

She bent beside him and took his hand. Michael looked
at her with a light once more in his eyes.

'Tell him to come. He shall hear nothing from me,
Jane.'

'And you will try to forget it?'

'I wish nothing better. Tell him to come here, my child.
When he's gone we'll talk together again.'

The interview did not last long, and Sidney left the house
without seeing Jane a second time.

She would have promised anything now. Seeing that
life had but one path of happiness for her, the path hopelessly
closed, what did it matter by which of the innumerable other
ways she accomplished her sad journey? For an instant,
whilst Sidney was still speaking, she caught a gleam of hope
in renunciation itself, the kind of strength which idealism is
fond of attributing to noble natures. A gleam only, and
deceptive; she knew it too well after the day spent by her
grandfather's side, encouraging, at the expense of her heart's
blood, all his revived faith in her. But she would not again
give way. The old man should reap fruit of her gratitude
and Sidney should never suspect how nearly she had proved
herself unworthy of his high opinion.

She had dreamed her dream, and on awaking must be
content to take up the day's duties. Just in the same way,
when she was a child at Mrs. Peckover's, did not sleep often
bring a vision of happiness, of freedom from bitter tasks, and
had she not to wake in the miserable mornings, trembling lest
she had lain too long? Her condition was greatly better than
then, so much better that it seemed wicked folly to lament
because one joy was not granted her.—Why, in the meantime
she had forgotten all about Pennyloaf. That visit must be
paid the first thing this morning.

CHAPTER XXXV

THE TREASURY UNLOCKED

A SUNDAY morning. In their parlour in Burton Crescent, Mr. and Mrs. Joseph Snowdon were breakfasting. The sound of church bells—most depressing of all sounds that mingle in the voice of London—intimated that it was nearly eleven o'clock, but neither of our friends had in view the attendance of public worship. Blended odours of bacon and kippered herrings filled the room—indeed, the house, for several breakfasts were in progress under the same roof. For a wonder, the morning was fine, even sunny; a yellow patch glimmered on the worn carpet, and the grime of the window-panes was visible against an unfamiliar sky. Joseph, incompletely dressed, had a Sunday paper propped before him, and read whilst he ate. Clem, also in anything but *grande toilette*, was using a knife for the purpose of conveying to her mouth the juice which had exuded from crisp rashers. As usual, they had very little to say to each other. Clem looked at her husband now and then, from under her eyebrows, surreptitiously.

After one of these glances she said, in a tone which was not exactly hostile, but had a note of suspicion :

' I'd give something to know why he's going to marry Clara Hewett.'

' Not the first time you've made that remark,' returned Joseph, without looking up from his paper.

' I suppose I can speak ? '

' Oh, yes. But I'd try to do so in a more lady-like way.'

Clem flashed at him a gleam of hatred. He had become fond lately of drawing attention to her defects of breeding. Clem certainly did not keep up with his own progress in the matter of external refinement; his comments had given her a sense of inferiority, which irritated her solely as meaning that she was not his equal in craft. She let a minute or two pass, then returned to the subject.

' There's something at the bottom of it ; I know that. Of course you know more about it than you pretend.'

Joseph leaned back in his chair and regarded her with a smile of the loftiest scorn.

' It never occurs to you to explain it in the simplest way, of course. If ever you hear of a marriage, the first thing you

ask yourself is: What has he or she to gain by it? Natural
enough—in you. Now do you really suppose that all mar-
riages come about in the way that *yours* did—on your side, I
mean?'

Clem was far too dull-witted to be capable of quick retort.
She merely replied:

'I don't know what you're talking about.'

'Of course not. But let me assure you that people sometimes think of other things besides making profit when they
get married. It's a pity that you always show yourself so
coarse-minded.'

Joseph was quite serious in administering this rebuke.
He really felt himself justified in holding the tone of moral
superiority. The same phenomenon has often been remarked
in persons conscious that their affairs are prospering, and
whose temptations to paltry meanness are on that account
less frequent.

'And what about yourself?' asked his wife, having found
her retort at length. 'Why did you want to marry *me*, I'd
like to know?'

'Why? You are getting too modest. How could I live
in the same house with such a good-looking and sweet-tem-
pered and well-behaved——'

'Oh, shut up!' she exclaimed, in a voice such as one hears
at the street-corner. 'It was just because you thought we
was goin' to be fools enough to keep you in idleness. Who
was the fool, after all?'

Joseph smiled, and returned to his newspaper. In satisfaction at having reduced him to silence, Clem laughed aloud
and clattered with the knife on her plate. As she was doing
so there came a knock at the door.

'A gentleman wants to know if you're in, sir,' said the
house-thrall, showing a smeary face. 'Mr. Byass is the
name.'

'Mr. Byass? I'll go down and see him.'

Clem's face became alive with suspicion. In spite of her
careless attire she intercepted Joseph, and bade the servant
ask Mr. Byass to come upstairs. 'How can you go down without a collar?' she said to her husband.

He understood, and was somewhat uneasy, but made no
resistance. Mr. Byass presented himself. He had a very long
face, and obviously brought news of grave import. Joseph
shook hands with him.

'You don't know my wife, I think. Mr. Byass, Clem. Nothing wrong, I hope?'

Samuel, having made his best City bow, swung back from his toes to his heels, and stood looking down into his hat. 'I'm sorry to say,' he began, with extreme gravity, 'that Mr. Snowdon is rather ill—in fact, very ill. Miss Jane asked me to come as sharp as I could.'

'Ill? In what way?'

'I'm afraid it's a stroke, or something in that line. He fell down without a word of warning, just before ten o'clock. He's lying insensible.'

'I'll come at once,' said Joseph. 'They've got a doctor, I hope?'

'Yes; the doctor had been summoned instantly.'

'I'll go with you,' said Clem, in a tone of decision.

'No, no; what's the good? You'll only be in the way.'

'No, I shan't. If he's as bad as all that, I shall come.'

Both withdrew to prepare themselves. Mr. Byass, who was very nervous and perspiring freely, began to walk round and round the table, inspecting closely, in complete absence of mind, the objects that lay on it.

'We'll have a cab,' cried Joseph, as he came forth equipped. 'Poor Jane's in a sad state, I'm afraid, eh?'

In a few minutes they were driving up Pentonville Road. Clem scarcely ever removed her eye from Joseph's face; the latter held his lips close together and kept his brows wrinkled. Few words passed during the drive.

At the door of the house appeared Bessie, much agitated. All turned into the parlour on the ground floor and spoke together for a few minutes. Michael had been laid on his bed; at present Jane only was with him, but the doctor would return shortly.

'Will you tell her I'm here?' said Joseph to Mrs. Byass. 'I'll see her in the sitting-room.'

He went up and waited. Throughout the house prevailed that unnatural, nerve-distressing quietude which tells the presence of calamity. The church bells had ceased ringing, and Sunday's silence in the street enhanced the effect of blankness and alarming expectancy. Joseph could not keep still; he strained his ears in attention to any slight sound that might come from the floor above, and his heart beat painfully when at length the door opened.

Jane fixed her eyes on him and came silently forward.

'Does he show any signs of coming round?' her father inquired.

'No. He hasn't once moved.'

She spoke only just above a whisper. The shock kept her still trembling and her face bloodless.

'Tell me how it happened, Jane.'

'He'd just got up. I'd taken him his breakfast, and we were talking. All at once he began to turn round, and then he fell down—before I could reach him.'

'I'll go upstairs, shall I?'

Jane could not overcome her fear; at the door of the bedroom she drew back, involuntarily, that her father might enter before her. When she forced herself to follow, the first glimpse of the motionless form shook her from head to foot. The thought of death was dreadful to her, and death seemed to lurk invisibly in this quiet room. The pale sunlight affected her as a mockery of hope.

'You won't go away again, father?' she whispered.

He shook his head.

In the meantime Bessie and Clem were conversing. On the single previous occasion of Clem's visit to the house they had not met. They examined each other's looks with curiosity. Clem wished it were possible to get at the secrets of which Mrs. Byass was doubtless in possession; Bessie on her side was reserved, circumspect.

'Will he get over it?' the former inquired, with native brutality.

'I'm sure I don't know; I hope he may.'

The medical man arrived, and when he came downstairs again Joseph accompanied him. Clem, when she found that nothing definite could be learned, and that her husband had no intention of leaving, expressed her wish to walk round to Clerkenwell Close and see her mother. Joseph approved.

'You'd better have dinner there,' he said to her privately. 'We can't both of us come down on the Byasses.'

She nodded, and with a parting glance of hostile suspicion set forth. When she had crossed City Road, Clem's foot was on her native soil; she bore herself with conscious importance, hoping to meet some acquaintance who would be impressed by her attire and demeanour. Nothing of the kind happened, however. It was the dead hour of Sunday morning, midway in service-time, and long before the opening of public-houses. In the neighbourhood of those places of refreshment were occasionally found small groups of men and boys, standing with their hands in their pockets, dispirited, seldom caring even to smoke; they kicked their heels against the kerbstone and sighed for one o'clock. Clem went by them with a haughty balance of her head.

As she entered by the open front door and began to descend the kitchen steps, familiar sounds were audible. Mrs. Peckover's voice was raised in dispute with some one; it proved to be a quarrel with a female lodger respecting the sum of three-pence-farthing, alleged by the landlady to be owing on some account or other. The two women had already reached the point of calling each other liar and thief. Clem, having no acquaintance with the lodger, walked into the kitchen with an air of contemptuous indifference. The quarrel continued for another ten minutes—if the head of either had been suddenly cut off it would assuredly have gone on railing for an appreciable time—and Clem waited, sitting before the fire. At last the lodger had departed, and the last note of her virulence died away.

'And what do *you* want?' asked Mrs. Peckover, turning sharply upon her daughter.

'I suppose I can come to see you, can't I?'

'Come to see me! Likely! When did you come last? You're a ungrateful beast, that's what you are!'

'All right. Go a'ead! Anything else you'd like to call me?'

Mrs. Peckover was hurt by the completeness with which Clem had established her independence. To do the woman justice, she had been actuated, in her design of capturing Joseph Snowdon, at least as much by a wish to establish her daughter satisfactorily as by the ever-wakeful instinct which bade her seize whenever gain lay near her clutches. Clem was proving disloyal, had grown secretive. Mrs. Peckover did not look for any direct profit worth speaking of from the marriage she had brought about, but she did desire the joy of continuing to plot against Joseph with his wife. Moreover, she knew that Clem was a bungler, altogether lacking in astuteness, and her soul was pained by the thought of chances being missed. Her encounter with the lodger had wrought her up to the point at which she could discuss matters with Clem frankly. The two abused each other for a while, but Clem really desired to communicate her news, so that calmer dialogue presently ensued.

'Old Snowdon's had a stroke, if you'd like to know, and it's my belief he won't get over it.'

'Your belief! And what's your belief worth? Had a stroke, has he? Who told you?'

'I've just come from the 'ouse. Jo's stoppin' there.'

They discussed the situation in all its aspects, but Mrs. Peckover gave it clearly to be understood that, from her point of view, 'the game was spoilt.' As long as Joseph continued living under her roof she could in a measure direct the course of events; Clem had chosen to abet him in his desire for removal, and if ill came of it she had only herself to blame.

'I can look out for myself,' said Clem.

'Can you? I'm glad to hear it.'

And Mrs. Peckover sniffed the air, scornfully. The affectionate pair dined together, each imbibing a pint and a half of 'mild and bitter,' and Clem returned to Hanover Street. From Joseph she could derive no information as to the state of the patient.

'If you will stay here, where you can do no good,' he said, ' sit down and keep quiet.'

'Certainly I shall stay,' said his wife, 'because I know you want to get rid of me.'

Joseph left her in the sitting-room, and went upstairs again to keep his daughter company. Jane would not leave the bedside. To enter the room, after an interval elsewhere, wrung her feelings too painfully; better to keep her eyes fixed on the unmoving form, to overcome the dread by facing it.

She and her father seldom exchanged a word. The latter was experiencing human emotion, but at the same time he had no little anxiety regarding his material interests. It was ten days since he had learnt that there was no longer the least fear of a marriage between Jane and Sidney, seeing that Kirkwood was going to marry some one else—a piece of news which greatly astonished him, and confirmed him in his judgment that he had been on the wrong tack in judging Kirkwood's character. At the same time he had been privily informed by Scawthorne of an event which had ever since kept him very uneasy—Michael's withdrawal of his will from the hands of the solicitors. With what purpose this had been done Scawthorne could not conjecture; Mr. Percival had made no comment in his hearing. In all likelihood the will was now in this very room. Joseph surveyed every object again and again. He wondered whether Jane knew anything of the matter, but

not all his cynicism could persuade him that at the present
time her thoughts were taking the same direction as his own.

The day waned. Its sombre close was unspeakably mourn-
ful in this haunted chamber. Jane could not bear it; she hid
her face and wept.

When the doctor came again, at six o'clock, he whispered
to Joseph that the end was nearer than he had anticipated.
Near, indeed; less than ten minutes after the warning had
been given Michael ceased to breathe.

Jane knelt by the bed, convulsed with grief, unable to hear
the words her father addressed to her. He sat for five minutes,
then again spoke. She rose and replied.

'Will you come with us, Jane, or would rather stay with
Mrs. Byass?'

'I will stay, please, father.'

He hesitated, but the thought that rose was even for him
too ignoble to be entertained.

'As you please, my dear. Of course no one must enter
your rooms but Mrs. Byass. I must go now, but I shall look
in again to-night.'

'Yes, father.'

She spoke mechanically. He had to lead her from the
room, and, on quitting the house, left her all but unconscious
in Bessie's arms.

CHAPTER XXXVI

THE HEIR

'AND you mean to say,' cried Clem, when she was in the cab
with her husband speeding back to Burton Crescent—'you
mean to say as you've left them people to do what they like?'

'I suppose I know my own business,' replied Joseph, wishing to convey the very impression which in fact he did—that
he had the will in his pocket.

On reaching home he sat down at once and penned a letter
to Messrs. Percival & Peel, formally apprising them of what
had happened. Clem sat by and watched him. Having sealed
the envelope, he remarked:

'I'm going out for a couple of hours.'

'Then I shall go with you.'

'You'll do nothing of the kind. Why, what do you mean, you great gaping fool?' The agitation of his nerves made him break into unaccustomed violence. 'Do you suppose you're going to follow me everywhere for the next week? Are you afraid I shall run away? If I mean to do so, do you think you can stop me? You'll just wait here till I come back, which will be before ten o'clock. Do you hear?'

She looked at him fiercely, but his energy was too much for her, and perforce she let him go. As soon as he had left the house, she too sat down and indited a letter. It ran thus:

'DEAR MOTHER,—The old feller has gawn of it apened at jest after six e'clock if you want to now I shall come and sea you at ten 'clock to-morow moning and I beleve hes got the will but hes a beest and theers a game up you may take your hothe so I remain C. S.'

This document she took to the nearest pillar-post, then returned and sat brooding.

By the first hansom available Joseph was driven right across London to a certain dull street in Chelsea. Before dismissing the vehicle he knocked at the door of a lodging-house and made inquiry for Mr. Scawthorne. To his surprise and satisfaction, Mr. Scawthorne happened to be at home; so the cabman was paid, and Joseph went up to the second floor.

In his shabby little room Scawthorne sat smoking and reading. It was a season of impecuniosity with him, and his mood was anything but cheerful. He did not rise when his visitor entered.

'Well now, what do you think brings me here?' exclaimed Joseph, when he had carefully closed the door.

'Hanged if I know, but it doesn't seem to be particularly bad news.'

Indeed, Joseph had overcome his sensibilities by this time, and his aspect was one of joyous excitement. Seeing on the table a bottle of sherry, loosely corked, he pointed to it.

'If you don't mind, Scaw. I'm a bit upset, a bit flurried. Got another wine-glass?'

From the cupboard Scawthorne produced one and bade the visitor help himself. His face began to express curiosity. Joseph tilted the draught down his throat and showed satisfaction.

'That does me good. I've had a troublesome day. It ain't often my feelings are tried.'

'Well, what is it?'

'My boy, we are all mortal. I dare say you've heard that observation before; can you apply it to any particular case?'

Scawthorne was startled; he delayed a moment before speaking.

'You don't mean to say——'

'Exactly. Died a couple of hours ago, after lying insensible all day, poor old man! I've just written your people a formal announcement. Now, what do you think of that? If you don't mind, old fellow.'

He filled himself another glass, and tilted it off as before. Scawthorne had dropped his eyes to the ground, and stood in meditation.

'Now what about the will?' pursued Joseph.

'You haven't looked for it?' questioned his friend with an odd look.

'Thought it more decent to wait a few hours. The girl was about, you see, and what's more, my wife was. But have you heard anything since I saw you?'

'Why, yes. A trifle.'

'Out with it! What are you grinning about? Don't keep me on hot coals.'

'Well, it's amusing, and that's the fact. Take another glass of sherry; you'll need support.'

'Oh, I'm prepared for the worst. He's cut me out altogether, eh? That comes of me meddling with the girl's affairs—damnation! When there wasn't the least need, either.'

'A bad job. The fact is, Percival had a letter from him at midday yesterday. The senior had left the office; young Percival opened the letter, and spoke to me about it. Now, prepare yourself. The letter said that he had destroyed his former will, and would come to the office on Monday—that's to-morrow—to give instructions for a new one.'

Joseph stood and stared.

'To-morrow? Why, then, there's *no will at all?*'

'An admirable deduction. I congratulate you on your logic.'

Snowdon flung up his arms wildly, then began to leap about the room.

'Try another glass,' said Scawthorne. 'There's still a bottle in the cupboard; don't be afraid.'

'And you mean to tell me it's all mine?'

'The wine? You're very welcome.'

'Wine be damned! The money, my boy, the money! Scawthorne, I'm not a mean chap. As sure as you and me stand here, you shall have—you shall have a hundred pounds! I mean it; dash me, I mean it! You've been devilish useful to me; and what's more I haven't done with you yet. Do you twig, old boy?'

'You mean that a confidential agent in England, unsuspected, may be needed?'

'Shouldn't wonder if I do.'

'Can't be managed under double the money, my good sir,' observed Scawthorne, with unmistakable seriousness. 'Worth your while, I promise you. Have another glass. Fair commission. Think it over.'

'Look here! I shall have to make the girl an allowance.'

'There's the filter-works. Don't be stingy.'

Joseph was growing very red in the face. He drank glass after glass; he flung his arms about; he capered.

'Damn me if you shall call me that, Scaw! Two hundred it shall be. But what was the old cove up to? Why did he destroy the other will? What would the new one have been?'

'Can't answer either question, but it's probably as well for you that *to-morrow* never comes.'

'Now just see how things turn out!' went on the other, in the joy of his heart. 'All the thought and the trouble that I've gone through this last year, when I might have taken it easy and waited for chance to make me rich! Look at Kirkwood's business. There was you and me knocking our heads together and raising lumps on them, as you may say, to find out a plan of keeping him and Jane apart, when all the while we'd nothing to do but to look on and wait, if only we'd known. Now this is what I call the working of Providence, Scawthorne. Who's going to say after this, that things ain't as they should be? Everything's for the best, my boy; I see that clearly enough.'

'Decidedly,' assented Scawthorne, with a smile. 'The honest man is always rewarded in the long run. And that reminds me; I too have had a stroke of luck.'

He went on to relate that his position in the office of Percival & Peel was now nominally that of an articled clerk, and that in three years' time, if all went well, he would be received in the firm as junior partner.

'There's only one little project I am sorry to give up, in connection with your affairs, Snowdon. If it had happened that your daughter had inherited the money, why shouldn't I have had the honour of becoming your son-in-law?'

Joseph stared, then burst into hearty laughter.

'I tell you what,' he said, recovering himself, 'why should you give up that idea? She's as good a girl as you'll ever come across, I can tell you that, my boy. There's better-looking, but you won't find many as modest and good-hearted. Just make her acquaintance, and tell me if I've deceived you. And look here, Scawthorne; by George, I'll make a bargain with you! You say you'll be a partner in three years. Marry Jane when that day comes, and I'll give you a thousand for a wedding present. I mean it! What's more, I'll make my will on your marriage-day and leave everything I've got to you and her. There now!'

'What makes you so benevolent all at once?' inquired Scawthorne, blandly.

'Do you think I've got no fatherly feeling, man? Why, if it wasn't for my wife I'd ask nothing better than to settle down with Jane to keep house for me. She's a good girl, I tell you, and I wish her happiness.'

'And do you think I'm exactly the man to make her a model husband?'

'I don't see why not—now you're going to be a partner in a good business. Don't you think I'm ten times as honest a man to-day as I was yesterday? Poor devils can't afford to be what they'd wish, in the way of honesty and decent living.'

'True enough for once,' remarked the other, without irony.

'You think it over, Scaw. I'm a man of my word. You shall have your money as soon as things are straight; and if you can bring about that affair, I'll do all I said—so there's my hand on it. Say the word, and I'll make you acquainted with her before—before I take that little trip you know of, just for my health.'

'We'll speak of it again.'

Thereupon they parted. In the course of the following day Scawthorne's report received official confirmation. Joseph pondered deeply with himself whether he should tell his wife the truth or not; there were arguments for both courses. By Tuesday morning he had decided for the truth; that would give more piquancy to a pleasant little jest he had in mind.

At breakfast he informed her, as if casually, and it amused him to see that she did not believe him.

'You'll be anxious to tell your mother. Go and spend the day with her, but be back by five o'clock; then we'll talk things over. I have business with the lawyers again.'

Clem repaired to the Close. Late in the afternoon she and her husband again met at home, and by this time Joseph's elation had convinced her that he was telling the truth. Never had he been in such a suave humour; he seemed to wish to make up for his late severities. Seating himself near her, he began pleasantly :

'Well, things might have been worse, eh ? '

'I s'pose they might.'

'I haven't spoken to Jane yet. Time enough after the funeral. What shall we do for the poor girl, eh ? '

'How do I know ? '

'You won't grudge her a couple of pounds a week, or so, just to enable her to live with the Byasses, as she has been doing ? '

'I s'pose the money's your own to do what you like with.'

'Very kind of you to say so, my dear. But we're well-to-do people now, and we must be polite to each other. Where shall we take a house, Clem ? Would you like to be a bit out of town ? There's very nice places within easy reach of King's Cross, you know, on the Great Northern. A man I know lives at Potter's Bar,* and finds it very pleasant ; good air. Of course I must be within easy reach of business.'

She kept drawing her nails over a fold in her dress, making a scratchy sound.

'It happened just at the right time,' he continued. 'The business wants a little more capital put into it. I tell you what it is, Clem ; in a year or two we shall be coining money, old girl.'

'Shall you ? '

'Right enough. There's just one thing I'm a little anxious about ; you won't mind me mentioning it ? Do you think your mother'll expect us to do anything for her ? '

Clem regarded him with cautious scrutiny. He was acting well, and her profound distrust began to be mingled with irritating uncertainty.

'What can she expect ? If she does, she'll have to be disappointed, that's all.'

'I don't want to seem mean, you know. But then she isn't so badly off herself, is she?'

'I know nothing about it. You'd better ask her.'

And Clem grinned. Thereupon Joseph struck a facetious note, and for half an hour made himself very agreeable. Now for the first time, he said, could he feel really settled; life was smooth before him. They would have a comfortable home, the kind of place to which he could invite his friends; one or two excellent fellows he knew would bring their wives, and so Clem would have more society.

'Suppose you learn the piano, old girl? It wouldn't be amiss. By-the-by, I hope they'll turn you out some creditable mourning. You'll have to find a West End dressmaker.'

She listened, and from time to time smiled ambiguously. . . .

At noon of the next day Clem was walking on that part of the Thames Embankment which is between Waterloo Bridge and the Temple Pier. It was a mild morning, misty, but illuminated now and then with rays of sunlight, which gleamed dully upon the river and gave a yellowness to remote objects. At the distance of a dozen paces walked Bob Hewett; the two had had a difference in their conversation, and for some minutes kept thus apart, looking sullenly at the ground. Clem turned aside, and leaned her arms on the parapet. Presently her companion drew near and leaned in the same manner.

'What is it you want me to do?' he asked huskily. 'Just speak plain, can't you?'

'If you can't understand—if you *won't*, that is—it's no good speakin' plainer.'

'You said the other night as you didn't care about his money. If you think he means hookin' it, let him go, and good riddance.'

'That's a fool's way of talkin'. I'm not goin' to lose it all, if I can help it. There's a way of stoppin' him, and of gettin' the money too.'

They both stared down at the water; it was full tide, and the muddy surface looked almost solid.

'You wouldn't get it all,' were Bob's next words. 'I've been asking about that.'

'You have? Who did you ask?'

'Oh, a feller you don't know. You'd only have a third part of it, and the girl 'ud get the rest.'

'What do you call a third part?'

So complete was her stupidity, that Bob had to make a laborious explanation of this mathematical term. She could have understood what was meant by a half or a quarter, but the unfamiliar 'third' conveyed no distinct meaning.

'I don't care,' she said at length. 'That 'ud be enough.'

'Clem—you'd better leave this job alone. You'd better, I warn you.'

'I shan't.'

Another long silence. A steamboat drew up to the Temple Pier, and a yellow shaft of sunlight fell softly upon its track in the water.

'What do you want me to do?' Bob recommenced. '*How?*'

Their eyes met, and in the woman's gaze he found a horrible fascination, a devilish allurement to that which his soul shrank from. She lowered her voice.

'There's lots of ways. It 'ud be easy to make it seem as somebody did it just to rob him. He's always out late at night.'

His face was much the colour of the muddy water yellowed by that shaft of sunlight. His lips quivered. 'I dursn't, Clem. I tell you plain, I dursn't.'

'Coward!' she snarled at him, savagely. 'Coward! All right, Mr. Bob. You go your way, and I'll go mine.'

'Listen here, Clem,' he gasped out, laying his hand on her arm. 'I'll think about it. I won't say no. Give me a day to think about it.'

'Oh, we know what your thinkin' means.'

They talked for some time longer, and before they parted Bob had given a promise to do more than think.

The long, slouching strides with which he went up from the Embankment to the Strand gave him the appearance of a man partly overcome with drink. For hours he walked about the City, in complete oblivion of everything external. Only when the lights began to shine from shop-windows did he consciously turn to his own district. It was raining now. The splashes of cool moisture made him aware how feverishly hot his face was.

When he got among the familiar streets he went slinkingly, hurrying round corners, avoiding glances. Almost at a run he turned into Merlin Place, and he burst into his room as though he were pursued.

Pennyloaf had now but one child to look after, a girl of

two years, a feeble thing. Her own state was wretched; professedly recovered from illness, she felt so weak, so lowspirited, that the greater part of her day was spent in crying. The least exertion was too much for her; but for frequent visits from Jane Snowdon she must have perished for very lack of wholesome food. She was crying when startled by her husband's entrance, and though she did her best to hide the signs of it, Bob saw.

'When are you going to stop that?' he shouted.

She shrank away, looking at him with fear in her red eyes.

'Stop your snivelling, and get me some tea!'

It was only of late that Pennyloaf had come to regard him with fear. His old indifference and occasional brutality of language had made her life a misery, but she had never looked for his return home with anything but anxious longing. Now the anticipation was mingled with dread. He not only had no care for her, not only showed that he felt her a burden upon him; his disposition now was one of hatred, and the kind of hatred which sooner or later breaks out in ferocity. Bob would not have come to this pass—at all events not so soon—if he had been left to the dictates of his own nature; he was infected by the savagery of the woman who had taken possession of him. Her lust of cruelty crept upon him like a disease, the progress of which was hastened by all the circumstances of his disorderly life. The man was conscious of his degradation; he knew how he had fallen ever since he began criminal practices; he knew the increasing hopelessness of his resolves to have done with dangers and recover his peace of mind. The loss of his daily work, in consequence of irregularity, was the last thing needed to complete his ruin. He did not even try to get new employment, feeling that such a show of honest purpose was useless. Corruption was eating to his heart; from every interview with Clem he came away a feebler and a baser being. And upon the unresisting creature who shared his home he had begun to expend the fury of his self-condemnation.

He hated her because Clem bade him do so. He hated her because her suffering rebuked him, because he must needs be at the cost of keeping her alive, because he was bound to her.

As she moved painfully about the room he watched her with cruel, dangerous eyes. There was a thought tormenting his brain, a terrifying thought he had pledged himself not to dismiss, and it seemed to exasperate him against Pennyloaf. He had horrible impulses, twitches along his muscles; every second the restraint of keeping in one position grew more unendurable, yet he feared to move.

Pennyloaf had the ill-luck to drop a saucer, and it broke on the floor. In the same instant he leapt up and sprang on her, seized her brutally by the shoulders and flung her with all his force against the nearest wall. At her scream the child set up a shrill cry, and this increased his rage. With his clenched fist he dealt blow after blow at the half-prostrate woman, speaking no word, but uttering a strange sound, such as might come from some infuriate animal. Pennyloaf still screamed, till at length the door was thrown open and their neighbour, Mrs. Griffin, showed herself.

' Well, I never! ' she cried, wrathfully, rushing upon Bob. 'Now you just stop that, young man! I thought it 'ud be comin' to this before long. I saw you was goin' that way.'

The mildness of her expressions was partly a personal characteristic, partly due to Mrs. Griffin's very large experience of such scenes as this. Indignant she might be, but the situation could not move her to any unwonted force of utterance. Enough that Bob drew back as soon as he was bidden, and seemed from his silence to be half-ashamed of himself.

Pennyloaf let herself lie at full length on the floor, her hands clutched protectingly about her head; she sobbed in a quick, terrified way, and appeared powerless to stop, even when Mrs. Griffin tried to raise her.

' What's he been a-usin' you like this for? ' the woman kept asking. ' There, there now! He shan't hit you no more, he shan't! '

Whilst she spoke Bob turned away and went from the room.

From Merlin Place he struck off into Pentonville and walked towards King's Cross at his utmost speed. Not that he had any object in hastening, but a frenzy goaded him along, faster, faster, till the sweat poured from him. From King's Cross, northwards; out to Holloway, to Hornsey. A light rain was ceaselessly falling; at one time he took off his hat and walked some distance bareheaded, because it was a pleasure to feel the rain trickle over him. From Hornsey by a great circuit he made back for Islington. Here he went into a public-house, to quench the thirst that had grown un-

bearable. He had but a shilling in his pocket, and in bringing it out he was reminded of the necessity of getting more
money. He was to have met Jack Bartley to-night, long
before this hour.

He took the direction for Smithfield, and soon reached
the alley near Bartholomew's Hospital where Bartley dwelt.
As he entered the street he saw a small crowd gathered about
a public-house door; he hurried nearer, and found that the
object of interest was a man in the clutch of two others. The
latter, he perceived at a glance, were police-officers in plain
clothes; the man arrested was—Jack Bartley himself.

Jack was beside himself with terror; he had only that
moment been brought out of the bar, and was pleading shrilly
in an agony of cowardice.

'It ain't me as made 'em! I never made one in my life!
I'll tell you who it is—I'll tell you where to find him—it's
Bob Hewett as lives in Merlin Place! You've took the wrong
man. It ain't me as made 'em! I'll tell you the whole truth,
or may I never speak another word! It's Bob Hewett made
'em all—he lives in Merlin Place, Clerkenwell. I'll tell
you——'

Thus far had Bob heard before he recovered sufficiently
from the shock to move a limb. The officers were urging their
prisoner forward, grinning and nodding to each other, whilst
several voices from the crowd shouted abusively at the pol-
troon whose first instinct was to betray his associate. Bob
turned his face away and walked on. He did not dare to run,
yet the noises behind him kept his heart leaping with dread.
A few paces and he was out of the alley. Even yet he durst
not run. He had turned in the unlucky direction; the crowd
was still following. For five minutes he had to keep advancing, then at last he was able to move off at right angles.
The crowd passed the end of the street.

Only then did complete panic get possession of him. With
a bound forward like that of a stricken animal he started
in blind flight. He came to a crossing, and rushed upon it
regardless of the traffic, Before he could gain the farther
pavement the shaft of a cart struck him on the breast and
threw him down. The vehicle was going at a slow pace, and
could be stopped almost immediately; he was not touched by
the wheel. A man helped him to his feet and inquired if he
were hurt.

'Hurt? No, no; it's all right.'

To the surprise of those who had witnessed the accident, he walked quickly on, scarcely feeling any pain. But in a few minutes there came a sense of nausea and a warm rush in his throat; he staggered against the wall and vomited a quantity of blood. Again he was surrounded by sympathising people; again he made himself free of them and hastened on. But by now he suffered acutely; he could not run, so great was the pain it cost him when he began to breathe quickly. His mouth was full of blood again.

Where could he find a hiding-place? The hunters were after him, and, however great his suffering, he must go through it in secrecy. But in what house could he take refuge? He had not money enough to pay for a lodging.

He looked about him; tried to collect his thoughts. By this time the police would have visited Merlin Place; they would be waiting there to trap him. He was tempted towards Farringdon Road Buildings; surely his father would not betray him, and he was in such dire need of kindly help. But it would not be safe; the police would search there.

Shooter's Gardens? There was the room where lived Pennyloaf's drunken mother and her brother. They would not give him up. He could think of no other refuge, at all events, and must go there if he would not drop in the street.

CHAPTER XXXVII

MAD JACK'S DREAM

IT was not much more than a quarter of an hour's walk, but pain and fear made the distance seem long; he went out of his way, too, for the sake of avoiding places that were too well lighted. The chief occupation of his thoughts was in conjecturing what could have led to Bartley's arrest. Had the fellow been such a fool as to attempt passing a bad coin when he carried others of the same kind in his pocket? Or had the arrest of some other 'pal' in some way thrown suspicion on Jack? Be it as it might, the game was up. With the usual wisdom which comes too late, Bob asked himself how he could ever have put trust in Bartley, whom he knew to be as mean-spirited a cur as breathed. On the chance of making things easier for himself, Jack would betray every secret in his possession. What hope was there of escaping capture, even if a hiding-place could be found for a day or two ? If he had his hand on Jack Bartley's gizzard !

Afraid to appear afraid, in dread lest his muddy clothing should attract observation, he kept, as often as possible, the middle of the road, and with relief saw at length the narrow archway, with its descending steps, which was one entrance to Shooter's Gardens. As usual, two or three loafers were hanging about here, exchanging blasphemies and filthy vocables, but, even if they recognised him, there was not much fear of their giving assistance to the police. With head bent he slouched past them, unchallenged. At the bottom of the steps, where he was in all but utter darkness, his foot slipped on garbage of some kind, and with a groan he fell on his side.

'Let him that thinketh he standeth take heed lest he fall,' cried a high-pitched voice from close by.

Bob knew that the speaker was the man notorious in this locality as Mad Jack. Raising himself with difficulty, he looked round and saw a shape crouching in the corner.

'What is the principal thing?' continued the crazy voice. 'Wisdom is the principal thing.'

And upon that followed a long speech which to Bob sounded as gibberish, but which was in truth tolerably good French, a language Mad Jack was fond of using, though he never made known how he had acquired it.

Bob stumbled on, and quickly came to the house where he hoped to find a refuge. The door was, of course, open; he went in and groped his way up the staircase. A knock at the door of the room which he believed to be still tenanted by Mrs. Candy and her son brought no reply. He turned the handle, but found that the door was locked.

It was not late, only about ten o'clock. Stephen Candy could not, of course, be back yet from his work, and the woman was probably drinking somewhere. But he must make sure that they still lived here. Going down to the floor below, he knocked at the room occupied by the Hope family, and Mrs. Hope, opening the door a few inches, asked his business.

'Does Mrs. Candy still live upstairs?' he inquired in a feigned voice, and standing back in the darkness.

'For all I know.'

And the door closed sharply. He had no choice but to wait and see if either of his acquaintances returned. For a few minutes he sat on the staircase, but as at any moment

some one might stumble over him, he went down to the back-
door, which was open, like that in front, and passed out into
the stone-paved yard. Here he seated himself on the ground,
leaning against a corner of the wall. He was suffering much
from his injury, but could at all events feel secure from the
hunters.

The stones were wet, and rain fell upon him. As he
looked up at the lighted windows in the back of the house, he
thought of Pennyloaf, who by this time most likely knew his
danger. Would she be glad of it, feeling herself revenged?
His experience of her did not encourage him to believe that.
To all his ill-treatment she had never answered with anything
but tears and submission. He found himself wishing she were
near, to be helpful to him in his suffering.

Clem could not learn immediately what had come to pass.
Finding he did not keep his appointment for the day after
to-morrow, she would conclude that he had drawn back. But
perhaps Jack Bartley's case would be in the newspapers on
that day, and his own name might appear in the evidence
before the magistrates; if Clem learnt the truth in that way,
she would be not a little surprised. He had never hinted to
her the means by which he had been obtaining money.

Voices began to sound from the passage within the house;
several young fellows, one or other of whom probably lived
here, had entered to be out of the rain. One voice, very loud
and brutal, Bob quickly recognised; it was that of Ned Higgs,
the ruffian with whom Bartley's wife had taken up. The
conversation was very easy to overhear; it contained no reference to the 'copping' of Jack.

' Fag ends!' this and that voice kept crying.

Bob understood. One of the noble company had been fortunate enough to pig up the end of a cigar somewhere, and it
was the rule among them that he who called out 'Fag-ends!'
established a claim for a few whiffs. In this way the delicacy
was passing from mouth to mouth. That the game should
end in quarrel was quite in order, and sure enough, before
very long, Ned Higgs was roaring his defiances to a companion who had seized the bit of tobacco unjustly.

' I 'ollered fag-end after Snuffy Bill!'

' You're a —— liar! I did!'

' You! You're a —— —— ——! I'll —— your —— in
arf a —— second!'

Then came the sound of a scuffle, the thud of blows, the

wild-beast bellowing of infuriate voices. Above all could be heard the roar of Ned Higgs. A rush, and it was plain that the combatants had gone out into the alley to have more room. For a quarter of an hour the yells from their drink-sodden throats echoed among the buildings. Quietness was probably caused by the interference of police; knowing that, Bob shrank together in his lurking-place.

When all had been still for some time he resolved to go upstairs again and try the door, for his breathing grew more and more painful, and there was a whirling in his head which made him fear that he might become insensible. To rise was more difficult than he had imagined; his head overweighted him, all but caused him to plunge forward; he groped this way and that with his hands, seeking vainly for something to cling to on the whitewashed wall. In his depth of utter misery he gave way and sobbed several times. Then once more he had the warm taste of blood in his mouth. Terror-stricken, he staggered into the house.

This time a voice answered to his knock. He opened the door.

The room contained no article of furniture. In one corner lay some rags, and on the mantel-piece stood a tin teapot, two cups, and a plate. There was no fire, but a few pieces of wood lay near the hearth, and at the bottom of the open cupboard remained a very small supply of coals. A candle made fast in the neck of a bottle was the source of light.

On the floor was sitting, or lying, an animated object, indescribable; Bob knew it for Mrs. Candy. Her eyes looked up at him apprehensively.

'I want to stay the night over, if you'll let me.' he said, when he had closed the door. 'I've got to hide away; nobody mustn't know as I'm here.'

'You're welcome,' the woman replied, in a voice which was horrible to hear.

Then she paid no more attention to him, but leaned her head upon her hand and began a regular moaning, as if she suffered some dull, persistent pain.

Bob crept up to the wall and let himself sink there. He could not reflect for more than a minute or two continuously; his brain then became a mere confused whirl. In one of the intervals of his perfect consciousness he asked Mrs. Candy if Stephen would come here to-night. She did not heed him till he had twice repeated the question, and then she started and looked at him in wild fear.

'Will Stephen be coming?'

'Stephen? Yes, yes. I shouldn't wonder.'

She seemed to fall asleep as soon as she had spoken; her head dropped heavily on the boards.

Not long after midnight the potman made his appearance. As always, on returning from his sixteen-hour day of work, he was all but insensible with fatigue. Entering the room, he turned his white face with an expression of stupid wonderment to the corner in which Bob lay. The latter raised himself to a sitting posture.

'That you, Bob Hewett?'

'I want to stop here over the night,' replied the other, speaking with difficulty. 'I can't go home. There's something up.'

'With Pennyloaf?'

'No. I've got to hide away. And I'm feeling bad—awful bad. Have you got anything to drink?'

Stephen, having listened with a face of a somnambulist, went to the mantel-piece and looked into the teapot. It was empty.

'You can go to the tap in the yard,' he said.

'I couldn't get so far. Oh, I feel bad!'

'I'll fetch you some water.'

A good-hearted animal, this poor Stephen; a very tolerable human being, had he had fair-play. He would not abandon his wretched mother, though to continue living with her meant hunger and cold and yet worse evils. For himself, his life was supported chiefly on the three pints of liquor which he was allowed every day. His arms and legs were those of a living skeleton; his poor idiotic face was made yet more repulsive by disease. Yet you could have seen that he was the brother of Pennyloaf; there was Pennyloaf's submissive beast-of-burden look in his eyes, and his voice had something that reminded one of hers.

'The coppers after you?' he whispered, stooping down to Bob with the teacup he had filled with water.

Bob nodded, then drained the cup eagerly.

'I got knocked down by a cab or something,' he added. 'It hit me just here. I may feel better when I've rested a bit. 'Haven't you got no furniture left?'

'They took it last Saturday was a week. Took it for rent.

I thought we didn't owe nothing, but mother told me she'd paid when she hadn't. I got leave to stop, when I showed 'em as I could pay in future; but they wouldn't trust me to make up them three weeks. They took the furniture. It's 'ard, I call it. I asked my guvnor if it was law for them to take mother's bed-things, an' he said yes it was. When it's for rent they can take everything, even to your beddin' an' tools.'

Yes; they can take everything. How foolish of Stephen Candy and his tribe not to be born of the class of landlords! The inconvenience of having no foothold on the earth's surface is so manifest.

'I couldn't say nothing to her,' he continued, nodding towards the prostrate woman. 'She was sorry for it, an' you can't ask no more. It was my fault for trustin' her with the money to pay, but I get a bit careless now an' then, an' forgot. You do look bad, Bob, an' there's no mistake. Would you feel better if I lighted a bit o' fire?'

'Yes; I feel cold. I was hot just now.'

'You needn't be afraid o' the coals. Mother goes round the streets after the coal-carts, an' you wouldn't believe what a lot she picks up some days. You see, we're neither of us in the 'ouse very often; we don't burn much.'

He lit a fire, and Bob dragged himself near to it. In the meantime the quietness of the house was suffering a disturbance familiar to its denizens. Mr. Hope—you remember Mr. Hope?—had just returned from an evening at the public-house, and was bent on sustaining his reputation for unmatched vigour of language. He was quarrelling with his wife and daughters; their high notes of vituperation mingled in the most effective way with his manly thunder. To hear Mr. Hope's expressions, a stranger would have imagined him on the very point of savagely murdering all his family.

Another voice became audible. It was that of Ned Higgs, who had opened his door to bellow curses at the disturbers of his rest.

'They'll be wakin' mother,' said Stephen. 'There, I knew they would.'

Mrs. Candy stirred, and, after a few vain efforts to raise herself, started up suddenly. She fixed her eyes on the fire, which was just beginning to blaze, and uttered a dreadful cry, a shriek of mad terror.

'O God!' groaned her son. 'I hope it ain't goin' to be

one of her bad nights. Mother, mother! what's wrong with you? See, come to the fire an' warm yourself, mother.'

She repeated the cry two or three times, but with less violence; then, as though exhausted, she fell face downwards, her arms folded about her head. The moaning which Bob had heard earlier in the evening recommenced.

Happily, it was not to be one of her bad nights. Fits of the horrors only came upon her twice before morning. Towards one o'clock Stephen had sunk into a sleep which scarcely any conceivable uproar could have broken; he lay with his head on his right arm, his legs stretched out at full length; his breathing was light. Bob was much later in getting rest. As often as he slumbered for an instant, the terrible image of his fear rose manifest before him; he saw himself in the clutch of his hunters, just like Jack Bartley, and woke to lie quivering. Must not that be the end of it, sooner or later? Might he not as well give himself up to-morrow? But the thought of punishment such as his crime receives was unendurable. It haunted him in nightmare when sheer exhaustion had at length weighed down his eyelids.

Long before daybreak he was conscious again, tormented with thirst and his head aching woefully. Someone had risen in the room above, and was tramping about in heavy boots. The noise seemed to disturb Mrs. Candy; she cried out in her sleep. In a few minutes the early riser came forth and began to descend the stairs; he was going to his work.

A little while, and in the court below a voice shouted, 'Bill! Bill!' Another worker being called, doubtless.

At seven o'clock Stephen roused himself. He took a piece of soap from a shelf of the cupboard, threw a dirty rag over his arm, and went down to wash at the tap in the yard. Only on returning did he address Bob.

'Feelin' any better?'

'I think so. But I'm very bad.'

'Are you goin' to stay here?'

'I don't know.'

'Got any money?'

'Yes. Ninepence. Could you get me something to drink?'

Stephen took twopence, went out, and speedily returned with a large mug of coffee; from his pocket he brought forth a lump of cake, which had cost a halfpenny. This, he thought, might tempt a sick appetite. His own breakfast he would take at the coffee-shop.

'Mother 'll get you anything else you want,' he said. 'She knows herself generally first thing in the morning. Let her take back the mug; I had to leave threepence on it.'

So Stephen also went forth to his labour—in this case, it may surely be said, the curse of curses. . . .*

At this hour Pennyloaf bestirred herself after a night of weeping. Last evening the police had visited her room, and had searched it thoroughly. The revelation amazed her; she would not believe the charge that was made against her husband. She became angry with Mrs. Griffin when that practical woman said she was not at all surprised. Utterly gone was her resentment of Bob's latest cruelty. His failure to return home seemed to prove that he had been arrested, and she could think of nothing but the punishment that awaited him.

'It's penal servitude,' remarked Mrs. Griffin, frankly. 'Five, or p'r'aps ten years. I've heard of 'em gettin' sent for life.'

Pennyloaf would not believe in the possibility of this befalling her husband. It was too cruel. There would be some pity, some mercy. She had a confused notion of witnesses being called to give a man a good character, and strengthened herself in the thought of what she would say, under such circumstances on Bob's behalf. 'He's been a good 'usband,' she kept repeating to Mrs. Griffin, and to the other neighbours who crowded to indulge their curiosity. 'There's nobody can say as he ain't been a good 'usband; it's a lie if they do.'

By eight o'clock she was at the police-station. With fear she entered the ugly doorway and approached a policeman who stood in the ante-room. When she had made her inquiry, the man referred her to the inspector. She was asked many questions, but to her own received no definite reply; she had better look in again the next morning.

'It's my belief they ain't got him,' said Mrs. Griffin. 'He's had a warnin' from his pals.'

Pennyloaf would dearly have liked to communicate with Jane Snowdon, but shame prevented her. All day she stood by the house door, looking eagerly now this way, now that, with an unreasoning hope that Bob might show himself. She tried to believe that he was only keeping away because of his behaviour to her the night before; it was the first time he had laid hand upon her, and he felt ashamed of himself. He would

come back, and this charge against him would be proved false;
Pennyloaf could not distinguish between her desire that something might happen and the probability of its doing so.

But darkness fell upon the streets, and her watch was kept
in rain. She dreaded the thought of passing another night in
uncertainty. Long ago her tears had dried up; she had a
parched throat and trembling, feverish hands. Between seven
and eight o'clock she went to Mrs. Griffin and begged her to
take care of the child for a little while.

'I'm goin' to see if I can hear anything about him. Somebody may know where he is.'

And first of all she directed her steps to Shooter's Gardens.
It was very unlikely that her mother could be of any use, but
she would seek there. Afterwards she must go to Farringdon
Road Buildings, though never yet had she presented herself
to Bob's father.

You remember that the Gardens had an offshoot, which
was known simply as The Court. In this blind alley there
stood throughout the day a row of baked-potato ovens, ten or
a dozen of them, chained together, the property of a local
capitalist who let them severally to men engaged in this business. At seven o'clock of an evening fires were wont to be
lighted under each of these baking-machines, preparatory to
their being wheeled away, each to its customary street-corner.
Now the lighting of fires entails the creation of smoke, and
whilst these ten or twelve ovens were getting ready to bake
potatoes the Court was in a condition not easily described. A
single lamp existed for the purpose of giving light to the alley,
and at no time did this serve much more than to make darkness visible; at present the blind man would have fared as
well in that retreat as he who had eyes, and the marvel was
how those who lived there escaped suffocation. In the Gardens themselves volumes of dense smoke every now and then
came driven along by the cold gusts; the air had a stifling
smell and a bitter taste.

Pennyloaf found nothing remarkable in this phenomenon;
it is hard to say what would have struck her as worthy of indignant comment in her world of little ease. But near the
entrance to the Court, dimly discernible amid sagging fumes,
was a cluster of people, and as everything of that kind just now
excited her apprehensions, she drew near to see what was
happening. The gathering was around Mad Jack; he looked
more than usually wild, and with one hand raised above his

head was on the point of relating a vision he had had the
night before.

'Don't laugh! Don't any of you laugh; for as sure as I
live it was an angel stood in the room and spoke to me.
There was a light such as none of you ever saw, and the angel
stood in the midst of it. And he said to me: "Listen, whilst
I reveal to you the truth, that you may know where you are
and what you are; and this is done for a great purpose."
And I fell down on my knees, but never a word could I have
spoken. Then the angel said: "You are passing through a
state of punishment. You, and all the poor among whom
you live; all those who are in suffering of body and darkness
of mind, were once rich people, with every blessing the world
can bestow, with every opportunity of happiness in yourselves
and of making others happy. Because you made an ill use of
your wealth, because you were selfish and hard-hearted and
oppressive and sinful in every kind of indulgence—therefore
after death you received the reward of wickedness. This life
you are now leading is that of the damned; this place to
which you are confined is Hell! There is no escape for you.
From poor you shall become poorer; the older you grow the
lower shall you sink in want and misery; at the end there is
waiting for you, one and all, a death in abandonment and
despair. This is Hell—Hell—Hell!"'

His voice had risen in pitch, and the last cry was so terrifying that Pennyloaf fled to be out of hearing. She reached
the house to which her visit was, and in the dark passage
leaned for a moment against the wall, trembling all over.
Then she began to ascend the stairs. At Mrs. Candy's door
she knocked gently. There was at first no answer, but when
she had knocked again, a strange voice that she did not recognise asked 'Who's that?' It seemed to come from low
down, as if the speaker were lying on the floor.

'It's me,' she replied, again trembling, she knew not with
what fear. 'Mrs. Hewett—Pennyloaf.'

'Are you alone?'

She bent down, listening eagerly.

'Who's that speakin'?'

'Are you alone?'

Strange; the voice was again different, very feeble, a thick
whisper.

'Yes, there's nobody else. Can I come in?'

There was a shuffling sound, then the key turned in the

lock. Pennyloaf entered, and found herself in darkness. She shrank back.

'Who's there? Is it you, mother? Is it you, Stephen?'

Some one touched her, at the same time shutting the door; and the voice whispered:

'Penny—it's me—Bob.'

She uttered a cry, stretching out her hands. A head was leaning against her, and she bent down to lay hers against it.

'O Bob! What are you doin' here? Why are you in the dark? What's the matter, Bob?'

'I've had an accident, Penny. I feel awful bad. Your mother's gone out to buy a candle. Have they been coming after me?'

'Yes, yes. But I didn't know you was here. I came to ask if they knew where you was. O Bob! what's happened to you? Why are you lyin' there, Bob?'

She had folded her arms about him, and held his face to hers, sobbing, kissing him.

'It's all up,' he gasped. 'I've been getting worse all day. You'll have to fetch the parish doctor. They'll have me, but I can't help it. I feel as if I was going.'

'They shan't take you, Bob. Oh no, they shan't. The doctor needn't know who you are.'

'It was a cab knocked me down, when I was running. I'm awful bad, Penny. You'll do something for me, won't you?'

'Oh, why didn't you send mother for me?'

The door opened. It was Mrs. Candy who entered. She slammed the door, turned the key, and exclaimed in a low voice of alarm:

'Bob, there's the p'lice downstairs! They come just this minute. There's one gone to the back-door, and there's one talkin' to Mrs. Hope at the front.'

'Then they've followed Pennyloaf,' he replied, in a tone of despair. 'They've followed Pennyloaf.'

It was the truth. She had been watched all day, and was now tracked to Shooter's Gardens, to this house. Mrs. Candy struck a match, and for an instant illuminated the wretched room; she looked at the two, and they at length saw each other's faces. Then the little flame was extinguished, and a red spot marked the place where the remnant of the match lay.

'Shall I light the candle?' the woman asked in a whisper.

Neither replied, for there was a heavy foot on the stairs. It came nearer. A hand tried the door, then knocked loudly.

'Mrs. Candy,' cried a stranger.

The three crouched together, terror-stricken, holding their breath. Pennyloaf pressed her husband in an agonised embrace.

'Mrs. Candy, you're wanted on business. Open the door. If you don't open, we shall force it.'

'No—no!' Pennyloaf whispered in her mother's ear. 'They shan't come in! Don't stir.'

'Are you going to open the door?'

It was a different speaker—brief, stern. Ten seconds, and there came a tremendous crash; the crazy door, the whole wall, quivered and cracked and groaned. The crash was repeated, and effectually; with a sound of ripping wood the door flew open and a light streamed into the room.

Useless, Pennyloaf, useless. That fierce kick, making ruin of your rotten barrier, is dealt with the whole force of Law, of Society; you might as well think of resisting death when your hour shall come.

'There he is,' observed one of the men, calmly. 'Hollo! what's up?'

'You can't take him away!' Pennyloaf cried, falling down again by Bob and clinging to him. 'He's ill. You can't take him like this!'

'Ill, is he? Then the sooner our doctor sees him the better. Up you get, my man!'

But there are some things that even Law and Society cannot command. Bob lay insensible. Shamming? Well, no; it seemed not. Send for a stretcher, quickly.

No great delay. Pennyloaf sat in mute anguish, Bob's head on her lap. On the staircase was a crowd of people, talking, shouting, whistling; presently they were cleared away by a new arrival of officials. Room for Law and Society!

The stretcher arrived; the senseless body was carried down and laid upon it—a policeman at each end, and, close clinging, Pennyloaf.

Above the noise of the crowd rose a shrill, wild voice, chanting:

'All ye works of the Lord, bless ye the Lord; praise Him and magnify Him for ever!'

CHAPTER XXXVIII

JOSEPH TRANSACTS MUCH BUSINESS

AMID the anguish of heart and nerve which she had to endure whilst her grandfather lay dead in the house, Jane found and clung to one thought of consolation. He had not closed his eyes in the bitterness of disappointment. The end might have come on that miserable day when her weakness threatened the defeat of all his hopes, and how could she then have borne it? True or not, it would have seemed to her that she had killed him; she could not have looked on his face, and all the rest of her life would have been remorsefully shadowed. Now the dead features were unreproachful; nay, when she overcame her childish tremors and gazed calmly, it was easy to imagine that he smiled. Death itself had come without pain. An old man, weary after his long journeys, after his many griefs and the noble striving of his thought, surely he rested well.

During the last days he had been more affectionate with her than was his habit; she remembered it with gratitude. Words of endearment seldom came to his lips, but since the reconciliation he had more than once spoken tenderly. Doubtless he was anxious to assure her that she had again all his confidence. Strengthening herself in that reflection, she strove to put everything out of her mind save the duty which must henceforth direct her. Happily, there could be no more strife with the promptings of her weaker self; circumstances left but one path open before her; and that, however difficult, the one she desired to tread. Henceforth memory must dwell on one thing only in the past, her rescue by Michael Snowdon, her nurture under his care. Though he could no longer speak, the recollection of his words must be her unfailing impulse. In her his spirit must survive, his benevolence still be operative.

At her wish, her father acquainted Sidney Kirkwood with what had happened. Sidney did not visit her, but he wrote a letter, which, having read it many times, she put carefully away to be a resource if ever her heart failed. Mr. Percival came to the house on Monday, in the company of Joseph Snowdon; he was sympathetic, but made no direct reference to her position either now or in the future. Whilst he and her father transacted matters of business in the upper rooms,

Jane remained downstairs with Mrs. Byass. Before quitting the house he asked her if she had had any communication with Miss Lant yet.

'I ought to write and tell her,' replied Jane.

'I will do so for you,' said the lawyer, kindly.

And on taking leave he held her hand for a moment, looking compassionately into her pale face.

On Thursday morning there arrived a letter from Miss Lant, who happened to be out of town and grieved that she could not return in time for the funeral, which would be that day. There was nothing about the future, excepting a promise that the writer would come very shortly.

Michael was buried at Abney Park Cemetery;* no ray of sunlight fell upon his open grave, but the weather was mild, and among the budded trees passed a breath which was the promise of spring. Joseph Snowdon and the Byasses were Jane's only companions in the mourning-carriage; but at the cemetery they were joined by Sidney Kirkwood. Jane saw him and felt the pressure of his hand, but she could neither speak nor understand anything that was said to her.

On Friday morning, before she had made a show of eating the breakfast Bessie Byass prepared for her, a visitor arrived.

'She says her name's Mrs. Griffin,' said Bessie, 'and she has something very important to tell you. Do you feel you can see her?'

'Mrs. Griffin? Oh, I remember; she lives in the same house as Pennyloaf. Yes: let her come in.'

The woman was introduced to the Byasses' parlour, which Bessie thought more cheerful for Jane just now then the room upstairs.

'Have you heard anything of what's been goin on with the Hewetts, Miss?' she began.

'No, I haven't been able to go out this week. I've had trouble at home.'

'I see at once as you was in mournin', Miss, an' I'm sorry for it. You're lookin' nothing like yourself. I don't know whether it's right to upset you with other people's bothers, but there's that poor Mrs. Hewett in such a state, and I said as I'd run round, 'cause she seems to think there's nobody else can come to her help as you can. I always knew as something o' this kind 'ud be 'appenin'.'

'But what is it? What has happened?'

Jane felt her energies revive at this appeal for help. It was the best thing that could have befallen, now that she was wearily despondent after yesterday's suffering.

'Her 'usband's dead, Miss.'

'Dead?'

'But that ain't the worst of it. He was took by the perlice last night, which they wanted him for makin' bad money. I always have said as it's a cruel thing that: 'cause how can you tell who gets the bad coin, an' it may be some pore person as can't afford to lose not a 'apenny. But that's what he's been up to, an' this long time, as it appears.'

In her dialect, which requires so many words for the narration of a simple story, Mrs. Griffin told what she knew concerning Bob Hewett's accident and capture; his death had taken place early this morning, and Pennyloaf was all but crazy with grief. To Jane these things sounded so extraordinary that for some time she could scarcely put a question, but sat in dismay, listening to the woman's prolix description of all that had come to pass since Wednesday evening. At length she called for Mrs. Byass, for whose benefit the story was repeated.

'I'm sure you oughtn't to go there to-day,' was Bessie's opinion. 'You've quite enough trouble of your own, my dear.'

'And that's just what I was a-sayin', mum,' assented Mrs. Griffin, who had won Bessie's highest opinion by her free use of respectful forms of address. 'I never saw no one look iller, as you may say, than the young lady.'

'Yes, yes, I will go,' said Jane, rising. 'My trouble's nothing to hers. Oh, I shall go at once.'

'But remember your father's coming at half-past nine,' urged Bessie, 'and he said he wanted to speak to you particular.'

'What is the time now? A quarter to nine. I can be back by half-past, I think, and then I can go again. Father wouldn't mind waiting a few minutes. I must go at once, Mrs. Byass.'

She would hear no objection, and speedily left the house in Mrs. Griffin's company.

At half-past nine, punctually, Mr. Snowdon's double knock sounded at the door. Joseph looked more respectable than ever in his black frock-coat and silk hat with the deep band. His bow to Mrs. Byass was solemn, but gallant; he pressed her fingers like a clergyman paying a visit of consolation, and in a subdued voice made affectionate inquiry after his daughter.

'She has slept, I hope, poor child?'

Bessie took him into the sitting-room, and explained Jane's absence.

'A good girl; a good girl,' he remarked, after listening with elevated brows. 'But she must be careful of her health. My visit this morning is on matters of business; no doubt she will tell you the principal points of our conversation afterwards. An excellent friend you have been to her, Mrs. Byass—excellent.'

'I'm sure I don't see how anyone could help liking her,' said Bessie, inwardly delighted with the expectation of hearing at length what Jane's circumstances really were.

'Indeed, so good a friend,' pursued Joseph, 'that I'm afraid it would distress her if she could no longer live with you. And the fact is'—he bent forward and smiled sadly— 'I'm sure I may speak freely to you, Mrs. Byass—but the fact is, that I'm very doubtful indeed whether she could be happy if she lived with Mrs. Snowdon. I suppose there's always more or less difficulty where step-children are concerned, and in this case—well, I fear the incompatibility would be too great. To be sure, it places me in a difficult position. Jane's very young—very young; only just turned seventeen, poor child! Out of the question for her to live with strangers. I had some hopes—I wonder whether I ought to speak of it? You know Mr. Kirkwood?'

'Yes, indeed. I can't tell you how surprised I was, Mr. Snowdon. And there seems to be such a mystery about it, too.'

Bessie positively glowed with delight in such confidential talk. It was her dread that Jane's arrival might put an end to it before everything was revealed.

'A mystery, you may well say, Mrs. Byass. I think highly of Mr. Kirkwood, very highly; but really in this affair! It's almost too painful to talk about—to *you*.'

Bessie blushed, as becomes the Englishwoman of mature years when she is gracefully supposed to be ignorant of all it most behoves her to know.

'Well, well; he is on the point of marrying a young person with whom I should certainly not like my daughter to associate—fortunately there is little chance of that. You were never acquainted with Miss Hewett?'

'Ye—yes. A long time ago.'

'Well, well; we must be charitable. You know that she is dreadfully disfigured?

'Disfigured? Jane didn't say a word about that. She only told me that Mr. Kirkwood was going to marry her, and I didn't like to ask too many questions. I hadn't even heard as she was at home.'

Joseph related to her the whole story, whilst Bessie fidgeted with satisfaction.

'I thought,' he added, 'that you could perhaps throw some light on the mystery. We can only suppose that Kirkwood has acted from the highest motives, but I really think—well, well, we won't talk of it any more. I was led to this subject from speaking of this poor girl's position. I wonder whether it will be possible for her to continue to live in your friendly care Mrs. Byass?'

'Oh, I shall be only too glad, Mr. Snowdon!'

'Now how kind that is of you! Of course she wouldn't want more than two rooms.'

'Of course not.'

Joseph was going further into details, when a latch-key was heard opening the front door. Jane entered hurriedly. The rapid walk had brought colour to her cheek; in her simple mourning attire she looked very interesting, very sweet and girlish. She had been shedding tears, and it was with unsteady voice that she excused herself for keeping her father waiting.

'Never mind that, my dear,' replied Joseph, as he kissed her cheek. 'You have been doing good—unselfish as always. Sit down and rest; you must be careful not to over-exert yourself.'

Bessie busied herself affectionately in removing Jane's hat and jacket, then withdrew that father and child might converse in private. Joseph looked at his daughter. His praise of her was not all mere affectation of sentiment. He had spoken truly when he said to Scawthorne that, but for Clem, he would ask nothing better than to settle down with this gentle girl for his companion. Selfishness, for the most part, but implying appreciation of her qualities. She did not love him, but he was sincere enough with himself to admit that this was perfectly natural. Had circumstances permitted, he would have tried hard to win some affection from her. Poor little girl! How would it affect her when she heard what he was going to say? He felt angry with Kirkwood; yes, truly indignant—men are capable of greater inconsistencies than this. She would not have cared much about the money had Kirkwood married her; of that he felt sure. She had lost her lover; now he was going to deprive her of her inheritance. Cruel! Yes; but he really felt so well-disposed to her, so determined to make her a comfortable provision for the future; and had the money been hers, impossible to have regarded her thus. Joseph was thankful to the chance which, in making him wealthy, had also enabled him to nourish such virtuous feeling.

How should he begin? He had a bright idea, an idea worthy of him. Thrusting his hand into his pocket he brought out half-a-crown. Then:

'Your humble friend's in a sad condition, I'm afraid, Jane?'

'She is, father.'

'Suppose you give her this! Every little helps, you know.'

Jane received the coin and murmured thanks for his kindness, but could not help betraying some surprise. Joseph was on the watch for this. It gave him his exquisite opportunity.

'You're surprised at me offering you money, Jane? I believe your poor grandfather led you to suppose that—that his will was made almost entirely in your favour?'

Jane could not reply; she searched his face.

'Would it disappoint you very much, my child,' he continued, sympathetically, 'if it turned out that he had either altered his mind or by some accident had neglected to make his will? I speak as your father, Janey, and I think I have some knowledge of your character. I think I know that you are as free from avarice as anyone could be.'

Was it true? he began to ask himself. Why, then, had her countenance fallen? Why did such a look of deep distress pass over it?

'The fact is, Janey,' he continued, hardening himself a little as he noted her expression, 'your grandfather left no will. The result—the legal result—of that is, that all his property becomes—ah—mine. He—in fact he destroyed his will a very short time, comparatively speaking, before he died, and he neglected to make another. Unfortunately, you see, under these circumstances we can't be sure what his wish was.'

She was deadly pale; there was anguish in the look with which she regarded her father.

'I'm very sorry it pains you so, my dear,' Joseph remarked, still more coldly. 'I didn't think you were so taken up with the thought of money. Really, Jane, a young girl at your time of life——'

'Father, father, how can you think that? It wasn't to be for myself; I thought you knew; indeed you did know!'

'But you looked so very strange, my dear. Evidently you felt——'

'Yes—I feel it—I do feel it! But because it means that grandfather couldn't get back his trust in me. Oh, it is too hard! When did he destroy his will? When, father?'

'Ten days before his death.'

'Yes; that was when it happened. You never heard; he promised to tell nobody. I disappointed him. I showed myself very foolish and weak in—in something that happened then. I made grandfather think that I was too selfish to live as he hoped—that I couldn't do what I'd undertaken. That was why he destroyed his will. And I thought he had forgiven me! I thought he trusted me again! O grandfather!'

Snowdon was astonished at the explanation of his own good luck, and yet more at Jane's display of feeling. So quiet, so reserved as he had always known her, she seemed to have become another person. For some moments he could only gaze at her in wonder. Never yet had he heard, never again would he hear, the utterance of an emotion so profound and so noble.

'Jane—try and control yourself, my dear. Let's talk it over, Jane.'

'I feel as if it would break my heart. I thought I had that one thing to comfort me. It's like losing him again—losing his confidence. To think I should have disappointed him in just what he hoped more than anything!'

'But you're mistaken,' Joseph exclaimed, a generous feeling for once getting the better of prudence. 'Listen, my dear, and I'll explain to you. I hadn't finished when you interrupted me.'

She clasped her hands upon her lap and gazed at him in eager appeal.

'Did he say anything to you, father?'

'No—and you may be quite sure that if he *hadn't* trusted you, he *would* have said something. What's more, on the very day before his death he wrote a letter to Mr. Percival, to say that he wanted to make his will again. He was going to do it on the Monday—there now! It was only an accident; he hadn't time to do what he wished.'

This was making a concession which he had expressly resolved to guard against; but Joseph's designs ripened, lost their crudity, as he saw more and more of his daughter's disposition. He was again grateful to her; she had made things smoother than he could have hoped.

'You really think, father, that he would have made the same will as before?'

'Not a doubt about it, my love; not a doubt of it. In fact—now let me set your poor little mind at rest—only two days before his death—when was it I saw him last? Friday? Thursday?—he said to me that he had a higher opinion of you than ever. There now, Jane!'

She would have deemed it impossible for anyone to utter less than truth in such connection as this. Her eyes gleamed with joy.

'Now you understand just how it was, Jane. What we have to talk about now is, how we can arrange things so as to carry out your grandfather's wish. I am your guardian, my dear. Now I'm sure you wouldn't desire to have command of large sums of money before you are twenty-one? Just so; your grandfather didn't intend it. Well, first let me ask you this question. Would you rather live with—with your stepmother, or with your excellent friend Mrs. Byass? I see what your answer is, and I approve it; I fully approve it. Now suppose we arrange that you are to have an allowance of two pounds a week? It is just possible—just possible—that I may have to go abroad on business before long; in that case the payment would be made to you through an agent. Do you feel it would be satisfactory?'

Jane was thinking how much of this sum could be saved to give away.

'It seems little? But you see——'

'No, no, father. It is quite enough.'

'Good. We understand each other. Of course this is a temporary arrangement. I must have time to think over grandfather's ideas. Why, you are a mere child yet, Janey. Seventeen! A mere child, my dear!'

Forgetting the decorum imposed by his costume, Joseph became all but gay, so delightfully were things arranging

themselves. A hundred a year he could very well afford just
to keep his conscience at ease; and for Jane it would be wealth.
Excellent Mrs. Byass was as good a guardian as could anywhere be found, and Jane's discretion forbade any fear on her
account when—business should take him away.

'Well now, we've talked quite long enough. Don't think
for a moment that you hadn't your grandfather's confidence,
my dear; it would be distressing yourself wholly without
reason—wholly. Be a good girl—why, there you see; I speak
to you as if you were a child. And so you are, poor little girl!
—far too young to have worldly troubles. No, no; I must
relieve you of all that, until—— Well now, I'll leave you
for to-day. Good-bye, my dear.'

He kissed her cheek, but Jane, sobbing a little, put her
pure lips to his. Joseph looked about him for an instant as
if he had forgotten something, then departed with what seemed
unnecessary haste.

Jane and Mrs. Byass had a long talk before dinner-time.
Mystery was at an end between them now; they talked much
of the past, more of the future.

At two o'clock Jane received a visit from Miss Lant. This
lady was already apprised by her friend Mr. Percival of all
that had come to pass; she was prepared to exercise much
discretion, but Jane soon showed her that this was needless.
The subject of pressing importance to the latter was Pennyloaf's disastrous circumstances; unable to do all she wished,
Jane was much relieved when her charitable friend proposed
to set off to Merlin Place forthwith and ascertain how help
could most effectually be given. Yes; it was good to be constrained to think of another's sorrows.

There passed a fortnight, during which Jane spent some
hours each day with Pennyloaf. By the kindness of fate only
one of Bob's children survived him, but it was just this
luckless infant whose existence made Pennyloaf's position so
difficult. Alone, she could have gone back to her slop-work,
or some less miserable slavery might have been discovered;
but Pennyloaf dreaded leaving her child each day in the care
of strangers, being only too well aware what that meant. Mrs.
Candy was, of course, worse than useless; Stephen the potman
had more than his work set in looking after her. Whilst Miss
Lant and Jane were straining their wits on the hardest of all
problems—to find a means of livelihood for one whom society
pronounced utterly superfluous, Pennyloaf most unexpectedly

solved the question by her own effort. Somewhere near the Meat Market, one night, she encountered an acquaintance, a woman of not much more than her own age, who had recently become a widow, and was supporting herself (as well as four little ones) by keeping a stall at which she sold children's second-hand clothing; her difficulty was to dispose of her children whilst she was doing business at night. Pennyloaf explained her own position, and with the result that her acquaintance, by name Mrs. Todd, proposed a partnership. Why shouldn't they share a room, work together with the needle in patching and making, and by Pennyloaf's staying at home each evening keep the tribe of youngsters out of danger? This project was carried out; the two brought their furniture together into a garret, and it seemed probable that they would succeed in keeping themselves alive.

But before this settlement was effected Jane's own prospects had undergone a change of some importance. For a fortnight nothing was heard of Joseph Snowdon in Hanover Street; then there came a letter from him; it bore a Liverpool post-mark, but was headed with no address. Joseph wrote that the business to which he had alluded was already summoning him from England; he regretted that there had not even been time for him to say farewell to his daughter. However, he would write to her occasionally during his absence, and hoped to hear from her. The allowance of two pounds a week would be duly paid by an agent, and on receiving it each Saturday she was to forward an acknowledgment to 'Mr. H. Jones,' at certain reading-rooms in the City. Let her in the meantime be a good girl, remain with her excellent friend Mrs. Byass, and repose absolute confidence in her affectionate father—J. S.

That same morning there came also a letter from Liverpool to Mrs. Joseph Snowdon, a letter which ran thus:

'Clem, old girl, I regret very much that affairs of pressing importance call me away from my happy home. It is especially distressing that this occurs just at the time when we were on the point of taking our house, in which we hoped to spend the rest of our lives in bliss. Alas, that is not to be! Do not repine, and do not break the furniture in the lodgings, as your means will henceforth be limited, I fear. You will remember that I was in your debt, with reference to a little

affair which happened in Clerkenwell Close, not such a long
time ago; please accept this intimation as payment in full.
When I am established in the country to which business
summons me, I shall of course send for you immediately, but
it may happen that some little time will intervene before I
am able to take that delightful step. In the meanwhile your
mother will supply you with all the money you need; she has
full authority from me to do so. All blessings upon you, and
may you be happy.—With tears I sign myself,

'YOUR BROKEN-HEARTED HUSBAND.'

Joseph's absence through the night had all but prepared
Clem for something of this kind, yet he had managed things
so well that up to the time of his departure she had not been
able to remark a single suspicious circumstance, unless, indeed,
it were the joyous affectionateness with which he continued
to behave. She herself had been passing through a time of
excitement and even of suffering. When she learned from
the newspaper what fate had befallen Bob Hewett, it was as
though someone had dealt her a half-stunning blow; in her
fierce animal way she was attached to Bob, and for the first
time in her life she knew a genuine grief. The event seemed
at first impossible; she sped hither and thither, making inquiries, and raged in her heart against everyone who confirmed the newspaper report. Combined with the pain of loss
was her disappointment at the frustration of the scheme Bob
had undertaken in concert with her. Brooding on her deadly
purpose, she had come to regard it as a certain thing that
before long her husband would be killed. The details were
arranged; all her cunning had gone to the contrivance of a
plot for disguising the facts of his murder. Savagely she had
exulted in the prospect, not only of getting rid of him, but
of being revenged for her old humiliation. A thousand times
she imagined herself in Bob's lurking-place, raising the weapon,
striking the murderous blow, rifling the man's pockets to
mislead those who found his body, and had laughed to herself
triumphantly. Joseph out of the way, the next thing was
to remove Pennyloaf. Oh, that would easily have been contrived. Then she and Bob would have been married.

Very long since Clem had shed tears, but she did so this
day when there was no longer a possibility of doubting that
Bob was dead. She shut herself in her room and moaned like
a wild beast in pain. Joseph could not but observe, when he

came home, that she was suffering in some extraordinary way. When he spoke jestingly about it, she all but rushed upon him with her fists. And in the same moment she determined that he should not escape, even if she had to murder him with her own hands. From that day her constant occupation was searching the newspapers to get hints about poisons. Doubtless it was as well for Joseph to be speedy in his preparations for departure.

She was present in the police-court when Jack Bartley came forward to be dealt with. Against him she stored up hatred and the resolve of vengeance; if it were years before she had the opportunity, Jack should in the end pay for what he had done.

And now Joseph had played her the trick she anticipated; he had saved himself out of her clutches, and had carried off all his money with him. She knew well enough what was meant by his saying that her mother would supply what she needed; very likely that he had made any such arrangement! You should have heard the sterling vernacular in which Clem gave utterance to her feelings as soon as she had deciphered the mocking letter!

Without a minute's delay she dressed and left the house. Having a few shillings in her pocket, she took a cab at King's Cross and bade the driver drive his hardest to Clerkenwell Close. Up Pentonville Hill panted the bony horse, Clem swearing all the time because it could go no quicker. But the top was reached; she shouted to the man to whip, whip! By the time they pulled up at Mrs. Peckover's house Clem herself perspired as profusely as the animal.

Mrs. Peckover was at breakfast, alone.

' Read that, will you? Read that!' roared Clem, rushing upon her and dashing the letter in her face.

' Why, you mad cat!' cried her mother, starting up in anger. ' What's wrong with you now?'

' Read that there letter! That's *your* doin', that is! Read it! Read it!'

Half-frightened, Mrs. Peckover drew away from the table and managed to peruse Joseph's writing. Having come to the end, she burst into jeering laughter.

' He's done it, has he? He's took his 'ook, has he? *What* did I tell you? Don't swear at me, or I'll give you something to swear about—such languidge in a respectable 'ouse! Ha, ha! What did I tell you? You wouldn't take

my way. Oh no, you must go off and be independent. *Serve*
you right! Ha, ha! *Serve* you right! You'll get no pity
from me.'

'You 'old your jaw, mother, or I'll precious soon set my
marks on your ugly old face! What does he say there about
you? You're to pay me money. He's made arrangements
with you. Don't try to cheat me, or I'll—soon have a summons out against you. The letter's proof; it's lawyer's proof.
You try to cheat me and see.'

Clem had sufficient command of her faculties to devise
this line of action. She half believed, too, that the letter
would be of some legal efficacy, as against her mother.

'You bloomin' fool!' screamed Mrs. Peckover. 'Do you
think I was born yesterday? Not one farden do you get out
of me if you starve in the street—not one farden! It's my
turn now. I've had about enough o' your cheek an' your
hinsults. You'll go and work for your livin', you great cart-
horse!'

'Work! No fear! I'll set the perlice after him.'

'The perlice! What can they do?'

'Is it law as he can go off and leave me with nothing to
live on?'

'Course it is! Unless you go to the work'us an' throw
yourself on the parish. Do, do! Oh my! shouldn't I like to
see you brought down to the work'us, like Mrs. Igginbottom,
the wife of the cat's-meat man, him as they stuck up wanted
for desertion!'

'You're a liar!' Clem shouted. 'I can make *you* support
me before it comes to that.'

The wrangle continued for some time longer; then Clem
bethought herself of another person with whom she must have
the satisfaction of speaking her mind. On the impulse, she
rushed away, out of Clerkenwell Close, up St. John Street
Road, across City Road, down to Hanover Street, literally
running for most of the time. Her knock at Mrs. Byass's
door was terrific.

'I want to see Jane Snowdon,' was her address to Bessie.

'Do you? I think you might have knocked more like
civilisation,' replied Mrs. Byass, proud of expressing herself
with superior refinement.

But Clem pushed her way forward. Jane, alarmed at the
noise, showed herself on the stairs.

'You just come 'ere!' cried Clem to her. 'I've got something to say to *you*, Miss!'

Jane was of a sudden possessed with terror, the old terror with which Clem had inspired her years ago. She shrank back, but Bessie Byass was by no means disposed to allow this kind of thing to go on in her house.

'Mrs. Snowdon,' she exclaimed, 'I don't know what your business may be, but if you can't behave yourself, you'll please to go away a bit quicker than you came. The idea! Did anyone ever hear!'

'I shan't go till I choose,' replied Clem, 'and that won't be till I've had my say with that little ——! Where's your father, Jane Snowdon? You just tell me that.'

'My father,' faltered Jane, in the silence. 'I haven't seen him for a fortnight.'

'You haven't, eh? Little liar! It's what I used to call you when you scrubbed our kitchen floor, and it's what I call you now. D'you remember when you did the 'ouse-work, an' slept under the kitchen table? D'you remember, eh? Haven't seen him for a fortnight, ain't you? Oh, he's a nice man, is your father! He ran away an' deserted your mother. But he's done it once too often. *I'*ll precious soon have the perlice after him! Has he left you to look after yourself? Has he, eh? You just tell me that!'

Jane and Mrs. Byass stared at each other in dismay. The letter that had come this morning enabled them to guess the meaning of Clem's fury. The latter interpreted their looks as an admission that Jane too was a victim. She laughed aloud.

'How does it taste, little liar, eh? A second disappointment! You thought you was a-goin' to have all the money; now you've got none, and you may go back to Whitehead's. They'll be glad to see you, will Whitehead's. Oh, he's a nice man, your father! Would you like to know what's been goin' on ever since he found out your old grandfather? Would you like to know how he put himself out to prevent you an' that Kirkwood feller gettin' married, just so that the money mightn't get into other people's 'ands? Would you like to know how my beast of a mother and him put their 'eds together to see how they could get hold of the bloomin' money? An' *you* thought you was sure of it, didn't you? Will you come with me to the perlice-station, just to help to describe what he looks like? An affectionate father, ain't he? Almost as good as he is a 'usband. You just listen to me, Jane Snowdon. If I find out as you're havin' money from him, I'll be revenged on you, mind that! I'll be revenged on you! D'you remember what my hand feels like? You've had it on the side of your —— 'ed often enough. You just look out for yourself!'

'And you just turn out of my house,' cried Bessie, scarlet with wrath. 'This minute! Sarah! Sarah! Run out by the arey-steps and fetch a p'liceman, this minute! The idea!'

Clem had said her say, however, and with a few more volleys of atrocious language was content to retire. Having slammed the door upon her, Bessie cried in a trembling voice :

'Oh, if only Sam had been here! My, how I should have liked Sam to have been here! *Wouldn't* he have given her something for herself! Why, such a creature oughtn't to be left loose. Oh, if Sam had been here!'

Jane had sat down on the stairs; her face was hidden in her hands. That brutal voice had carried her back to her wretched childhood; everything about her in the present was unreal in comparison with the terrors, the hardships, the humiliations revived by memory. As she sat at this moment, so had she sat many a time on the cellar-steps at Mrs. Peckover's. So powerfully was her imagination affected that she had a feeling as if her hands were grimy from toil, as if her limbs ached. Oh, that dreadful voice! Was she never, never to escape beyond hearing of it?

'Jane, my dear, come into the sitting-room,' said Bessie 'No wonder it's upset you. What *can* it all mean?'

The meaning was not far to seek; Jane understood everything—yes, even her father's hypocrisies. She listened for a few minutes to her friend's indignant exclamations, then looked up, her resolve taken.

'Mrs. Byass, I shall take no more money. I shall go to work again and earn my living. How thankful I am that I can!'

'Why, what nonsense are you talking, child! Just because that—that *creature*—— Why, I've no patience with you, Jane! As if she durst touch you! Touch you? I'd like to see her indeed.'

'It isn't that, Mrs. Byass. I can't take money from father. I haven't felt easy in my mind ever since he told me about it, and now I *can't* take the money. Whether it's true or not, all she said, I should never have a night's rest if I consented to live in this way.'

'Oh, you *don't* really mean it, Jane?'

Bessie all but sobbed with vexation.

'I mean it, and I shall never alter my mind. I shall send back the money, and write to the man that he needn't send any more. However often it comes, I shall always return it. I couldn't, I couldn't live on that money! Never ask me to, Mrs. Byass.'

Practical Bessie had already begun to ask herself what arrangement Jane proposed to make about lodgings. She was no Mrs. Peckover, but neither did circumstances allow her to disregard the question of rent. It cut her to the heart to think of refusing an income of two pounds per week.

Jane too saw all the requirements of the case.

'Mrs. Byass, will you let me have one room—my old room upstairs? I have been very happy there, and I should like to stay if I can. You know what I can earn; can you afford to let me live there? I'd do my utmost to help you in the house; I'll be as good as a servant, if you can't keep Sarah. I should so like to stay with you!'

'You just let me hear you talk about leaving, that's all! Wait till I've talked it over with Sam.'

Jane went upstairs, and for the rest of the day the house was very quiet.

Not Whitehead's; there were other places where work might be found. And before many days she had found it. Happily there were no luxuries to be laid aside; her ordinary dress was not too good for the workroom. She had no habits of idleness to overcome, and an hour at the table made her as expert with her fingers as ever.

Returning from the first day's work, she sat in her room—the little room which used to be hers—to rest and think for a moment before going down to Bessie's supper-table. And her thought was:

'He, too, is just coming home from work. Why should my life be easier than his?'

CHAPTER XXXIX

SIDNEY

LOOK at a map of greater London, a map on which the town paper shows as a dark, irregularly rounded patch against the whiteness of suburban districts, and just on the northern limit of the vast network of streets you will distinguish the name of Crouch End. Another decade, and the dark patch will have spread greatly further; for the present, Crouch End is still able to remind one that it was in the country a very short time ago. The streets have a smell of newness, of dampness; the bricks retain their complexion, the stucco has not rotted more than one expects in a year or two; poverty tries to hide itself with venetian blinds, until the time when an advanced guard of houses shall justify the existence of the slum.

Characteristic of the locality is a certain row of one-storey cottages—villas, the advertiser calls them—built of white brick, each with one bay window on the ground floor, a window pretentiously fashioned and desiring to be taken for stone, though obviously made of bad plaster. Before each house is a garden, measuring six feet by three, entered by a little iron gate, which grinds as you push it, and at no time would latch. The front-door also grinds on the sill; it can only be opened by force, and quivers in a way that shows how unsubstantially it is made. As you set foot in the pinched passage, the sound of your tread proves the whole fabric a thing of lath and sand. The ceilings, the walls, confess themselves neither water-tight nor air-tight. Whatever you touch is at once found to be sham.

In the kitchen of one of these houses, at two o'clock on a Saturday afternoon in September, three young people were sitting down to the dinner-table: a girl of nearly fourteen, her sister, a year younger, and their brother not yet eleven. All were decently dressed, but very poorly; a glance at them, and you knew that in this house there was little money to spend on superfluities. The same impression was produced by the appointments of the kitchen, which was disorderly, too, and spoke neglect of the scrubbing-brush. As for the table, it was ill laid and worse supplied. The meal was to consist of the fag-end of a shoulder of mutton, some villainously cooked potatoes (*à l'Anglaise*) and bread.

'Oh, I can't eat this rot again!' cried the boy, making a dig with his fork at the scarcely clad piece of bone. 'I shall have bread and cheese. Lug the cheese out, Annie!'

'No, you won't,' replied the elder girl, in a disagreeable voice. 'You'll eat this or go without.'

She had an unpleasing appearance. Her face was very thin, her lips pinched sourly together, her eyes furtive, hungry, malevolent. Her movements were awkward and impatient, and a morbid nervousness kept her constantly starting, with a stealthy look here or there.

'I shall have the cheese if I like!' shouted the boy, a very ill-conditioned youngster, whose face seemed to have been damaged in recent conflict. His clothes were dusty, and his hair stood up like stubble.

'Hold your row, Tom,' said the younger girl, who was quiet and had the look of an invalid. 'It's always you begins. Besides, you can't have cheese; there's only a little bit, and Sidney said he was going to make his dinner of it to-day.'

'Of course—selfish beast!'

'Selfish! Now just listen to that, Amy! when he said it just that we mightn't be afraid to finish the meat.'

Amy said nothing, but began to hack fragments off the bone.

'Put some aside for father first,' continued Annie, holding a plate.

'Father be blowed!' cried Tom. 'You just give me that first cut. Give it here, Annie, or I'll crack you on the head!'

As he struggled for the plate, Amy bent forward and hit his arm violently with the handle of the knife. This was the signal for a general scrimmage, in the midst of which Tom caught up a hearth-brush and flung it at Amy's head. The missile went wide of its mark and shivered one of the window-panes.

'There now!' exclaimed Annie, who had begun to cry in consequence of a blow from Tom's fist. 'See what father says to that!'

'If I was him,' said Amy, in a low voice of passion, 'I'd tie you to something and beat you till you lost your senses. Ugly brute!'

The warfare would not have ended here but that the door opened and he of whom they spoke made his appearance.

In the past two years and a half John Hewett had become a shaky old man. Of his grizzled hair very little remained, and little of his beard; his features were shrunken, his neck scraggy; he stooped much, and there was a senile indecision in his movements. He wore rough, patched clothing, had no collar, and seemed, from the state of his hands, to have been engaged in very dirty work. As he entered and came upon the riotous group his eyes lit up with anger. In a strained voice he shouted a command of silence.

'It's all that Tom, father,' piped Annie. 'There's no living with him.'

John's eye fell on the broken window.

'Which of you's done that?' he asked sternly, pointing to it.

No one spoke.

'Who's goin' to pay for it, I'd like to know? Doesn't it cost enough to keep you, but you must go makin' extra expense? Where's the money to come from, I want to know, if you go on like this?'

He turned suddenly upon the elder girl.

'I've got something to say to you, Miss. Why wasn't you at work this morning?'

Amy avoided his look. Her pale face became mottled with alarm, but only for an instant; then she hardened herself and moved her head insolently.

'Why wasn't you at work? Where's your week's money?'

'I haven't got any.'

'You haven't got any? Why not?'

For a while she was stubbornly silent, but Hewett constrained her to confession at length. On his way home to-day he had been informed by an acquaintance that Amy was wandering about the streets at an hour when she ought to have been at her employment. Unable to put off the evil moment any longer, the girl admitted that four days ago she was dismissed for bad behaviour, and that since then she had pretended to go to work as usual. The trifling sum paid to her on dismissal she had spent.

John turned to his youngest daughter and asked in a hollow voice:

'Where's Clara?'

'She's got one of her headaches, father,' replied the girl, trembling.

He turned and went from the room.

It was long since he had lost his place of porter at the
filter-works. Before leaving England, Joseph Snowdon managed to dispose of his interest in the firm of Lake, Snowdon,
& Co., and at the same time Hewett was informed that his
wages would be reduced by five shillings a week—the sum
which had been supplied by Michael Snowdon's benevolence.
It was a serious loss. Clara's marriage removed one grave
anxiety, but the three children had still to be brought up, and
with every year John's chance of steady employment would
grow less. Sidney Kirkwood declared himself able and willing
to help substantially, but he might before long have children
of his own to think of, and in any case it was shameful to
burden him in this way.

Shameful or not, it very soon came to pass that Sidney
had the whole family on his hands. A bad attack of rheumatism
in the succeeding winter made John incapable of earning anything at all; for two months he was a cripple. Till then
Sidney and his wife had occupied lodgings in Holloway;
when it became evident that Hewett must not hope to be able
to support his children, and when Sidney had for many weeks
paid the rent (as well as supplying the money to live upon) in
Farringdon Road Buildings, the house at Crouch End was
taken, and there all went to live together. Clara's health
was very uncertain, and though at first she spoke frequently
of finding work to do at home, the birth of a child put an end
to such projects. Amy Hewett was shortly at the point when
the education of a board-school child is said to be 'finished;'
by good luck, employment was found for her in Kentish Town,
with three shillings a week from the first. John could not
resign himself to being a mere burden on the home. Enforced
idleness so fretted him that at times he seemed all but out of
his wits. In despair he caught at the strangest kinds of casual
occupation; when earning nothing, he would barely eat enough
to keep himself alive, and if he succeeded in bringing home a
shilling or two, he turned the money about in his hands with
a sort of angry joy that it would have made your heart ache to
witness. Just at present he had a job of cleaning and white-
washing some cellars in Stoke Newington.

He was absent from the kitchen for five minutes, during
which time the three sat round the table. Amy pretended to
eat unconcernedly; Tom made grimaces at her. As for
Annie, she cried. Their father entered the room again.

'Why didn't you tell us about this at once?' he asked, in

a shaking voice, looking at his daughter with eyes of blank misery.

'I don't know.'

'You're a bad, selfish girl!' he broke out, again overcome with anger. 'Haven't you got neither sense nor feelin' nor honesty? Just when you ought to have begun to earn a bit higher wages—when you ought to have been glad to work your hardest, to show you wasn't unthankful to them as has done so much for you! Who earned money to keep you when you was goin' to school? Who fed and clothed you, and saw as you didn't want for nothing? Who is it as you owe everything to?—just tell me that.'

Amy affected to pay no attention. She kept swallowing morsels, with ugly movements of her lips and jaws.

'How often have I to tell you all that if it wasn't for Sidney Kirkwood you'd have been workhouse children? As sure as you're livin', you'd all of you have gone to the workhouse! And you go on just as if you didn't owe thanks to nobody. I tell you it'll be years and years before one of you'll have a penny you can call your own. If it was Annie or Tom behaved so careless, there'd be less wonder; but for a girl of your age—I'm ashamed as you belong to me! You can't even keep your tongue from bein' impudent to Clara, her as you ain't worthy to be a servant to!'

'Clara's a sneak,' observed Tom, with much coolness. 'She's always telling lies about us.'

'I'll half-knock your young head off your shoulders,' cried his father, furiously, 'if you talk to me like that! Not one of you's fit to live in the same house with her.'

'Father, I haven't done nothing,' whimpered Annie, hurt by being thus included in his reprobation.

'No more you have—not just now, but you're often enough more trouble to your sister than you need be. But it's you I'm talkin' to, Amy. You dare to leave this house again till there's another place found for you! If you'd any self-respect, you couldn't bear to look Sidney in the face. Suppose you hadn't such a brother to work for you, what would you do, eh? Who'd buy your food? Who'd pay the rent of the house you live in?'

A noteworthy difference between children of this standing and such as pass their years of play-time in homes unshadowed by poverty. For these, life had no illusions. Of every mouthful that they ate, the price was known to them. The roof over their heads was there by no grace of Providence, but solely because such-and-such a sum was paid weekly in hard cash, when the collector came ; let the payment fail, and they knew perfectly well what the result would be. The children of the upper world could not even by chance give a thought to the sources whence their needs are supplied ; speech on such a subject in their presence would be held indecent. In John Hewett's position, the indecency, the crime, would have been to keep silence and pretend that the needs of existence are ministered to as a matter of course.

His tone and language were pitifully those of feeble age. The emotion proved too great a strain upon his body, and he had at length to sit down in a tremulous state, miserable with the consciousness of failing authority. He would have made but a poor figure now upon Clerkenwell Green. Even as his frame was shrunken, so had the circle of his interests contracted ; he could no longer speak or think on the subjects which had fired him through the better part of his life ; if he was driven to try and utter himself on the broad questions of social wrong, of the people's cause, a senile stammering of incoherencies was the only result. The fight had ever gone against John Hewett ; he was one of those who are born to be defeated. His failing energies spent themselves in conflict with his own children ; the concerns of a miserable home were all his mind could now cope with.

'Come and sit down to your dinner, father,' Annie said, when he became silent.

'Dinner? I want no dinner. I've no stomach for food when it's stolen. What's Sidney goin' to have when he comes home?'

'He said he'd do with bread and cheese to-day. See, we've cut some meat for you?'

'You keep that for Sidney, then, and don't one of you dare to say anything about it. Cut me a bit of bread, Annie.'

She did so. He ate it, standing by the fireplace, drank a glass of water, and went into the sitting-room. There he sat unoccupied for nearly an hour, his head at times dropping forward as if he were nearly asleep ; but it was only in abstraction. The morning's work had wearied him excessively, as such effort always did, but the mental misery he was suffering made him unconscious of bodily fatigue.

The clinking and grinding of the gate drew his attention ; he stood up and saw his son-in-law, returned from Clerkenwell.

When he had heard the house-door grind and shake and close, he called ' Sidney ! '

Sidney looked into the parlour, with a smile.

' Come in here a minute ; I want to speak to you.'

It was a face that told of many troubles. Sidney might resolutely keep a bright countenance, but there was no hiding the sallowness of his cheeks and the lines drawn by ever-wakeful anxiety. The effect of a struggle with mean necessities is seldom anything but degradation, in look and in character ; but Sidney's temper, and the conditions of his life, preserved him against that danger. His features, worn into thinness, seem to present more distinctly than ever their points of refinement. You saw that he was habitually a grave and silent man ; all the more attractive his aspect when, as now, he seemed to rest from thought and give expression to his natural kindliness. In the matter of attire he was no longer as careful as he used to be ; the clothes he wore had done more than just service, and hung about him unregarded.

' Clara upstairs ? ' he asked, when he had noticed Hewett's look.

' Yes ; she's lying down. May's been troublesome all the morning. But it was something else I meant.'

And John began to speak of Amy's ill-doing. He had always in some degree a sense of shame when he spoke privately with Sidney, always felt painfully the injustice involved in their relations. At present he could not look Kirkwood in the face, and his tone was that of a man who abases himself to make confession of guilt.

Sidney was gravely concerned. It was his habit to deal with the children's faults good-naturedly, to urge John not to take a sombre view of their thoughtlessness ; but the present instance could not be made light of. Secretly he had always expected that the girl would be a source of more serious trouble the older she grew. He sat in silence, leaning forward, his eyes bent down.

' It's no good whatever *I* say,' lamented Hewett. ' They don't heed me. Why must I have children like these ? Haven't I always done my best to teach them to be honest and good-hearted ? If I'd spent my life in the worst ways a man can, they couldn't have turned out more worthless. Haven't I wished always what was right and good and true ? Haven't I always spoke up for justice in the world ? Haven't I done what I could, Sidney, to be helpful to them as fell into

misfortune ?   And now in my old age I'm only a burden, and
the children as come after me are nothing but a misery to all
as have to do with them.   If it wasn't for Clara I feel I
couldn't live my time out.   She's the one that pays me back
for the love I've given her.   All the others—I can't feel as
they're children of mine at all.'

It was a strange and touching thing that he seemed nowadays utterly to have forgotten Clara's past.   Invariably he
spoke of her as if she had at all times been his stay and comfort.   The name of his son who was dead never passed his
lips, but of Clara he could not speak too long or too tenderly.

'I can't think what to do,' Sidney said.   'If I talk to her
in a fault-finding way, she'll only dislike me the more ; she
feels I've no business to interfere.'

'You're too soft with them.   You spoil them.   Why, there's
one of them broken a pane in the kitchen to-day, and they know
you'll take it quiet, like you do everything else.'

Sidney wrinkled his brow.   These petty expenses, ever
repeated, were just what made the difficulty in his budget ;
he winced whenever such demands encroached upon the poor
weekly income of which every penny was too little for the
serious needs of the family.   Feeling that if he sat and
thought much longer a dark mood would seize upon him, he
rose hastily.

'I shall try kindness with her.   Don't say anything more
in her hearing.'

He went to the kitchen-door, and cried cheerfully, 'My
dinner ready, girls ? '

Annie's voice replied with a timorous affirmative.

'All right ; I'll be down in a minute.'

Treading as gently as possible, he ascended the stairs and
entered his bedroom.   The blind was drawn down, but sunlight shone through it and made a softened glow in the
chamber.   In a little cot was sitting his child, May, rather
more than a year old ; she had toys about her, and was for the
moment contented.   Clara lay on the bed, her face turned so
that Sidney could not see it.   He spoke to her, and she just
moved her arm, but gave no reply.

'Do you wish to be left alone ? ' he asked, in a subdued
and troubled voice.

'Yes.'

'Shall I take May downstairs ? '

'If you like.   Don't speak to me now.'

He remained standing by the bed for a minute, then turned his eyes on the child, who smiled at him. He could not smile in return, but went quietly away.

'It's one of her bad days,' whispered Hewett, who met him at the foot of the stairs. 'She can't help it, poor girl!'

'No, no.'

Sidney ate what was put before him without giving a thought to it. When his eyes wandered round the kitchen the disorder and dirt worried him, but on that subject he could not speak. His hunger appeased, he looked steadily at Amy, and said in a kindly tone:

'Father tells me you've had a stroke of bad luck, Amy. We must have a try at another place, mustn't we? Hollo, there's a window broken! Has Tom been playing at cricket in the room, eh?'

The girls kept silence.

'Come and let's make out the list for our shopping this afternoon,' he continued. 'I'm afraid there'll have to be something the less for that window, girls; what do *you* say?'

'We'll do without a pudding to-morrow, Sidney,' suggested Annie.

'Oh come, now! I'm fond of pudding.'

Thus it was always; if he could not direct by kindness, he would never try to rule by harsh words. Six years ago it was not so easy for him to be gentle under provocation, and he would then have made a better disciplinarian in such a home as this. On Amy and Tom all his rare goodness was thrown away. Never mind; shall one go over to the side of evil because one despairs of vanquishing it?

The budget, the budget! Always so many things perforce cut out; always such cruel pressure of things that *could* not be cut out. In the early days of his marriage he had accustomed himself to a liberality of expenditure out of proportion to his income; the little store of savings allowed him to indulge his kindness to Clara and her relatives, and he kept putting off to the future that strict revision of outlay which his position of course demanded. The day when he had no longer a choice came all too soon; with alarm he discovered that his savings had melted away; the few sovereigns remaining must be sternly guarded for the hour of stern necessity. How it ground on his sensibilities when he was compelled to refuse some request from Clara or the girls! His generous nature suffered pangs of self-contempt as often as there was talk of economy.

To-day, for instance, whilst he was worrying in thought over Amy's behaviour, and at the same time trying to cut down the Saturday's purchases in order to pay for the broken window, up comes Tom with the announcement that he lost his hat this morning, and had to return bareheaded. Another unforeseen expense! And Sidney was angry with himself for his impulse of anger against the boy.

Clara never went out to make purchases, seldom indeed left the house for any reason, unless Sidney persuaded her to walk a short distance with him after sundown, when she veiled herself closely. Neither Amy nor Annie could be trusted to do all the shopping, so that Sidney generally accompanied one or other of them for that purpose on Saturday afternoon. To-day he asked Amy to go with him, wishing, if possible, to influence her for good by kind, brotherly talk. Whilst she was getting ready he took John aside into the parlour, to impart a strange piece of news he had brought from Clerkenwell.

'Mrs. Peckover has had a narrow escape of being poisoned. She was found by one of her lodgers all but dead, and last night the police arrested her daughter on the charge.'

'Mrs. Snowdon?'

'Yes. The mother has accused her. There's a man concerned in the affair. One of the men showed me a report in to-day's paper; I didn't buy one, because we shall have it in the Sunday paper to-morrow. Nice business, eh?'

'That's for the old woman's money, I'll wager!' exclaimed Hewett, in an awed voice. 'I can believe it of Clem; if ever there was a downright bad 'un! Was she living in the Close?'

'Mrs. Snowdon wasn't. Somewhere in Hoxton. No doubt it was for the money—if the charge is true. We won't speak of it before the children.'

'Think of that, now! Many's the time I've looked at Clem Peckover and said to myself, "You'll come to no good end, my lady!" She was a fierce an' bad 'un.'

Sidney nodded, and went off for his walk with Amy. . . .

It was a difficult thing to keep any room in the house orderly, and Sidney, as part of his struggle against the downward tendency in all about him, against the forces of chaos, often did the work of housemaid in the parlour; a little laxity in the rules which made this a sacred corner, and there would have been no spot where he could rest. With some success, too, he had resisted the habit prevalent in working-class homes of prolonging Saturday evening's occupations until the early hours of Sunday morning. At a little after ten o'clock to-night John Hewett and the children were in bed; he too, weary in mind and body, would gladly have gone upstairs, but he lingered from one five minutes to the next, his heart sinking at the certainty that he would find Clara in sleepless misery which he had no power to allay.

Round the walls of the parlour were hung his own drawings, which used to conceal the bareness of his lodging in Tysoe Street. It was three years since he had touched a pencil; the last time having been when he made holiday with Michael Snowdon and Jane at the farm-house by Danbury Hill. The impulse would never come again. It was associated with happiness, with hope; and what had his life to do with one or the other? Could he have effected the change without the necessity of explaining it, he would gladly have put those drawings out of sight. Whenever, as now, he consciously regarded them, they plucked painfully at his heart-strings, and threatened to make him a coward.

None of that! He had his work to do, happiness or no happiness, and by all the virtue of manhood he would not fail in it—as far as success or failure was a question of his own resolve.

The few books he owned were placed on hanging shelves; among them those which he had purchased for Clara since their marriage. But reading was as much a thing of the past as drawing. Never a moment when his mind was sufficiently at ease to refresh itself with other men's thoughts or fancies. As with John Hewett, so with himself; the circle of his interests had shrivelled, until it included nothing but the cares of his family, the cost of house and food and firing. As a younger man, he had believed that he knew what was meant by the struggle for existence in the nether world; it seemed to him now as if such knowledge had been only theoretical. Oh, it was easy to preach a high ideal of existence for the poor, as long as one had a considerable margin over the week's expenses; easy to rebuke the men and women who tried to forget themselves in beer-shops and gin-houses, as long as one could take up some rational amusement with a quiet heart. Now, on his return home from labour, it was all he could do not to sink in exhaustion and defeat of spirit. Shillings and pence; shillings and pence—never a question of pounds, unfortunately; and always too few of them. He understood how men have gone mad under pressure of household cares; he realised the horrible temptation which has made men turn dastardly from the path leading homeward and leave those there to shift for themselves.

When on the point of lowering the lamp he heard some-one coming downstairs. The door opened, and, to his surprise, Clara came in. Familiarity could not make him insensible to that disfigurement of her once beautiful face; his eyes always fell before her at the first moment of meeting.

'What are you doing?' she asked. 'Why don't you come up?'

'I was that minute coming.'

His hand went again to the lamp, but she checked him. In a low, wailing, heart-breaking voice, and with a passionate gesture, she exclaimed, 'Oh, I feel as if I should go mad! I can't bear it much longer!'

Sidney was silent at first, then said quietly, 'Let's sit here for a little. No wonder you feel low-spirited, lying in that room all day. I'd gladly have come and sat with you, but my company only seems to irritate you.'

'What good can you do me? You only think I'm making you miserable without a cause. You won't say it, but that's what you always think; and when I feel that, I can't bear to have you near. If only I could die and come to the end of it! How can you tell what I suffer? Oh yes, you speak so calmly—as good as telling me I am unreasonable because I can't do the same. I hate to hear your voice when it's like that! I'd rather you raged at me or struck me!'

The beauty of her form had lost nothing since the evening when he visited her in Farringdon Road Buildings; now, as then, all her movements were full of grace and natural dignity. Whenever strong feeling was active in her, she could not but manifest it in motion unlike that of ordinary women. Her hair hung in disorder, though not at its full length, massing itself upon her shoulders, shadowing her forehead. Half-consumed by the fire that only death would extinguish, she looked the taller for her slenderness. Ah, had the face been untouched!

'You are unjust to me,' Sidney replied, with emotion, but not resentfully. 'I can enter into all your sufferings. If I speak calmly, it's because I *must*, because I daren't give way. One of us must try and be strong, Clara, or else——'

He turned away.

'Let us leave this house,' she continued, hardly noticing what he said. 'Let us live in some other place. Never any change—always, always the same walls to look at day and night—it's driving me mad!'

'Clara, we can't move. I daren't spend even the little money it would cost. Do you know what Amy has been doing?'

'Yes; father told me.'

'How can we go to the least needless expense, when every day makes living harder for us?'

'What have we to do with them? How can you be expected to keep a whole family? It isn't fair to you or to me. You sacrifice me to them. It's nothing to you what I endure, so long as they are kept in comfort!'

He stepped nearer to her.

'What do you really mean by that? Is it seriously your wish that I should tell them—your father and your sisters and your brother—to leave the house and support themselves as best they can? Pray, what would become of them? Kept in *comfort*, are they? How much comfort does your poor father enjoy? Do you wish me to tell him to go out into the street, as I can help him no more?'

She moaned and made a wild gesture.

'You know all this to be impossible; you don't wish it; you couldn't bear it. Then why will you drive me almost to despair by complaining so of what can't be helped? Surely you foresaw it all. You knew that I was only a working man. It isn't as if there had been any hope of my making a larger income, and you were disappointed.'

'Does it make it easier to bear because there is no hope of relief?' she cried.

'For me, yes. If there *were* hope, I might fret under the misery.'

'Oh, I had hope once! It might have been so different with me. The thought burns and burns and burns, till I am frantic. You don't help me to bear it. You leave me alone when I most need help. How can *you* know what it means to me to look back and think of what might have been? You say to yourself I am selfish, that I ought to be thankful someone took pity on me, poor, wretched creature that I am. It would have been kinder never to have come near me. I should have killed myself long ago, and there an end. You thought it was a great thing to take me, when you might have had a wife who would——'

'Clara! Clara! When you speak like that, I could almost believe you are really mad. For Heaven's sake, think what you are saying! Suppose I were to reproach you with having consented to marry me? I would rather die than let such a word pass my lips—but suppose you heard me speaking to you like this?'

She drew a deep sigh, and let her hands fall. Sidney continued in quite another voice:

'It's one of the hardest things I have to bear, that I can't make your life pleasanter. Of course you need change; I know it only too well. You and I ought to have our holiday at this time of the year, like other people. I fancy I should like to go into the country myself; Clerkenwell isn't such a beautiful place that one can be content to go there day after day, year after year, without variety. But we have no money. Suffer as we may, there's no help for it—because we have no money. Lives may be wasted—worse, far worse than wasted —just because there is no money. At this moment a whole world of men and women is in pain and sorrow—because they have no money. How often have we said that? The world is made so; everything has to be bought with money.'

'You find it easier to bear than I do.'

'Yes; I find it easier. I am stronger-bodied, and at all events I have some variety, whilst you have none. I know it. If I could take your share of the burden, how gladly I'd do so! If I could take your suffering upon myself, you shouldn't be unhappy for another minute. But that is another impossible thing. People who are fortunate in life may ask each day what they *can* do; we have always to remind ourselves what we *can't*.'

'You take a pleasure in repeating such things; it shows how little you feel them.'

'It shows how I have taken to heart the truth of them.'

She waved her hand impatiently, again sighed, and moved towards the door.

'Don't go just yet,' said Sidney. 'We have more to say to each other.'

'I have nothing more to say. I am miserable, and you can't help me.'

'I can, Clara.'

She looked at him with wondering, estranged eyes. 'How? What are you going to do?'

'Only speak to you, that's all. I have nothing to give but words. But——'

She would have left him. Sidney stepped forward and prevented her.

'No; you *must* hear what I have got to say. They may be only words, but if I have no power to move you with my words, then our life has come to utter ruin, and I don't know what dreadful things lie before us.'

'I can say the same,' she replied, in a despairing tone.

'But neither you nor I shall say it! As long as I have strength to speak, I won't consent to say that! Clara, you must put your hand in mine, and think of your life and mine as one. If not for my sake, then for your child's. Think; do you wish May to suffer for the faults of her parents?'

'I wish she had never been born!'

'And yet you were the happier for her birth. It's only these last six months that you have fallen again into misery. You indulge it, and it grows worse, harder to resist. You may say that life seems to grow worse. Perhaps so. This affair of Amy's has been a heavy blow, and we shall miss the little money she brought; goodness knows when another place will be found for her. But all the more reason why we should help each other to struggle. Perhaps just this year or two will be our hardest time. If Amy and Annie and Tom were once all earning something, the worst would be over— wouldn't it? And can't we find strength to hold out a little longer, just to give the children a start in life, just to make your father's last years a bit happier? If we manage it, shan't we feel glad in looking back? Won't it be something worth having lived for?'

He paused, but Clara had no word for him.

'There's Amy. She's a hard girl to manage, partly because she has very bad health. I always think of that—or try to—when she irritates me. This afternoon I took her out with me, and spoke as kindly as I could; if she isn't better for it, she surely can't be worse, and in any case I don't know what else to do. Look, Clara, you and I are going to do what we can for these children; we're not going to give up the work now we've begun it. Mustn't all of us who are poor stand together and help one another? We have to fight against the rich world that's always crushing us down, down —whether it means to or not. Those people enjoy their lives. Well, I shall find *my* enjoyment in defying them to make me despair! But I can't do without your help. I didn't feel very cheerful as I sat here a while ago, before you came down; I was almost afraid to go upstairs, lest the sight of what you were suffering should be too much for me. Am I to ask a kindness of you and be refused, Clara?'

It was not the first time that she had experienced the constraining power of his words when he was moved with passionate earnestness. Her desire to escape was due to a fear of yielding, of suffering her egotism to fail before a stronger will.

'Let me go,' she said, whilst he held her arm. 'I feel too ill to talk longer.'

'Only one word—only one promise—now whilst we are the only ones awake in the house. We are husband and wife, Clara, and we must be kind to each other. We are not going to be like the poor creatures who let their misery degrade them. We are both too proud for that—what? We can think and express our thoughts; we can speak to each other's minds and hearts. Don't let us be beaten!'

'What's the good of my promising? I can't keep it. I suffer too much.'

'Promise, and keep the promise for a few weeks, a few days; then I'll find strength to help you once more. But now it's your turn to help me. To-morrow begins a new week; the rich world allows us to rest to-morrow, to be with each other. Shall we make it a quiet, restful, hopeful day? When they go out in the morning, you shall read to father and me—read as you know how to, so much better than I can. What? Was that really a smile?'

'Let me go, Sidney. Oh, I'm tired, I'm tired!'

'And the promise?'

'I'll do my best. It won't last long, but I'll try.'

'Thank you, dear.'

'No,' she replied, despondently. 'It's I that ought to thank you. But I never shall—never. I only understand you now and then—just for an hour—and all the selfishness comes back again. It'll be the same till I'm dead.'

He put out the lamp and followed her upstairs. His limbs ached; he could scarcely drag one leg after the other. Never mind; the battle was gained once more.

CHAPTER XL

JANE

'The poisoning business startled me. I shouldn't at all wonder if I had a precious narrow squeak of something of the kind myself before I took my departure; in fact, a sort of fear of the animal made me settle things as sharp as I could. Let me know the result of the trial. Wonder whether there'll be any disagreeable remarks about a certain acquaintance of yours, detained abroad on business? Better send me newspapers—same name and address. . . . But I've something considerably more important to think about. . . . A big thing; I scarcely dare tell you how big. I stand to win $2,000,000! . . . Not a soul outside suspects the ring. When I tell you that R.S.N. is in it, you'll see that I've struck the right ticket this time. . . . Let me hear about Jane. If all goes well here, and you manage that little business, you shall have $100,000, just for house-furnishing, you know. I suppose you'll have your partnership in a few months?'

Extracts from a letter, with an American stamp, which Mr. Scawthorne read as he waited for his breakfast. It was the end of October, and cool enough to make the crackling fire grateful. Having mused over the epistle, our friend took up his morning paper and glanced at the report of criminal trials. Whilst he was so engaged his landlady entered, carrying a tray of appetising appearance.

'Good-morning, Mrs. Byass,' he said, with much friendliness. Then, in a lower voice, 'There's a fuller report here than there was in the evening paper. Perhaps you looked at it?'

'Well, yes, sir; I thought you wouldn't mind,' replied Bessie, arranging the table.

'She'll be taken care of for three years, at all events.'

'If you'd seen her that day she came here after Miss Snowdon, you'd understand how glad I feel that she's out of the way. I'm sure I've been uneasy ever since. If ever there comes a rather loud knock at—there I begin to tremble; I do indeed. I don't think I shall ever get over it.'

'I dare say Miss Snowdon will be easier in mind?'

'I shouldn't wonder. But she won't say anything about it. She feels the disgrace so much, and I know it's almost more than she can do to go to work, just because she thinks they talk about her.'

'Oh, that'll very soon pass over. There's always something new happening, and people quickly forget a case like this.'

Bessie withdrew, and her lodger addressed himself to his breakfast.

He had occupied the rooms on the first floor for about a year and a half. Joseph Snowdon's proposal to make him acquainted with Jane had not been carried out, Scawthorne deeming it impracticable; but when a year had gone by, and Scawthorne, as Joseph's confidential correspondent, had still to report that Jane maintained herself in independence, he one day presented himself in Hanover Street, as a total stranger, and made inquiry about the rooms which a card told him were to let. His improved position allowed him to live somewhat more reputably than in the Chelsea lodging, and Hanover Street would suit him well enough until he obtained the promised partnership. Admitted as a friend to Mr. Percival's house in Highbury, he had by this time made the acquaintance of Miss Lant, whom, by the exercise of his agreeable qualities, he one day led to speak of Jane Snowdon. Miss Lant continued to see Jane, at long intervals, and was fervent in her praise as well as in compassionating the trials through which she had gone. His position in Mr. Percival's office of course made it natural that Scawthorne should have a knowledge of the girl's story. When he had established himself in Mrs. Byass's rooms, he mentioned the fact casually to his friends, making it appear that, in seeking lodgings, he had come upon these by haphazard.

He could not but feel something of genuine interest in a girl who, for whatever reason, declined a sufficient allowance and chose to work for her living. The grounds upon which Jane took this decision were altogether unknown to him until an explanation came from her father. Joseph, when news of the matter reached him, was disposed to entertain suspicions; with every care not to betray his own whereabouts, he wrote to Jane, and in due time received a reply, in which Jane told him truly her reasons for refusing the money. These Joseph communicated to Scawthorne, and the latter's interest was still more strongly awakened.

He was now on terms of personal acquaintance, almost of friendship, with Jane. Miss Lant, he was convinced, did not speak of her too praisingly. Not exactly a pretty girl, though far from displeasing in countenance ; very quiet, very gentle, with much natural refinement. Her air of sadness—by no means forced upon the vulgar eye, but unmistakable when you studied her—was indicative of faithful sensibilities. Scaw-thorne had altogether lost sight of Sidney Kirkwood and of the Hewetts ; he knew they were all gone to a remote part of London, and more than this he had no longer any care to discover. On excellent terms with his landlady, he skilfully elicited from her now and then a confidential remark with regard to Jane ; of late, indeed, he had established something like a sentimental understanding with the good Bessie, so that, whenever he mentioned Jane, she fell into a pleasant little flutter, feeling that she understood what was in progress. . . . . Why not ?—he kept asking himself. Joseph Snowdon (who addressed his letters to Hanover Street in a feigned hand) seemed to have an undeniable affection for the girl, and was constant in his promises of providing a handsome dowry. The latter was not a point of such importance as a few years ago, but the dollars would be acceptable. And then, the truth was, Scawthorne felt himself more and more inclined to put a certain question to Jane, dowry or none. . . .

Yes, she felt it as a disgrace, poor girl ! When she saw the name ' Snowdon ' in the newspaper, in such a shameful and horrible connection, her impulse was to flee, to hide herself. It was dreadful to go to her work and hear the girls talking of this attempted murder. The new misery came upon her just as she was regaining something of her natural spirits, after long sorrow and depression which had affected her health. But circumstances, now as ever, seemed to plot that at a critical moment of her own experience she should be called out of herself and constrained to become the consoler of others.

For some months the domestic peace of Mr. and Mrs. Byass had been gravely disturbed. Unlike the household at Crouch End, it was to prosperity that Sam and his wife owed their troubles. Year after year Sam's position had improved ; he was now in receipt of a salary which made—or ought to have made—things at home very comfortable. Though his children were now four in number, he could supply their wants. He could buy Bessie a new gown without very grave consideration, and could regard his own shiny top-hat, when he donned it in the place of one that was really respectable enough, without twinges of conscience.

But Sam was not remarkable for wisdom; indeed, had he been anything more than a foolish calculating-machine, he would scarcely have thriven as he did in the City. When he had grown accustomed to rattling loose silver in his pocket, the next thing, as a matter of course, was that he accustomed himself to pay far too frequent visits to City bars. On certain days in the week he invariably came home with a very red face and a titubating* walk; when Bessie received him angrily, he defended himself on the great plea of business necessities. As a town traveller there was no possibility, he alleged, of declining invitations to refresh himself; just as incumbent upon him was it to extend casual hospitality to those with whom he had business.

'Business! Fiddle!' cried Bessie. 'All you City fellows are the same. You encourage each other in drink, drink, drinking whenever you have a chance, and then you say it's all a matter of business. I won't have you coming home in that state, so there! I won't have a husband as drinks! Why, you can't stand straight.'

'Can't stand straight!' echoed Sam, with vast scorn. 'Look here!'

And he shouldered the poker, with the result that one of the globes on the chandelier came in shivers about his head. This was too much. Bessie fumed, and for a couple of hours the quarrel was unappeasable.

Worse was to come. Sam occasionally stayed out very late at night, and on his return alleged a 'business appointment.' Bessie at length refused to accept these excuses; she couldn't and wouldn't believe them.

'Then don't!' shouted Sam. 'And understand that I shall come home just when I like. If you make a bother I won't come home at all, so there you have it!'

'You're a bad husband and a beast!' was Bessie's retort.

Shortly after that Bessie received information of such grave misconduct on her husband's part that she all but resolved to forsake the house, and with the children seek refuge under her parents' roof at Woolwich. Sam had been seen in indescribable company; no permissible words would characterise the individuals with whom he had roamed shamelessly on the pavement of Oxford Street.* When he next met her, quite sober and with exasperatingly innocent expression, Bessie refused to open her lips. Neither that evening nor the next would she utter a word to him—and the effort it cost her was tremendous. The result was, that on the third evening Sam did not appear.

It was a week after Clem's trial. Jane had been keeping to herself as much as possible, but, having occasion to go down into the kitchen late at night, she found Bessie in tears, utterly miserable.

'Don't bother about me!' was the reply to her sympathetic question. 'You've got your own upsets to think of. You might have come to speak to me before this—but never mind. It's nothing to you.'

It needed much coaxing to persuade her to detail Sam's enormities, but she found much relief when she had done so, and wept more copiously than ever.

'It's nearly twelve o'clock, and there's no sign of him. Perhaps he won't come at all. He's in bad company, and if he stays away all night I'll never speak to him again as long as I live. Oh, he's a beast of a husband, is Sam!'

Sam came not. All through that night did Jane keep her friend company, for Sam came not. In the morning a letter, addressed in his well-known commercial hand. Bessie read it and screamed. Sam wrote to her that he had accepted a position as country traveller, and *perhaps* he might be able to look in at his home on that day month.

Jane could not go to work. The case had become very serious indeed; Bessie was in hysterics; the four children made the roof ring with their lamentations. At this juncture Jane put forth all her beneficent energy. It happened that Bessie was just now servantless. There was Mr. Scawthorne's breakfast only half prepared; Jane had to see to it herself, and herself take it upstairs. Then Bessie must go to bed, or assuredly she would be so ill that unheard-of calamities would befall the infants. Jane would have an eye to everything; only let Jane be trusted.

The miserable day passed; after trying in vain to sleep, Bessie walked about her sitting-room with tear-swollen face and rumpled gown, always thinking it possible that Sam had only played a trick, and that he would come. But he came not, and again it was night.

At eight o'clock Mr. Scawthorne's bell rang. Impossible for Bessie to present herself; Jane would go. She ascended

to the room which had once—ah, once!—been her own
parlour, knocked and entered.

'I—I wished to speak to Mrs. Byass,' said Scawthorne,
appearing for some reason or other embarrassed by Jane's
presenting herself.

'Mrs. Byass is not at all well, sir. But I'll let her
know——'

'No, no ; on no account.'

'Can't I get you anything, sir ? '

'Miss Snowdon—might I speak with you for a few
moments ? '

Jane feared it might be a complaint. In a perfectly
natural way she walked forward. Scawthorne came in her
direction, and—closed the door.

The interview lasted ten minutes, then Jane came forth
and with a light, quick step ran up to the floor above. She
did not enter the room, however, but stood with her hand on
the door, in the darkness. A minute or two, and with the same
light, hurried step, she descended the stairs, sprang past the
lodger's room, sped down to the kitchen. Under other circumstances Bessie must surely have noticed a strangeness in
her look, in her manner ; but to-night Bessie had thought for
nothing but her own calamities.

Another day, and no further news from Sam. The next
morning, instead of going to work (the loss of wages was most
serious, but it couldn't be helped), Jane privately betook herself to Sam's house of business. Mrs. Byass was ill; would
they let her know Mr. Byass's address, that he might immediately be communicated with ? The information was
readily supplied; Mr. Byass was no farther away, at present,
than St. Albans. Forth into the street again, and in search
of a policeman. ' Will you please to tell me what station I
have to go to for St. Albans ?' Why, Moorgate Street would
do ; only a few minutes' walk away. On she hastened.
' What is the cost of a return ticket to St. Albans, please ? '
Three-and-sevenpence. Back into the street again ; she must
now look for a certain sign, indicating a certain place of business. With some little trouble it is found ; she enters a dark
passage, and comes before a counter, upon which she lays—
a watch, her grandfather's old watch. 'How much ?' 'Four
shillings, please.' She deposits a halfpenny, and receives four
shillings, together with a ticket. Now for St. Albans.

Sam ! Sam ! Ay, well might he turn red and stutter and

look generally foolish when that quiet little girl stood before
him in his 'stock-room' at the hotel. Her words were as
quiet as her look. 'I'll write her a letter,' he cries. 'Stop;
you shall take it back. I can't give up the job at once, but
you may tell her I'm up to no harm. Where's the pen?
Where's the cursed ink?' And she takes the letter.

'Why, you've lost a day's work, Jane! She gave you the
money for the journey, I suppose?'

'Yes, yes, of course.'

'Tell her she's not to make a fool of herself in future.'

'No, I shan't say that, Mr. Byass. But I'm half-tempted
to say it to someone else!'

It was the old, happy smile, come back for a moment; the
voice that had often made peace so merrily. The return
journey seemed short, and with glad heart-beating she hastened from the City to Hanover Street.

Well, well; of course it would all begin over again; Jane
herself knew it. But is not all life a struggle onward from
compromise to compromise, until the day of final pacification?

Through that winter she lived with a strange secret in her
mind, a secret which was the source of singularly varied feelings—of astonishment, of pain, of encouragement, of apprehension, of grief. To no one could she speak of it; no one
could divine its existence—no one save the person to whom
she owed this surprising novelty in her experience. She
would have given much to be rid of it; and yet, again, might
she not legitimately accept that pleasure which at times came
of the thought?—the thought that, as a woman, her qualities
were of some account in the world.

She did her best to keep it out of her consciousness, and
in truth had so many other things to think about that it was
seldom she really had trouble with it. Life was not altogether easy; regular work was not always to be kept; there
was much need of planning and pinching, that her independence might suffer no wound. Bessie Byass was always in
arms against that same independent spirit; she scoffed at it,
assailed it with treacherous blandishment, made direct attacks
upon it.

'I must live in my own way, Mrs. Byass. I don't want
to have to leave you.'

And if ever life seemed a little too hard, if the image of
the past grew too mournfully persistent, she knew where to go

for consolation. Let us follow her, one Saturday afternoon early in the year.

In a poor street in Clerkenwell was a certain poor little shop—built out as an afterthought from an irregular lump of houses; a shop with a room behind it and a cellar below; no more. Here was sold second-hand clothing, women's and children's. No name over the front, but neighbours would have told you that it was kept by one Mrs. Todd, a young widow with several children. Mrs. Todd, not long ago, used to have only a stall in the street; but a lady named Miss Lant helped her to start in a more regular way of business.

'And does she carry it on quite by herself?'

No; with her lived another young woman, also a widow, who had one child. Mrs. Hewett, her name. She did sewing in the room behind, or attended to the shop when Mrs. Todd was away making purchases.

There Jane Snowdon entered. The clothing that hung in the window made it very dark inside; she had to peer a little before she could distinguish the person who sat behind the counter. 'Is Pennyloaf in, Mrs. Todd?'

'Yes, Miss. Will you walk through?'

The room behind is lighted from the ceiling. It is heaped with the most miscellaneous clothing. It contains two beds, some shelves with crockery, a table, some chairs—but it would have taken you a long time to note all these details, so huddled together was everything. Part of the general huddling were five children, of various ages; and among them, very busy, sat Pennyloaf.

'Everything going on well?' was Jane's first question.

'Yes, Miss.'

'Then I know it isn't. Whenever you call me "Miss," there's something wrong; I've learnt that.'

Pennyloaf smiled, sadly but with affection in her eyes. 'Well, I have been a bit low, an' that's the truth. It takes me sometimes, you know. I've been thinkin', when I'd oughtn't.'

'Same with me, Pennyloaf. We can't help thinking, can we? What a good thing if we'd nothing more to think about than these children! Where's little Bob? Why, Bob, I thought you were old clothes; I did, really! You may well laugh!'

The laughter was merry, and Jane encouraged it, inventing

all sorts of foolish jokes. 'Pennyloaf, I wish you'd ask me to stay to tea.'

'Then that I will, Miss Jane, an' gladly. Would you like it soon?'

'No; in an hour will do, won't it? Give me something that wants sewing, a really hard bit, something that'll break needles. Yes, that'll do. Where's Mrs. Todd's thimble? Now we're all going to be comfortable, and we'll have a good talk.'

Pennyloaf found the dark thoughts slip away insensibly. And she talked, she talked—where was there such a talker as Pennyloaf nowadays, when she once began?

Mr. Byass was not very willing, after all, to give up his country travelling. That his departure on that business befell at a moment of domestic quarrel was merely chance; secretly he had made the arrangement with his firm some weeks before. The penitence which affected him upon Jane's appeal could not be of abiding result; for, like all married men at a certain point of their lives, he felt heartily tired of home and wished to see the world a little. Hanover Street heard endless discussions of the point between Sam and Bessie, between Bessie and Jane, between Jane and Sam, between all three together. And the upshot was that Mr. Byass gained his point. For a time he would go on country journeys. Bessie assented sullenly, but, strange to say, she had never been in better spirits than on the day after this decision had been arrived at.

On that day, however—it was early in March—an annoying incident happened. Mr. Scawthorne, who always dined in town and seldom returned to his lodgings till late in the evening, rang his bell about eight o'clock and sent a message by the servant that he wished to see Mrs. Byass. Bessie having come up, he announced to her with gravity that his tenancy of the rooms would be at an end in a fortnight. Various considerations necessitated his living in a different part of London. Bessie frankly lamented; she would never again find such an estimable lodger. But, to be sure, Mr. Scawthorne had prepared her for this, three months ago. Well, what must be, must be.

'Is Miss Snowdon in the house, Mrs. Byass?' Scawthorne went on to inquire.

'Miss Snowdon? Yes.'

'This letter from America, which I found on coming in, contains news she must hear—disagreeable news, I'm sorry to say.'

'About her father?' Bessie inquired anxiously.

Scawthorne nodded a grave and confidential affirmative. He had never given Mrs. Byass reason to suppose that he knew anything of Joseph's whereabouts, but Bessie's thoughts naturally turned in that direction.

'The news comes to me by chance,' he continued. 'I think I ought to communicate it to Miss Snowdon privately, and leave her to let you know what it is, as doubtless she will. Would it be inconvenient to you to let me have the use of your parlour for five minutes?'

'I'll go and light the gas at once, and tell Miss Snowdon.'

'Thank you, Mrs. Byass.'

He was nervous, a most unusual thing with him. Till Bessie's return he paced the room irregularly, chewing the ends of his moustache. When it was announced to him that the parlour was ready he went down, the letter in his hand. At the half-open door came a soft knock. Jane entered.

She showed signs of painful agitation.

'Will you sit down, Miss Snowdon? It happens that I have a correspondent in the United States, who has lately had—had business relations with Mr. Joseph Snowdon, your father. On returning this evening I found a letter from my friend, in which there is news of a distressing kind.'

He paused. What he was about to say was—for once—the truth. The letter, however, came from a stranger, a lawyer in Chicago.

'Your father, I understand, has lately been engaged in—in commercial speculation on a great scale. His enterprises have proved unfortunate. One of those financial crashes which are common in America caused his total ruin.'

Jane drew a deep breath.

'I am sorry to say that is not all. The excitement of the days when his fate was hanging in the balance led to illness—fatal illness. He died on the sixth of February.'

Jane, with her eyes bent down, was motionless. After a pause, Scawthorne continued:

'I will speak of this with Mr. Percival to-morrow, and every inquiry shall be made—on your behalf.'

'Thank you, sir.'

She rose, very pale, but with more self-command than on

entering the room. The latter part of his communication seemed to have affected her as a relief.

'Miss Snowdon—if you would allow me to say a few more words. You will remember I mentioned to you that there was a prospect of my becoming a partner in the firm which I have hitherto served as clerk. A certain examination had to be passed that I might be admitted a solicitor. That is over; in a few days my position as a member of the firm will be assured.'

Jane waited, her eyes still cast down.

'I feel that it may seem to you an ill-chosen time; but the very fact that I have just been the bearer of such sad news impels me to speak. I cannot keep the promise that I would never revive the subject on which I spoke to you not long ago. Forgive me; I *must* ask you again if you cannot think of me as I wish? Miss Snowdon, will you let me devote myself to making your life happy? It has always seemed to me that if I could attain a position such as I now have, there would be little else to ask for. I began life poor and half-educated, and you cannot imagine the difficulties I have overcome. But if I go away from this house, and leave you so lonely, living such a hard life, there will be very little satisfaction for me in my success. Let me try to make for you a happiness such as you merit. It may seem as if we were very slightly acquainted, but I know you well enough to esteem you more highly than any woman I ever met, and if you could but think of me——'

He was sincere. Jane had brought out the best in him. With the death of Snowdon all his disreputable past seemed swept away, and he had no thought of anything but a decent rectitude, a cleanly enjoyment of existence, for the future. But Jane was answering:

'I can't change what I said before, Mr. Scawthorne. I am very content to live as I do now. I have friends I am very fond of. Thank you for your kindness—but I can't change.'

Without intending it, she ceased upon a word which to her hearer conveyed a twofold meaning. He understood; offer what he might, it could not tempt her to forget the love which had been the best part of her life. She was faithful to the past, and unchanging.

Mrs. Byass never suspected the second purpose for which her lodger had desired to speak with Jane this evening. Scawthorne in due time took his departure, with many expressions of goodwill, many assurances that nothing could please him better than to be of service to Bessie and her husband.

'He wished me to say good-bye to you for him,' said Bessie, when Jane came back from her work.

So the romance in her life was over. Michael Snowdon's wealth had melted away; with it was gone for ever the hope of realising his high projects. All passed into the world of memory, of dream—all save the spirit which had ennobled him, the generous purpose bequeathed to those two hearts which had loved him best.

To his memory all days were sacred; but one, that of his burial, marked itself for Jane as the point in each year to which her life was directed, the saddest, yet bringing with it her supreme solace.

A day in early spring, cloudy, cold. She left the work-room in the dinner-hour, and did not return. But instead of going to Hanover Street, she walked past Islington Green, all along Essex Road, northward thence to Stoke Newington, and so came to Abney Park Cemetery; a long way, but it did not weary her.

In the cemetery she turned her steps to a grave with a plain headstone. Before leaving England, Joseph Snowdon had discharged this duty. The inscription was simply a name, with dates of birth and death.

And, as she stood there, other footsteps approached the spot. She looked up, with no surprise, and gave her hand for a moment. On the first anniversary the meeting had been unanticipated; the same thought led her and Sidney to the cemetery at the same hour. This was the third year, and they met as if by understanding, though neither had spoken of it.

When they had stood in silence for a while, Jane told of her father's death and its circumstances. She told him, too, of Pennyloaf's humble security.

'You have kept well all the year?' he asked.

'And you too, I hope?'

Then they bade each other good-bye. . . .

In each life little for congratulation. He with the ambitions of his youth frustrated; neither an artist, nor a leader of men in the battle for justice. She, no saviour of society by the force of a superb example; no daughter of the people, holding wealth in trust for the people's needs. Yet to both was their work given. Unmarked, unencouraged save by their love of uprightness and mercy, they stood by the side of those more hapless, brought some comfort to hearts less courageous than their own. Where they abode it was not all dark. Sorrow certainly awaited them, perchance defeat in even the humble aims that they had set themselves; but at least their lives would remain a protest against those brute forces of society which fill with wreck the abysses of the nether world.

EXPLANATORY NOTES

In these notes reference is made to Gissing's scrap-book. This substantial collection of jottings, entries copied from books and newspapers, and newspaper cuttings, is in the Carl H. Pforzheimer 'Shelley and His Circle' Collection at The New York Public Library. I am grateful to the Carl and Lily Pforzheimer Foundation, Inc. for permission to quote from it. I am also very grateful to David Grylls and Pierre Coustillas for drawing my attention to the scrap-book and for providing me with a working transcript.

EPIGRAPH: 'A painting of a dung-heap might be justified if a beautiful flower grew out of it; otherwise the dung-heap is merely repulsive.' Ernest Renan (1823–92) was a historian of religion, whose most famous book was *Vie de Jésus* (1863).

2 *Clerkenwell Green*: although it is often classed as an 'East End novel', *The Nether World* is not set in the East End—the dark continent 'discovered' by the later Victorians—but in Clerkenwell. Gissing's use of real names of streets and buildings invites the reader to look at a map. Much has changed, but for the most part the street pattern of the novel's teeming, claustrophobic world still exists. Its perimeter is (roughly) from King's Cross east to the Angel, Islington; on to Old Street via City Road; City Road as the crow flies to St Paul's; and then back up Farringdon Road to Pentonville Road and King's Cross. Much of the story takes place, in fact, in a much smaller area, the centre of Clerkenwell itself. Chancery Lane, Furnivall's Inn, and Lincoln's Inn Fields, the law area which figures in Chapter XVIII, are just off the south-western corner of the area delimited above.

Unless Gissing draws attention to a specific feature of a street or building which requires comment, further topographical annotation will not be supplied. The whereabouts of most streets can be ascertained from any map of London, and historical information about churches and other public buildings will be found in the second volume of *London* (1952) in Nikolaus Pevsner's *The Buildings of England*.

mechanics: labourers; without modern English association with machinery necessarily.

petasus: 'a low-crowned broad-brimmed hat worn by the ancient Greeks' (*OED*).

4 *coppers*: common term for the non-silver coins—farthings, halfpennies, and pennies—in pre-decimal coinage.

5 *next room*: the frontispiece to Arnold White's *The Problems of a Great City* (1886), which Gissing read, depicts a corpse lying in a living-room. In his account of conditions in working-class homes, White dwells on this practice and on the considerable time that sometimes elapses before burial, a horror which is also attested in one of the most influential pamphlets of the period, Andrew Mearns' *The Bitter Cry of Outcast London* (1883). As an entry in the scrap-book reveals, Gissing himself saw a dead child laid out on a sitting-room table in a house in Eastbourne.

burial-club: self-help, mutual-aid savings schemes, common amongst the working classes, in which a small sum was invested regularly to ensure that money would be available for funeral expenses. The indignity of a pauper's burial, 'on the parish', was greatly feared.

6 *farden*: a farthing; a small coin worth a quarter of one penny in pre-decimal currency.

8 *bonnes bouches*: appetizing morsels.

15 *washhand stand*: a piece of furniture designed to carry a basin, ewer, soap dish, and so on. Few working-class houses had any piped water, let alone hot water. All water had to be carried in large ewers. See Enid Gauldie, *Cruel Habitations: A History of Working-Class Housing 1780–1918* (1974) and Anthony S. Wohl, *The Eternal Slum: Housing and Social Policy in Victorian London* (1977).

25 *Her features*: the significance of detailed description of features, which are common in Victorian novels, is examined in detail (with fascinating illustrations) by Mary Cowling in *The Artist*

as Anthropologist: The Representation of Type and Character in Victorian Art (1989). It was widely believed that facial characteristics—notably shape of forehead, rear skull, and chin, and set of eyes—were a reliable indicator of personality: 'all human beings carry charts of their mentality and character at their mast-heads, legible, even in detail, by all who know how to read them' (Cowling, p. 12, quoting L. N. Fowler, 'How to Read Character', *Lectures on Man*, 1864). In the scrap-book Gissing made a number of entries under the heading, 'Faces etc. Hints of Character'.

31 *subdued . . . worked in*: allusion to Shakespeare's sonnet 111, lines 6–7: 'my nature is subdued | To what it works in, like the dyer's hand.'

40 *a doctor*: Gissing noted in the scrap-book: 'At East End it is common for a doctor to have his name displayed in half a dozen different chemists' shops. His work is really done by unqualified assistants, provided with death certificates signed & partially filled in, in advance.' Quoted by permission of the Carl and Lily Pforzheimer Foundation, Inc.

41 *prints*: engraved reproductions of paintings were as common in nineteenth-century households as photographic ones are in the twentieth. A scrap-book entry reveals that Gissing saw the engravings described here adorning a sitting-room in Eastbourne. The collection has a distinctly moral aspect. The Earl of Strafford (d. 1641) and William Lord Russell (d. 1683) were both great men whose lives ended on the scaffold. John Martin (1789–1854) specialized in huge and generally apocalyptic biblical and historical scenes. His *The Fall of Nineveh* (1829) depicts the fall of the greatest Assyrian city, sacked in the seventh century BC, whose ruin was foretold in the Old Testament Book of Nahum.

42 *a moulder*: the scrap-book notes: ' "moulder". Engaged by builder. Makes mouldings for ceilings.' The main rooms of even quite lowly houses were often ornamented with highly wrought cornices and ceiling 'roses' moulded in plaster.

Pactolus: a river of gold. King Midas, whose touch turned everything to gold, bathed in the River Pactolus, which thereafter flowed through golden sand.

costermonger: trader who sells fruit and vegetables from a barrow.

43 *Mad Jack*: an entry in the scrap-book contains the germ of this character: ' "Mad Jack" who sings psalms. His dream in which he is told that slums are Hell, & the people in them were once wicked rich in a former life.' Submerged here is a reference to the parable of Dives and Lazarus, which figures repeatedly in writing on the poor. In the parable (Luke 16: 19–31), Dives the rich man goes to Hell while Lazarus, the beggar, rests in Abraham's bosom. In his *Problems of a Great City*, Arnold White observes: 'Between Dives and Lazarus the great gulf fixed becomes deeper, wider and blacker month by month and year by year' (p. 13).

45 *to the 'Ouse*: workhouses, generally large and forbidding institutions (commonly called 'Bastilles'), were, and were intended to be, the last resort of the indigent. For a readable account see Norman Longmate, *The Workhouse* (1974).

50 *Marquis of Northampton*: a substantial landowner in Clerkenwell. The Northampton estate included some 600 working-class houses.

51 *St. John's Square . . . impransus*: Clerkenwell Road was created by the Metropolitan Board of Works in 1878 to join Oxford Street to Old Street. It cut through the square which was once the courtyard of the Priory of St John, the chief seat in England of the Knights of St John of Jerusalem. St John's Arch, all that survived of the priory, was the residence of Edward Cave when he began the highly successful and long-lived *Gentleman's Magazine* (1731–1914). The anecdote about Dr Johnson '*impransus*', that is, supperless, is related in Boswell's *Life*.

54 *mantle-making*: A mantle is a loose, sleeveless cloak. In the scrap-book Gissing notes: '*Mantle-finisher*. Makes button-holes, puts on buttons, faces fronts & collars, trims with 6 yds of gimp & 16 yds of lace, & with waist-tape, sews ticket on & sends out finished—for 1/– [one shilling]. Can do 1 in 6 hrs. A girl paying 5/– for room makes 5/6 [five shillings and six pence] to 6/– to live on. Slack season from Nov. 9th to first week in Feb., & from beg. of May to July.' Gissing is

highlighting 'here one of the nineteenth century's most intractable industrial problems, the appalling conditions which obtained in the clothing industry. They were exposed repeatedly throughout the century, notably by Henry Mayhew in 1849–50, whose sensational disclosures spurred Charles Kingsley to write his influential polemic 'Cheap Clothes and Nasty' and provided many of the details for *Alton Locke*. But no matter how often outrage was expressed, little essentially changed.

Whereas conditions in factories and mines were alleviated throughout the Victorian period by successive phases of legislation, the tailoring industry remained resistant to amelioration largely because of the nature of its organization. Master tailors gave work out to middle-men, who in turn parcelled work out to home-workers, such as Margaret Barnes. The middle-men were squeezed and so they squeezed in turn. The invention of the sewing-machine, in common use by the late 1850s, actually worsened the lot of those at the bottom of the pile. Alexander Hay Japp noted in his *Industrial Curiosities. Glances here and there in the World of Labour* (1880), which Gissing read: 'we are sorry to find that there is a class of masters in London . . . who totally regardless of this new means of bettering the condition of their needle-women, have adopted measures which defeat its value to them, and tend to grind them to earth as of old. The great ready-made clothiers, instead of employing women in factories under their own eye, buy machines and let them out to *middle-men*; these again employ the women, and deprive them of all the advantages of the invention.'

For a striking account of 'sweating', the general term for this kind of labour organization, see William J. Fishman, *East End 1881: A Year in a London Borough among the Labouring Poor* (1988), 60–81.

56 *die-sinker's craft*: a die is an engraved stamp used to impress a design on metal or paper. A die-sinker engraves the die. In his entries on London occupations in the scrap-book Gissing notes of die-sinkers: 'Some artistic turn required. Workmen "wear collars." Skilled man, £3 a week. Lad of 19, £1 a week. Work, 54 hrs. Begin at 8 or 8.30, & on Friday work late.

Average of 9'hrs a day. Work on vast variety of things: medals, dies for coins, metal tickets &c. &c.' These details are worked in at the beginning of Chapter 8. Gissing visited a die-sinkers on 26 March 1888 and recorded in his diary that he 'Got useful ideas for "Nether World" '.

74 *model lodgings*: In an attempt to tackle the problem of working-class housing various bodies in the later nineteenth century, notably philanthropic trusts, erected high-density tenement blocks to provide low-cost accommodation for the working poor. Although an improvement on slum dwellings, the model lodgings were not always welcomed, for two reasons. One was that the buildings were almost always 'heavy and monotonous . . . having all the pretensions of warehouses and barracks' (Donald J. Olsen, *The Growth of Victorian London* (1976), 280, quoting *Building News*, 1883). The other was that such lodgings were under a degree of supervision. They were intended to mark off the more 'deserving' from the rest of the poor. For details and many photographs see John Nelson Tarn, *Five Per Cent Philanthropy: An account of housing in urban areas between 1840 and 1914* (1973), esp. 42–106; Enid Gauldie, *Cruel Habitations: A History of Working-Class Housing 1780–1918* (1974), esp. 213–35; and Anthony S. Wohl, *The Eternal Slum: Housing and Social Policy in Victorian London* (1977), esp. 141–78.

75 *pot-man*: barman and general factotum for the pub.

pledge of total abstinence: that is, abstinence from alcohol. For an account of the campaign waged for temperance and total abstinence, and the distinction between pubs and Mrs Candy's favoured beer-shop, see Brian Harrison, *Drink and the Victorians: The Temperance Question in England 1815–1872* (1971), and the same author's 'Pubs', in H. J. Dyos and Michael Wolff (eds.), *The Victorian City: Images and Realities*, 2 vols. (1973), i, 161–90.

77 *Sadler's Wells Theatre*: the site of a pleasure-garden from as early as 1683. Gissing refers to Samuel Phelps, who directed the theatre with great success from 1844 to 1862. After his retirement the theatre suffered many vicissitudes, being at various times a skating-rink, a venue for prize-fighting, a

melodrama theatre, and a music-hall, before closing down in 1906.

namesake: that is, a 'bob', a common term for one shilling (12 pennies) in pre-decimal coinage. A substantial sum: Penny-loaf has just bought seven pounds of coal for one penny.

80 *State Education . . . orthodoxy*: this paragraph could easily be misunderstood. The Education Act of 1870 empowered compulsory education for children between the ages of 5 and 12, either in new schools, under School Boards, or in the existing Anglican or other denominational establishments. Board schools, free to children in need, would teach Christianity, but not any one branch of it—hence would suit Hewett's desire for 'education on an independent basis', that is, independent of Church control. But like many other institutions in Great Britain provided by the state, Board schools were regarded by many of those they were designed to help as necessarily inferior. Clara Hewett uses the religious argument, but she actually declines to attend a Board School out of straightforward snobbery—she will not sit next to children lower in the pecking-order than herself.

99 *truckle-bed*: strictly, a low bed on castors, designed to be pushed out of view during the day. Commonly used of any collapsible bed.

parable of the Samaritan: the Samaritan succours a man who has been left for dead by thieves, while others pass him by on the other side of the road (Luke, 10: 30–7). Jesus tells this parable in answer to the question, 'And who is my neighbour?'

104 *'Io Saturnalia' . . . pileus*: 'Io' is merely an exclamation, like 'Ho!' 'Saturnalia', referring to the Roman festival of Saturn, is any time of licensed disorder. The August Bank Holiday was instituted in 1871. One of Arnold White's stranger assertions in *The Problems of a Great City* is that the new Bank Holidays are to some considerable extent to blame for imprudent early marriage amongst the poor. The *pileus* is a 'felt cap without a brim, worn by ancient Greeks and Romans' (OED.)

105 *Crystal Palace*: the building, designed by Joseph Paxton,

which housed the Great Exhibition of 1851. The greatest iron-and-glass building in the world, the Crystal Palace was taken down from its site in Hyde Park once the exhibition was over and re-erected at Sydenham in South London. It burned down in 1936. For splendid photographs of it *in situ*, being dismantled, and at Sydenham, see Gavin Stamp, *The Changing Metropolis: Earliest Photographs of London 1839–1879* (1984), 187–95. Gissing's diary for 2 April 1888 records that he 'Spent day at Crystal Palace, and brought back a lot of good notes'.

a dolman: a cape with a 'dolman' sleeve, that is, a sleeve cut in one piece with the rest of the garment.

106 *'Javan or Gadire'*: quotation from Milton's *Samson Agonistes* (715–16), referring to Dalila.

107 *a sovereign*: a one-pound coin in pre-decimal currency.

120 *caryatid*: Gissing means that Clem looks broad and immensely strong. A caryatid is a masonry female figure supporting an entablature, that is, all of the masonry above the column.

121 *tonsure*: shaving the crown of the head as a sign of the priesthood. On the description of Snowdon's facial characteristics, 'which gave him a curiously animal aspect', see note to p. 25 above.

122 *yellow promise*: various kinds of margarine were available from *c.*1870. Developments in food production, preservation, and marketing very greatly affected daily life in the railway and machine age. See, for a good introduction, J. C. Drummond and Anne Wilbraham, *The Englishman's Food: A History of Five Centuries of English Diet* (1939), revised edn. Dorothy Hollingsworth (1957). Gissing observed in his scrap-book: 'That the vulgar classes are in general fond of vinegar & such things is greatly due to the fact that their food (even when they have enough of it) is so vilely cooked that it has no savour.'

123 *davy*: affidavit; a written sworn statement for a court of law.

127 *time-workers*: in time-work one is paid, on an agreed hourly rate, for the time spent on a job. In piece-work one is only paid for each item produced or job done. When demand slackens, piece-workers are always the first to be laid off.

134 *bassinette*: a basket-work cradle.

145 *ad libitum*: without restraint.

152 *Salvation Army*: founded in 1865 by William Booth. Originally an East End mission, the movement was named the Salvation Army in 1878 and its organization codified on military lines: officers and troops made campaigns into darkest London to save the lost and relieve urban poverty. Gissing saw the Christmas Day procession of the Army in 1886 and noted in his scrap-book: 'Booth standing up in the carriage. Many bands, marching & playing at intervals; girls with tambourines. The only healthy faces were those of a few girls evidently making sport of the outing. No pretty faces. The men poor cripples, epileptic & cretinous. Grotesque religious inscripts. round their hats. Sudden outbursts of hymns, & gesticulation. The pathos of it all.'

164 *Liverpool Street*: Liverpool Street station, built in 1875 for the Great Eastern Railway company, served eastern England.

181 *modern Agora*: from Greek, meaning a place of assembly.

doctrine . . . vaccination: subjects being discussed are Christianity, vegetarianism, contraception, and vaccination. The doctrine of the Trinity—the ground of Christianity's conception of God—is that God is both three and one: God the Father, God the Son, God the Holy Spirit. The Malthusian League—named after the population theorist Thomas Malthus (1766–1834)—advocated birth-control, to near-universal hostility. Compulsory vaccination for children against smallpox was introduced in 1853. Further legislation extended the measure and in 1871 penalties were imposed for non-compliance. For an account of both of the latter topics see F. B. Smith, *The People's Health 1830–1910* (1979).

186 *kitchen*: squalid or low accommodation, as in 'thieves'-kitchen'.

217 *half-crown and a florin*: coins worth two shillings and sixpence and two shillings respectively.

230 '*sic volo, sic jubeo* : a very slight misquotation of Juvenal, *Satire* 6, line 223: 'Thus I wish, thus I order.'

231 *Highbury*: Bessie means that Sidney might signal his rise in

the world by moving to one of the more salubrious suburbs which grew rapidly in the second half of the century. Highbury is north of Islington. See Francis Sheppard, *London 1808–1870: The Infernal Wen* (1971) and Donald J. Olsen, *The Growth of Victorian London* (1976).

241 *Financial Reform Almanack*: published by The Financial Reform Association, whose aims, emblazoned on the title-page of each annual issue, were 'To Advocate Economical Government, Just Taxation, & Perfect Freedom of Trade'. The *Almanack* contained tables of figures relating to fiscal and commercial matters, as well as a polemic each year about the need for economic reform.

249 *An interesting house . . . four-and-sixpence*: Charles Booth's researchers discovered that slum housing mimicked higher-class housing in one respect, namely, that pressure of demand kept rents high, even though the accommodation rented was disgusting. Overcrowding that beggars belief, insanitary conditions, pest infestation, and high rents were all endemic to lower-class housing.

picking of rags . . . home: sorting of rags for reuse. The emphasis in 'of course at home' is important. The vast number of outworkers, who toiled for piece-rates in their own homes, were the most exploited group amongst the urban proletariat. As Beatrice Webb observed, when reviewing a House of Lords Select Committee report on the Sweating System: 'Alike from the obligations and the expenses of the factory owner, the sweater is free. Meanwhile the slum landlord is receiving, for his cellars and attics, the double rent of workshop and dwelling, without incurring the expensive sanitary obligations of the mill-owner. In short, it is home work which creates all the difficulties of our problem. For it is home work which, with its isolation, renders trade combination impracticable; which enables the manufacturer to use as a potent instrument, for the degradation of all, the necessity of the widow or the greed of the Jew. And more important still, it is home work which, by withdrawing the workers from the beneficent protection of the Factory Acts, destroys all legal responsibility on the part of the employer and the landlord for conditions of employment.' *My Apprenticeship* (1926), 337.

251 *the soup-kitchen*: Gissing records this episode in detail in the scrap-book.

264 *downy*: wide-awake, knowing.

274 *Farringdon Road Buildings*: Farringdon Buildings, Farringdon Road, architect Frederick Chancellor, were built in 1874 by the Metropolitan Association for Improving the Dwellings of the Industrious Classes—one of the oldest established (1841) bodies of its kind. For discussion and photograph (p. 97) see John Nelson Tarn, *Five Per Cent Philanthropy: An Account of Housing in Urban Areas between 1840 and 1914* (1973), esp. 42–106.

319 *grande toilette*: full readiness in clothing, make-up, hair, and so on to receive callers or to go out.

330 *Potter's Bar*: once again a detail indicates the topicality of the novel when first published. The Great Northern Railway company only pushed its suburban line further out to Potter's Bar in the early 1880s. See Jack Simmons, *The Victorian Railway* (1991), 328.

343 *the curse of curses*: in the *Genesis* story of the Fall of Man, God pronounces a curse on the fallen Adam—that he will have to labour all his life. Stephen's is the curse of curses because his livelihood depends on others drinking.

349 *Abney Park Cemetery*: founded 1840 in Stoke Newington, by Congregationalist trustees who from the outset refused to countenance sectarianism or Anglican dominance. As Chris Brooks points out in *Mortal Remains: The History and Present State of the Victorian and Edwardian Cemetery* (1989), 'its clientele remained overwhelmingly nonconformist throughout the nineteenth century' (p. 28). William and Catherine Booth, founders of the Salvation Army, are buried there.

356 *slop-work*: 'slop' was the general term for cheap, ready-made (that is, not made to measure) garments.

383 *titubating*: staggering, reeling.

383 *Oxford Street*: prostitution was common and visible in London to a degree which astonished overseas visitors and troubled social commentators at home. James Greenwood numbered it among *The Seven Curses of London* (1869), and so did everyone else who wrote on the problems of urban life. The area including Oxford Street, Regent Street, and the Haymarket was the liveliest for the trade. For a succinct introductory account see Kellow Chesney, *The Victorian Underworld* (1970).

TROLLOPE IN OXFORD WORLD'S CLASSICS

THE OXFORD SHERLOCK HOLMES

The Oxford World's Classics Website

www.worldsclassics.co.uk

- Information about new titles
- Explore the full range of Oxford World's Classics
- Links to other literary sites and the main OUP webpage
- Imaginative competitions, with bookish prizes
- Peruse *Compass*, the Oxford World's Classics magazine
- Articles by editors
- Extracts from Introductions
- A forum for discussion and feedback on the series
- Special information for teachers and lecturers

www.worldsclassics.co.uk

American Literature

British and Irish Literature

Children's Literature

Classics and Ancient Literature

Colonial Literature

Eastern Literature

European Literature

History

Medieval Literature

Oxford English Drama

Poetry

Philosophy

Politics

Religion

The Oxford Shakespeare

A complete list of Oxford Paperbacks, including Oxford World's Classics, OPUS, Past Masters, Oxford Authors, Oxford Shakespeare, Oxford Drama, and Oxford Paperback Reference, is available in the UK from the Academic Division Publicity Department, Oxford University Press, Great Clarendon Street, Oxford OX2 6DP.

In the USA, complete lists are available from the Paperbacks Marketing Manager, Oxford University Press, 198 Madison Avenue, New York, NY 10016.

Oxford Paperbacks are available from all good bookshops. In case of difficulty, customers in the UK can order direct from Oxford University Press Bookshop, Freepost, 116 High Street, Oxford OX1 4BR, enclosing full payment. Please add 10 per cent of published price for postage and packing.